Henry Gay Hewlett

The Heroes of Europe

A biographical outline of European history A.D. 700 to A.D. 1700

Henry Gay Hewlett

The Heroes of Europe
A biographical outline of European history A.D. 700 to A.D. 1700

ISBN/EAN: 9783337214302

Printed in Europe, USA, Canada, Australia, Japan

Cover: Foto ©Raphael Reischuk / pixelio.de

More available books at **www.hansebooks.com**

THE
HEROES OF EUROPE:

A

Biographical Outline of European History

FROM A.D. 700 TO A.D. 1700.

By HENRY G. HEWLETT.

"All history resolves itself very easily into the biography of a few stout and earnest persons." — EMERSON'S *Essays on Self-Reliance*.

BOSTON:
TICKNOR AND FIELDS
M DCCC LXI.

University Press, Cambridge:
Stereotyped and Printed by Welch, Bigelow, & Co.

PREFACE.

THIS work has been intended as a companion to Mr. J. G. Edgar's *Heroes of England.* The intention must serve as the Author's apology for his otherwise inexcusable omission of Englishmen. The plan and scope of the two volumes, however, are materially different, — Mr. Edgar confining himself to the biographies of " those heroes who, against the enemies of their country, have fought the battles of England at sea and on the land;" while the Author of the present work has given a wider meaning to the word "Hero," and endeavored to furnish a biographical outline of European history from the eighth to the eighteenth century. With this aim, he has been influenced in his selection of heroes less by a consideration of their personal eminence, than of their representative value. Particular epochs, movements, and episodes have

thus been illustrated in a single sketch, and threads
of connection preserved throughout the series.
The lives of *savans*, artists, and men of letters,
which it has been found impossible to connect
with the history of any such general events, have
been reluctantly omitted. The work being intended for popular use, explanations of technical
terms, and translations of foreign words have been
carefully supplied. While disavowing any pretensions to original research, the Author may be
permitted to state that he has uniformly consulted
the most trustworthy historians.

August 2d, 1860.

CONTENTS.

LIST OF ILLUSTRATIONS.

THE

HEROES OF EUROPE.

Introduction.

DURING the three centuries which elapsed from the commencement of the Christian era to the division of the Roman empire by Diocletian, the history of Europe is identical with that of Rome. The following three centuries and a half witnessed the gradual growth of the northern nations, resulting in the fall of the empire of the West and the decline of that of the East, — a decline still further augmented towards the close of the period by the sudden rise of the religious despotism of Mohammed in Asia. Weakened by the immensity of its extent, the excess of its military power, and the contrasting luxury and wretchedness attendant upon the unequal distribution of its wealth, the Western empire became less and less able to resist the tides of barbarian invasion which flowed in rapid succession from the North. The Goths were followed by the Huns; the Huns by the Vandals and Heruli. In A.D. 476, Odoacer, king of the latter tribe, finally abolished the last vestige of empire. From the

1   A

Heruli, the sceptre of Italy passed into the hand of the
Eastern or Ostro-Goths, who, under the wise rule of The-
odoric and his successors, for a brief space restored the
ancient dignity of Rome. At the expiration of about
half a century, the Eastern empire also, for as brief a
space, revived under the heroic influence of Belisarius,
and Italy was reconquered from the Ostro-Goths. The
invitation of a disgraced general, however, in 568, brought
on a new invasion from the Lombards, a tribe from Pannonia. Gifted with strength, courage, and sagacity, this
people retained for two centuries the northern provinces
of Italy, which it conquered. At the period when the
present historical outline commences, the remaining districts of that country were nominally governed by the officers of the Eastern empire, of whom the Bishop of Rome
was the most distinguished and the least dependent.

Passing from Italy to Greece, we find the emperors
maintaining a precarious stand against the strange and
formidable force which, in the space of less than a century, wrested from their grasp the richest provinces of
Asia and Africa. Mohammed, born at Mecca, in Arabia,
in 569, announced himself in 609 as the apostle of a new
creed. By the influence of his genius and enthusiasm,
Arabia was soon converted from polytheism to the worship of One God. The fire of fanaticism, once kindled,
spread from thence over the whole East. The love of
conquest allied itself with zeal for the faith; and Khaled,
Amroo, Omar, and the early caliphs, triumphantly bore
the sword and the Koran into Persia, Syria, and Egypt.
Though as yet Constantinople had been besieged without
success, the fate of the Eastern empire was doomed.

The most important European nation during the sixth century was that of the Franks, a tribe which, originally springing from the Lower Rhine, had successively conquered the petty states into which Gaul was then divided. Clovis, chief of the Salian Franks, from the close of the fifth to the early part of the sixth century, founded a powerful kingdom, embracing most of modern France and a large portion of Western Germany. Though suffering, at the period when our narrative opens, from the degradation of the original dynasty, it still preserved in itself a principle of life.

The condition of the rest of Europe at this time may be described in a few lines. Spain was still governed by the Western or Visi-Goths, who conquered it in the fifth century; but their rule was falling into decay, and was on the eve of being snatched from them by the Mohammedan conquerors of Africa. The Saxons occupied Westphalia and part of Saxony; the Frisii, the Low Countries; the Sclavonians, Bohemia; the Huns, Pannonia. Scandinavia was peopled by a hardy Gothic race, which, under the various names of Norsemen, Swedes, Danes, Norwegians, &c., made itself feared throughout the North of Europe. Russia, inhabited by rude tribes of Sclavonic and Gothic origin, had as yet no true history. Our own country, under the Saxon Heptarchy, had no unity or constitution.

The state of religion, although still unsettled, was in progress of reduction into one form. Catholic Christianity, so called, — viz. the doctrine prescribed by the Council of Nice in 325, — was professed by the Eastern emperors and their subjects, real or nominal. The Bishop of

Rome, as the alleged successor of St. Peter, had for some time arrogated to himself a supremacy over other bishops, and his pretensions to be the fount of Catholic doctrine were gradually obtaining ground. The adoption of Catholicism by the Frank monarchs gave it the ascendency in Christian Europe. The tenets of Arius (who, in the fourth century, taught that the Second Person of the Trinity was of inferior nature to the First) were, however, still held by the Lombards. The Visi-Goths of Spain, and the Saxons of England, were Christianized; but Germany, Scandinavia, and the remaining countries of Europe, save in a few scattered districts, were wrapt in Paganism.

The love of a contemplative and devotional life, which had manifested itself early in the history of Christianity, was still strong in Europe. The most illustrious monastic order was that of St. Benedict, established in the preceding century, and which, from its wise regulations for the government of the body as well as of the mind, was destined to exert a permanent and beneficial influence within the limited scope of its sway. The monasteries were the chief, if not the sole hiding-places of learning, which was restricted to the smallest possible compass in Europe at this era. Within the countries which had formed part of the Roman empire Latin was still spoken, but in a mixed and corrupt shape, which was gradually assuming the modern forms of Italian, French, Spanish, &c. The common art of writing was a rare accomplishment among the clergy, and the highest men of rank among the laity were seldom able to read. The fine arts, also, were scantily cultivated, their only seat of de-

sign being the metropolis of the Eastern empire; whence
the Byzantine architecture and painting, then prevalent
throughout Europe, derived their name. The state of
society, both as to morality and manners, was in keeping
with the political and religious condition above described.
Those general principles of justice and honor, which
everywhere govern mankind in a greater or less degree,
preserved the social fabric from ruin; but this comparative order was not inconsistent with the frequent exhibition of barbarian violence and crime.

Such is the condition of Europe towards the close of
the seventh century after Christ, — a condition of semi-
civilization; whence it is difficult to see which nation will
be the first to emerge. The first step forward proves to
be taken by France, — a country which, with all its short-
comings, has, from that era to the present, been ever distinguished in the vanguard of human progress.

Charles Martel.

CHRISTIANITY AND MOHAMMEDANISM IN EUROPE.

TOWARDS the close of the seventh century of our era, the kingdom which we now name France was peopled by a half-barbarous, professedly Christian race, of mixed tribes, the ruling portion of which originally sprang from Germany. The Frankish kingdom, as it was called, had risen upon the ruins of the Roman empire, and for about a century was remarkable for the ability of its sovereigns. But after the death of King Dagobert I. in A. D. 638, the royal family seemed devoid of any mental or moral strength whatsoever, and the kings of this line have been always known as *fainéans*, — weak idlers. The real power of the government was held by a succession of chief officers of the household, styled "Mayors of the Palace." The most distinguished of these noblemen was Pépin d'Héristal, who, from the year 688 to his death in 715, was virtually king of France, — the nominal sovereigns being but puppets in his hands. The country was then divided into two great districts, — the eastern, known as Austrasia; and the western, as Neustria. At his death Pépin left the reins of government to his grandson, Theodebald, an infant under the guardianship of his mother, Plectrude. The lawful king, Dagobert III., was also a child. It was clear that a fierce race of warriors required a strong arm to keep them in check, and could not long brook an infant's sway. The Neustrians commenced the revolt by expelling Theodebald and his mother, and choosing for their ruler a Mayor of the Palace named Raginfred. They then attacked Austrasia, which had not joined in the revolt. It was without fitting defences, and had no able man to direct its resistance against this assault. What course should the Austrasians take? Pépin, as we have said, left the government of France to a grandson; but he had a natural son, Charles, then in the flower of his youth. Whether on account of his not having been born in wedlock, or his having offended Pépin by some misconduct, Charles had been slighted, and even hated, by his father, who banished him to a monastery at Cologne, far from the intrigues of statecraft and the tumult of war. " Here," said the Austrasians, " is the likeliest man for our leader; a son of the wisest and firmest ruler the kingdom has yet acknowledged." It was agreed, therefore, by the people, that he should be invited to come, and a summons was sent from Metz, the then capital of the district, to the cloister at Cologne. Young and brave, pining in uncongenial society, and debarred from the employment of his talents, Charles seized this opportunity of release. Eagerly accepting the invitation, he hastened to return with the messengers, and soon, amidst the shouts of the delighted Austrasians, put himself at their head, under the title of Duke. The family of Pépin was not royal, and Charles doubtless saw the wisdom of yielding to the popular reverence for the ancient race of kings. The Neustrians had the same prejudice; and, accordingly, while Charles in the one district, and Raginfred in the other, virtually governed, their respective tools were Clothaire IV., king of Austrasia, and Chilperic II., king of Neustria, two descendants of the old dynasty. These events took place in A. D. 716.

The two countries now prepared for war. The Franks of Neustria were not so thoroughly and habitually warlike as their brethren of Austrasia, whose military system was better developed, in consequence of their position near the Rhine continually exposing them to conflicts with bands of Germans, which crossed the river in hopes of conquest. Nevertheless, the Austrasian Franks were now at a disadvantage, by reason of the unprepared state in which the Neustrian attack found them. Charles and Raginfred collected each an army, and marched at its head. The encounter was for some time doubtful, but the Neustrians gained a considerable advantage in the first campaign, and Charles was obliged to seek an asylum in the forests of the Ardennes region. Here, however, he did not long remain in concealment. Issuing forth at the head of a fresh body of men, he came upon the Neustrian army by surprise. A fearful slaughter took place, which he followed up by a vigorous pursuit. The Neustrians made a stand at Vincy, near Cambray. Charles met them here, and after a gallant struggle completely routed the force of Raginfred. This victory decided the fate of Neustria, and the crown of both countries was, in the year 719, placed on the head of Chilperic II. Either from motives of policy or of generosity, Charles did not abuse his success by the punishment of his rival, Raginfred, on whom he conferred the earldom and prov-

ince of Anjou. He himself was content to remain sole
Mayor of the Palace, under a show of obedience to a
powerless king.

A brave, iron-willed man, this Charles Martel appears
to us, — dimly as the light of historic tradition permits us
to behold him. He made his army the sole engine of his
power, and cultivated it to the fullest extent then possible
to him. Even the Church was not able to resist him;
and at his pleasure he seized on benefices which he
deemed too important to be placed in priestly hands, and
bestowed them on his warriors. A rebellion among the
nobles of Aquitaine demanded his attention; and thither
he marched with ruthless determination, stemming revolt
and establishing order. But he had a work to do in his
generation far more important to Europe than any he
had yet performed.

The Arab tribes, which in the last century had been
converted, by the genius of Mohammed, from idolatry to
the worship of God, and from lawless bandits into disciplined soldiers, were at this period pursuing their career
of religious conquest into the heart of Christendom. The
Gothic monarchy of Spain, under its last king, Roderick,
had fallen beneath the invading force, which now threatened France. The Duchy of Aquitaine, which considered itself independent of France, but which Charles had
reduced to comparative submission, opposed the only
barrier to Arabian aggression. Eudes (or Eudin), then
Duke, was a gallant prince, and did all that in him lay to
resist the claim which the new lords of Spain asserted to
his province of Septimania (Languedoc). He defeated
one invading army before Toulouse in the year 721; but

1*

the tide of invasion still flowed in. He then tried intrigue,
and bestowed his daughter on Musa, a revolted general
of the great Arabian leader, Abd-er-rahman. But all was
in vain. In 732 the Moslem once more appeared, in tremendous force, all over the South of France, ravaging as
they came, finally besieging Arles, and defeating its relieving army.

The wives and children of the invaders followed in
their train, as though they intended to settle in the country. Abd-er-rahman was advancing yet further on his
victorious way, when Eudes, as a last resource, applied
for aid to his enemy, Charles. What were personal en-
mities now? This common, national danger must be
averted at all hazards. So thought Eudes when he sent
to Charles. So thought Charles when he quickly summoned an army, and marched towards the plains between
Poitiers and Tours, where the Arabs were quartered.
The importance of the struggle that ensued cannot well
be over-estimated. Christianity and Mohammedanism
were at issue for the possession of Europe. The difficulties that lay in the way of the success of Charles were
very great. The Arabs were animated with the fanatical zeal of a new faith, and a greedy desire of domination. The Franks, on the other hand, were probably not
at all conscious of, or concerned for, the religious interests
which were at stake, and aimed at no more than a vigorous rebuff of an unprovoked assault. They had the advantage of familiarity with the country and climate; but
were outmatched, beyond comparison, in numbers. The
old monkish chroniclers tell us that the battle lasted seven
days. The Arab army was mainly composed of cavalry

and bowmen, and the Franks suffered greatly from the charges of the former and the unerring shots of the latter. But on the seventh day the combatants closed with each other. Heavily fell the iron hands of the sturdy Franks upon the sinewy, but slender frames, of their Asiatic opponents. Nevertheless, Charles had no cavalry; and the swift steeds of Arabia, with their daring riders, trampled down his battalions. Suddenly, there was a cry in the rear of the Moslem army that the infidels were spoiling the camp. More eager to save their treasure than to slay their foes, the Arabs turned in this direction. Skilfully interpreting the movement as a flight, Charles cheered on his men to pursue. The crisis was fatal to Abd-er-rahman. He tried to rally his cavalry. It was too late; and he fell, pierced through with many a Frankish spear. The incredible number of 30,000 Arabs is said to have fallen in this memorable defeat. The remainder fled through Aquitaine before the avenging sword of Charles. Well was he named "Martel," from the hammer-like might of his good arm! Who can say whether France and Germany, ay, England and all Europe, might not at this hour be sunk in such poverty and degradation of moral and intellectual life as Turkey now exhibits, had Charles Martel and his bold Franks fought less valiantly and enduringly at Tours?

History tells us but little more of Charles. He carried his arms into the Netherlands, conquered the Frisians and other tribes which then dwelt there, made them Christians by force, and vassals of the Frankish crown. In Saxony, and other parts of Germany also, his power was feared and obeyed. Pope Gregory II. offered to transfer to him the allegiance due from Rome to the Greek emperor, but the scheme was ended by the death of Charles. After the decease of King Chilperic II., in 720, Thierry IV. reigned in the same feeble manner as the other kings of his degenerate race. On his death, in 736, the people did not care to appoint a successor, being satisfied with the government which Charles continued to exercise under the title of "Duke of the Franks." He died in 741, at the age of forty-seven, leaving the monarchy to his three sons, Pépin, Carloman, and Griffo. Of the elder of these, we shall hear more anon. Charles Martel is the first hero who succeeded in stamping his image upon the surface of European history, after the chaos of the broken Roman empire had in some measure yielded to the spirit of order. He was chieftain of an unruly tribe, rather than king of a settled state. In this light we must regard him, if we would judge his character fairly; and thus considered, he may be said to have governed France wisely and well. If his memory cannot be cleared from the reproach of certain deeds of violence, we can afford to pardon him when we remember the good service that his strong hammer once wrought for Europe.

Pepin-le-Bref.

THE CARLOVINGIAN DYNASTY OF FRANCE.

CHARLES MARTEL, as we have seen, was never king of the Franks, and his sons were too politic to assume the title on his death. Griffo, the third son, may be dismissed from our notice at once, as he was from the government of the kingdom; his brothers, Carloman and Pépin, taking advantage of his weakness to dispossess him. After this act of supremacy they were for some time content to act as Mayors of the Palace, in the districts of Neustria and Austrasia respectively, under the nominal sovereignty of Childeric III., the last of the *faineant* kings whom they set up as a puppet. Carloman distinguished himself by attacking the Saxons and other tribes which threatened aggression; and in 744 Pépin severely punished a revolt of his father's old enemy (Eudes, duke of Aquitaine), who, as already stated, had been compelled to do homage to the Frankish crown. Pépin soon had no sharer in his power or fame. Carloman was not made for a soldier, and, under the sudden impulse of devotional feeling, resigned his office in 747, and retired into a Roman monastery.

Pépin, thus left sole lord of France, did not hastily attempt to cut prejudice against the grain. Feeling his

way gradually, he sounded popular opinion, for three
years, on the subject of changing the royal dynasty, and
placing the crown on the head of one who had a good
right arm to defend it.   Finding himself strong enough
at last to take decided measures, he quietly dethroned
Childeric III.; and shaving off his long hair, the symbol
of royalty among the early Frankish kings, sent him to
one monastery at St. Omer, and his son Thierry to another at Fontenelle.   This accomplished, Pépin proceeded
to obtain justification for his acts from the Pope.   This
was a novel step; for although the Bishops of Rome had
great spiritual influence over Christendom, in virtue of
their alleged descent from St. Peter, their temporal authority was by no means admitted out of their own diocese.   Pépin was a wise man in his generation, though
short-sighted as far as posterity was concerned.   He saw
clearly enough that no sanction which he could obtain for
his acts was likely to be so binding upon the minds of his
subjects, and the world at large, as that pronounced by a
power which had already fastened its yoke on the soul
and conscience.   The Pope, Zachariah, was not insensible to the importance of the Frankish monarchy, being at
the time of Pépin's accession especially in need of help
against Astolpho, king of the Lombards, who threatened
to seize on the Eternal City itself.   When, therefore,
Pépin's envoys arrived at Rome, and conveyed their
master's application, the pontiff did not hesitate to answer
that it was truly fitting for one to be king in name who
was king in deed.   Thus fortified against opposition, Pépin proceeded to fulfil all the ceremonies attaching to the
kingly dignity.   He and his queen (Bertrada) were duly

crowned and consecrated by Boniface, the "Apostle of
Germany," and Bishop of Mainz. This rite was performed at Soissons in 752, with all the pomp that the
Jewish kings had been wont to employ on such occasions.
The national assembly was summoned; and in the presence of the great Frank nobles Boniface produced a vial
of oil, announcing it as that which had fallen from heaven
on the day when the first king of the Franks (Clovis)
had received baptism. The sacred oil was then poured
upon the head of Pépin; and amid the acclamations of
nobles, soldiers, and peasants, he was crowned their king.

He was a man, like his father, well fitted to rule over a
warlike and rude people. What was most admired in a
king at that period was personal courage, and, what was
most needed, strength of will. Pépin had both; but he
had one defect, which, though to us it may seem a trifle,
to men who prized the body far more than soul or mind,
was a serious matter. He was of small stature, and acquired the name of "le Bref" in consequence. Fully
conscious that this was a disadvantage to him, — and, indeed, hearing his name once derided by his courtiers, —
Pépin took a speedy opportunity of proving that what he
lacked in height he more than made up in strength and
bravery. It was common in those days to exhibit animal-
fights at the Frankish court, as indeed, to her shame be
it spoken, is common in Spain to this day. On one of
these occasions a lion and a bull were engaged in a savage and mortal struggle. Pépin and his courtiers were
seated round the arena looking on, when suddenly the
king started up, and cried: "Who will dare to separate
those beasts?" There was a dead silence. The at-

tempt was madness, — certain destruction. Unsheathing
his sword, and glancing scornfully round upon his courtiers, Pépin leapt into the arena, and drew the attention
of the combatants upon himself. Raging with fury, they
turned to attack him; but with cool and measured steps
he evaded their onset, and by a succession of well-aimed
blows struck off one by one the heads of lion and bull.
Then, throwing down his streaming sword, he accosted
the astonished courtiers, "Am I worthy to be your
king?" A deafening shout was the reply, and the name
of "Pépin the Short" was no longer a term of derision
but of honor.

Having thus established his reputation for those qualities which were most essential to his influence, Pépin
took measures to render it permanent by acts of wisdom
and liberality. He frequently called together the national assemblies, and included in the summons bishops
as well as chieftains. Consulting with them as to the
most prudent course of action, he preserved their affection to his person and obedience to his orders. He especially courted the favor of the Church, and showed his
gratitude for the sanction which Pope Zachariah had
given to his accession by assisting the next pope, Stephen III., in a serious contest which broke out in 753
with the Lombards. Their king Astolpho took an active
part in the great religious quarrel which then agitated
Christendom with respect to the worship of images, es-
pousing the cause of the image-breakers, while Pope
Stephen supported the opposite side. Threatened with
invasion, the Pope flew to the court of Pépin, who received him with much reverence, and in return was

crowned king for the second time. Stephen even pronounced sentence of excommunication against all who
should dare to choose a king of France from any other
than Pépin's family. At the Pope's request the King
assembled an army, and marched against Astolpho. The
war lasted for two years, but eventually terminated in
the success of Pépin, who compelled Astolpho to yield
up to the Pope the exarchate of Ravenna, the last relic
of the great Roman empire in Italy, and of which the
Lombards had deprived the Eastern emperors.

Pépin, however, had in view a more national war than
this. The duchy of Aquitaine was perpetually in a state
of resistance to the authority of the Frankish kings.
This was owing in some measure, to the difference of
language and civilization which prevailed between the
people of the duchy and those of the kingdom. A spirit
of hostility was also fostered by the increase of population which Aquitaine obtained from the Gascons, a tribe
from the Pyrenees, not subject to the Franks. After a
long period of uncertain warfare, Pépin determined to
decide the struggle by active operations. He accordingly, in 759, took advantage of a rising of the people
of Septimania against their Arabian rulers. He made
himself master of Narbonne and other towns, and freed
the Septimanians. Then turning upon Guaifer, duke
of Aquitaine, he summoned him to disgorge the spoils
which he had seized from the Aquitanian lands of certain churches of France. Guaifer replied in defiant
terms, and for nine years resisted the attempts of Pépin
to reduce him to submission. It was a sanguinary and
desolating war. The fairest districts of Auvergne, Li-

B

mousin, and Berry, were laid waste and burnt by Pépin; and in the Frankish territories Guaifer levied an equally terrible retribution. He was murdered at last by his own subjects, and Aquitaine was annexed to the kingdom.

This was Pépin's last and most important achievement. He did not, as we might have expected he would, die in harness on the battle-field, but of dropsy, at the age of fifty-four. This event occurred in 768, at St. Denis. Long before his death he had obtained the coronation of his two sons, Charles and Carloman, jointly with his own, and directed his territories to be divided between them.

To be the successful founder of a new dynasty demands a genius which we may justly entitle heroic, expressive as that word is of strength of character merely, without regard to moral worth. Pépin, however, was not devoid of the latter, to a limited extent, and has left a memory which, if not remarkable for virtue, is at least not disfigured by vice.

Charlemagne.

THE common remark that great men have no sons —
founded upon very superficial observation, and offending
the natural probability, that genius is inheritable like
any other human quality — meets with a striking con-
tradiction in the case of Charlemagne, the third, if not
the fourth, of a family of heroes.

Charles, as his real name was, — " Magne," or Great,
being added as a title of honor, — succeeded on the death
of his father to the western half of his dominions only;
Carloman, the second son, ruling in the east. After a
brief junction of their forces to put down a revolt in
Aquitaine, the brothers quarrelled. The death of Carloman, however, in 770, prevented an internal war.
Charles forcibly seized upon his brother's inheritance,
and his nephews flew to Lombardy. He now reigned
alone over a large and imposing territory, stretching in
influence, if not in extent, from Holland to Spain, and
from Bohemia to the northern limits of France. But he
projected a far wider empire even than this, and, either
from zeal for religion, or love of power, — probably from
both motives combined, — set himself to conquer the barbarian and heretical nations on either side of him. To

the southeast were the Arian Lombards; to the northeast the Pagan Frisians, and Saxons; to the southwest the Moslem Arabs. The Catholic Church must first be freed from the galling insults which the heresy and arrogance of the Lombard monarchy inflicted on the Papal See. At the prayer of Pope Adrian I., Charles crossed the Alps, and marched against the Lombard king Desiderius, or Didier. Resisted in vain by the mountaineers of the passes and the garrison of Pavia, which held out for two years, Charles finally entered that city, and took the king prisoner; extinguishing the Lombards as a nation forever. After this success the conqueror visited Rome. Splendid, indeed, was the pomp of his triumphal entry. At a distance of thirty miles from the city he was met by the chief nobles and officers with banners. The path was lined with men of all the nations which acknowledged the authority of the Pope or the Greek Emperor. Bands of children chanted the victor's fame in chorus, and preceded him with branches of olive and palm. Arrived at the Vatican, he prostrated himself before his spiritual lord, and kissed each step of the palace stairs. But although thus humble in outward seeming, Charles was inwardly ambitious, and looked forward to the possession of a dominion with which the Pope could not presume to compete.

He turned next upon the Saxons, who had rejected with violence a mission which he sought to force upon their acceptance in 770. For thirty years these small republics struggled against the oppression of his despotic will. Under a warrior named Witikind they perpetually revolted, but with ever unavailing courage. After a decisive campaign Charles transported large numbers of the conquered race to other districts, but permitted to those who remained the exercise of their own laws, and even the government of their own chieftains.

In Spain he was less successful. though his conquests were considerable. A dispute between two leading Arab families led to his being invited to interfere. Electing to support the cause of the family whose territories were at the greatest distance, he crossed the Pyrenees, drove the Arabs beyond the Ebro, and then subjugated parts of Navarre and other Christian states, which he annexed to the Frankish throne. One great battle, however, he is said to have lost there, — famous in romance as that of Roncesvalles, — where Roland, one of his mightiest chiefs or paladins, was slain.

In Hungary, Pépin, the son of Charles, was victorious over the Avari ; a bold race of horsemen, who had for years despoiled the East of treasures, which they guarded in strong camps, called ringes. On these Pépin seized, and carried the spoil to his father in triumph.

A second boon conferred on the Pope (now Leo III.), in 800, namely, his restoration to the Papal Chair, whence a conspiracy of his own clergy had driven him, called for the highest reward which his gratitude could bestow on Charles. The conqueror again visited Rome, and on Christmas-day attended the great Cathedral of St. Peter to worship. As he knelt in prayer, the Pope came to his side, and placed on his head the crown of the Western Empire. And at the same moment the walls echoed to an universal shout of " Life and victory to Charles, the most pious Augustus, crowned by God the great and peaceful Emperor of the Romans!" Thus was Rome severed from her connection with the eastern empire of Greece; a new western empire founded; and the ambition of Charles achieved.

His dominion extended east and west between the rivers Ebro and Elbe, and from the river Eyder, the frontier line of Germany and Denmark, on the north, to the duchy of Benevento in Italy, on the south. His title of Emperor of the West was acknowledged by the Eastern Emperor, Nicephorus, and the boundaries of the two territories were fixed between them. As an instance of the vanity which Charles displayed on his accession to this honor, it is related that when the Greek ambassadors arrived they were conducted into a majestic hall, wherein was a man so superbly dressed, and seated on so rich a chair, that they concluded he must be the Emperor, and fell on their knees. The man rose, however, announcing that he was but Master of the Horse to the Emperor; whereupon the ambassadors, deeply impressed with the dignity of a king possessing such subjects, proceeded to the next hall. Here they prostrated themselves before another and yet more gorgeously dressed personage, on a grander throne, but were again entreated to rise, — the object of their adoration being but an officer of state. In two more rooms this illusion was repeated, until the wonder of the strangers was sufficiently excited, and they became overwhelmed with awe at the sight of Charles himself, in the last apartment to which they were shown, seated on a throne as costly, and surrounded with a pomp as magnificent, as any to which they had been accustomed at the Court of Constanti-

nople. This may have been politic affectation, rather than vanity, on the part of Charles, who dressed very plainly on ordinary occasions, in the fashion of his poorer subjects, and was simple and temperate in diet. His private life in other particulars will not bear strict scrutiny, being disfigured by the usual vices of his time and position. Yet, though his character was flawed, he has a great name in spite of it. It should always be remembered that, while a conqueror, he was far more. He was perhaps the most influential civilizer that the world ever knew. Whatever selfish motives may have prompted his policy, it resulted in schemes the most wise and beneficent. Stern and cruel, after the fashion of his age, in effecting his conquests, he was liberal far beyond his fellows in his method of governing the conquered. Like Alexander the Great, he attempted to make no rash changes in the constitution or laws of a people which he subdued. In one point, however, he differed from the Macedonian conqueror, who allowed the existence of every variety of creed in his vast dominions, whereas Charles made the adoption of Christianity an essential mark of obedience to his authority. It was his scheme to make a common faith the main tie of union between the various and dissimilar nations which acknowledged him as king. He accordingly parcelled out each conquered province into bishoprics, and established numerous monasteries and schools. Although regulating his empire according to the despotic principles of the feudal system (into the nature of which we shall elsewhere inquire), he endeavored to insure the permanence of his rule by allowing his people the right of self-government to a limited extent. With this view he summoned national assemblies, which included, not the nobles and clergy only, but also a certain number of persons chosen by each province to represent itself. These assemblies discussed the laws, which were afterwards affirmed by the Emperor's will. Literature and art were not neglected in his plan of government, although he himself was but scantily educated. He favored learned men of all nations, and gave generous encouragement to art, especially that of architecture. His anxiety to diffuse learning was shown by the personal attention which he gave to the progress of the schools which he set on foot. It is told of him that he thus addressed the pupils of a school which was founded in his own palace, and numbered among its members the sons of many leading men in the country : " Being rich, and sons of the first men in my realm, you think birth and wealth are sufficient, and these studies needless which would honor you in their pursuit. You care only for dress, play, and amusement. But I swear that I count as nothing the rank and riches for the sake of which you are reverenced, and that unless you quickly make up by hard work the time which you have wasted in trifling, you need never look for any boon at the hands of Charles."

A better stimulus to industry than threat or promise — as one may fancy — must have been the stately presence and solemn voice of the mighty Emperor to the trembling students.

How was it, then, — prudently and carefully as Charles planned and ruled, — that his schemes failed ; and the vast empire, which he had toiled to unite, broke up at his death? The empire was too vast; the work too difficult. The nations which he subdued were reduced by force, not inclination. The changes which he made in their faith were sudden, not gradual. The magnet of his genius kept the huge framework of his dominions together while he lived; but the attraction once removed, the whole fell asunder.

Lasting changes are effected in nature and history by calm and slow processes. Man, however mighty, in vain attempts to hasten the speed of the Almighty's mechanism, in the turning of the minutest wheel.

The symptoms of decay showed themselves in the lifetime of Charles. The national assemblies were not appreciated by the people, for whose advantage they were intended. They grudged the time and expense requisite to attend meetings of which they were too little civilized to perceive the value. The military service and taxes, enjoined by the great capitulars, or ordinances of Charles, however essential to the well-being of the State, were burdensome to individuals, and the encroachments of the nobles and the clergy increased the distress of the people. Added to these internal disorders, came attacks from without. Pirate bands of Norsemen perpetually harassed the coasts of the empire, and demanded the strictest vigilance and the strongest defences to prevent invasion. On one occasion, when Charles was resident in a town in the south of France, a vessel of Norse freebooters ventured to enter the harbor. The Emperor stood by a window to watch them, as they fled from the pursuit of his officers, and wept as he gazed. Observing the surprise of his nobles, he turned and said:—

2

"Do ye not know wherefore I weep, friends? It is not, verily, that I fear the harm which these robbers can do me, but I am deeply grieved to see how, even while I live, they dare to come so near: and am troubled to think of the evil which they will do to my successors and their people."

These disappointments, together with the loss of his two eldest sons, preyed upon the mind of Charles during his declining years. Though a tall, broad-shouldered man, of great natural strength, he sank into such helplessness, that he could not move unassisted. He retired from the duties of government during the last year of his life ; occupying his thoughts in devotion and his labors in charity. Towards the close he became utterly prostrate, for many days taking nothing but water as nourishment.

On the 28th January, 814, at the age of seventy-one, the great conqueror, after signing with his hand a figure of the cross, and uttering, " Into thy hands I commend my spirit," breathed his last.

They buried him in the cathedral of Aix-la-Chapelle, clothed in his emperor's robes, crowned and girt with his sword. His sceptre and shield lay at his feet ; and beside him a Bible and a purse, which he had carried after the manner of a pilgrim during his journeys to Rome. His tomb has been rifled ; but the name of Charlemagne may yet be read on the cathedral pavement.

The pages of history will forever preserve the same name. Great Charles truly was, both in grasp of mind and vigor of action. Though his empire, as a whole, fell with him, its ruin did not result in anarchy, nor did any relapse into barbarism occur among the nations which he had civilized. The principles of life and stability yet remained in the broken members, and the present partition of central Europe may be said to have originated with the dissolution of his Empire of the West.

Hildebrand.

WE have seen the Bishops of Rome, under their title
of Universal Fathers, or Popes, taking a prominent part
in politics, and extending their originally spiritual empire
to temporal domination also. This was gradually obtained
by the encroachments of successive Popes, not without
resistance on the part of the states whose power was thus
diminished. Charlemagne, though a devoted son of the
Church, was by no means its slave, and while he lived
the Papal See was governed by his influence. On the
dissolution of his empire, however, the interests of the
kingdoms which were formed out of it frequently clashed
with those of Rome. Throughout the middle ages, indeed, a contest for supremacy between the Popes and the
Emperors of Germany raged incessantly. It was an unequal fight. The Church in those days held the exclusive possession of learning, and offered the highest prizes
of rank and power to candidates, as well of the humblest
as of the noblest birth. It claimed, moreover, the direct
sanction of God for its authority: against its decrees in
matters of religion there was no earthly appeal, and excommunication from its pale was held to deprive the
sinner of the bliss of heaven. To these immense forces

the mightiest emperor could only oppose an army —
brave, yet superstitious — the very generals of which
were ignorant, unlettered men, however naturally gifted.
Brute strength might, and often did, prevail over intellect
for a time; but victory was certain to the owner of the
best weapon. A duel between two men, one armed with
a rifle and the other with a mace, can have but one termination.

During the eleventh century, however, this contest was
in process of action. Italy was in an unsettled state, and
a succession of weak or profligate Popes had disgraced
the See, which was bought and sold by the Emperors of
Germany and the Marquises of Tusculum, as one or the
other got the upper hand. The same disorder prevailed
in France, where bishoprics were disposed of by the
kings and nobles at their pleasure. The people, thus
deprived of that humane shelter which the Church had
afforded from the oppression of their lords, were ground
down to slavery. A firm arm was needed to restore the
dignity of the clergy and depress the tyranny of the
nobles, and at the appointed time it was uplifted.

Early in the eleventh century, Hildebrand, the son of
a Tuscan carpenter, was dedicated to the vows of a monk
in the convent of Cluny, in Burgundy. The youth was
thoughtful, pious, and staid, — devoted to the duties of
his calling, zealous in study, and rigid in self-discipline.
He soon acquired a high reputation in the convent, and
on his departure for Rome carried with him such testi-
monials as secured him a welcome reception. Benedict
IX. was then Pope, having been raised to that post at
the age of twelve by the influence of his father, the

Marquis of Tusculum. A life of shameless profligacy, however, led to this pontiff's deposition, shortly after the arrival of the young monk. A contest for the title ensued, in which the stranger took a leading part. The nobles supported the deposed Pope, who was one of their order; but the clergy gave their voice for a candidate who took the name of Gregory the Sixth. Hildebrand, it is said, undertook to obtain by the power of gold what would otherwise have been disputed by that of steel. Benedict was open to a bribe, and resigned in favor of his opponent, who ascended the chair of St. Peter in 1044. In gratitude for this service, Gregory at his death made Hildebrand his heir. During the brief reigns of the two next Popes, who were murdered by their political enemies, the monk was comparatively quiet; but attached himself to the Bishop of Toul, who was elected Pope Leo IX. by the Emperor of Germany in 1048. Hildebrand's genius now began to develop itself. Under his direction, the Pope set about the work of reforming abuses in the Church, and repressing heresy. Councils were held with this view, and the decrees there pronounced rigorously carried into effect. On the defeat of Leo in his expedition against the Normans, and his death in 1054, Benedict IX. again attempted to recover the Papal See, but was still opposed by Hildebrand. By the aid of the monks, who looked up to him as their great champion, he won over the Romans to submit to a second Imperial election, rather than the yoke of the deposed profligate. Henry III. of Germany nominated Victor II., and the choice was accepted at Rome. As the legate of this Pope, Hildebrand proceeded to France, where the abuses of the Church were most notorious. Here he remained a year, which he spent in making a searching inquiry into the prevalence of disorder, and ordaining stern measures of reform. The accession of Henry IV., a child of six years old, to the empire of Germany, in 1056, gave Hildebrand an opportunity of partially unfolding the schemes which he had hitherto concealed with respect to the exaltation of the priesthood. Two years afterwards, on the death of Stephen IX., who succeeded Victor II., a fresh contest occurred for the popedom. The Italian nobility chose Benedict X., in opposition to the voice of the cardinals, who, at the desire of Hildebrand, elected Nicholas II. Immediately on the accession of the new Pope a council was summoned, from which Hildebrand obtained a decree that cardinals alone should elect a candidate for the See on any future vacancy, — the emperors to retain the right of confirmation only. This bold act was managed with such art as not to offend Henry or his counsellors. His sanction was asked to the next election of Pope Alexander II., in 1061, and though it was refused, and an anti-pope set up by the Imperial party, Hildebrand carried his point by unceasing firmness. In 1073, on the death of Alexander, he himself was chosen to succeed. Before accepting the dignity, however, he disarmed opposition by expressing his anxiety to obtain the Imperial sanction, which he considered essential to the validity of his title. Henry gave this assurance accordingly, and Hildebrand took the name of Gregory VII. From this period, the genius of this extraordinary man fully manifested itself.

The aims of his life were to purify the Church from all

earthly taints, and with this purified Church to rule the
world. A mighty scheme, verily! one that an earnest
and faithful follower of Christ might lawfully conceive
and execute, but one that might easily delude the schemer
himself with its vastness, and lead him to glorify with the
name of zeal what was in truth nothing but ambition.
Hildebrand commenced by an attack on two leading corruptions of the Church. He summoned a council in 1074,
which pronounced a curse on all who committed the crime
of simony, — that is, the trafficking in spiritual benefices,
— and forbade the marriage of the clergy. The former
of these ecclesiastical offences was, as we have said, shame-
lessly and repeatedly practised, by no one so much as by
Henry the Emperor of Germany. The latter corruption,
as it was called, was scarcely less common, the tendency
of humanity to obey the laws which God gave for its government having hitherto proved too strong to be repressed
by the decrees of unnatural councils. Simony truly deserved the severest checks that Hildebrand could place
upon it, destructive as it was to the spiritual character of
a priest's office and the effect of his teaching on his flock.
For the prohibition of marriage to the clergy, there is
only to be said that the enforcement of this rule, inhuman
and monstrous as it was, procured for the Church the
advantages of undivided allegiance and stern discipline.
Men who would consent to cut asunder their heartstrings
for the sake of an idea, would worship it henceforth as an
idol. To the first ordinance of this council, the Emperor,
at whom it was chiefly directed, paid little regard, and
continued his sale of benefices as before. The second ordinance, however, created a painful excitement through-

out Christendom; the Milanese clergy, who followed the practice of the Greek Church, and were generally married men, being especially loud in their complaints. All protest availed nothing; the decree of the council was final; and the iron heel of the ascetic Hildebrand has trampled down thousands of loving hearts through eight long centuries since.

Finding Henry obstinate in his claims to the disposal of Church livings, Hildebrand ventured on a further and more daring step. At a council summoned in 1075, he caused a decree to be passed (or at least revived) abolishing the usage of what were called "lay investitures." This term was employed to signify the authority, which the Emperors of Germany and other monarchs exercised, of investing a bishop with his possession of the temporalties of his see; that is, the lands from which his income was derived. These lands were fairly enough considered by the great lay lords to be parts of their territories, and a bishop as one among other tenants. The form of investing a bishop was to put a ring and crosier into his hand, as symbols of office. Gregory used mild language in announcing this decree to the Emperor, but Henry showed no signs of yielding. He even entered into secret alliance against the Pope with the Normans, who were then ravaging parts of Italy. At the same time, some of the Roman nobles, either friendly to the Emperor, or jealous of Hildebrand's increasing power, executed a desperate plan of dispossessing him. It was Christmas-day, and the great church of St. Peter's was thronged with worshippers, before whose eyes the vicegerent of Christ was performing the sacred mystery of the mass. He was yet pronouncing the solemn words which accompany the supposed alteration of bread and wine into flesh and blood, and the ignorant yet devout people were listening rapt to the sound of his revered voice, when suddenly the doors were burst open, and a body of armed men dashed through the crowd, and seized on the person of Hildebrand. He was haled to prison, and his authority for a season usurped by the nobles who had thus sacrilegiously displaced him. But the clergy and the people were his warm adherents: a counter-faction was soon formed, Hildebrand was released from his prison in triumph, and his captors were banished from the city. He hesitated no longer to act decisively against Henry. He declared that monarch's investitures void without the Papal sanction; excommunicated his ministers on the charge of simony; and, after exciting the hopes of the Saxons and others who were in rebellion against him, actually summoned the Emperor to appear on his trial at Rome.

The young man's blood was stirred, and his imperial dignity chafed, by this insulting summons. His reply was an order for an assembly of certain of his lords, including both nobles and bishops, to be held at Worms. Here, after stating the demands of Gregory, Henry obtained a decree, by which the Pope was deposed on the very same grounds alleged against the Emperor himself, namely, simony and murder; to which the assembly added the charge of atheism. Gregory's anger at this audacity was only equalled by his determination to surpass it. He immediately, namely, in 1076, held another council, at which the Emperor was solemnly excommunicated, — his kingdoms adjudged to be forfeited, and his

subjects absolved from their allegiance. At the same
time were pronounced the great decrees which have
been called "the Pope's Dictates." These contain the
main features of that system of universal supremacy
which Hildebrand desired to establish. They announced
that the Pope alone had the power to depose emperors
and prelates; that he was the chief lord in Christendom,
to whom all monarchs were to kneel; that he might absolve subjects from their oaths to impious kings; that he
could alone make absolute decrees which might annul
those of lesser lords, but be annulled by none; that the
Catholic Church in all times must be held infallible, and
those out of its pale no longer Christians. It may seem
strange that these pretensions were so little resisted by
the sovereigns, whose power they not only weakened but
undermined; but when it is considered how sacred was
the sanction which the Pope could claim for his acts,
and how formidable the instruments with which he was
able to enforce them, we shall rather admire the courage
of a prince like Henry in occupying the position of resistance single-handed. He attempted this manfully for
some time, fortified by the support of the great cities of
Lombardy, which Gregory had offended by his decree
against the marriage of the clergy. But the excommunication of their sovereign was an excellent plea for
revolt with the rebellious Saxons, and a natural cause
of dread to those bishops who had been at first disposed
to side with him. A league, headed by the Dukes of
Suabia and Carinthia, was formed against him, and the
unhappy prince found himself deserted both by the
church and the laity. He nevertheless determined to

test the strength of his Lombard allies, and, although it was winter, set out for the Alps. The journey was painful and tedious, and its effects on the courage and spirits of the naturally brave and sanguine Henry were very depressing. Superstition, too, began to work upon his mind, and the result was that, although joined by a large body of Lombards, he considered it vain to contend with his powerful enemy, and resolved to yield. The Countess Matilda of Tuscany was Gregory's great ally, and both were then residing at her fortress of Canossa, near Reggio, in Northern Italy. Thither, in January, 1077, the Emperor repaired to seek absolution. Judging it best to adopt the outward tokens of submission, he put on the garb of penance, and appeared before the castle in a woolen shirt, and barefooted. On arriving, his guards were separated from him, and he awaited an audience in the outer court. Gregory was occupied, it was said, with the Countess, and the Emperor must wait. Thus scantily clothed, and fasting, in an atmosphere of intense cold, his naked feet resting on the snow, did Henry remain for three days, from morning till evening. Gregory at last considered the penance sufficiently severe, and admitted the Emperor to his presence. The spirit of the proud prince was tamed, and he humbly asked for absolution, which was granted. He, however, could not obtain permission to reassume the Imperial Crown until a decision on the subject had been given by a general assembly. Forced to accept these degrading terms, Henry withdrew from the Pope's presence, and found that his Lombard allies had deserted him in disgust.

Instead of further depressing, this intelligence served

to restore his fallen spirit. He repudiated his late cowardice, and prepared for fresh resistance, but failed for some time to recover his lost ground. The German nobles assembled, and formally deposed him in favor of Rudolph, Duke of Suabia. Henry led an army against the rebels, but was defeated. Gregory supported Rudolph's claims, and sent him the crown with an inscription, signifying that it was given in right of the Papal authority, transmitted from St. Peter. Henry's strength of mind was stimulated by this new insult. He called together a council in the Tyrol, at which he obtained the deposition of Gregory, and elected in his stead Guibert, Archbishop of Ravenna, as Pope Clement III. In the next encounter between the Emperor's army and the rebels, which took place at Merseberg, October 2, 1081, Rudolph fell by the hand of a young hero, of whom we shall hear more. Herman of Luxembourg proved an inefficient successor, — the spirit of revolt was crushed, and Henry remained victor. War was now declared by him against Gregory, whose allies were Robert Guiscard, the Norman leader, and the Countess Matilda. This War of Investiture, as it was called, from its original occasion, was continued for some years. Henry three times attacked Rome, but was repulsed, and withdrew to ravage the territories of the Countess. Negotiations were at length agreed on in 1083, and Gregory showed some signs of yielding at least a part of his vast demands. But in the next year a faction arose in Rome itself against the Pope's authority, and Henry was invited to enter the city. Advancing rapidly with an army, he appeared before the walls on the 21st of March, 1084, and

made himself master of the Lateran palace and the chief
bridges. Gregory was taken by surprise at the assault,
but contrived to escape to the Castle of St. Angelo.
Henry immediately took measures to install the new Pope.
On Palm Sunday, Guibert was solemnly consecrated by
several bishops who were opposed to Gregory, and the
shouts of the populace must have struck with most unme-
lodious concord on the ear of the fugitive through the
grim walls of his fortress. To complete the agony of
defeat, Henry was on the following Sunday (Easter-day)
crowned Emperor by the hands of the new Pope, amid
the renewed rejoicings of the people. But Gregory's
imprisonment was not of long duration. His ally, Guiscard, marched towards Rome with an army to aid him,
and fearing the result of an encounter, Henry deemed it
prudent to retire. The fierce Normans, who numbered a
body of Saracens also in their ranks, entered at Henry's
departure, and released Gregory. Unable to appreciate
the glory and beauty of the Eternal City, the barbarians
availed themselves of the plea of conquest to plunder on
every hand, — Gregory feeling either too enraged at the
late conduct of the Romans, or too powerless in the
hands of his allies, to prevent their violence. He soon
summoned a council, and again pronounced Henry and
Clement excommunicated. War might have recommenced if Guiscard and his Normans had remained at
Rome; but, sated with plunder, they retired to Salerno;
whither Gregory, feeling insecure at Rome, soon followed.

Here, in 1085, shortly after performing the solemn act
of consecration in a church which the Normans had lately
erected, he was seized with illness. Worn with recent

excitement and fatigue, his frame rapidly gave way. Mentally strong to the last, and persuaded of the truth of his pretensions, he repeated his decrees against Henry and the upstart who called himself Pope. With the proud words on his lips, " I have loved justice and hated iniquity, and therefore I die in exile," the great Hildebrand expired.

We seem to see in this extraordinary man a strong, earnest, and upright nature, distorted by pride, and overwhelmed with the greatness of a scheme which it was in the power of no single being to accomplish. His aims were perhaps pure throughout : they were, at least, noble in the outset, — as far as we can judge : but the fatal error of making self the representative of a principle, perverted the reformer into the despot. He thus accomplished as much evil as good. If he succeeded in freeing the Church from the interference of lay powers, he united such a vast temporal authority to the spiritual office of the Popes as speedily outweighed the importance of the latter, and corrupted the Church at its fountain. In short, he only changed one tyranny for another. Yet, let him have his full praise for a praiseworthy deed. He was martyred, but his work survived. His successors carried on the same struggle with the German emperors, and finally prevailed.

In 1122, Pope Calixtus II. and the Emperor Henry V. agreed to a compromise of the long outstanding question of investiture. By the terms of this concordat, as it was called, the Church was henceforth privileged to choose its own bishops, without any interference of the Emperors ; who also surrendered their claim to invest with the ring and crosier, retaining only the right to be present, through their officers, at the election of a bishop, and to receive his homage by the sceptre, as in the case of other tenants. Even this limited power was still further diminished by the concessions of later emperors. The growth of a practice, that the cathedral clergy (deans and chapters) should choose their bishops, finally centred all spiritual government in the Church. Thus Hildebrand's good work was accomplished. Would that his evil work had not lived also! But he had sullied his righteous ends with unrighteous means; and his successors imitated these no less than those. The arrogance and despotism of Innocent III., Innocent IV., and Boniface VIII., stretched the doctrine of Papal Supremacy so tightly, that it broke beneath the strain. The yoke of tyranny became insupportable; and at last, arming herself with the weapons of intellect, which Rome had so long wielded alone, Europe rose to her feet, and made herself free.

The Cid.

THE MOORS IN SPAIN.

As the heroes of whom we are treating belong to history, and not romance, we feel some hesitation in numbering the Cid in our list, — the narratives concerning his life and exploits being, to a great extent, merely poetic. Yet it has been wisely said, that much which must be rejected as not fact may still be accepted as truth: that is, there is often to be found, under the husks of legend and myth, a sound kernel of historical reality. This may be the case with respect to the Cid, — who, probably, was a warrior so remarkable for genius or bravery above his fellows, that he gathered up in a single fame the reputations of many others, with whose deeds he was credited, and whom, as a class, he accordingly represents in history.

Spain, long one of the most flourishing provinces of the Roman empire, was amongst the first to fall under the sway of the Visi-Goths, a warlike but enlightened race, which soon embraced Christianity. For three centuries the country remained under Gothic rule, but fell in 712 by the invasion of the Arabian conquerors of Africa, — a remnant of Christians only preserving an independent monarchy in the mountains of Asturia. This little seed of freedom grew and bore fruit. France, as we have seen, proved a formidable barrier against further invasion; and in Spain itself internal jealousies among the Arab families weakened the Moslem and strengthened the Christian power. In the eleventh century there were several states in Spain wholly unfettered by a foreign yoke. The enmity between the two races and creeds was bitter, and war raged perpetually. Yet it often happened that, at the prompting of private revenge or family quarrels, alliances were made between kingdoms thus naturally opposed to each other. A recollection of this fact is essential to a clear understanding of Spanish history at this period.

At the commencement of the eleventh century the chief Christian states of Spain became, through divers marriages, united under one king, Sancho, who died in 1034, dividing his territories among his three sons: of whom Garcia took Navarre; Ferdinand, Castile; and Ramirez, Aragon. Leon, the remaining Christian monarchy, was ruled by Bermudez III., whose sister Ferdinand of Castile had married. Just as this apparent junction of interests occurred among the warriors of the Cross, the greatest confusion prevailed among those of the Crescent. The mighty house of the Ommiades — perhaps the most illustrious of the factions into which the successors of the Prophet were divided — no longer commanded the allegiance of the Arabs of Spain. Its last prince fled, and the chief cities fell into the hands of independent lords, who constituted themselves petty Emirs in their own dominions. Instead, however, of taking full advantage of this state of anarchy to extend their united power,

the Christian kings weakened each other by unnatural
and deadly quarrels. Ferdinand, king of Castile, seems
to have been the principal aggressor. His great captain
in his wars, both with Moslem and Christian states, was
Rodrigo Laynez, who was called also by the Spaniards
Ruy Diaz de Rivar, from the name of his birthplace;
and by the Arabs *El Sayd* (Lord), which has been altered into *Cid*. He was probably born about the year
1026, or rather later, at the castle of Rivar, near Burgos,
in Old Castile, of a noble but not wealthy family. He
joined the army of Ferdinand, and rose by his talents,
strength, and courage, to the highest place in that king's
service. Among the romantic stories told of his early
career is one concerning his marriage, which forms the
subject of a popular ballad. The father of Rodrigo having been injured by a Count Gomez, the young knight
defied him to duel, and slew him. The Count's daughter,
Ximena, in a storm of grief and rage, flew to the king,
and cried for vengeance on Rodrigo, who met her face to
face, and awaited the result of her entreaties.

No one, however, was hardy enough to offer himself as
the damsel's champion against so doughty a warrior, and
Rodrigo calmly retired. His manly bearing and fame
won him a place in the very heart which he had so deeply
offended; and, with truly Spanish impetuosity, Ximena
gave him, not only pardon, but love. She again repaired
to the king, and asked leave to bestow her hand upon the
knight, — urging the curious plea, that she foresaw he
would one day be the most powerful subject in the realm.
Informed of this request, of which the king approved,
Rodrigo consented to the marriage, as an act of obedience

to his sovereign and of justice to the lady. The meeting of this strangely matched pair is thus described in the ballad (Lockhart's translation) : —

> " But when the fair Ximena came forth to plight her hand,
> Rodrigo, gazing on her, his face could not command:
> He stood, and blushed before her: thus at the last said he,
> ' I slew thy sire, Ximena, but not in villany:
> In no disguise I slew him; man against man I stood;
> There was some wrong between us, and I did shed his blood:
> I slew a man; I owe a man; fair lady, by God's grace,
> An honored husband shalt thou have in thy dead father's place.' "

It is unfortunate that this charming story is supposed to have but little foundation in fact. Many of Rodrigo's legendary exploits are still less authentic; but history and fable unite in declaring him a warrior of no common stamp. His master, King Ferdinand, as we have said, invaded the territories of his brothers and friends, besides those of his enemies. Garcia, Ramirez, and Bermudez, successively fell before his attacks, which Rodrigo, in the true spirit of knightly obedience to his lord, did not hesitate to lead. Sancho, the king's eldest son, was Rodrigo's most intimate friend; and on the accession of the prince to his father's throne on the death of Ferdinand, in 1065, Rodrigo became Campeador (or, as the Arabs called him, *El Cambitur*), that is, head of the army. The new king followed in his father's courses of injustice, and drove his brother, Alfonso, King of Leon, into exile.

In 1072 Sancho besieged Zamora; which one of his sisters, whom he had likewise despoiled, held out against him. The King was killed during the siege; and, as it was suspected, by the agency of his exiled brother, Alfonso, who succeeded to the throne. Rodrigo felt his

friend's death deeply, and did not scruple to avow his
suspicions of Alfonso. Before promising allegiance, the
Campeador insisted that the King should cleanse himself
by an oath of the accusation which popular rumor had
brought against him. To this Alfonso, whether innocent
or guilty, not unnaturally demurred; but the powerful
warrior was firm, and the King at last yielded. When
the appointed day arrived, Alfonso made his appearance,
surrounded by his courtiers, all obsequiously vying in
praise of his glory and virtue, and contemptuous denunci-
ations of his daring accuser. Rodrigo stood alone, and
gazed on the king sternly. Some of the nobles endeavored to dissuade him from holding this attitude of opposition, and to induce him to forego the demand which he
had made; but he put them aside, and repeated his challenge. Alfonso dared not refuse to accept it, and accordingly recited aloud the form of oath prescribed on such
occasions, — affirming, in the presence of his Maker and
the Saints of Heaven, that he was guiltless of the death
of his brother. He had no sooner concluded, than all
eyes were turned upon the Cid, who, in deep, solemn
tones, and with the most impressive earnestness of manner, imprecated on the head of his king every curse that
heaven or hell could inflict, if, in taking that oath, he had
committed perjury. The awed assembly then broke up.
Rodrigo, from that hour, was hated by the king and
shunned by the court.

Yet, aware of the Cid's value, Alfonso seems to have
concealed his resentment for some time, and even endeavored to win the affection of his great subject, by allying
him in marriage with one of the royal family. Rodrigo's

wife was now dead, and he consented to marry the princess proposed to him, whose name was also Ximena.
The marriage took place in 1074. It had not the effect,
however, of uniting the King and the Cid. After having
achieved a brilliant success over the Arabs of Granada,
who were at war with two other Moslem states in alliance with Castile, and having signalized his humanity by
releasing all his prisoners, the great Campeador was disgraced and banished by his ungrateful master. At the
court of the Emir of Saragossa the exile found a ready
welcome, and was appointed to a high post in the government of the kingdom. He did not bear arms against his
own sovereign, but headed the Arabs in several battles
with the Christians of Aragon and other states. The
invasion of a Moorish host into Spain, under the eminent
Caliph Jusef Ben Taxfin, chief of the Almoravides and
conqueror of Morocco, — the rapid subjugation of the independent Emirs, — and the defeat of Alfonso's army by
that prince at the battle of Zalaka, in 1087, recalled the
Castilians to a sense of Rodrigo's worth. He was invited
to return by Alfonso, and with great generosity consented; bringing with him a large body of men raised by
his own exertions and cost. For two years he made his
name terrible to the Moors, as the great Christian champion.

But even this fame was not sufficient to secure his
influence at court, and about the year 1090 he was once
more banished, and his estates were seized. He appears
from this time to have commenced a life of adventurous
and independent warfare with the Moors. He besieged
Alcocer, a strong Moorish fortress on the borders of Ara-

gon, and finally took it. With a band of determined warriors of his own stamp he ravaged, consumed, and spoiled all the Moslem territories which he invaded, — making a castle on a rock in Ternel his chief stronghold, and thence sallying out in forays. The place has been ever since called the Rock of the Cid.

The last and greatest achievement of this hero was the taking of Valencia. This city was in the hands of a Moslem prince, Alcadir by name, who had refused to acknowledge the authority of Jusef and the Almoravides over Spain, which they were attempting to subdue. The Cid, either as an ally of Alcadir, or from motives of policy, assisted him in the defence of the city; but it was taken through the treachery of its Cadi, Ahmed. For this service, the traitor was made governor in the room of Alcadir, who fell fighting bravely. A kinsman of the betrayed king determined to avenge his death, and asked the Cid's aid, which was promptly given. The Arabian historians relate that Ahmed yielded after a brief siege, on conditions of safety for himself and family. It is further related that this promise was faithlessly broken, and the guilty Ahmed sentenced by Rodrigo to be burnt alive for his crimes. The Christian historians happily acquit the Cid's memory of this barbarity; but all unite in recording the successful siege of the city, which he took in 1094. While he lived, the Moors vainly tried to retake it; but on his death, which is supposed to have occurred in 1099, Valencia again fell. Romance has colored with glowing tints this scanty historic outline of the Cid's life. Spanish literature, for two or three hundred years after his death, is almost confined to epic or ballad poetry, of which he is the hero.   To acquire such a fame demanded a force of character, which, if not accurately painted by these loving and fanciful narrators, cannot have fallen far short of the glory with which the world will forever associate the name of the Cid Campeador.

Godfrey de Bouillon.

THE FIRST CRUSADE.

THE Asiatic tribes which embraced the religion of
Mohammed, though presenting many diversities of character, were, during the middle ages, generally confounded
under the name of Saracens, the original title of an Arab
race on the borders of Egypt. As the Mohammedan
conquests extended, the sceptre of domination passed
from the hands of one tribe to another, and jealousies led
to the formation of independent states at various times.
The names of three only of the great Mohammedan factions need be borne in mind. The Fatimites, or followers of Ali, who married the Prophet's daughter Fatima;
the Abbassides, followers of his uncle Abbas; and the
Ommiades, who took their name from an eminent chieftain, Ommiyah. The hatred of these factions to each
other was intense. In the eleventh century the chief
power in the East passed into the hands of the Turks, a
tribe from the plains of Tartary, which, under color of
supporting the Abbassides of Persia, rapidly rose into
superior importance, and finally absorbed many of the
greatest Mohammedan powers into itself.

The "Holy Land" of Palestine, or Judæa, was one
of the most remarkable, if not valuable, portions of the

Saracen empire, to which it was annexed by Omar in the seventh century. Under the wise rule of the Abbassides, especially of such caliphs as the famous Haroun Alraschid, the sanctity with which Jerusalem was regarded alike by Jews and Christians was respected. Pilgrimages to the Holy Sepulchre were tolerated, and the pilgrims protected. This just and liberal treatment was exchanged in the eleventh century for cruel and bigoted persecutions, under one of the Fatimite caliphs, who had displaced the Abbassides as Commanders of the Faithful. Hakem even destroyed the great Christian Church of the Resurrection, and wantonly insulted the ceremonies of Easter-day. Succeeding caliphs, however, restored the toleration which Hakem had violated, and pilgrimages were renewed with increased enthusiasm. As many as 3,000 pilgrims, under the Bishop of Cambrai, set out for Jerusalem in 1054. None, indeed, succeeded in reaching the Holy City, — the majority perishing by famine and shipwreck. Undaunted, notwithstanding this failure, a body of 7,000, among whom were several bishops, undertook a similar expedition ten years later, and about half of the number arrived at their destination. A pilgrimage to Jerusalem was indeed one of the most common forms of penance for crime prescribed by the superstition of the age, and men, and even women, as well of the highest as the lowest rank, vied for honors in an ambition so holy as that of kissing the spot where the Saviour's body had lain.

Such was the state of feeling in Europe when, in the year 1094, the Turks (of whom we have spoken) besieged the Holy City, then ruled by the Fatimite Caliphs,

and took it. The bigotry and persecution of Hakem
were revived, and the pilgrims subjected to every form
of violence and insult. The Greek Emperor, Alexius
Commenus, whom the Turks had recently defeated, implored the assistance of the great Christian states against
this new and formidable foe. Pope Urban II., to whom
his letter was addressed, was then engaged in the same
War of Investiture which Gregory VII. had so long carried on with Henry IV., Emperor of Germany. The
Council of Plaisance, which Urban summoned to decide
upon the measures to be taken against the Turks, was
attended by the partisans on both sides of the quarrel,
and politics were angrily discussed instead of religion.
Meantime, however, the enthusiasm of the people of
France, Germany, and Italy, had been aroused to a
pitch of frenzy by the glowing and pathetic eloquence of
a French monk, named Peter the Hermit, who had recently returned from Jerusalem, where he had witnessed
the barbarities inflicted on the Christians. This earnest
and imaginative fanatic, deeply impressed with the holi-
ness of his mission, kindled in all whom he addressed
a like zeal. Urban gave him full sanction to awaken
Christendom to the duty of expelling the infidel from the
holy places; and in a marvellously brief space of time
the work was accomplished. France was the great
centre of excitement; and here, therefore, Urban, on
learning Peter's success, summoned his next assembly.
It was held at Clermont, in Auvergne, during the winter
of 1095, nobles and prelates, with thousands of lower
rank, crowding the cities and towns of the neighborhood.
At the tenth sitting the vast concourse was addressed by

Peter the Hermit, who pictured, in passionate and touching language, which drew tears from his hearers, the sufferings of the Christians in Palestine. Then Pope Urban, with more solemn and weighty words, appealed to the princes and soldiers of France who were seated before him. He reminded them of the national exploits of their fathers, whom Charles Martel and Charlemagne led against the Saracens; and called on the sons of such fathers to achieve yet greater deeds. As the burning words dropped from his lips they lighted a flame in every heart, and the whole assembly suddenly rose and shouted with one voice, " It is God's will! It is God's will!" Urban caught up the cry: "Yes, without doubt, it is God's will. He has dictated to you the words, let them be your war-cry, and be this your badge!" As he spoke, he held up a crucifix. The great meeting was moved like one man; and, falling on their knees, all confessed their sins, received absolution, and took vows of service in the Holy War. A red cross, embroidered on the right shoulder, was the common sign assumed by all the soldiers, who thence acquired the name of "Crusaders." The departure of the army was fixed for the 15th August, 1096; but the rude and undisciplined people whom Peter's teaching had aroused required no preparation, and were eager to set out at once. The result of this misguided expedition was such as might have been expected. As many as 300,000 persons (including women and children) are said to have set out under the guidance of Peter and a knight named Walter the Penniless. Ignorant of the route, blindly looking for miraculous support, and on the failure of this reduced to plunder, they fell into the hands of the fierce tribes of Hungary and Bulgaria, who massacred them by hundreds. Those who escaped the Hungarians, and reached Bithynia, there perished by the attacks of the Turks, and only Peter returned to record the fate of the expedition. Meantime, the highest nobles of France and Germany were arming and preparing in earnest for the enterprise to which they were vowed. Estates were pawned and sold to obtain money for the expenses of the undertaking, and many commercial cities purchased important liberties from their lords at this favorable opportunity. The chief of one of three great divisions into which the Christian army was formed was a man whom we have taken as the very type and model of a true crusader, — Godfrey de Bouillon.

He was the son of Gustavus, Count of Bouillon, or Boulogne, in the district of Ardennes and province of Luxembourg, and was born about the year 1060. His profession had been from his youth that of arms, and his earliest services in the field were rendered to his lord, the Emperor of Germany. In the war of Investiture he had taken an active part against Gregory VII., and bore the Imperial standard at the battle of Merseberg. By his hand (as we have previously hinted) the usurper, Rudolph, Duke of Suabia, fell in that decisive encounter. Godfrey's sword, swayed by his young and powerful wrist, is said to have shorn off the right arm of Rudolph at a single stroke. For this valiant deed, Henry IV. created Godfrey Duke of his province of Bouillon ; or, according to some historians, Lower Lorraine. At the subsequent siege of Rome, which we have already described, Godfrey

made himself again prominent by scaling the city walls
among the first. This action colored his whole life. All
his contemporaries portray his nature as displaying the
loftiest integrity and the deepest piety. Sound and clear
as his intellect was, he yet shared in the superstition of
his times, and was led by reflection to believe that, in
bearing arms against God's vicegerent, and attacking a
city where so many apostles and martyrs lay buried, he
had been guilty of a heinous sin. Remorse worked on
his mind so heavily that he took a vow to join in the
Crusade, from a conviction that his glaring crime could
only be blotted out by a heroism equally conspicuous.
His noble birth, and yet nobler character, won for him
so high a place in the estimation of his fellows, that, on
announcing his intention of undertaking the Crusade,
hundreds flocked to his standard. A worthy general,
truly, of soldiers thus ardent in a cause which they
deemed divine! To the qualities of bodily strength and
beauty, which in those days were chiefly valued in the
head of an army, Godfrey happily united the more dura-
ble strength of intellect and beauty of soul. His knightly heart and statesman's mind never ran counter; and
whatever generous policy the one dictated, was carried
into effect by the wisdom of the other. Although averse
to distinction, it was thrust upon him by the votes of his
fellow-chiefs, and their decision was gladly hailed by the
common soldiers, who loved Godfrey as a father. He
would not, therefore, refuse the post of general, but applied himself to its duties with activity. He first set an
example of unselfish zeal to his brother nobles, by disposing of his duchy for the purpose of his expedition, —

an example faithfully followed by the leading nobility of
France and the Rhine. He then summoned his army to
join him in August, 1096, on the banks of the rivers
Meuse and Moselle. At the appointed time, a force of
80,000 foot and 10,000 horse assembled under his banner,
and set out on its march through Germany, — the two
other divisions of the Christian army taking a different
route. On reaching Hungary, Carloman, who then ruled
that country, showed some signs of objection to the passage of so formidable a body, — remembering the licentious excesses that had been committed by the rabble
which followed Peter the Hermit. Here Godfrey's wisdom was admirably displayed. By his firm measures of
restraint on the impetuosity of his troops he first proved
that they were under the influence of strict discipline.
Then, confiding himself to the justice and good faith of
Carloman, he disarmed that monarch's suspicions by
frankness and simplicity. The result was that, instead
of opposition, the Hungarian prince gave him help, and
escorted the Crusaders with a body of cavalry into the
territories of Greece. Alexius Comnenus was by this
time alarmed at the eagerness with which the Christian
states had responded to his appeal for aid against the
infidel. He mistrusted, not without reason, the intentions
of some of the chiefs of the expedition, — mere adventurers, like the Norman Boemond of Tarentum for example, who was his avowed foe, — and therefore deemed
it politic to guard against danger to himself by demanding
homage from all the Crusaders who entered his dominions. The two other divisions of the Christian army
were now on their way to Constantinople, by a different

road from that taken by Godfrey. One of the French
nobles, the Count de Vermandois, was shipwrecked on
the coast of Epirus, and Alexius unjustifiably detained
him as a prisoner or hostage for the good faith of the
other leaders. On learning these tidings, Godfrey, who
was now in Thrace, sent to the Emperor, requiring the
Count's release. This was not accorded ; and Godfrey,
therefore, treated the country as hostile ; levying contributions on the people as he marched through. The Emperor immediately saw his error, and promised to grant
the Count's release on the arrival of the French army.
This promise satisfied Godfrey, and his march was once
more peaceful. The wily Emperor, in the mean while,
obtained from his prisoner an oath of homage, hoping to
induce the other Crusaders to follow the example. Godfrey, on his arrival, at first refused this, as unbecoming
the rank and character which he bore ; but, finding that
the act would appease the jealousies which had already
broken out between the Greeks and Franks, and put a
check on the schemes of those leaders in the crusading
ranks whom Alexius especially dreaded, at last consented.
The other chieftains made a like submission ; and this
sacrifice of pride, by healing internal discords, served for
a season to promote the success of the Crusade.

After a sojourn of some time at Constantinople, the
Crusaders, now formed into one army, crossed the Bos-
phorus, and entered Bithynia. Here the sight of the
carnage which the Turks had inflicted on the weak and
disorderly body that Peter had led forth, stimulated the
zeal and indignation of the Christian host. Its passage
through the Turkish kingdom of Roum was not unre-

sisted. David, then Sultan, a valiant prince, had already prepared an army, and fortified his capital of Nice, — a position of great natural strength.

The Crusaders advanced in excellent order; and, after twice routing the Turkish army of defence, commenced the siege. Godfrey is said to have distinguished himself by a feat of skill on one occasion during this assault. A gigantic Turk, who was the hero of the Moslem army, had greatly harassed the Christians by his wondrous success in the use of the javelin. Having spent his shafts one day, he ascended a tower, and showered masses of rock on the besiegers, whom he at the same time abused, and defied to combat. The Christian archers played upon his person, without bringing him down; until Godfrey grasped a crossbow, and at one shot pierced the giant's heart. The siege lasted seven weeks; and was prosecuted with such vigor and ingenuity by the Crusaders that the Turks were on the point of yielding, when Alexius, who had sent a body of Greeks with the army, craftily procured to himself the glory of conquest by instructing his general to intrigue with the Nicæans secretly, and persuade them to yield to his power, on condition of protection. The Greek general so worked upon the fears and hopes of the garrison, that his advice was accepted; and, to the surprise and anger of the Franks, the Emperor's flag one day appeared on the towers of Nice, and the city surrendered. This act of perfidy reopened the jealousy between the Eastern and Western Christians, which Godfrey had labored to extinguish; and from this time may be dated the rise of those internal divisions which eventually proved so fatal to the

3 *

Crusades. The seeds of disunion, indeed, existed from
the first among the Franks themselves. There was no
bond of alliance between the score of different European
nations which were thus assembled together, — save a
common faith and a common cause. How truly religious
was the feeling which animated the whole enterprise is
strikingly shown by the influence which it exerted in
keeping under control for so long a time the evil passions
which the unwonted junction of so many various races
perpetually excited. When we remember that the army
was governed by no single general, and that the troops of
one officer refused to acknowledge the authority of another, we shall rather wonder at the maintenance of any
sort of order than at the prevalence of so much contention.

Leaving Nice, the Crusaders advanced in two divisions;
both without guides, and through a hostile and desert
country. The Turks, in great numbers, followed in their
rear. Godfrey and the Count of Thoulouse headed one
division; Boemond, prince of Tarentum, and Robert,
Duke of Normandy (son of our William the Conqueror),
the other. The latter body had separated from the former at some distance, and was traversing the plains near
Dorylæum, in Phrygia, when a sudden attack was made
upon it by a powerful army of Turks. The Christians
were taken by surprise, while exhausted with heat and
fatigue, and in an unfavorable situation. In spite of the
heroic valor of Boemond, Robert, and other knights, the
battle was turning against them; when Godfrey's division,
to which a message had been despatched, came up. He
shouted aloud the Crusaders' war-cry: "It is God's

will!" and the whole army, echoing the shout, by a
gallant charge retrieved the fortunes of the day, and
completely routed the Turks. After this success the
Crusaders resolved to march in a single body, and thus
prevent a recurrence of the hazard which they had
escaped. The Turks preceded them, burning the crops
as they went; and the Christians, in consequence, suffered fearful privations from famine during the march.
Hundreds perished from exhaustion. The horses died
for want of sufficient food and water; and knights were
seen either walking on foot, or riding on oxen and asses,
carrying their own armor. In passing through Pisidia,
an anecdote is related of Godfrey which is characteristic
of his courage and gallantry. He was wandering among
the recesses of a forest in pursuit of game, which was
needed for the supply of the troops, when he came upon
a private soldier of the army, who was defending himself
from the attack of a bear. Godfrey struck at the beast,
which at once turned on its new assailant, inflicting a
deep wound in his thigh. Another stroke from the skilful hunter's arm terminated the contest; but the blood
streamed from his wound so rapidly, that he scarcely
reached the camp alive. The grief of his soldiers was
intense, as they beheld their beloved leader stretched on
a litter, and borne into his tent as if dead. The skill of
his physicians and a long interval of rest triumphed over
the weakness occasioned by the loss of blood, and Godfrey once more appeared at the head of his army.

Antiochetta, the capital of Pisidia, attempted no resistance; and here the main body of the Christians recruited
for some time. Meanwhile, a party of Crusaders, headed

by Baldwin, brother of Godfrey, and a famous knight named Tancred, had been sent forward to clear a passage for the army. Tancred subdued the city of Tarsus; but his victory was usurped by Baldwin, whose ambitious and covetous nature bore no resemblance to that of his brother. Tancred, a man after Godfrey's heart, surrendered this conquest for the sake of peace; but when Baldwin showed symptoms of repeating his injustice, resisted by force. Tancred was defeated, but a reconciliation took place between the combatants. Baldwin, who had no real interest in the success of the Crusade, soon afterwards turned aside into Mesopotamia, where he made himself master of Edessa, and formed a Christian state there. Though founded by merely personal ambition, this eventually proved of great assistance to the Crusaders, by checking the progress of the Turkish arms in Asia.

The main body now crossed the Taurus, after a tedious and painful passage, and presented itself before the walls of Antioch, then ruled by an independent Turkish emir named Accien. This city was especially dear to the Christians, as the first in which their title had been assumed; and the sight of its walls roused their flagging spirits. Some of the generals advised that the siege should be deferred for some months, until reinforcements arrived, and the winter was over; but the majority of the chiefs, among whom Godfrey was conspicuous, confident of success, and dreading the depressing influences of delay, urged an immediate attack, which was accordingly made. The Turks adopted the stratagem of apparently neglecting to defend the city; and the Christians,

falling into the snare, scattered their forces. The licentiousness of some of their number, moreover, proved fatal
to their vigilance, and a sudden sortie of the garrison
inflicted deadly havoc. The siege was then commenced
in earnest; but the city was so strongly guarded, that
months elapsed without any impression being made upon
its walls; and disease, famine, and the inclemency of the
season, united with the missiles of the Turks to weaken
the Christian force. Many of the leaders (Robert, Duke
of Normandy, among them) withdrew in cowardly disgust at the failure of the siege and the pressure of want;
while despair drove many of those who remained to
courses of reckless vice. Godfrey, firm to his duty and
strong in faith, aided the exertions of the clergy in encouraging the spirits of his troops, and restraining their
profligate excesses. A timely supply of provisions from
some of the Armenian monasteries, and a brilliant victory obtained by Boemond and the Count of Thoulouse
over an army which the Sultans of Aleppo and Damas-
cus had sent to the succor of Antioch, rewarded Godfrey's confidence, and infused new vigor into the hearts
of his army. This was needed to sustain the brunt of a
desperate encounter which shortly afterwards took place
between the besieged and their besiegers. A reinforcement of Italian Crusaders having arrived, it was suddenly attacked by a large Turkish force, and thrown into
disorder. Godfrey, who had been engaged on the siege,
rapidly marshalled his men, and fell upon the enemy.
A sortie of the garrison was immediately made, and a
fearful conflict ensued under the walls of the city. The
Turks were put to flight with immense loss, and the

Christians pursued them up to the very gates. In this scene of carnage, Godfrey's recorded feats of valor approached the incredible. His sword clave the stoutest armor asunder at a blow. A gigantic Arab horseman offered him single combat, and broke his shield by way of challenge. Godfrey rose in his stirrups, and smote the Arab on the shoulder with such tremendous force as to split his whole body in twain; half of which, with the head, fell into the river Orontes, while the remainder, yet clinging to the terrified horse, was carried back into the city.

Notwithstanding all these exploits, the Turks held out, and were only defeated at last by stratagem. This was achieved by the skill of Boemond, who intrigued with Phirous, one of the leaders of the garrison, for the surrender of the city, upon favorable terms to himself. Boemond stipulated with his fellow-chiefs that the principality of Antioch should be granted him in return for his services; and after some opposition, this was conceded. Phirous managed the perilous task of admitting the Crusaders with the utmost adroitness. At the dead of night the walls were scaled by Boemond and his followers; and Antioch was taken, in June, 1098, after a siege of eight months. Accien, its prince, and 6,000 Turks, are said to have fallen on this eventful night.

The Crusaders had no sooner obtained this signal success than they were in their turn besieged by an army raised by the Sultans of Mossoul and other cities. Antioch had just sustained so long a siege, that the Christians found scarcely any provisions on their entrance, and their besiegers now cut off all supplies from without.

Famine soon raged in the city to such an extent, that horses, roots, leaves, leathern shoes, and even human bodies, were eagerly devoured by the starving soldiers. Godfrey shared his scanty meals with his comrades, and is related to have slain his last charger for food. Desertions from the ranks now occurred in great numbers, and despair led many to blaspheme who were ashamed to fly. To add to the misery of the Christians, they learnt that the Emperor Alexius, who was advancing with reinforcements, had judged their case hopeless, and retraced his steps. The city was now scarcely defended, and many proposed to surrender it, even on degrading terms, so that their lives were spared.

Godfrey and the clergy again exerted themselves successfully. Religion, though under the form of superstition, proved the defence of the Crusaders. Miracles and revelations, it was believed, were vouchsafed, to cheer their hearts with a sense of Divine support. The Saviour and the Virgin appeared in person to one of the Lombard priests, and assured him of the final triumph of the Crusade. The iron lance, which had pierced the Reedemer's side, was found buried near the altar of one of the city churches, in the very spot which had been revealed to another priest by St. Andrew in a vision. These announcements, whether the result of fraud or delusion, had the effect of stimulating the enthusiasm of the besieged to an extraordinary pitch. They ventured to challenge the Turkish army to a combat of picked troops; and when the proposal was spurned, boldly advanced to attack the whole force. The appearance of the Crusaders, as they marched out of the city, must have been indeed pitiable.

Privations had so reduced them, that many had no clothing. Some were nearly fainting from weakness. The barons and knights proceeded chiefly on foot; and camels and asses supplied the place of horses to most of those who rode. Yet the burning zeal of the Christians made the march seem like a triumphal procession; and while the clergy sang hymns of consolation and victory, the soldiers responded with the war-cry, "It is God's will! It is God's will!" The Turkish general, fearing nothing from an army so scantily provided with the means of war, was taken by surprise, but hastily arranged his troops in order of battle. The sight of several natural prodigies, such as the sudden appearance of a meteor, and the favorable direction of the wind, acting upon the superstitious fancy of the Christians, impelled them to extraordinary exertions. The Moslem forces, on the other hand, were weakened by the existence of rivalries and discords in their midst, and lacked the stimulus which the Christians derived from desperation. The attack was commenced by a volley of arrows, followed by a charge of the Turkish and Arabian archers, which the Crusaders not only steadily sustained, but vigorously returned. Godfrey, who commanded their right wing, broke the left wing of the Moslem; but the latter had encompassed the river with a large force, and attacked the Christians in the rear. In spite of the heroism of Godfrey and Tancred, who slaughtered all that ventured to compete with them, and the brave resistance of the whole army, the enemy was evidently gaining ground, when (according to the historians) three horsemen, in brilliant armor, suddenly appeared at the head of a reinforcement descending from the adjacent mountains. Some of the clergy seized on this circumstance to reanimate the Crusaders. " Behold your heavenly succor!" cried a bishop. " Heaven has sent the holy martyrs, George, Demetrius, and Theodore to fight for you!" As he spoke, the whole army seemed inspired with irresistible strength; and, shouting the well known war-cry, made another vigorous charge, which broke the Moslem ranks. The Sultan of Mossoul fled, and his immense force dispersed in the utmost disorder. The extravagant number of 100,000 is said to have fallen in this engagement.

The Crusaders, instead of proceeding at once to Jerusalem, remained for several months in Antioch, employing the time in re-establishing Christianity in that city, and sending to their brethren in the West for further aid. The delay was prejudicial; as the disputes between the rival chiefs, which the din of war had silenced, again broke out, and disease committed terrible ravages in the camp. Certain expeditions, however, were made in the neighborhood, and several towns fell into the hands of the Christians. Meantime, news arrived that an army of Egyptian Arabs — who acknowledged the Fatimite Caliphs, and had as yet resisted the attempt of the Turks to usurp dominion over all the followers of the Prophet — had captured Jerusalem. The Crusaders, filled with indignation, resumed their march to the Holy City, conquering on their way several towns. Ambassadors were sent from the Caliph of Cairo with superb presents to the Christian leaders, and proposals of peace between them and the Egyptians. But Godfrey would not be bribed to accept the humiliating terms proposed; one of which was, that only unarmed Christians should be admitted into the city. The ambassadors were sent back with the answer that the Crusaders were on their march; and, if opposed, might extend their conquests even to the Nile.

By daybreak on the 10th June, 1099, the Christian army came in sight of Jerusalem. The spectacle transported all with mingled feelings of joy, reverence, and remorse. Some fell on their knees and prayed; others kissed the sacred soil; many wept for their sins; and the air ever and anon resounded with the shout: "It is God's will!" The siege was commenced at once, Godfrey fixing his camp on Mount Calvary. The Egyptians had prepared for a protracted defence, by strengthening the fortifications and furnishing the garrison with ample provisions. They had likewise ravaged the neighboring country, and filled up the cisterns, so as to harass the besiegers as much as possible. Owing to these impediments the Christians made slow progress. After various disappointments, however, they at length manufactured engines of great size and strength, shaped like towers, which were to be wheeled up to the walls, so as to enable the besiegers to enter by means of drawbridges. On the 14th of July, 1099, at daybreak, the Crusaders were in arms, and at the same moment the assault was made on various points. Godfrey stood on his wooden tower, which was stationed near one of the gates, and by voice and action stimulated his soldiers to deeds of daring. His death-dealing javelin never missed its aim. The Egyptians employed every possible agent of defence, — showering down boiling oil, combustible materials, and various

descriptions of missile, on the heads of their assailants.
During the first day the Crusaders were repulsed at
every point; but on the morrow fortune turned. The
first half of the day was with the Egyptians, who cast
lighted torches against the wooden engines of the Crusaders, and effected the destruction of many. Godfrey was
as usual conspicuous, and became the mark of repeated
attacks, — the cross of gold which surmounted his tower
especially enraging the Moslem. An incident, supposed
to be supernatural, was the immediate cause of the Christians' success. Godfrey and the Count of Thoulouse at
the same time observed the figure of a knight on the
Mount of Olives, who with his buckler signalled to the
Christians that they should enter the city. The two
leaders, animated by a common feeling, cried out, "Behold St. George!" The enthusiasm of the Crusaders
from this moment was irresistible. Godfrey's tower was
first pushed close beside the walls, and in spite of flame
and missile the drawbridge was lowered. Then, accompanied by several of his bravest knights, he dashed into
the city. Others followed at the same point; the gates
were broken down, and Jerusalem was taken. A horrible carnage of the Moslem ensued, in which Godfrey, although unable to check, refused to share. His first act
was to retire from his comrades, and with three attendants to repair, unarmed and barefooted, to the Church of
the Sepulchre. His vow was accomplished, and the des-
ecration of one holy site atoned for by the preservation
of another yet holier. This act of devotion, so worthy of
the true Crusader, recalled from carnage those who had
forgotten their vows in the thirst for vengeance, and the

whole army, led by the clergy, followed him to the same church in penitential procession.

Godfrey's work was now nearly ended, and his reward came. The leaders of the army, soon after the capture of the city, held a council for the purpose of deciding to whom should be given the crown of Jerusalem. No decision was arrived at; so many various opinions being expressed, and so many interests at stake. Ten of the most esteemed chiefs were then formed into an elective body, and proceeded to make careful inquiries into the fitness of those who were proposed for the kingly office. Godfrey took no part, it would seem, in either discussion or inquiry, and displayed no sort of anxiety as to his own claims. But the clergy and the mass of the soldiers were devoted to him, — endeared as he was by a thousand memories of his piety, courage, and generosity. On all hands the electors heard his praises sounded, and, to the joy of the whole army, they concluded their labors by announcing the choice to have fallen upon him. But, to the surprise of all, he declined the offered rank. " I will not wear a golden crown," said he, " in a city where my King and Saviour has been only crowned with thorns." All that his fellow-chiefs could persuade him to accept was the title of Defender and Baron of the Holy Sepulchre, though he did not deem it right to refuse the kingly authority. He soon had occasion to exert his power, for the Caliph of Cairo had by this time collected a large army, and was on his march to Jerusalem. The Crusaders, though unfitted for a fresh campaign, prepared to defend their conquest, and, at the head of his troops, Godfrey advanced towards Ascalon, where the enemy was stationed. A battle took place on the adjoining plains, in which the Moslem force was routed with terrific slaughter. The city itself would have fallen but for the covetous spirit displayed by the Count of Thoulouse, who, unable to obtain a promise that the possession of the place should be given him, deserted Godfrey with all his men. A quarrel ensued between the two leaders, but was terminated through the influence of their brothers in arms, — Godfrey being ready to forgive any injury to himself for the sake of the common cause.

The Crusade was now completed, but Godfrey's duties as king were yet to commence. He set about fulfilling them with activity, fortifying various important positions, subduing revolts of hostile tribes, dividing the conquered territories equally among his generals, according to the feudal system, and summoning an Assize, or Assembly of his wisest councillors to draw up a code of laws. This code, which long remained in operation, amply testified to the legislative wisdom of the Crusaders. But the new state was not long favored with his presence to enforce and exemplify its constitution. In returning from a successful expedition against some Arabs of Galilee, he was met by the Emir of Cæsarea, who offered him a present of fruits. Godfrey tasted a cedar apple, and immediately was seized with illness. He died, not without suspicion of poison having been thus administered, shortly after reaching Jerusalem, commending to his comrades the care of the holy places, and the state which he had founded. His age scarcely exceeded forty years.

One of the most celebrated and beautiful Italian poems, the *Jerusalem Delivered* of Tasso, has " the pious

Godfrey for the presiding hero of the glorious scenes which it narrates. But there are no grounds for supposing that his fame belongs to romance rather than history. Contemporary writers have painted his portrait in no less flattering colors than Tasso has used, and the poet's affectionate fancy has scarcely exaggerated the tribute which the soberest historian may feel warranted in rendering to the memory of the great and good Crusader, Godfrey de Bouillon.

St. Bernard.

MORAL POWER OF THE CHURCH.

In 1091, on the day when the renowned Christian
champion of whom we have before spoken — the Cid —
died in Spain, a yet greater Christian champion was born
in France : greater, if only in this, that the weapons of
his warfare were not carnal. We have had occasion to
praise Hildebrand for his efforts to restore the dignity
and influence of the clergy, — fatally as the power which
he thus conferred on them has since been abused. That
the work was good in itself we think will be clear from a
perusal of the life of the warrior-monk, St. Bernard.

His birthplace was Fontaines, near Dijon, in Burgundy; his father, Tecelin, a knight of honorable reputation, and so absorbed in his profession that he was compelled to leave the care of his seven sons, of whom Bernard was the third, to his wife Aleth. She was a pious
and gentle woman, strictly attached to the duties of religion, and anxious for the spiritual rather than the temporal
welfare of her children, whom she therefore devoted to
the cloister. A dream, it is said, had indicated to her
the future fame of her third son, before his birth. He
rapidly displayed signs of possessing no ordinary character. His education was undertaken by the then cele-

brated school of Chantillon and the University of Paris, where he remained some years, actively pursuing his studies. His mother died soon after his return home, and he then proceeded to fulfil her wish, which accorded with his own, of becoming a monk. His father and friends endeavored to dissuade him from this step, but they had miscalculated in attempting argument with a youth so singularly decided in opinions and convincing in eloquence as Bernard. Instead of being dissuaded, he persuaded five of his brothers and twenty-five other friends to join him in the career which he had chosen. His father and remaining brothers subsequently followed him, and the whole family took monastic vows. Bernard did not select for his abode one of those monasteries whose wealth and splendor had corrupted the intention of their founders, and softened the severity of the original discipline. His motive was truly religious, and took the superstitious form then almost inseparable from earnest piety. He and his comrades entered the poor convent of Citeaux, near Dijon, where the rules of life enjoined by St. Benedict in the sixth century were observed with great rigor. Frequent watchings, fasts, bleedings, and scourgings, for the purpose of mortifying the body; abstinence from conversation or laughter; habits of perpetual devotion, laborious exertion, and humble obedience to the abbot, were the main features of the system. Bernard undertook the duties of his office with such incessant zeal, and displayed such amazing control over his appetites, that he seriously weakened his health, but at the same time enlarged his reputation to such an extent that the convent became overcrowded with the number

of those whom he had attracted thither. He was therefore appointed, after three years' residence at Citeaux, to
head a colony of monks, which was to be fixed in the
valley of Clairvaux, — a desolate, though beautiful spot,
in the bishopric of Langres. The tears of their brethren
accompanied the departure of Bernard and the twelve
others who composed the band. It was in the year 1115,
and at the age of twenty-six, that he was made Abbot of
Clairvaux. His appearance at the consecration is described as that of a corpse rather than a man, so emaci-
ated with the rigors of devotion had he become. The
privations of the members of the colony were most severe.
The season for sowing had been spent in building the
convent, and when the winter came they were reduced to
little better than starvation. Coarse bread, and beech-
leaves steeped in salt, were their only food. This scanty
sustenance, together with the strict adherence to the
Benedictine rule, in which Bernard still persisted, so
shattered his health, that the bishop of the diocese, who
was his personal friend, at last interfered, and released
him from the active duties of abbot. But as soon as a
brief respite had restored his strength, Bernard renewed
his self-mortifying practices. A fresh attack of illness
followed, and he was obliged permanently to relax his
habits. In after years he lamented the error into which
his early enthusiasm and mistaken zeal had led him, the
effects of which greatly marred his future influence for
good.

Though debarred from laboring in his own sphere,
Bernard's energetic mind would not let him rest, and he
began from this time to exercise the power, which his

reputation for sanctity had brought him, in political life. He well knew the nature of the position which he was thus enabled to take, and did not shrink from its perils. " Bernard! wherefore art thou here on earth?" is said to have been his constant self-appeal. Poor and unarmed, a priest or monk in those days had nothing wherewith to oppose the tyranny of the powerful nobility, save the weapons of religion and intellect. How strong these were we have already seen in the case of Hildebrand; how righteously they could be used we shall see in the case of Bernard. In repeated instances he interposed the weight of his authority between the anger of a king or noble and the weakness of a subject or tenant, and scarcely ever failed in his object. One of the most remarkable examples of this kind was his conduct towards the Count of Aquitaine. This nobleman, a man of immense strength of will no less than body, and violent and despotic beyond his fellows, having espoused the cause of one rival Pope against another, dismissed from their sees several excellent bishops in his territory, who were adverse to his views, and supplied their places without regard to fitness of character. Bernard, having twice remonstrated in vain, after the last interview held a solemn mass in the church near the Count's castle, at which that nobleman, as excommunicated, could not be present, but stood outside. The consecration of the wafer was duly performed, and the blessing bestowed upon the people, when Bernard suddenly made his way through the crowd, bearing in his hand the Host on its paten (or plate), and confronted the astonished Count as he stood at the church-door amid his soldiery. With pale, stern face,

and flashing eyes, the daring monk thus addressed the
haughty chief: "Twice have the Lord's servants entreated you, and you have despised them. Lo! now the
blessed Son of the Virgin — the Head and Lord of that
Church which you persecute — appears to you! Behold
your Judge, to whom your soul must be rendered! Will
you reject Him like His servants?" A hush of awe and
expectation among the by-standers followed these words,
broken by a groan from the conscience-stricken Count,
whose imagination was filled with such lively terror
of Divine wrath that he fell fainting to the ground.
Though raised up by his men, he again fell speechless.
Bernard, seizing the opportunity, called to his side one of
the deposed bishops, and on the Count's recovery ordered
that the kiss of reconciliation should be bestowed, and the
exile restored. The effect of this scene was not transient, for the proud spirit had been subdued in the Count's
heart, and he performed penance for his offences by
going on pilgrimage.

Various other instances of Bernard's boldness in rebuking kings, nobles, and even Popes, might be adduced.
His most remarkable appearance as a political peacemaker was in the dispute which took place after the death
of Pope Honorius II., as to the succession to the Popedom. Two rival factions at Rome contended for the claims
of separate candidates; one a wealthy and worldly, — the
other a learned and pious cardinal. Bernard, as we may
suppose, supported the cause of the latter, who took the
name of Innocent II. At the Council of Etampes, where
Louis VI. of France and his nobles were assembled, the
monk's eloquence prevailed over all the arguments of

diplomacy; and the influence of France was pledged to
the side of Innocent. Bernard next engaged aid from
our Henry I. and Lothaire the Emperor of Germany.
He then proceeded to Milan, where the party of the rival
Pope, Anaclete, and his supporter, Conrad, Duke of
Suabia, — Lothaire's antagonist, — was strongest. Bernard's fame was so great, and the imaginations of those
who beheld him so fascinated by his force of will, that on
his way the sick were carried forth to meet him, and
numerous miracles were said to be wrought by the
touch of his garments. In Milan, through his eloquence,
Anaclete's party was completely vanquished, and the
Milanese so impressed that they offered to displace their
archbishop in Bernard's favor. But on this and other
occasions he steadily refused any such rank, content to
live and die in a sphere where he could be more useful,
if less exalted. He returned to France, after a length-
ened absence, in 1135, meeting on his way with a royal
reception.   .

He was once more absorbed in the duties of his office,
as Abbot of Clairvaux, when again summoned to Italy
by Innocent II., to oppose the power of Roger, the Norman King of Sicily, whose aid Anaclete had obtained.
Bernard first passed into Germany, and successfully
mediated between the Emperor and the Suabian princes,
inducing the latter to relinquish their rebellion. Lothaire
was then prevailed upon to aid Innocent by force of
arms, while Bernard proceeded to employ force of intellect in the same service. He first won over, by his
arguments, many of Anaclete's chief supporters, and then
accepted a challenge, which King Roger threw out, to

dispute publicly in the Court of Salerno, as to the claims
of the rival Popes, with Anaclete's champion, Cardinal
Pietro di Pisa. At this public contest Bernard not only
confuted but converted the Cardinal, and reconciled him
to Innocent. With Roger Bernard was not so successful, and a battle ensued between the armies of the contending Popes. Innocent was captured, but contrived to
make favorable terms with Roger; and a peace was
agreed to, which was finally ratified by the death of Anaclete in 1138. Another anti-Pope having been set up,
Bernard used his personal influence with the pretender,
and induced him to yield. Thus the schism in the
Church was healed, and the good Abbot returned to
Clairvaux.

In 1146 he was mainly instrumental in promoting the
second Crusade. News reached Europe that, two years
before, the Christian state of Edessa (which, as we have
already seen, was founded by Baldwin, brother of Godfrey de Bouillon) had, through the weakness of its government, fallen into the hands of the Sultan of Bagdad,
and Jerusalem was again in peril. Inflamed with enthusiasm, Bernard stirred up the hearts of his countrymen
to zeal in the cause of the Cross. Louis VII. of France
was readily persuaded to undertake the Crusade, as a
penance for his crimes; but the Emperor Conrad of
Germany was indisposed to exertion; and to him, therefore, Bernard hastened, rousing the people of France
and Germany as he travelled through. The frozen reluctance of the monarch could not withstand the fiery
earnestness of the monk. Conrad is said to have dis-
solved into tears at the discourse, and eagerly accepted

the cross which was proffered. While in Germany, Bernard showed his liberality of thought, — rare in those days, — by sternly rebuking the ignorance of a monk, who was denouncing the Jews as the cause of the recent calamities. At the Council of Vezelai (in Burgundy), held in 1146, Bernard's eloquence was as exciting in its influence on his hearers as that of Pope Urban had been on a previous occasion. As the speaker, at the end of his oration, held up the cross, which was to be the badge of the enterprise, Louis VII. threw himself at the feet of his subject, and the whole assembly thronged round him, shouting the old war-cry, "It is God's will!" Bernard distributed to thousands of eager hands all the crosses which he had brought with him; and finding these insufficient for the demand, took off the Benedictine robe which he wore, and tore it into cross-shaped pieces. So impressed were the chiefs of the Crusading army with his power over the people, that at a subsequent assembly they even offered the command of the expedition to him, — an unwarlike monk.

He declined the post, on the ground of unfitness; but had he accepted it the issue of the Crusades might have been different from what it was. His authority would at least have kept in check the discords, perfidies, and excesses to which he, probably with justice, afterwards attributed the failure of the enterprise. From these causes, together with a fatal incapacity on the part of the French and German generals, the second Crusade resulted in nothing but the wholesale massacre of the Christian armies by the Turks. Bernard, who had predicted the success of the expedition, was deeply distressed at the unfortunate result; the more as, with great injustice, the weight of popular indignation fell upon him, and seriously damaged his influence. This disappointment, however, did not discourage him, and only served to concentrate his attention for the rest of his life on the more immediate duties of his calling.

These he had never neglected, even while immersed in religious politics. By advice and example he greatly reformed the discipline of monastic life. He continually preached in his own convent; and, either personally or through agents, is said to have founded upwards of sixty monasteries in alliance with Clairvaux. Among them the Hospice of Mont St. Bernard, in Switzerland, has distinguished itself by loving deeds worthy of its founder. Bernard was an eminent theologian, both in theory and practice, and many of his works are extant. They disclose very forcibly his strong intellect and warm heart. Many of his opinions were most liberal for his age, and he rejected several tenets on which the Roman Catholic Church has since insisted, with a decision which would have ranked him among heretics had he lived a few centuries later. He manifested, nevertheless, a want of freedom in his conduct towards the great Abelard, who in that age represented the true Protestant spirit of inquiry into the received doctrines of the Church. Against this daring thinker Bernard unjustifiably employed the weight of authority which he possessed, to silence what he deemed a dangerous boldness of opinion. Towards Abelard personally, however, he displayed nothing but generous and respectful courtesy, even in the heat of controversy; and it is satisfactory to know that a cordial interchange of kindly feeling passed between these two eminent men long before their deaths.

Many of Bernard's wise and good deeds are recorded, which cannot be noticed here. We may refer to but one, which greatly influenced the world for centuries after his death; namely, the sanction and aid which he gave to the establishment of the Knight-Templars, a body of soldier-priests, who devoted their lives to the preservation of the Holy Places and the protection of pilgrims. Had they faithfully adhered to the statutes which he drew up for their conduct, the exhibition of zeal which they were designed to make might have been as blessed to Christendom as their arrogance was cursed.

A few years before his death, Bernard had the gratification of seeing one of his own disciples raised to the Papal chair, as Pope Eugenius III. The new Pontiff recognized his master's authority no less than before his accession, and Bernard's counsel and influence were repeatedly used in his behalf. But the over-activity of the good Abbot too soon decayed the slender strength which his firm will had wrested, as it were, from death, in a hand-to-hand struggle, that lasted for more than forty years. Always sickly, frequently reduced to the brink of the grave, yet perpetually at work, his constitution gave way in 1153, at the age of sixty-three. His last act was worthy of his life. He was on a dying-bed when a discord broke out between the nobles and the burghers of the town of Mentz. Bernard rose, and once more entered the arena of strife with the olive-branch of peace in his hand. The proud barons and the angry citizens listened humbly to his gentle words, and shrank from the

mild glances of those eyes which his biographers scarcely
ever mention without calling *dovelike*. The turbulence
of passion was hushed, and Bernard returned to die.
The filial tears of his disciples at Clairvaux, and the re-
grets of all the nation, followed him to the grave. About
twenty years after his death a decree of canonization
awarded him the title of Saint, which, considering how
it has been disgraced by unholy bearers, will not seem so
fitly to recognize his merit as that name which the reverence of the Church has further bestowed on him, — the
last of the Fathers.

4 *   F

Frederick Barbarossa.

THE GERMAN EMPERORS AND THE LOMBARD CITIES.

THE German empire of Charlemagne was formed by him out of five separate nations, — Saxony, Suabia, Franconia, Bavaria, and Lorraine, — whose constant rivalries this arbitrary union wholly failed to extinguish. On the termination of his dynasty, in 911, the empire became alternately elective and hereditary, — the former, as the desire of the people, — the latter, as the ambition of the reigning family preponderated.

Conrad, Duke of Franconia, was first nominated Emperor. On his death without an heir, Henry the Fowler, Duke of Saxony, was chosen to succeed him, and the title of Emperor continued for four generations in the Saxonian house. In 1002, on the death of Otho III., Henry, Duke of Bavaria, was elected; and on his death, in 1024, the choice of the nation fell upon Conrad II., of the Franconian house. Four emperors succeeded him of the same family; one of them being Henry IV., whom we have seen engaged in the War of Investiture with the Popes. On the death of his son, Henry V., in 1125, the Franconian line ended; but the heir to the estates of the family was Frederick, Duke of Suabia. A struggle ensued for the throne, and eventually Lothaire, Duke of Saxony,

was elected, — a prince who entertained an ancestral
hatred to the house of Hohenstauffen, or Suabia. His
daughter married Henry the Proud, Duke of Bavaria,
whom he hoped to procure as his successor, and therefore largely endowed. But on Lothaire's death, in 1138,
the Suabian party made choice of Conrad, the brother
of Frederick, Duke of Suabia, as Emperor: the Saxonian
party was compelled to yield, and Henry was shorn of
all his vast possessions. The whole of German and Italian history for centuries after this period is occupied
more or less with the progress of the contest thus arising
between these rival houses. It was finally grafted upon
the old quarrel between the Emperors and the Popes;
the latter taking part with the Guelphs — the name of
the Saxonian family — against the Ghibelines, a title
given to the partisans of the house of Suabia (or Franconia), from the name of a Franconian town.

Conrad III. died in 1152; on his death-bed admitting
the incapacity of his son, and recommending the electors
to choose as Emperor his nephew Frederick, surnamed,
from his red beard, Barbarossa, whose ability and judgment were undeniable. This prince was the son of Frederick, Duke of Suabia, of whom we have spoken as the
heir to Henry the Fifth's estates, and was born in 1121.
Impelled by youthful enthusiasm, he joined the second
Crusade, and much distinguished himself for courage.

Just and generous, accomplished in mind, and gifted
with a stately presence, he justified his uncle's praise,
and satisfied the desires of the German nobles. At a
Diet, or Assembly of both spiritual and temporal lords,
held at Frankfort, he was chosen Emperor, and imme-

diately crowned at Aix-la-Chapelle. Among his first acts was the extension of his power in the North, where two candidates, Canute and Sweno, were contending for the Danish crown. Frederick settled the dispute by deciding in favor of the latter, whom he obliged to do homage to the Empire. In 1154 commenced the most important events of his reign.

Italy, the darling of Nature, has long been, and is to this day, the victim of Man. It would almost seem as if, by some terrible law of compensation, Europe had been permitted to avenge, by a series of despotic and violent attacks, the tyranny which Rome succeeded in establishing for so many centuries over the whole known world. Pagan and Christian, barbarous and civilized nations, have successively trampled on the necks of the Italians ever since the fall of Rome. Foremost and latest in the number of their oppressors has been the German race, — one opposed in every quality of soul, mind, and body, to the Italian. The ground for this unceasing spirit of oppression has been the claim of conquest, originating in the feudal sovereignty acquired by Charlemagne through his victory of the Lombards.

This authority was for some time exercised with comparative mildness by his successors, and admitted without much opposition by the Italians. Periodical entrances of the emperors were made into Lombardy, where feudal service was rendered to them, and laws were issued for the government of the country. These visits were few; and the distance was too great to allow of the Imperial rule being rigidly enforced. Cities and towns meantime arose in various parts of Italy, and rapidly gained

strength ; while, on the other hand, there grew up a powerful order of nobles, who constituted themselves the
patrons or the despots of these communities. The one
were the germs of the famous Italian republics, and the
other the ancestors of those who became the kings or
dukes of the states into which dissension and corruption
eventually reduced those once free governments.

The War of Investiture disordered the whole of Italy,
some cities and nobles joining the Emperor, and others
the Pope. It served also to distract the attention of
Germany from its distant province, and gave time for
the growth of republican tendencies in the several communities. In Lombardy, especially, a large number of
cities practically asserted their freedom by settling their
own constitutions, and conducting their affairs on the
principles of self-government. They were stimulated to
this assertion of liberty by the spectacle of several scattered cities, which were nominally as well as virtually
independent. Such were Venice, Ravenna, Genoa, Pisa,
and others, which originally acknowledged the supremacy
of the Greek Emperor, but gradually attained their freedom, and were at this time in the most flourishing condition of social and commercial prosperity. In the south
of Italy, Naples, Gaeta, and Amalfi had for a considerable period maintained a republican character, and resisted alike the encroachments of the Lombard duchy
of Benevento, which Charlemagne had not reduced, and
the inroads of the Saracens, who from time to time ravaged Sicily and the Neapolitan coast. Before the accession of Frederick, however, the Normans had displaced
the Saracens, and subjugated not only these three repub-

lies, but all Southern Italy and Sicily likewise. Rome, under its spiritual lord and municipal constitution, enjoyed, like the North Italian cities, a virtual independence of the German Emperor; while Florence, Bologna, and other communities, were still more unshackled.

Such was the state of Italy when Frederick Barbarossa ascended the throne. A long period of strife between the the two powers which they had reason to fear, as their temporal and spiritual tyrants, had enabled the Lombard cities to acquire no little strength. Their commerce was extensive, their armies well disciplined, their fortifications secure. They kept in check the pride and violence of the neighboring nobility by forming leagues among themselves, which soon extended to an important and formidable association of interests. Yet these alliances, which naturally involved the domination of one of the larger cities over the smaller, often led to collisions. Milan and Pavia, for example, were constant rivals, and the minor states in their vicinity enrolled themselves under one or other of these powerful leaders. The injustice of the former towards Lodi, which in 1111 the Milanese razed to the ground for resisting their commands, gave occasion to the attempts of Frederick Barbarossa on the liberty of Italy at large. He had been bred and encouraged in the belief that to him, as the successor of the Roman and Frank Emperors, of right belonged the sovereignty of the world. The self-assertion of a city like Milan, therefore, must have seemed to him the height of arrogance; and he took occasion of the first act of misgovernment on its part to vindicate his authority. In 1154, two of the inhabitants of Lodi, which had remained in slavery since

its fall, made an expedition into Germany, and laid a
complaint on behalf of their city before Frederick in person. He contented himself at first with writing a letter
to the chief magistrates of Milan, in which he ordered
them to set Lodi free. On the Imperial ambassador arriving at Milan and presenting his letter, it was read
aloud by the magistrates. In the excess of their self-con-
fidence the Milanese tore the missive in pieces, and so ill-
treated the envoy that he barely escaped with his life.
Enraged at this insult, Frederick at once summoned an
army, and in October, 1154, made his appearance on the
Italian side of the Alps. He held a Diet on the plains
of Roncaglia, near Piacenza, where that assembly was
usually held, and was met by numerous complaints of the
nobility against the cities, and of these against each other.
Without deciding on the various questions thus raised, he
set out to visit each place in person. The Milanese, who
were bound by their feudal service to supply the Imperial army with provisions, performed this duty so ineffi-
ciently that the Germans plundered the villages on their
way to obtain food. The inhabitants of those cities in
league with Milan fled as he came, and Asti, in particular,
suffered from the ravages of his army. Tortona was bold
enough to resist the orders of Frederick that it should
relinquish its alliance. He thereupon laid siege to the
city, which a body of Milanese troops aided to defend.
The garrison held out for more than two months with the
utmost courage ; but water at last fell short, and the inhabitants agreed to surrender. Frederick spared their
lives, and allowed them to withdraw to Milan with the
personal effects which each could carry, but dismantled

and burnt the city. Dreading probably the chance of defeat if he attacked Milan itself, the Emperor proceeded to Pavia, where he received the iron crown of Lombardy, and then marched to Rome. Though ill-received by the Romans generally, he manifested a cordial spirit towards Pope Adrian IV., who in his turn was friendly, having reasons of his own for peace, to which he attached a condition.

Frederick was anxious to be crowned with the golden crown of Rome; but before this ceremony was performed, and even before he could obtain the accustomed "kiss of peace," he had to consent to a humiliating mark of homage to his spiritual superior, namely, to hold the stirrup of the Pope as he sat on horseback. The Emperor thought it wise to yield this point, and was accordingly crowned in the Vatican. Rome was at this time disturbed by the contests of those who looked upon the Pope as their temporal governor no less than Head of the Church, with those who had been roused by the eloquence of Arnold of Brescia to desire a republic. Arnold was a pupil of Abelard, and a reformer both in religion and politics. The Pope feared and hated him on both accounts, as he had considerable influence with the people. Before Frederick's entrance an embassy of the republican party met him, and in somewhat high-flown language vaunted the glories of the Eternal City. Frederick answered, with conscious pride, that the dignity of Rome had been transferred from Italy to Germany, whose sons were now the true representatives of the old Romans; and the ambassadors gained nothing from the interview. Urged by the Pope, who doubtless painted in the blackest colors the

danger of Arnold's teachings, Frederick delivered him
up, and the unfortunate man was burnt alive before the
city gates. One would fain acquit the Emperor of sanctioning this barbarity. It led to a vain attempt at revolution by the Romans, which nearly proved fatal to Frederick; but it was soon crushed, and he withdrew to the
mountains. Spoleto being remiss in providing supplies
to his troops, he captured and burnt it, — an act of cruelty which exasperated the Lombard cities. His army
was now weakened by losses and sickness, and he therefore returned home by way of Verona and the Tyrol.
The Veronese refused his troops admittance, but made
him a bridge of boats across the river Adige. This only
just served to land the army in safety, and then broke
by the violence of the current. Frederick attributed this
disaster to intention on the part of the Veronese, and it
added to his wrath against the Italians generally. He
returned to Germany, and occupied some time in preparing another and yet more powerful army. He found affairs, moreover, in Germany which required his presence.
It was at this period that he performed the generous act
of restoring Henry the Lion, son of Henry the Proud, to
the duchy of Bavaria and other ancestral possessions, of
which, as has been stated, Conrad had deprived the Saxonian house.

During the interval the Lombards recovered themselves. Tortona and other cities which Frederick had
destroyed were rebuilt by the bold Milanese, who gloried
in their advocacy of the cause of liberty against despotism, and provoked a fresh vengeance from the Emperor,
by attacking Pavia and other cities which had supported

him. In 1158 he had completed his duties in Germany, and collected a prodigious army, which eagerly gathered round him who was regarded as the rightful avenger of rebellion against German supremacy. By all the Alpine passes at once he poured his troops into Lombardy, and advanced to Milan by way of Brescia. This city was in alliance with its great sister, but the inhabitants were so terrified at the aspect of the Imperial army that they consented to break off the connection and pay a large ransom. Milan resolved to resist. The bridges of the river Adda were fortified, — but to no purpose, for Frederick's cavalry swam across the stream, and having captured one of the bridges, the whole army entered the Milanese territory. Having summoned assistance from Pavia and other cities, and ordered the rebuilding of Lodi. he laid siege to Milan in August, 1158. Finding its walls too strong to be beaten down he cut off the supplies of food, and reduced the inhabitants by famine. One of the neighboring nobles at last proposed terms of mediation, which were agreed on. The Milanese preserved their city from injury, and even from the entry of the Germans, and were allowed to retain their self-government and some of their allies, but agreed to pay a heavy tribute and homage to the Emperor, and guarantee the freedom of Lodi and Como. At a Diet of the kingdom, however, held at Roncaglia, a month or two after this treaty, Frederick announced a novel system of government, which in the opinion of Milan subverted its whole constitution. Instead of the Italian cities having consuls as before, a single foreigner, to be chosen by the Emperor, and called a *Podesta*, was to administer justice. Other ordinances were made, which seriously injured the Milanese; among them a decree for altering the boundaries of cities, whereby those of Milan no longer included the town of Monza and other ancient possessions.

The Milanese were so displeased with what they considered Frederick's breach of faith, that they expelled the Imperial Podesta on his arrival, and prepared for war. The Emperor did not at once attack the city, but after denouncing it as rebellious, at a Diet held in 1159, he attempted to reduce its allies. Of these Crema was among the most faithful, a small but strongly built and well-manned town. It was besieged by Frederick himself, assisted by troops sent from the Ghibeline city of Cremona, and heroically defended by the garrison, of which a portion was Milanese. The siege lasted six months, in spite of the Emperor's utmost endeavors. He was not naturally cruel, but on this occasion, either for the sake of making an example, or exasperated beyond his wont, was betrayed into deeds of great barbarity. He hanged within sight of the town some of the hostages which Milan and Crema had sent to his camp. Others were children and members of the highest families in Crema. These he ordered to be bound to a tower, — similar to that which we have seen was used by Godfrey de Bouillon at the siege of Jerusalem, — and thus drawn up to the side of the walls. By this stratagem he hoped to soften the rebels into submission, or to obtain an entrance into the city. But he mistook the characters of those against whom he fought, — true descendants as they were of Brutus and Manlius. It must have been fearful to watch the faces of fathers and sons thus brought close to each other under circumstances so strange and tragical. Not a thrust from lance or sword, not a cast from a sling or an arrow's shot, could be made by the besieged without wounding or killing their children. Yet the patriot would not give way to the father. Many thus terribly situated prayed that they might be put to death by their fellow-citizens; but all united to urge the children to meet their fate bravely. The assault was made, and the tower with its precious burden was driven back, after nine youths had been slain. The miseries of privation from food at last compelled the Cremese to surrender. The city was pillaged, but Frederick permitted the garrison to retire to Milan.

Many of the Germans returned home after this success, but the Emperor remained in Italy, and, with the aid of Pavia and other Ghibeline cities, carried on the blockade of Milan for a year, vigorously preventing the entrance of provisions, and destroying the neighboring country. In June, 1161, he was joined by a large German army, and so exhausted the Milanese by famine that in March, 1162, they were forced to yield. All expected some signal vengeance would be wreaked on a city which had revolted so often, and withstood so long. A month passed before Frederick gave his decision. It was one of mingled severity and mercy. "Milan," he declared, "shall be a desert; but the inhabitants may, if they will, settle in four villages outside the walls, and at a distance of ten miles from each other." He then returned to Germany. The city was razed to the ground, and the people dispersed; some near the site of their old dwell-

ings; others in various cities, both Ghibeline and Guelph.
Here the fame of their bold deeds preceded them, and the
endurance of Milan excited the highest admiration in
men of both parties. The oppression of the Podestas
and the burden of taxation further alienated the Ghibeline cities from the Emperor, and strengthened the growth
of liberty. The Lombard cause was now taken up by
one of the rival Popes, Alexander III., whom, on the
death of Adrian IV., in 1159, half the conclave of Cardinals had elected, in opposition to Victor III., chosen by
the other half, and supported by the Emperor. The two
Popes respectively held councils, and excommunicated
each other. Alexander fled to France, and obtained
recognition from nearly all the European states save
Germany. Victor, nevertheless, remained at Rome, and
relied on the Emperor's alliance.

In 1163 Frederick visited Italy once more, attended
by a small force and a train of nobles, with which he travelled, as if in triumph. But meantime the chief cities
of Lombardy and Venetia — some of which, as Cremona, had previously been Ghibeline, and others, as
Verona, had kept aloof from the war — entered into a
league to defend themselves, and endeavor to diminish
the Imperial power. Frederick was on his way towards
Rome, with the intention of supporting Victor III. by
his presence; but hearing of the League, stopped, and
summoned the Ghibeline cities to supply an army against
it. But he soon discovered that they appreciated liberty
too much to be anxious about his interests; and meeting
with no sufficient response, he returned home in anger.

For some time his attention was occupied in Germany

and France, to the exclusion of Italian affairs. Negotiations were pending between him and Louis VII. of
France, for the purpose of putting an end to the contest
between the rival Popes, when, in 1164, Victor III. died.
Finding that his ambassador had, without consulting him,
agreed with the Imperialist party of Cardinals to choose
Paschal III. as Pope, Frederick broke off negotiations,
and sanctioned the new appointment. Meantime, however, Alexander III. had returned to Italy, and employed
all his influence with the Norman King of Sicily, as well
as the Lombard cities, to resist the Emperor's tyranny.
It was time for Frederick to bestir himself, and accordingly, in October, 1166, he marched over the Grison
Alps to Lodi. Here he held a Diet, and promised to
redress any acts of injustice that his officers had committed. Finding himself in need of assistance from the
Italians of his own party, he proceeded into Tuscany,
where the Ghibelines were numerous. But the cause
of liberty had taken root here, and in Romagna also, and
he was disappointed of the support he expected. Ancona
resisted his entrance, and he was obliged to take hostages
from Bologna as pledges of fealty. He determined, therefore, to march to Rome. On arriving, he was opposed by
a Roman army, which Alexander, who was master of the
city, had collected for his defence. Frederick's German
troops defeated the Italians, and he obtained possession of
the suburb outside the Vatican. Alexander fled, and Paschal III. was solemnly installed as Pope, exercising his
pontifical authority by crowning anew Frederick and his
Empress Beatrice.

It was now the summer of 1167, when that wild and

beautiful plain which surrounds Rome, known as the
Campagna, is always pestilential. A terrible fever broke
out in the German camp, several of the most able and
valiant nobles, with thousands of knights and soldiers,
falling victims. The Emperor, therefore, hastily left the
city, returning into Tuscany with a shattered and continually lessening force. He was refused admittance by
the small town of Pontremoli, and actually was too weak
to force a passage. He crossed the Apennines by a difficult route, and reached Pavia in September.

During the past year the Lombard cities had strengthened their confederation into a compact and formidable
body. It was called "The League of Lombardy," and
both Guelph and Ghibeline cities were members. Its
object was the preservation of liberty, which the Emperor's aim, as his former partisans now clearly saw, was
to destroy. Cremona, which had helped to raze the
walls of Milan, proved its sincere recantation of error
by proposing to the League that the great city, which
had defended the common cause so bravely, should be
rebuilt. This was accordingly done in the course of a
few weeks, so strenuously did the citizens of all the con-
federated towns labor at this generous task. Milan was
again fortified, and its dispersed inhabitants flocked within
the walls. Such were the tidings which reached Frederick's ears when, saddened and mortified by the loss of
his brave army, he reached Pavia. He angrily summoned a Diet of his Ghibeline allies; but Pavia, Como,
Novara, and Vercelli, alone sent deputies. His spirit
was roused at the obstinate determination manifested by
the League; and though, in truth, almost powerless

against it, he would not yield. He addressed the assembly in a violent and haughty speech, and concluded by an imperious challenge to his rebel subjects, throwing down his glove on the floor, and defying them to battle. During the winter he tested his strength against theirs: finding his weakness but too apparent, he hastily terminated the campaign in March, 1168, and returned into Germany.

Here he found enough to occupy him for six years. He obtained the consent of the nobles to the coronation of his son Henry, a child of five years old, as King of the Romans, in 1169, — a step probably taken to secure the future possession of his Italian rights. Discords between Henry the Lion, head of the Saxonian house, and other princes, and a revolt of the Duke of Poland, demanded the interference and authority of Frederick, and prevented his personal presence in Italy. But at last he felt the necessity of taking measures to recover his lost ground in that country, which daily became more and more alienated from him. Novara, Como, and other Ghibeline cities had joined the League, which was fomented by the influence of Alexander III., and rapidly increased in strength.

In honor of the Pope, and as a protection against the yet powerful party of the Imperialists in Pavia, a new city was built in the plain, near the spot where the rivers Tanaro and Bormida join their waters. It was called Alessandria; and though rapidly built, was amply peopled and fortified. Another anti-Pope, Calixtus III., had been set up by the Ghibelines, on the death of Paschal, against Alexander; but the cause of the latter was gaining ground, and on all hands Frederick's supporters deserted him.

In 1173 he sent an army, under Christian, the Archbishop of Mentz, into Tuscany. The prelate succeeded in animating some members of the Ghibeline party there by intrigues and bribes ; promising the Emperor's aid to those cities which desired to be revenged on their personal foes ; flattering the despotic nobles, and humbling the independent burghers. Ancona boldly resisted all attempts to seduce it from the League, and Christian accordingly besieged it in 1174, with a Tuscan army.

The citizens, secure in their sense of right, and confiding in the promised succor of their confederates, as well as in the natural strength of the town, held out bravely. Blockaded both by land and sea, cut off from all supplies from without, and as yet unassisted by their allies, the Anconese were reduced to the utmost extremity of famine. Rock-herbs, shell-fish, and even leather, were eagerly eaten by the starving garrison. A touching instance of patriotism is recorded of a young mother, who offered her breast to a fainting soldier, unable, without such support, to fulfil his duty in the ranks. In spite of all their privations, the Archbishop failed in persuading the inhabitants to surrender. His army was weakened by losses, and when he saw the beacon fires of the Ferrarese, who at last came to the help of Ancona, gleaming on the neighboring mountains, he judged it wise to raise the siege and withdraw.

Frederick was by this time on his way to Italy in person, — entering Piedmont in October, 1174. He captured Suza, and so threatened Asti that it yielded

without opposition. Alessandria, however, resisted; and
for four months its newly built walls, manned by brave
soldiers, defied his assaults. Baffled by this obstinacy,
straitened in his resources through the sickness of his
troops, and menaced by the approach of the League's
army against him, he was forced to follow the example
of Christian, and raise the siege.

Arrived at Pavia, he attempted to negotiate with both
the Lombards and the Pope. They were willing to
listen to reasonable terms, but Frederick still clung to
his old prerogatives, inherited, as he said, from his ancestors. He claimed so much that the commissioners
appointed to draw up a treaty could come to no satisfactory result, and war was resumed. Joined by another
German army in 1176, he planned to attack Milan, and
punish the insolence of her citizens. The two armies
encountered each other on the 29th of May, at Lignano,
within a few miles of the city. The Lombard forces
were chiefly composed of Milanese militia, with a few
allies. In the centre of the body was placed the *caroc-
cio*, or sacred car of the city, after ·a fashion adopted
throughout the free Italian states. This car contained
an altar, at which mass was daily said; and above it rose
the municipal standards, flaunting their heraldic colors in
the sunshine, — the figure of Christ, with outstretched
arms, surmounting all. Round this holy ark of liberty
fought a band of young Milanese, who were sworn to
defend it. They were nine hundred in number, and
known as "The Company of Death," from their desperate patriotism.

At the first onset of Frederick's cavalry the Lombards

gave way, and the battle might have been lost, had not "the Company of Death," fearful for the safety of their treasure, nobly vindicated their vow. All knelt down to renew it,—calling upon God and the patron saint of Milan, St. Ambrose, to aid them. Excited to a pitch of unwonted zeal, they rose, and charged the Germans. The attack was so sudden and furious that the tide of victory turned. The rest of the Lombards followed up the advantage, and the enemy was forced back. The defeat was so general that the camp fell into the hands of the Italians. Frederick himself was obliged to flee; and the Empress, who was at Pavia, believed him slain. After a concealment of some days, and encountering great perils, he reached that city in safety.

He was now convinced of the power of the League, and weary of ill-success. Having opened fresh negotiations with the Pope, the two met at Venice, by arrangement, in March, 1177. But while ready to be reconciled to the Church, he could not even yet brook the idea of making concessions to his subjects. A truce of six years was at last agreed to, during which time freedom was guaranteed to the leagued cities; but a final decision was postponed.

Frederick returned to Germany, after reconciling himself to Alexander III., whom he consented to acknowledge in lieu of the anti-Pope, Calixtus. During the six years of truce with Italy, the Emperor's active mind was not at rest. He had married Beatrice, heiress of the throne of Burgundy, and must needs visit that country to take its crown. He went to Arles, and was there crowned with his Queen. He returned home to punish

Henry the Lion, Duke of Saxony, who had offended him deeply, by ungratefully refusing to aid him in the last Italian campaign. Certain complaints having been brought against this nobleman, Frederick summoned him to appear at a Diet of the empire. He resisted, but in vain; being finally banished for seven years, and his estates confiscated. This further rupture between the Ghibeline and Guelph party led to results which may be noticed hereafter.

Frederick's son Henry was now anxious to secure his future rights in Italy; and this, coupled with the loss of the Imperial revenue, which was not paid during the truce, induced the Emperor to yield reluctantly what he doubtless saw he could not longer withhold from the Italians, — a recognition of their liberty. A great Diet was accordingly held at Constance, in 1183, and a treaty signed on the 25th of June in that year. By it the Lombard League was allowed, and the right of the cities to raise armies, fortify their walls, and govern themselves, was acknowledged. On the other hand, certain rights of the Emperor were admitted by the cities, — such as the investiture of their officers by his legates, and the appointment of a supreme Judge of Appeal. These claims, however, could be compounded for by a money fine if preferred. Thus ended the first great attempt of the Emperors of Germany on the liberties of Italy.

Frederick's power was not really weakened by the concessions he had thus made, and in Germany he had always maintained order by the wisdom and firmness of his government. Peace now prevailed in all his domin-

ions, and he took advantage of the opportunity to secure
their possession to his family. In 1184 he summoned a
general Diet at Mentz, at which his Empress, with his
five sons, and a crowd of nobles, both spiritual and lay-
ambassadors, and knights, amounting it is said to 70,000,
besides a multitude of untitled persons, assembled to do
him honor. Here he secured the fealty of the nobles
and people to his sons, and a festival of unexampled
magnificence was held on the occasion. Every species
of rejoicing was celebrated, and the Diet of Mentz has
never since been forgotten. To this day the Rhenish
peasants sing the ballads which were composed by the
Court minstrels at that splendid scene. Anxious to preserve what he still retained in Italy, and perhaps stimulated by real magnanimity of feeling, he once more visited that country in 1185 : not now in triumph or anger,
but dignified conciliation. The Lombard cities met his
advances in the same generous spirit, receiving him cordially and honorably. With Milan he even formed a
friendly alliance, and won the affection of the people by
his geniality and frankness. He was less amicable with
the new Pope, Lucius III., who succeeded Alexander
III. in 1181, touching the right to the Duchy of Spoleto
and the March of Ancona, territories always held of the
Empire, but which the Papal See, in virtue of a grant by
the Countess Matilda of Tuscany, now claimed as the
"patrimonial inheritance of St. Peter." The dispute did
not proceed far, as Frederick's son, Henry, had married
the daughter and heiress of the Norman King of Sicily,
whose alliance was therefore lost to the Pope.

The last years of Frederick's life were spent, like the

first, in a campaign of a very different character to that in which most of his reign had been passed. The Christian kingdom of Jerusalem, after the death of Godfrey de Bouillon, had long maintained a successful stand against the Moslem states in its vicinity, under the able rule of his immediate successors. The unfortunate result of the second Crusade did not for some time affect its prosperity. The ambition of Amaury, a prince of the House of Anjou, who filled the throne in the middle of the twelfth century, led him to make an attempt upon Egypt, which not only failed, but drew upon him the vengeance of its Caliph, Saladin, the Moslem hero of his time, and a prince of singular ability. Amaury's successors were yet weaker than himself, and quarrels for the government ensued; which, coupled with the licentiousness of other Christian princes in Antioch and elsewhere, destroyed the effects of the first Crusade, and left Palestine once more a prey to the Moslem. Saladin was completely successful in his invasion, and Jerusalem fell into his hands in 1187. The news reached Europe, where it excited mingled feelings of grief, shame, and indignation. Popes Gregory VIII. and Clement III. roused Christendom to the duty of revenge; and the third Crusade was actively set on foot.

Under the pressure of religious conviction, Frederick adopted the Cross, and with an army of upwards of 150,000 men marched, in the spring of 1189, through Hungary and Asia Minor. The Greek Emperor, like his predecessor during the first Crusade, was jealous of the success of other European powers, and broke faith with the Crusaders, by making a secret agreement with

Saladin and the Sultan of Iconium, that every obstacle should be thrown in the way of the Germans. But, in spite of this perfidy, Frederick's army was victorious in two engagements with the Turks, and took the city of Iconium. He had advanced as far as the banks of the river Calycadnus (or Selef), in Cilicia, when he was stopped at the ford by a crowd of pack-horses. Impatient of delay, though now nearly seventy years of age, he set spurs to his horse and plunged into the river. The current was rapid at the time, and the Emperor's strong charger struggled in vain against it. In the sight of his army the gallant old man was swept down out of reach, stunned against a tree which overhung the water, and drowned. This event occurred on the 10th of June, 1190.* His troops proceeded on their march, after duly mourning for their loss; but not many survived him long, — his son Frederick, Duke of Suabia, dying of fever at the siege of Acre, in 1191, and only a small body of the German Crusaders returning home at the end of the expedition. The result of the third Crusade is well known to all who are familiar — and what Englishman is not? — with the history of our first Richard.

Frederick was greatly revered and beloved by his German subjects, and the common people among them long refused to believe him dead. Two famous legends have floated down to our own times respecting his fate. One describes him as still sleeping in a deep trance among the Thuringian mountains, his head resting on his arm, his red beard having grown through the granite

* According to some historians, he was struck with apoplexy while bathing.

by which he sits. When the ravens cease to fly round the mountain he will awake, and restore the reign of good. The other legend places the scene of his slumbers at Salzburg, and makes the blossoming of a mysterious pear-tree the token of his awaking. Such fond superstitions imply no ordinary genius on the part of him who inspired them.

Frederick will obtain much obloquy from those who regard him only as the oppressor of the Italians. This, indeed, he was, but not from sheer cruelty of nature. He must be regarded from his own position, — as a powerful and able monarch, bred up in a belief that a despotic government was not only his inheritance, but a Divine institution. Much allowance must therefore be made for his imperious attempts to put down what he considered revolutionary principles and practices. As a despot, he contrasts very favorably with our Charles I., who occupied a similar position with respect to his subjects. Frederick and Charles were both conscientious, however mistaken, in resisting the opposition of those whom they held little better than slaves. But whereas Charles violated honor and good faith in all his dealings with the Parliament, Frederick's integrity and generosity won him respect from his bitterest foes. We have taken him as the hero of a principle, which he vindicated with greater strength, courage, and honesty, than perhaps any other despot before or since. The failure of such a man to enslave a few commercial cities manifests with the utmost clearness how strong even the weakest may become, by a wise union of forces, and the common consciousness of a righteous cause.

Frederick the Second of Germany.

On the death of Frederick Barbarossa, his son Henry, who was married to Constance, the heiress of the King of Sicily, succeeded to the empire of Germany, under the title of Henry VI. He lived but a few years, — leaving the crowns of both Germany and Sicily (with which was united Naples) to his son Frederick, a child of three years old, whose election as his successor he had obtained from the German nobles. The widowed mother of the young Emperor, anxious to secure to him all his rights, appointed Pope Innocent III. his guardian. That pontiff was a true successor of Hildebrand in ambition, if not earnestness, and employed his whole life in the steadfast endeavor to unite the highest possible temporal with the highest possible spiritual power of the Papal See. To him Europe owed the persecution of the Albigenses, and the Inquisition. He undertook the guardianship of Frederick, on the condition that the Duchy of Spoleto and the March of Ancona (which, as we have stated, were claimed by the Popes as their inheritance, through the grant of the Countess Matilda of Tuscany) should be surrendered to the Church. As really portions of the empire, the Countess could not justly have disposed of them, and the

5 *

grant was therefore worthless; but Innocent sustained his claim by a true or pretended will of the late Emperor Henry, bequeathing these territories to the See; and Constance felt compelled to comply. She died soon afterwards. But though thus secured in his South Italian dominions, Frederick could not obtain possession of Germany, where a civil war had broken out between the Guelph and Ghibeline parties. Disregarding their oath to Henry, the nobles of the last-named faction elected his brother Philip, Duke of Suabia, as Emperor; while the Guelphs chose Otho, Duke of Brunswick, the son of Henry the Lion, Duke of Saxony. The rival Emperors disputed for the title until 1208, when Philip was assassinated in a private quarrel. Otho, as the head of the Guelph house, was favored by Innocent III., whom he conciliated by yielding all pretensions to investitures, &c. He took an oath of obedience, and was accordingly crowned as Otho IV. But once on the throne, he showed himself as much averse to Papal interference as any Ghibeline emperor, and brought down upon himself as surely the anger of the Pope. Innocent tried to enforce obedience by excommunication, but in vain; and therefore resorted to what he deemed the safe expedient of reviving the Ghibeline party in the person of his ward, Frederick.

The young prince was now eighteen years of age. His mental and bodily accomplishments were of a very high order. Enterprising, vigorous, brave, and learned, he was fitted in an unusual degree for the difficult post of Emperor at such a time; and, to an extent that Innocent little foresaw, for the task of grappling with the increasing power of the Papacy. His immediate work was to sustain the rights of the Suabian house, and he performed it with activity. Marching through Lombardy, and cutting his way through the Milanese, who refused him a passage, he presented himself to the Ghibelines of Germany, and was crowned at Aix-la-Chapelle King of the Germans and Romans. He was well received by all, save in Saxony, where Otho's ancestral dominions lay, and which still clung to him as Emperor. A contest ensued, which lasted six years; finally terminating by the death of Otho in 1218. Frederick then succeeded to the Imperial dignity without opposition.

During this struggle the Italian cities had not been inactive. The treaty of Constance had secured their freedom to levy wars at will; and they unfortunately abused it to their own injury, by repeated disputes among themselves and with the adjoining nobles. The latter had now found it politic to become enrolled as citizens of the neighboring communities; and their influence in the state soon became formidable.

Allied by birth, marriage, or traditionary sentiment, to one or other of the two contending houses, the nobles brought with them a political leaven which rapidly fermented the whole republic. Thus it happened that cities which had on previous occasions been distinguished adherents of the Guelph party now supported the Ghibeline interests, while a converse change occurred in the politics of former Ghibeline cities. The inconsistency of Innocent III., moreover, created much confusion. Milan, for example, which had been foremost in the Guelph cause, headed the list as its opponent, despite the excommunication of the Pope, whom the Pavian Ghibelines readily supported.

Innocent III. died in 1216, and the confusion occasioned by his countenance of the Suabian against the Saxonian house ceased. The old quarrel between Emperor and Pope was soon reopened, and the terms Ghibeline and Guelph returned to their ordinary sense of expressing the opposite interests of these two potentates.

There was sufficient cause of uneasiness on the part of the Popes, touching the security of their temporal power, in the fact of the Emperor's possessing, in addition to Germany, the kingdom of Naples and Sicily, so long an ally and safeguard of the Church. To dissever this union of crowns was a favorite object of Innocent III. and his successor, Honorius III. Disaffection in the Neapolitan states was encouraged by Papal agents; and the rigor of the Imperial Government, thereby rendered necessary, was used as an argument to its disadvantage. As a general principle, moreover, the Popes exerted all their influence to strengthen the Guelph party.

In Tuscany a Guelph League was formed, of the cities of Florence, Sienna, Lucca, and Pistoia, among others, though the Ghibelines were predominant in Pisa, and still numerous in Florence, which was the scene of frequent strifes between the rival factions. The same quarrels raged in Lombardy, where the Ghibelines were successful in a battle fought at Ghibello, in 1218. Milan, nevertheless, still continued the stronghold of the Guelphs, and soon found occasion to display its hostility to the new Emperor.

He seems to have been fully alive to the nature of the struggle in which he was called upon to engage. Far

from shrinking, his youthful ambition was roused at the
idea of waging a successful contest with a power so
usurping as the Papacy, against which his great ancestors had so often fought unsuccessfully. The free opinions which he is reported to have held on theological subjects may have further strengthened his avowed desire to
render the Pope no more than the first bishop in Christendom. An opportunity of asserting his rights was not
long wanting. By his wife, Constance of Aragon, he
had a son, Henry, whom he had already crowned King
of Sicily. This child he now crowned King of Germany
also, by the consent of his nobles, so as to unite the two
kingdoms. Enraged at this act, so fatal to his hopes,
Honorius complained of it as arbitrary; but his anger
was appeased by Frederick's assurance that the step was
necessary for the security of his family, before he could
undertake a Crusade in which he had promised to embark at the Pontiff's solicitation. Frederick visited Italy
in 1220, and Honorius consented to crown him Emperor.
The ceremony took place at Rome, on the 22d November, 1220. Frederick proceeded from Rome to Naples,
where he occupied some time in settling the disturbances
which afflicted the country, evincing much wisdom in the
code of laws which he drew up for its government, respecting its ancient institutions, promoting education, and
patronizing literature and art. Honorius, rigorously exacting from him the fulfilment of his promise to join the
Crusade, persuaded him (as the Empress had recently
died) to give countenance to his claims on Jerusalem by
marrying, as a second wife, Iolante, daughter of John,
Count de Brienne, heiress, through her ancestors, the

Counts of Anjou, to the nominal kingdom of that city. The marriage took place in 1225, and the Crusade was fixed for 1227. Before starting, Frederick endeavored to obtain the crown of Lombardy, which the Milanese Guelphs guarded jealously at Monza. He summoned a Diet at Cremona, but urged his plea to no purpose with the obstinate Milanese, whose opposition was secretly encouraged by the Pope. Their refusal was unjustified by any acts of oppression on the part of Frederick, who had always respected the treaty of Constance, and claimed no more than was thereby accorded to the Emperors by the Lombard League. His real offence to Milan was that he represented the Suabian house, and to the Pope, that he united the crowns of Germany and Sicily, and thus overbalanced the power of the Church. The Milanese renewed the Lombard League, and occupied the Alpine passes, so as to prevent any reinforcements arriving to Frederick's assistance. He therefore relinquished the attempt for a time, leaving it to the Pope, his professed ally, to prosecute the claim, and proceeded to undertake the Crusade. Honorius, of course, took no steps in Frederick's behalf, and gave the Milanese an amnesty on condition of their joining in the Crusade also. He died soon after, and was succeeded by Gregory IX., an able and learned Pontiff, nephew of Innocent III., whom in character he greatly resembled.

Frederick was by no means enthusiastic for the Crusade against the Moslem rulers of Palestine, esteeming the expedition foolhardy and needless. Since the conclusion of the third Crusade, which guaranteed to the Christians the peaceful exercise of their devotions at Jerusalem, another expedition had been raised in 1198, under the leadership of Baldwin, Count of Flanders, which resulted only in the temporary conquest of Constantinople by the Venetians and French, who thus revenged themselves on the Greeks for their perfidies. The weakness and disunion of the Christians in Asia, and the uncertain fulfilment of their treaty with the Moslem, afforded ample food for the superstitious appetite of the European clergy, who incessantly preached the duty of a Crusade which should effectually secure the possession of Palestine. Honorius III. had been very active in these endeavors, and was especially importunate with Frederick, whose absence he desired. Gregory IX. was more exacting still.

After many delays, the Emperor prepared to start in 1227, when a pestilence suddenly broke out in the army, and he himself fell sick. He set out, nevertheless, but was compelled to put back, and land at Otranto. The fleet sailed without him, but reached no further than Greece, and the expedition wholly failed. Aware of Frederick's reluctance to set out on the Crusade, and perhaps believing his illness feigned, Gregory manifested the utmost indignation at his conduct, and excommunicated him. In the next year, however, Frederick prepared another fleet, and started in earnest. This seemed to Gregory an act of even greater audacity than the previous delay, for an excommunicated person was held wholly unfit to embark in so sacred an undertaking. The perverse Pontiff now threw every obstacle in the way of the Crusade, and instructed the Patriarch of Jerusalem to oppose the Emperor at all points. Meantime a body

of troops was sent to waste and disturb the Neapolitan
states. Frederick heard of this while in the East, but
would not return without achieving something to show
for his expedition. He tried diplomacy, rather than
force, with the Sultan of Egypt, and succeeded in making
a treaty, which secured to the Christians the possession
of Jerusalem, and other privileges in Palestine. The
Emperor then proceeded to Jerusalem, where he desired
to be crowned. He vainly tried to persuade the clergy
who attended him to perform the due rites. Not one
would consent. As excommunicated, he was beyond the
pale of the Church and the influence of her sacraments,
and to administer these would be sacrilege. Such was
the reply given to his command. His proud and daring
spirit could not brook submission to such authority. " I
will crown myself, then!" was his retort, and he performed what he said, — with his own hands placing the
crown of Jerusalem on his head, in the presence of his
army. While returning home, the Knight-Templars,
who hated him, betrayed his movements to the Sultan;
but that generous prince refused to aid in any schemes
against a monarch with whom he was now in treaty, and
revealed the conspiracy.

Frederick returned to Italy in haste after this success,
and entered his Neapolitan dominions. Gregory was assisted by a body of troops sent from the Guelph League
of Lombardy, but the Emperor's force was victorious;
and in 1230 he not only conquered back his old estates,
but compelled the Pope to withdraw the sentence of excommunication. A treaty of peace was then agreed to
between the Emperor and the Pope, in which the Lombards were included.

The peace was hollow, and each party knew it. On both sides active measures were taken to strengthen their respective interests. Frederick occupied himself for some time in his Neapolitan dominions, by carrying out his scheme of a temporal government, which should be independent of the overdue influence alike of the Church and the nobles. At a great Diet held at Capua, in 1231, he announced this system in a code of laws. Its principles, which were based on the freedom of the Empire, were of course radically opposed to those of the Papacy; and Gregory endeavored to thwart the Imperial policy by a collection of ecclesiastical laws, published in 1234, according to which the root of all power was the Church. The first open quarrel broke out in consequence of Frederick's attempt, in 1233, to enforce his legal claim on the crown of Lombardy, which the Milanese still withheld. As a preparatory step, he summoned from Sicily a strong force of Saracens in his pay, on whom he much relied, as being, both from religion and race, quite inaccessible to the influence of the Pope. At the same time he stimulated into activity the Ghibeline party in the North of Italy, at the head of which he placed Eccelino III. of Romano, a powerful noble, who held immense possessions in the Veronese Marches; a man of remarkably vigorous intellect and practised military skill, but of cruel and malignant heart. Gregory and the Guelph party had meantime not been inactive. They raised up an antagonist to the Emperor in the person of his own son, Henry, whom, as has been stated, he caused, when a mere child, to be crowned *King* of Germany, — a title equivalent to that of Viceroy. During his father's protracted absence this

young prince had displayed an ambitious and passionate
temper, which made him an easy prey to the wiles of
Frederick's foes.   In 1233 the Milanese offered to bestow on him the crown of Lombardy, which they had
declined to surrender to his father; and calculating on an
equal support in Germany, Henry summoned the nobles,
whom he had recently gratified by an edict which rendered them less dependent on the Empire, and declared
his intention of seizing the crown of Germany.   Before,
however, he or his partisans could take any decisive steps,
the active Frederick hastened into Germany, and commanded his disobedient son to meet him at Worms.   The
Emperor's presence sufficed to restore the wavering allegiance of most of his nobles; and Henry, finding himself
deserted, dared not persist in rebellion.   Relying on
Frederick's clemency, he came to Worms, and threw
himself at the feet of his father, imploring forgiveness.
The generous Emperor gave it, but the ungrateful prince
took advantage of this clemency to conspire against his
life.   Frederick no longer hesitated to inflict a just punishment, and accordingly imprisoned his son in various
fortresses, till 1240, when he died.   The Emperor remained two years in Germany, during which he married,
for the third time, Isabella, the sister of our Henry III.
He employed himself in numerous reforms for the preservation of order and peace; some of them too liberal for
the time, and consequently of but transient duration.   His
general policy in Germany, as in Italy, was to check the
violence of the nobility and the encroachments of the
Church.   With this view he forbade, under penalties,
any acts of tyranny committed by feudal lords against

their tenants, or the neighboring cities; and confided the
government of the German Church to the Imperial Archbishop, instead of the Pope. The sanction which Frederick gave to the Feme, or Secret Tribunal of Justice,
may perhaps be considered a step of doubtful wisdom;
but it must be remembered that this was founded only for
the suppression of vice too strong to be openly attacked,
and was not an agent of the Church.

In the summer of 1236 he crossed into Italy with a
small body of cavalry, and arrived at Verona. Here,
and at Pisa, the Ghibelines were predominant, but elsewhere the Guelph party had widely extended its power.
The Lombard League had been renewed in 1235, and
the Este family of Ferrara (allied by marriage to the
Saxonian Guelphs) aided Gregory in rousing Eastern
and Central Italy to resist the Emperor's claims.

The first blood was drawn in Vicenza, a Guelphic city,
which Eccelino stormed with a Saracen army, captured,
and plundered with the utmost barbarity. The Emperor
himself was recalled home in consequence of an attack
made by the Duke of Austria — a constant rebel — on an
army which was marching to join the Imperialists in
Italy. By his vigorous measures, in concert with his
son Conrad, Frederick defeated the Duke, whom he
forced to retire into a fortress, and dismembered Austria
of many valuable possessions. He then returned to
Italy, where Eccelino had already captured and pillaged
Padua, the stronghold of the Guelphs in the East. With
a large body of Saracens Frederick advanced towards
Mantua, so as to encourage the Ghibelines, who were
outnumbered in that city, and then turned to meet the

army of the Lombard League, which, under the leadership of Milan, was stationed between Brescia and Cremona. By a series of skilful manœuvres he managed to
cut off any chance of retreat in the direction of Milan,
and offered battle to the Guelphs at Cortenuova on the
Oglio. on the 26th and 27th of November, 1237. A desperate conflict ensued. The Milanese fought bravely,
but were outmatched in foresight and tact by the Emperor, and unused to fight with the warlike and savage
Saracens. The defeat of the League was decisive, —
ten thousand fell or were taken, and the beloved *caroc-
cio* of Milan was among the trophies which Frederick
bore away in triumph on an elephant which he had
brought back with him from the Crusades.

This success induced some of the leagued cities to relinquish their confederation, and Frederick seized the
opportunity to strengthen the Ghibeline party in Asti and
other cities of Piedmont, which he visited in the next
year. He rewarded with the hand of his natural daughter
the services of Eccelino, and made another of his illegitimate children, Hans or Enzio, King of Sardinia.

Milan, Brescia, and other cities still resisted the Emperor, and he laid siege to the last named for some weeks,
but its inhabitants defended themselves so bravely that he
withdrew. The secession of some of the Guelphic cities
and nobles so alarmed Gregory that he no longer re-
frained from offensive measures against Frederick. He
prevailed on Venice and Genoa to join his party, by exciting their fears for the preservation of their commerce.
In 1239 he took the additional step of excommunicating
his enemy. This engine of attack was among the most

formidable and successful that could possibly be used.
A man of Frederick's independent will and strong nerve
might and did despise it, and political partisanship was
often superior to its superstitious influence ; but it had a
great effect on the minds of the weak and credulous, who
felt their souls in peril if they abetted the rebellion of an
excommunicant against the Church. Frederick himself
became suspicious of some of his new allies, and they, in
their turn, fearful of him. Many accordingly, one by one,
deserted his camp. Following up this advantage, Gregory promoted an accusation of heresy against Frederick,
who, being notoriously free, both in opinions and speech,
may have unguardedly laid himself open to the charge.

In 1241 a General Council on the subject was summoned at Rome, and prelates from France and other
parts of Europe set out to attend it. Frederick meanwhile was carrying on the war with varying fortune, —
losing Ferrara, but capturing Faenza. Hearing of the
intended Council, he determined, if possible, to prevent
it, and accordingly repaired to the republic of Pisa, his
faithful ally, and a bitter opponent of Genoa, its commercial rival. Many of the French bishops had embarked at Nice in Genoese galleys, bound for Ostia, the
port of Rome. The Pisans promised him help, and his
son Enzio was recalled from Hungary, where he had
successfully repelled an invasion of Mongols, to head the
fleet. Under this prince, and their admiral Sismondi,
the Pisans lay in wait for the Genoese fleet at the island
of Meloria, near Leghorn. The assault was victorious,
three vessels being sunk, and nineteen, with their freight
of bishops, ambassadors, and money, captured. The

Pisans treated their prisoners with respect, but kept them in close confinement. This unforeseen disaster, together with the triumphant march of Frederick towards Rome, which he besieged, so affected the aged Gregory that he did not survive the shock, and died in the summer of 1241.

Frederick would not put any obstacle in the way of a new Pope's being elected, and therefore set free the cardinals whom the Pisans had captured. Two years, however, elapsed before the election was made, and it then fell upon Cardinal Fiesco, a Guelph, noble by birth, but a personal friend of the Emperor. The latter, however, well knew to what policy the Church was pledged, and when told of the choice, remarked, " He will become my enemy instead of remaining my friend. No Pope can be a Ghibeline." Innocent IV., as Fiesco was styled, fully justified Frederick's suspicion, and carried out to the full the designs of Gregory, renewing the alliance of the Papacy with the Lombard cities, and convoking a new General Council. This he fixed at Lyons instead of Rome, so as to procure the support of the French, who were then ruled by Louis IX., a faithful son of the Church. Frederick sent his chancellor, Thaddeus, to attend the Council, which met in 1245. This eloquent man in vain protested against the unjust charges brought against his master, who was accused by Innocent of desiring to uproot religion and enslave the Church. The Pope and his party prevailed, and the most terrible curses were pronounced against the Emperor. According to the usual form, the assembled prelates, who held lights in their hands, suddenly let them fall to the ground

as the words of condemnation were uttered. Amid the
gloom and smoke of the extinguished torches was heard
the loud, stern voice of Innocent: " Thus may the Emperor's glory vanish for evermore !"

By this solemn act of excommunication — one of the
most daring assumptions of Papal authority on record —
Frederick was declared a heretic, his subjects were released from their oaths, and even involved in the same
sentence if they adhered to his cause. The Electors of
the Empire were empowered to choose another Emperor
in his stead ; while the Pope reserved in his own hands
the choice of a King of Sicily. It was now a sheer trial
of strength between the Church and the Emperor. Frederick's strong soul was not abashed or unnerved by this
insulting challenge. He vindicated himself of the charge
of heresy before the European states, and summoning an
assembly of his nobles, he placed the Imperial crown on
his head, and swore to defend it. He performed his oath
valiantly against fearful odds. The German Church,
which he had tried to render independent of Rome,
turned against him, and the mendicant monks of the
Franciscan and Dominican orders, who were the agents
of the Pope and the Inquisition, travelled through Germany to excite the terrors of the people, and prevent
their supporting him. At the same time the Pope caused
Henry, Landgrave of Thuringia, to be crowned Emperor.

To their credit, the chief German nobles did not sanction this choice. but they generally contented themselves
with neutrality in the struggle ; and Conrad, Frederick's
son, and Regent in his absence, was defeated in an engagement with the Landgrave's troops at Frankfort.

Frederick, however, was not deserted by many of his German subjects; several of the cities which he had protected, as Metz, Ratisbon, &c., proving their gratitude by actively resisting their bishops, who attempted to enforce the Pope's authority. Conrad was eventually successful over the Landgrave, who fled after being defeated at Ulm, and died in 1247.

In Italy, however, the effect of the curse on Frederick had been very injurious to his personal popularity, as well as to his political interests. The Neapolitans, whom he had governed so well, were disaffected, and the inhabitants of the Veronese Marches, which he had intrusted to Eccelino, attributed the acts of that barbarous man to his master. Worst of all, conspiracies broke out amongst the Imperial courtiers, and Pietro delle Vigne, Frederick's intimate friend and secretary, was detected in an attempt to poison him. This extorted a bitter groan from Frederick, who exclaimed, "Alas! whom now can I trust?" In 1247 Parma, whence the Guelph nobles had been driven out by the Ghibelines, readmitted the exiles. This exasperated the Emperor, who was at the time at Turin, negotiating with Louis IX. of France to obtain his mediation with the Pope. Summoning a body of Saracens from Apulia, the Emperor advanced into Lombardy, where he likewise assembled the Lombard Ghibelines under his son Enzio, and the troops of Eccelino from Verona. Milan, Mantua, and other Guelph cities, both in Lombardy and Central Italy, on the other hand, sent men to the help of Parma. Frederick besieged it, but to no purpose; his camp was suddenly surprised by a sortie; his crown captured, and his soldiers scattered. This defeat determined him to secure himself in his Sicilian kingdom, whither he accordingly went in 1248, leaving Enzio to carry on the war. In Florence the Ghibelines were successful, driving out, by a sudden and concentrated movement, all the Guelph families in a single night. But in Eastern Italy Enzio received a fatal check. Bologna was there the stronghold of the Guelphs, and its citizens, after putting down the Ghibeline party in several small cities of Romagna, turned to attack the Modenese troops of Enzio. A battle was fought at Fossalta, in May, 1249, in which the Ghibelines were routed and Enzio himself captured. His father, who was much attached to him, offered in vain the most costly ransom, — a silver ring equal in size to the circumference of Bologna ; but the offer was refused, and the young and gallant Enzio, famed alike for his talents, beauty, and courage, was kept a state prisoner in that city till his death, after a captivity of twenty-two years.

In Germany also the Church was, in great measure, triumphant. On the death of the Landgrave of Thuringia, Innocent put up William, Count of Holland, as a competitor for the Empire ; and he obtained assistance from Flanders and Burgundy, which enabled him to defeat Conrad in 1247. All these misfortunes weighed heavily on the spirit of Frederick, who was now waxing into years. He endeavored to appease Innocent by offering to embark in the Crusade which Louis IX. of France was then about to undertake, and whose influence he again urged as a mediator. But the relentless Pope would hear of no concessions, and the gallant Em-

peror was again roused. Eccelino, his son-in-law, and
greatest general, proved perfidious; but even this did not
shake Frederick's indomitable courage. He summoned
another army of Saracens, and was again successful in
Lombardy, when suddenly overtaken by illness at Firen-
zuola, in December, 1250.

He died in the arms of his son Manfred, at the age of
fifty-six. His body was carried to Palermo, and there
buried. Here, in 1781, it was found, when the tomb was
opened, — the head still adorned with the crown of the
Empire, the hand still holding the sceptre and the ball.

Though disfigured by many of the moral failings from
which few in that age were free, Frederick was eminent
for those virtues which may be called political, as being
chiefly desirable in a monarch, — honor, justice, and
mercy. Intellectually he was, perhaps, the first man of
his day, — conspicuous alike for native power and acquired knowledge. It is for this reason that we have
selected him as the hero of the laity in their great struggle with the Church for temporal supremacy. His reign
suggests similar reflections to those which were called
forth by the life of Hildebrand, — the hero of the Church.

The most powerful Emperor had no chance of success
against a despotism such as the Pope was able to wield,
in virtue of his union of spiritual and temporal dominion.
Thought alone can compete with thought. Frederick was
personally a match for any Pope; but he was single-
handed, and the Church could command the brains of all
Christendom in its service. We shall see the same fight
renewed, upon equal terms, when we have to speak of
Luther, and shall have to record a very different issue.

With respect to the Italian republics, it is lamentable
to remark how speedily those in Lombardy had declined
from their allegiance to the principles which animated
them in the contest with Frederick Barbarossa. They
fought against Frederick II., not for the defence of their
liberties, which he always respected, but in support of a
faction. The result, as we shall see, was fatal to their
liberties. The nobles, whom they called in as allies,
proved their tyrants. The Church, with whose cause
they were content to be identified, asked, in return, a
surrender of faith and conscience; and placed a yoke on
their necks, which to this day has not been shaken off.

St. Louis.

THE LAST CRUSADE.

THE leading events of the history of France, since the death of Charlemagne, have already been alluded to in passing, but demand a brief notice separately. The throne of France remained in the hands of his descendants till the year 987, when Louis V., surnamed *le Fainéant*, died. Their dynasty had been unable to maintain the dignity which Charlemagne transmitted. The radical defect in his policy, to which we have referred, namely, the arbitrary nature of the union which he established between dissimilar races, proved fatal to his Empire. Germany and Italy, as we have seen, shook off allegiance to his successors, who quarrelled among themselves. On the death of Charles *le Gros* (the Fat), in 888, the final partition of the Empire was made, and his son was only recognized as King of France. This title was indeed but nominal; for the family of a powerful noble, the Count of Anjou, virtually governed the kingdom. Through the weakness of successive monarchs, and the encroachments of successive counts, even the title at last dropped; and in 987 Hugues Capet, Count of the Isle of France and Anjou, was duly crowned King. In his dynasty the legitimate monarchy of France has ever since descended.

The most striking features of the political history of France during the tenth and eleventh centuries are the conflict of the feudal aristocracy on the one hand, with monarchical and democratical power on the other, — and the influence exerted by the Crusades on both.

The feudal system was the natural growth of conquest. A territory having been conquered by the chief of a race, or the leader of an army, was divided by him between his generals, who, in their turn, parcelled out small portions of land amongst their soldiers. A chain of ties was thus created between the *Suzerains*, or paramount lords, and their tenants or vassals. Military service, and formal acts of homage, were the symbols of allegiance paid by the latter to the former. The lands thus held were called fiefs, and were generally inheritable from father to son. This system placed immense power in the hands of the nobles, who, while recognizing the king as their chief lord, exercised an authority over their tenants only inferior to his. They erected fortresses; raised armies, administered law; disposed of offices, spiritual and lay; levied taxes; and coined money at their pleasure. Their tenants were often cruelly oppressed, and in their turn treated their own inferiors as slaves, under the name of *villeins*, buying and selling them, with the soil to which they were attached, like cattle or furniture. The whole system was, indeed, but an organized slavery. The most powerful noble could not legally marry a wife, or transfer his property to another, without a license from the king; and during the minority of the tenant, the lord might dispose of him in marriage without his consent. The natural propensity of man to order, and the necessity of some great law of obedience for its preservation, account for the strong hold which feudalism, in spite of its abuses, so long retained on Europe.

The vigor of the early sovereigns of the House of Capet, which had risen from the aristocracy, obtained for them an authority over their nobles which had never been exercised since the time of Charlemagne. Philip Augustus, who reigned from 1179 to 1233, was especially successful in his attempts to bend his potent subjects beneath his sway. His citation of our King John, who owed him homage for Normandy, &c., to appear before him to answer for the murder of Prince Arthur, and the confiscation of the English fiefs in France for John's non-appearance, were daring displays of Philip's imperious will. He firmly riveted the bonds of law upon his hitherto lawless nobility, and obtained the respect and obedience of his subjects generally. To his grandfather, Louis VI., the *communes*, or municipal leagues of France, owed their first legal sanction and encouragement. From the time of the Romans, who always favored the growth of borough interests, several cities in the south of France, peopled by traders and artisans, had retained their self-government, which made them independent of feudalism. Gradually new cities arose, which won or purchased their liberties from the weakness or poverty of the neighboring barons. But the possession of a warlike soldiery and strong castles enabled a feudal lord to injure and oppress an unarmed body of peaceful citizens with impunity. The French cities, therefore, like the Italian, found it needful to league together for their common advantage. These federations were known as *communes*, the members

of which were sworn to mutual protection. Louis VI.,
and other Capetian kings, soon perceived the value of
these bodies as assistants in the work of restraining the
power of the aristocracy. He gave many of them charters, which legally insured their rights; and in return
the communes sided with the Crown whenever its interests clashed with those of the nobles.

The Crusades aided much to the accomplishment of
the same result. In the first place, they glorified the
character of feudalism by enforcing the principles of
chivalry. To be a *true knight*, a man must be devout,
just, merciful, and pure. Many Crusaders, indeed, fell
far short of this high ideal; but there can be no doubt
that, on the whole, it elevated the standard of morality,
and checked the rampant tyranny which had previously
prevailed. Founded on a principle of sincere though
mistaken piety, the Crusaders recognized all who took
the cross as brethren: hence the meanest serf became,
in some measure, free; and the same benign sentiment
extended its effect to all classes. The attraction of a
common cause in foreign lands further contributed to
wean the Crusaders from the class quarrels and domestic
feuds which occupied them at home. During their absence, the Crown was enabled to acquire a strength which
had previously been spent in the repression of constant
rebellions. And the need of money for the expedition
obliged many feudal lords to contract with the communes
for the sale of lands or liberties.

Such was the condition of France at the commencement of the thirteenth century. The balance of power,
however, was only sustained by the activity of all the

parties concerned. The slightest wavering on the part of the Crown would be fatal, — the least opportunity seized. A wise, sincere, and humane ruler was needed to confirm and enlarge the vantage ground which law and order had already obtained; and such a ruler arose in the person of Louis IX., who ascended the throne in 1226.

His father, Louis VIII., was a man of weak character, whose reign was chiefly signalized by the horrible persecution of the Protestant Albigenses of Provence, which, under the sanction of Innocent III. and later Popes, had been carried on by Simon de Montfort, and other fanatics, since 1209. Louis himself had died of fever, when about to commence the siege of Thoulouse.

The Queen Dowager, Blanche of Castile, was a woman of great energy; and during the minority of her son she bravely contested her claims to the regency of the kingdom with those of Philip, her husband's brother, whom our Henry III. supported. She appealed, not in vain, to the gratitude of the metropolis, which the Capetian Kings had befriended; and at her call a large force of citizens joined her. With their aid she defeated Philip and other nobles, who opposed her son's coronation, and by two treaties, in 1229 and 1231, she both extended the limits of her kingdom and put an end to civil war. Over Louis, who was but eleven years old when his father died, she exercised a somewhat rigorous, but a holy and prudent discipline, to which he was much indebted for strengthening his moral and mental constitution. Though not remarkable for talents, this young prince possessed considerable decision of character, and a large share of

personal courage. It is, however, by the piety, purity, and benevolence of his soul, that he stands forth so prominently in the history of Europe. A nature more truly loving and lovable has rarely been bestowed on any member of the human family. Yet, with all these paramount excellences, his life presents a tragedy, — the fatal consequences of unreasoning faith. All his errors — we cannot justly call them faults — proceeded from this prolific source. Before recording these, it will be gratifying to point out the happier results of those noble and wise qualities which have consecrated his name.

After the treaty of 1231, France remained at peace for some years; during which time Louis married Margaret of Provence, a princess only inferior in worth to himself. Soon after attaining his majority he was called upon to conflict with the Count of Brittany and other nobles who resisted his authority. At the head of his vassals Louis marched against the rebels, and was so prompt and energetic in his measures that the Count was forced to yield and sue for pardon in the attitude of a criminal, with a rope round his neck. Henry III. crossed with an army to support the rebellion, and recover, if possible, the possessions which John had surrendered to Philip. The armies met at Saintes, in 1242, where the French were victorious, — the rebels subsequently submitting, and Henry returning home.

In 1244 Louis had a severe illness, which was attended with danger to his life. During the progress of it, he vowed to undertake a new Crusade, should he recover. The fulfilment of this vow was opposed by Blanche of Castile (who still had great influence over her son) and

6 * •   I

many of his best counsellors; but Louis was inflexible where religion and honor demanded a sacrifice.

In 1248 he collected a large army, and prepared to start by way of Sicily, the nearest route to Palestine, when he remembered that the island belonged to Frederick II. of Germany, who was under excommunication by the Pope. All attempts to shake the decision of Innocent IV. failed; and yielding to the pious weakness of fearing to rest in an excommunicant's territory, Louis changed his plans, and determined to pass by way of Cyprus and Egypt, — a route which proved the ruin of the expedition. He committed the regency of France to his mother; assumed the staff of pilgrimage, and, accompanied by his wife and brothers, left Paris on the 12th of June, 1248. He stayed for several months in Cyprus, until his armament amounted to 50,000 men, and then sailed for Egypt.

Arrived at the port of Damietta, he caused the oriflamme (the national standard of France) to be waved above his head; and, arrayed in complete armor, he unsheathed his sword, and leaped into the sea, followed by his knights. The inhabitants fled, and the French took possession of the city. The inundation of the Nile prevented their further movements for several months. Licentiousness and disease were fostered by this delay, in spite of the King's remonstrances; and their unopposed success made the Crusaders careless as to the tactics of the enemy.

On the subsidence of the Nile, Louis fortified Damietta, and left his Queen and her ladies there, while he with the main army advanced on Cairo, the metropolis of Egypt, where the Sultan resided. Near Mansourah the Crusaders became perplexed by the intricacy of the canals; and a hasty dash across one of these, made by the King's brother, the Count of Artois, with 2,000 men, led to a calamitous result. Mansourah was apparently deserted; and the Count's troops, who preceded their comrades at some distance, commenced pillaging the houses. The inhabitants, who were only concealed, showered down stones from the roofs; and at the same moment a large body of the Sultan's army made an attack in front. Louis reached Mansourah in time to save a few of his men, but found his brother and several others slain. The Moslem camp was captured, but proved a doubtful prize. The plains were barren and scorching; and the harassing assaults of the Egyptians, who poured "Greek fire" (missiles filled with combustible materials) on their foes, rendered the situation more intolerable still. Pestilence broke out, and the King himself fell dangerously ill. He then ordered a retreat to Damietta, whither the sick were to be conveyed in galleys. These were intercepted, and the sick murdered by the Egyptians; while, at the same time, an attack was made on the Christian camp.

Louis was so weak that he could scarcely ride, but nevertheless would not desert his post. He rode between the ranks, encouraging his men, till he fainted, and was obliged to withdraw from the field. His quaint and affectionate biographer, the Lord of Joinville, who was with him in this expedition, thus describes the scenes which ensued: "Of all his men-at-arms there was only one with him, the good knight, Sir Geoffrey de Sergine; and who, I heard say, did defend him like as a faithful servant doth guard his master's cup from flies, — for every time that the Saracens did approach the King he defended him with vigorous strokes of the blade and point of his sword, and his strength seemed doubled. At last he brought the King to a house where there was a woman from Paris; and laying him on the ground, placed his head on the woman's lap, expecting every moment that he would breathe his last." In this half-dying condition a body of Egyptians found him, and bore him to the tent of the Sultan. The defeat of the Christians, who were weakened by the climate, disease, and want of food, was general; many fell by the sword, and the rest were taken prisoners with their King.

In captivity Louis showed a noble resignation and courage amid the apostasy of many. He won the respect of the Sultan, who treated him with generosity, and listened to the terms of ransom which he proposed. The Queen remained at Damietta, which was strongly garrisoned. Fearful, nevertheless, of falling into the hands of the Moslem, who would have carried her into the Sultan's harem, she prayed an old knight in her suite to slay her with his sword, should there be any danger of that event. "I had determined on so doing, madam," was the answer. Margaret's heroism was not put to this severe test, for the surrender of Damietta was one of the conditions of her husband's release; and after paying in addition a sum of 400,000 livres, Louis was on the point of being set free. An insurrection, however, suddenly arose among the Mamelukes, or Tartarian troops, in whose hands the real power of the state was placed, and the Sultan was murdered. A party of the assassins, it is said, entered the chamber of Louis with their scimitars drawn; but his calm dignity saved him, and the treaty was carried out by the new Sultan.

Many of the French nobles returned home, but the King, faithful to his vow, proceeded to Syria, and spent four years in strengthening the fortresses of Tyre and other Christian towns, redeeming many Crusaders from slavery, and reducing to order the disturbed condition of the country.

The death of the Queen-Dowager Blanche, who had governed France wisely during her regency, recalled him in 1254, after an absence of six years. He still wore the cross upon his shoulder, as a token that his oath as a Crusader was not yet fulfilled; but he never once neglected the more pressing and necessary duties which devolved on him as a monarch. His immediate work was to supersede the arbitrary legislation which the nobles exercised in their manorial courts over their tenants. He accordingly introduced into general use the famous code of Roman laws known as the Pandects of Justinian, and constituted the chief civil lawyers, who had studied its contents and were best acquainted with its principles, into a Parliament, or Court of Justice. The nobles and the clergy were duly represented in this assembly; but its clerks, or lawyers, were especially favored by the King, who seconded their own efforts to absorb the business of the court as much as possible. Louis further mediated between the tyranny of the nobles and the weakness of their tenants, by encouraging the practice of appealing to the Crown in case of injustice. This he even extended to ecclesiastical matters; a bold step for

one so devoted to the Church. The prohibition of the
barbarous custom of duelling to decide personal quarrels
was another of his humane laws. These, and divers
other ordinances, founded in a like spirit of equity, are
known in a collected shape as the *Institutes of St. Louis.*
His enactment touching appeals from the Church to the
Crown, and the prohibition which he likewise issued
against the levying of money in France for the use of
the Pope without the King's license, are known as a
Pragmatic Sanction, — a term applied to any especially
important national decree. Louis set the example of
keeping the laws in his own person, and none was fitter
to administer them than he. Under an oak in the forest
of Vincennes, near Paris, often sat the good King to hear
appeals and petitions from his poor subjects. His social
and foreign relations were as fully attended to as his
political reforms. He first placed the French navy on a
substantial footing. To him Paris owed a public library,
a hospital for the blind, and the establishment of a body
of police. Under his sanction, also, his confessor, Robert
de Sorbon, founded the famous theological college called
by his name. So scrupulously just and honorable was
Louis, that he appointed a commission to ascertain what
restitution of territory should be made to nations which
had been mulcted by the conquests of his predecessors,
and he thus more than once sacrificed extensive possessions for the sake of a principle. By a treaty of 1255,
made with Henry III., Louis restored to the English
Crown the provinces of which Philip Augustus had deprived it, and obtained in return the surrender of Henry's rights in Normandy and other fiefs. The reputation

which Louis thus acquired among his fellow-monarchs
led to his being asked to act as mediator in several quarrels, and gave him many opportunities of exhibiting his
peaceful and loving policy.

The mental blindness of which we have spoken led
him to commit errors, which, if his misled conscience had
not sanctioned them, would deserve the name of crimes
Towards Jews and heretics he showed no mercy, issuing
severe and unjust laws against them "for the good of his
soul." The duty of the historian is to record these failings of a noble nature as impartially as its beauties; but
the evil must, in all fairness, be credited to the Church
and system which taught, and not to the believer who
practised.

In 1270 the affairs of the East again attracted the attention of Europe, and recalled Louis to the fulfilment of
his vow, which he had only postponed. The Greeks had
retaken the city of Constantinople from the French and
Venetian Crusaders some years previously, yet the re-
constitution of the Christian Empire of the East had not
availed to check the aggressions of the Moslem in Palestine. Benocdar, the Sultan of Egypt, had already taken
Cæsarea and Jaffa; and news now came that Antioch
had fallen, 100,000 Christians having been massacred in
the siege. The seventh and last Crusade was at once set
on foot by outraged Europe, and Louis led the expedition, in which France was, as usual, foremost. He raised
an army of 6,000 horse and 30,000 foot, and was accompanied by his three sons, the King of Navarre, and several nobles of high rank. His brother, Charles of Anjou
(the new King of Naples), and our first Edward (then

prince), were to join the French in the course of the year. Some romantic intelligence that the Moslem King of Tunis was desirous of being baptized, induced the pious Louis again to try the African, instead of the Asiatic, route to Palestine. He narrowly escaped with his life, in a tempest which overtook the fleet in the Mediterranean, but landed in Sardinia, and after recruiting here, again set sail, and anchored off Carthage. He met with opposition, instead of welcome, from the inhabitants of the coast, and was obliged to besiege Tunis. The excessive heat of the climate and the unhealthiness of the soil proved a second time fatal to the army. Plague at last broke out, and Louis was himself seized. Finding himself dying, he sent for Philip, his eldest son and successor. Placing in his hand a written paper, the good King prayed his son to follow the directions which it contained, — directions for the conduct of his life, as king and individual; enforcing those principles of love to God and man which had guided his own career. Then, requesting to be lifted from his bed, Louis instructed his attendants to strew the floor of his tent with ashes, and place him thereon, that he might die, as he had lived, in an attitude of humiliation and penitence towards his Creator. This was done, and shortly afterwards, as though in vision fulfilling the vow which he was not permitted to realize, he uttered, " I will enter thy house, — I will worship in thy sanctuary ! " and expired. His age was but fifty-four.

A few moments elapsed, and the sound of a trumpet echoed through the plague-stricken and half-deserted camp. It was the note of Charles of Naples, whose fleet had just arrived off the coast. Meeting with no response, he rode rapidly towards the tent of the king, and on entering, saw his body lying still warm upon the ashes. The rites of burial were not performed with the usual formalities, his remains being distributed among his relatives. The flesh was kept by Charles, who buried it, on his return to Sicily, in the great Abbey of Monreale, at Palermo. The bones and other parts were conveyed back to France. Those who have visited Paris will not forget the exquisite Gothic structure known as the "Sainte Chapelle," which is attached to the Palais de Justice, containing the Courts of Law. It was erected by Louis as a receptacle for certain supposed relics of Christ. The windows of the chapel are entirely composed of stained glass, and as the sunbeams strike upon them, their tints of crimson, blue, and orange, blend into a rainbow-like harmony of glowing and lustrous color, which recalls the heart of Louis IX., enshrined within those walls, as its fitting human antitype. He was canonized about thirty years afterwards, under the title of St. Louis.

After three months vainly spent upon the siege of Tunis, Charles of Naples, who, during the illness of his nephew Philip, now King of France, had undertaken the command of the expedition, relinquished it, and made a treaty with the Moslem king upon favorable terms. The Crusaders then returned to Europe; the Egyptians retained their conquests in Palestine; and, though many subsequent schemes to recover it were proposed, the Crusades were never resumed.

Some of the effects of these memorable expeditions have already been mentioned; but a brief notice of their general results will not here be out of place. Though barren of final success in their immediate object, and probably availing little to extend the sway of Christianity, they no doubt contributed much to check the aggressive spirit of Mohammedan conquest, which, as we have seen, had frequently threatened Europe. By promoting a sentiment of religious brotherhood in Christendom, they were of some service in diminishing, though they could not subdue, the ceaseless rivalries which previously and subsequently deluged in blood the leading European states. The unknown land of the East, with its stores of learning, wealth, and natural produce, was thrown open to the enterprise of the West, and commerce and navigation received a stimulus, the results of which have never since declined. To the Crusades we probably owe the introduction of novel ideas of art, in the cultivation of which the East was then much more advanced than the West. Literature was certainly fostered by these events, history finding ample scope for narrating, and poetry perpetual food for glorifying, the heroism and virtue which signalized so many scenes both of success and misfortune. The lyrical and narrative poems sung and written by the Troubadours of Southern, and the Trouvères of Northern France, are the literary growth of that spring-time of imagination which actively blossomed in the Crusades. Chanted or recited by the minstrels at the festive board of a baronial castle, the mimic battle-field of the tournament, or the camp-fire of the bivouac, these lays and romances gave a zest to pleasure, a solace to weariness, and an impulse to enthusiasm, without which the history of the period might have had a different aspect from that it wears. The growth of municipal liberty, and the partial emancipation of the serf, also due to the Crusades, have been mentioned in connection with France especially, but were not confined to that country alone. And last, but not least of these results, must again be noticed the firm hold which the principles of chivalry obtained in Europe. The enunciation of precepts so ennobling as the laws of knighthood bears witness at least to the presence of a moral consciousness in that age which our own cannot afford to despise. We can scarcely over-estimate the advantage of such a standard of honor in a comparatively unenlightened period; and sufficient evidences are on record of the integrity, generosity, and courtesy, which the Crusaders evinced, — so unlike the ordinary practices of their rank and character, — to justify us in attributing these effects to that cause. Chief perhaps among the best features of the chivalric spirit was the romantic enthusiasm which it inspired for woman, as an object of reverent, pure, and tender regard. "God and my lady!" was the true knight's war-cry; and if his imagination led him to an extravagant adoration of the creature above the Creator, it was certainly a nobler error than the abuse of power and license of appetite, displayed by his devouter Moslem antagonist, in relation to the weaker sex. The influence that women have so beneficially exercised in Christendom, as elements of purity and gentleness in the social framework, which the the ruder passions of men have mainly contributed to form, may not improbably be attributed to the enthusiastic impulse of chivalric feeling, fostered by the warmth and lustre of the Crusades.

And as we have taken Godfrey de Bouillon as the first hero of these enterprises, we take St. Louis as the last, — twin-brothers in earnest devotion, self-denying patience, unsullied honor, and cordial courtesy. If the Crusades had brought no more result to Europe than the exhibition of such virtues and the memory of such names, it had been enough for the historian to record, as tokens of the presence of God in the lives of his children.

Rudolph of Hapsburg.

RISE OF THE HOUSE OF AUSTRIA.

On the death of Frederick II. of Germany, his son Conrad IV. succeeded to the unenviable position of representing the Suabian line of emperors with the shadow of their former authority. By the Ghibelines of Italy, and his ancestral province of Suabia, he was acknowledged as their head; but the Pope repudiated his claims, and the Guelphs flocked to the side of his rival, William of Holland. Manfred, the natural son of Frederick, assisted his brother in securing the possession of Naples; but in 1254 Conrad's life was cut short in his twenty-sixth year, by an illness which was ascribed to poison administered by Papal agents. On his death the Duchy of Franconia made itself free, though that of Suabia acknowledged his son, Conradin, as Emperor till his death.

The relentless vengeance of the Church pursued to the grave all the descendants of Frederick II. After the death of Conrad, the kingdom of Naples and Sicily acknowledged Manfred as its sovereign. Uniting the Ghibelines by his genius and address, he soon proved a worthy successor of his father, and a formidable foe to the Guelphs. Pope Urban IV., therefore, set up an antagonist to him in the person of Charles, Count of Anjou, brother of Louis IX. of France. This nobleman was of an ambitious and restless temperament, which kept France in a perpetual state of turmoil. Louis was, therefore, by no means unwilling that his brother should accept the offer of a foreign crown, made him by the Pope, the sovereign disposer of all temporal titles. Charles eagerly caught at the proposal, and, aided by a Provençal army, Charles defeated Manfred at Grandella, near Benevento, in 1266. Manfred fell in the battle, and Charles took possession of the crown. A gallant attempt was made in the next year by the youthful Conradin, the last Suabian Emperor of Germany, to recover his ancestral dominions in Italy; but he was defeated by Charles, and beheaded with great cruelty. On the scaffold the young prince threw down his glove; praying that one of the by-standers would bear it to his kinsmen, who would accept it as a symbol of inheritance, and avenge his untimely death. The glove was picked up by a knight named Truches, and carried to Pedro III. of Aragon, the son-in-law of Manfred, who, some years afterwards, avenged the execution of Conradin, both by the re-conquest of Sicily, and the horrible massacre of the French in that island, so well known as the Sicilian Vespers.

The death of William of Holland left Germany without an Emperor of either the Ghibeline or Guelph faction. An interregnum ensued; for the College of Electors was divided between the partisans of two candidates, — Richard, Earl of Cornwall (brother of our Henry III), and Alfonso X. of Castile. Each party tried by

intrigues and bribes to succeed in its object, and Richard
having the fullest coffers, won over the largest number
of adherents, and a partial recognition as Emperor.

On his death, in 1271, another struggle ensued. The
title was now admittedly elective, and the power of choice
was principally, though not exclusively, in the hands of
an Electoral College, composed of a few chief nobles, —
viz. the three Archbishops of Mentz, Trèves, and Cologne, the Rhenish Palatine, the Duke of Saxon-Witten-
berg, the Margrave of Brandenburg, and the King of
Bohemia. This college possessed vast influence, and
much lessened the importance of the Imperial dignity,
as did also the increased strength of the inferior nobles,
who, on the dismemberment of some of the great German
duchies, made themselves nearly independent, and formed
a second Electoral College of the Princes of the Empire.
The growth of the commercial cities in Northern Germany, which were leagued into a Hanse (or association),
contributed to the same result.

The Diet of election was held in 1273, at Frankfort, —
the principal candidates being Ottocar, King of Bohemia,
and Alfonso X., King of Castile, both men of rank and
wealth. The choice of the Electors, nevertheless, fell
upon a comparatively unknown nobleman, — Rudolph,
Count of Hapsburg. The reasons for the selection must
be found in a sketch of his antecedent history.

He was born in 1218, the descendant of an ancient
and illustrious family, whose territories were situate in
the district of Aargau, Switzerland. His youth was unsettled, — occupied in warfare, more or less justifiable,
with his neighboring fellow-lords. His name was more

honorably known as a terror to the banditti, who infested
the country round his castle. He fought also in Italy
under the Guelphic banner. In 1264 he inherited the
estates of his uncle, the Count of Kyburg, which were
of considerable extent and value, including much of what
are now the Cantons of Berne, Lucerne, Zurich, Uri,
Schwyz, and Unterwalden. Rudolph's laudable repression of robbery in these and other of his territories, was
fitly rewarded by the gratitude of Werner, Archbishop
of Mentz. This prelate, in travelling from Strasburg to
Rome, applied to Rudolph for the protection of a band
of horse as far as the frontiers of Italy. The request
was abundantly fulfilled. Rudolph's cavaliers accompanied the Archbishop as far as to Rome itself, and then
returned to Strasburg. Werner felt so indebted for this
courtesy, that when the election of an emperor was
mooted, he determined to repay Rudolph with a costly
recompense. The powerful Burgrave of Nuremburg
was interested in his behalf, but the Electors of the two
colleges were not won over without difficulty; and the
Count's three daughters, who were marriageable, were
offered as bribes to three of the Princes of the Empire,
who were bachelors. He himself promised to support
the Guelph cause in both Germany and Italy, and to
consult the colleges in all questions of state policy. The
only remonstrant was Ottocar, King of Bohemia, who
was a candidate as well as an elector. His ambassadors were unavailing in their arguments, and Rudolph
was duly elected.

When the news reached the Count, he was attacking
the city of Basle, against whose bishop he had grounds

of complaint for the murder of some relatives. The citizens, either weary of the siege, or anxious to win appro-
bation from their new sovereign, relinquished the defence
at once; and admitting him into the city, hailed his election with joy. He then proceeded to Aix-la-Chapelle,
and was there crowned King of the Romans. Gregory
X., then Pope, was of a temperate and conciliating temper, and no difficulty was experienced in procuring his
ratification of the appointment. Rudolph, indeed, was
ready to concede to the Church almost all the questions
which had been so bitterly and bloodily contested between it and the Empire for so many centuries. He
renounced any assumption of authority over Rome, the
March of Ancona, and Duchy of Spoleto, and all interference in ecclesiastical elections, save only the presence
of his officers at the investiture of bishops. These concessions. which were the result of prudence, rather than
fear, healed the long-standing feud between the two greatest powers of Central Europe.

Rudolph's election to the Empire was, of course, disputed by the indignant King of Bohemia. His vast
possessions comprised nearly all the present Empire of
Austria. Certain acts of cruelty towards his Styrian
subjects, committed by this monarch, and complained of
at the Diet, in 1275, gave the Emperor an opportunity
of punishing his rebellious vassal. He raised an army,
with which he invaded and subdued Austria; while his
relative, Meinhard, Count of the Tyrol, attacked Carinthia and other provinces. Ottocar's army was finally
opposed to Rudolph's on the banks of the Danube, which
the former relied on as a barrier. But the Emperor or-

7   J

dered a bridge of boats to be made, crossed the river, and
forced Ottocar to yield. Austria, Styria, Carniola, and
Carinthia were surrendered to the Empire; and only
Bohemia and Moravia retained. For these the King
was obliged to do homage, and accordingly, in 1276, he
came dressed in his regal robes to the tent of Rudolph,
which was fixed on an island in the Danube. The Emperor was dressed in a common military dress, adopted,
doubtless, to render Ottocar's submission the more complete. This was the motive also for a rather unusual
proceeding at this interview. As the King knelt before
the Emperor in the tent which screened them from the
gaze of the spectators, it was suddenly lifted, and the act
of homage rendered conspicuous to all. Rudolph's conduct seems, at first sight, an ungenerous trampling on a
fallen foe, but is so exceptional in this respect from all
else recorded of him, that we may reasonably believe it
justified by the occasion. Ottocar was a proud man, and
naturally wounded at this insult. He was not appeased
by the amends which Rudolph made by intermarrying
their families. Stimulated to revenge by his wife, the
King once more revolted. The attempt was not successful, and he was slain in a battle which took place near
Vienna in 1278. His son, Wenceslaus, then did homage
to the Emperor, whose son-in-law he afterwards became.

Rudolph now strengthened his authority by dividing
the government of the newly conquered provinces among
his family. He further endeavored to restore peace and
order throughout Austria and other parts of his dominions, by travelling through them in person. Sanguinary
feuds between spiritual and lay nobles, and commercial

cities, then disgraced Germany. Many of the less potent barons were mere titled robbers, whose fortresses were dens of plunder. Though unable to put an end to all these abuses, he exerted himself successfully in numerous instances. He persuaded, or commanded, several nobles engaged in feuds to submit their quarrels to arbitration, and repeatedly punished with the severest penalties acts of fraud and injustice committed by other lords. In Thuringia he destroyed more than sixty castles of robber-barons, and hanged about thirty of the owners. He favored the growth of free cities, to which he gave charters; and in all parts of the empire he enforced the just execution of the law. The people much loved him, for he was always accessible to the meanest of his subjects. On one occasion his guard refused admittance to some poor persons who asked for the Emperor. Rudolph, who beheld the scene, ordered that they should be admitted. "I was not made Emperor," said he, "to be excluded from my fellow-men." From his personal attendance in so many places, and constant enforcement of justice, he was called "the Living Law," and his subjects delighted to repeat anecdotes of his gratitude, generosity, and piety. A specimen of each may be given.

When seated one day in the great Court of Mentz, he noticed among the crowd a citizen of Zurich, who had once, long before his election, saved his life. The man was in humble circumstances, but the Emperor treated him like an equal, — rising from the throne, accosting his old friend in cordial terms, and finally bestowing on him the then valuable dignity of knighthood.

The generosity of Rudolph was signally displayed dur-

ing the Bohemian campaign. All the army — himself
included — suffered severely from a scarcity of water. A
pitcher full was at last procured, and brought to Rudolph,
but he refused it. He would share the troubles of his
troops, he said, and not touch anything of which they
were as much in want as himself.

His piety was exhibited on an occasion when it is
hardly possible that unworthy motives could have actuated its display. He was hunting in a mountainous district alone, when he met a priest toiling along a steep and
miry footpath, to carry the consecrated wafer to a sick
person. Rudolph immediately dismounted, and requested
the priest to ride. " For you," said he, " to walk with
the body of Christ in your hand, while I ride, were truly
an unbecoming sight!" Many such acts, bearing witness
to a real nobleness of heart, are still affectionately recorded in the popular traditions of Germany respecting
Rudolph of Hapsburg.

He was tainted with the weakness of over-ambition in
spite of his high qualities, and desired to render the empire hereditary, instead of elective. With this view he
made application to the electing princes for the coronation of his son Albert as King of the Romans. The request was refused, and it is said that the old man died of
chagrin. This event occurred in 1291.

Rudolph of Hapsburg has been called "the Second
Restorer of the German Empire." He has had some
severe censurers of his policy with respect to the Papacy,
as being weak and mean; but most historians unite in
awarding him high praise for wisdom, justice, and good-
faith. He at least succeeded in his main objects of calm-

ing and regulating the empire at a time when the Imperial dignity was weakest. Success, indeed, is not invariably the measure of right, but it is usually the measure
of sound judgment; and for the possession of a large
share of this all-important qualification, under difficult
circumstances, we think Rudolph of Hapsburg well entitled to rank among the heroes of Europe.

William Tell.

THE refusal of the Electors of Germany to secure the throne to Albert, son of Rudolph the First, was perhaps dictated as much by personal as public feeling, — by dislike to the individual as to hereditary monarchy. Albert certainly merited hatred as a cruel and perfidious tyrant. As Duke of Austria, in his father's lifetime, his conduct had been such as to excite his Viennese subjects to revolt, — an offence which he punished by the most barbarous mutilations, as well as civil penalties. On the death of Rudolph, the Archbishop of Mentz — a man of strong will and great influence — won over his fellow-Electors, to place on the throne his cousin Adolph, Count of Nassau, who was a weak tool in his hands. Albert was constrained to give way, and even acquiesced in the appointment by taking an oath of fealty to the new Emperor. Adolph soon excited contempt by his mean and paltry policy, and having quarrelled with the Archbishop, was deserted by him in favor of Albert. The armies of the rivals met near Worms in 1298, and Adolph was slain. The Electors had previously been induced to give their votes for Albert, who thereupon took the title of Albert the First. An indifferently worthy successor of his father in

intellect, he inherited none of his probity, being, on the
contrary, insincere, ungenerous, and covetous. He, nevertheless, was for some time successful in subduing the
independent spirit of the King of Bohemia, and resisting
the pretensions of Pope Boniface VIII., who carried the
arrogance of the Roman See to a higher pitch than any
of his predecessors. Albert won the bitter hatred of his
subjects by his tyrannical conduct, and more especially
of the Swiss, who were his patrimonial retainers, or serfs.

The power of the Counts of Hapsburg in Switzerland
was originally only that of a feudal lord over the tenants
of his own domain. Switzerland, as a whole, was nominally included in the kingdom of Burgundy, and acknowledged the supremacy of the German Empire. Gradually,
however, various nobles, both among the clergy and
laity, had acquired strength and influence over large
districts. Berne, Basle, Zurich, and other commercial
cities, had also risen into importance. A spirit of independence, natural and almost universal among mountaineers, animated the Swiss middle class and peasantry, and
it only required the provocation of tyranny to excite this
spirit into open revolt. The Counts of Hapsburg claimed
feudal rights in Lucerne, Schwyz, and Unterwalden
especially; and both as Imperial judges and "advo-
cates," or lay guardians of certain convents in those Cantons, ventured to exercise authority over Uri also, — a
district inhabited by a free community of shepherds, singularly tenacious of their liberties. Rudolph had used
his power temperately; but Albert took advantage of his
accession to abuse his authority, by placing deputy-gov-
ernors in these Cantons, — officers whose duties were

twofold, — those, namely, of Imperial viceroys and managers of the Hapsburgian possessions. He evidently intended to reduce the Swiss into slavery, by abolishing all their ancient customs and privileges. The opposition he met with in this scheme forms the subject of the present brief sketch.

Nothing is known of the early life of William Tell, and his very existence is disputed by some writers. As his name signifies a *Simpleton*, it has been conjectured that he is a legendary character, created by popular imagination to convey an idea of the humble and ignoble instruments by which the work of freedom was accomplished. But this description of poetry is so unlike what we usually find in similar cases, — a popular hero being always extravagantly grand and imposing; and the narratives of Tell, on the other hand, are so straightforward and natural that, although we cannot receive them as strictly accurate without further evidence, there is, we think, no ground for rejecting them altogether. William Tell, therefore, in our judgment, is, upon the whole, a real personage, and to be believed in accordingly.

He was not the prime mover in the revolt whose successful issue has been always associated with his name. In 1307, the cruelty of Von Landenburg, the Emperor's governor of Unterwalden, in putting out the eyes of an old yeoman named Melchthal, for an offence committed by his son Arnold, so exasperated that young man that he excited the peasantry of both Unterwalden and Uri (where he had fled) to share his feelings and promise aid in his plans. At the same time Gessler, the Imperial governor over Uri and Schwyz, was equally hated for his tyrannical conduct. A fortress-prison, which he built in Uri, especially aroused the wrath of the peasantry, which was further stimulated by his insulting order that all persons who passed through the town of Altorf should do homage by kneeling to the Ducal hat of Austria (or according to some writers, his own), which he fixed on the top of a pole in the market-place. Disobedience to this order was punishable with corporal pains and confiscation of property. This, and other acts of injustice, at last so provoked a wealthy and esteemed land-owner of Schwyz, named Werner Stauffacher, that, in concert with Arnold Melchthal, and an honorable yeoman of the Canton of Uri, named Walter Furst, he formed a committee of thirty-three tried men, who met by night in a secret haunt, and there planned measures for the enfranchisement of Switzerland from the tyrannous yoke of the Empire.

Tell, though not the prime mover, was the immediate agent of the scheme. His wife was the daughter of Furst; and it was probably by the influence of the latter that our hero, who seems to have been a peasant of ordinary standing in the Canton of Uri, joined in the league, though without taking a prominent part in it. The only noticeable feature concerning him was his reputation for skill as an archer. His avocations often took him to Altorf, where the Ducal hat was conspicuously fixed in the central market-place; but he would not dissemble his independent spirit, and continually passed the badge of slavery without sharing in the homage paid to it by the trembling townsmen. This boldness was at last reported to Gessler, ever on the watch to punish disobedience; and one day, in the winter of 1307, Tell re-

7 *

ceived a summons to attend the Governor. On presenting himself, he was sternly asked by Gessler what were
the reasons of his refusal to do homage to the hat. Tell
was not as yet disposed to be a martyr, and with a somewhat undignified show of cowardice excused his neglect
on the plea of ignorance, and promised compliance.
Gessler probably suspected the man's real character, and
would not discharge him without punishment. We give
the memorable story which follows, as the old chroniclers
relate it, and without vouching for its truth.

Ordering Tell's children to be sent for, the Governor
asked which of them was most dear to the father. Tell
replied that they were alike dear to him; upon which
Gessler selected a boy of six years old, placed him at
several paces distant from the group in an open space of
ground, set an apple on his head, and thus accosted the
astonished father : —

" Tell, I hear that you are a marksman good and true.
You shall prove it before me, by shooting that apple off
the head of your child ! Be careful to strike the apple;
for should your first shot miss it shall cost you your life !"

" For the sake of God, sir, I entreat you to spare me
this trial ! " cried the horror-struck Tell. " Consider how
unnatural it were to shoot at my own dear son ! "

The reply of the Governor was brief and stern : —

" Unless you shoot the apple, you or your child shall
die ! "

Tell turned from the cold eyes and hard lips of the
merciless man to the unseen presence of a merciful God,
whom he implored to give his hand firmness in this
dreadful moment. Taking up his crossbow, and fixing

one arrow in it, he placed another behind in his collar ; and then drawing a long breath, took his aim and shot. The arrow cleft the apple through the core, and the child's head was untouched. Gessler was amazed at this feat of skill, on which he had not reckoned, and did not withhold his applause, but suddenly turned to Tell with the question : —

"Why did you place that other arrow in your collar?"

Tell evaded the question at first, but on receiving a promise that his life should be spared, answered : —

"My lord, I will tell you the truth. Had I struck my child with one arrow, I would not have missed you with the other."

Enraged at this daring speech, Gessler ordered his servants to seize and bind so dangerous a rebel ; whom, though pledged to save alive, he vowed to punish with perpetual imprisonment. Tell was accordingly hand-cuffed, and led to Fluellen, a village still standing at the head of the beautiful Waldstädten, or Lake of Lucerne. Here a boat awaited him, and the Governor entered, accompanied by a small party of servants. Some of them guarded the prisoner, while the others managed the vessel ; which was steered for Brunnen, on the Schwyz coast of the lake. From thence the Governor proposed taking Tell to the Castle of Küssnacht, where a dungeon was to be his doom for life.

It was a stormy winter's day, and the clouds hung heavily over the steep brow of the Righi, and the jagged peaks of that wild range of mountains which the Swiss have named Mount Pilate, from a legend that, in one of its desolate tarns, the deposed procurator of Judæa, and

remorseful judge of the Saviour, perished by self-murder.
The blue waters of the lake were now darkened, and
heaving with the violence of the wind; and when the
boat reached Achsen, where the coast-line curves, the
storm was at such a height that the crew became terrified.
Tell all this time — a strong and good steersman — was
lying useless, with his hands bound. One of Gessler's
servants at last ventured to ask the Governor's permission
to make use of Tell's assistance, considering the peril in
which all were placed. Gessler, who was in great terror
of drowning, readily consented; promising Tell his release if he succeeded in saving him. The fetters being
removed, Tell hasted to the helm, keeping an eye on
his crossbow, which was lying near, while he skilfully
steered the vessel round the corner of Achsen. He soon
reached a spot where a ledge of rock projected into the
lake, affording a good landing-place. Calling to the crew
to be careful of the vessel in this dangerous locality, he
steered straight for the rock, drove the vessel against it,
seized his crossbow, and leaped ashore. Then with a
vigorous exertion of his sturdy arm, he pushed off the
vessel into the lake, and left it tossing in the waves,
while he swiftly ran across the Canton to a steep bank
overhanging the road from Brunnen to Küssnacht, along
which he knew that the Governor must pass. Meantime,
after a perilous buffet with the storm, Gessler and his
servants, full of wrath against Tell, reached Brunnen,
and took horses for the castle. The cavalcade passed
the spot of Tell's concealment, as he expected, who,
watching his opportunity, while Gessler was in the act
of devising schemes for the capture of the fugitive, once

more drew the crossbow, and an avenging arrow pierced the Governor's heart. Tell made good his escape forthwith.

This act of violence, which, as revengeful and insidious, cannot be defended, was displeasing to the Swiss patriots generally, who desired, if possible, to avoid blood-shed. This, however, was not possible. After capturing the chief fortresses of Unterwalden, Uri, and Schwyz, the peasantry, in 1308, formed at Brunnen an extensive confederation, which was to last for ten years, whereby they swore to defend their privileges, although acknowledging the Imperial supremacy.

The assassination of Albert I. by his nephew, about the same time, removed a tyrant; and the election of Henry, Count of Luxembourg, to the vacant throne, as Henry VII.,—a wise, brave, and just prince,—procured for Switzerland a temporary exemption from the revenge of Austria. He, however, was also assassinated in 1313, and a struggle ensued for the throne between the partisans of Albert's son, Frederick, and Louis, Duke of Bavaria. Leopold, Duke of Austria, Frederick's brother, was his chief ally. Exasperated, as a member of the house of Hapsburg, at the revolt of his Swiss tenants, and as Frederick's general at the support which they naturally gave to the cause of the Duke of Bavaria, Leopold eagerly seized an opportunity of invading the free Cantons.

The Swiss, though undisciplined and scantily armed, made up for the deficiency by steady courage and unfailing ardor, and at the battle of Morgarten, in 1315, utterly routed the Austrians. Tell, who had returned to his former humble position since his exploits, took part in this battle.

The independence of the three great Cantons was fully confirmed by this victory. A perpetual league was formed, which some years later was strengthened by the adhesion of Lucerne, and subsequently of other Cantons. The Austrians frequently attempted to recover their lost territories, but in vain. At the battle of Sempach, in 1385, occurred the famous act of Winkelried, a gentleman of Unterwalden, who, when the Swiss were unable to pass a barrier of spear-heads which the Austrian knights presented, grasped in his arms, as many spears as he could hold, buried their points in his breast, and thus gave his countrymen a passage. This defeat put an end to the attempts of Austria for many years; and Switzerland continued nominally tributary to the Empire, but virtually free, till the beginning of the sixteenth century, when a last attack was made upon her independence by the Emperor Maximilian. It failed; and eventually, by a solemn treaty of peace, the Cantons of Switzerland were declared free.

Tell, so far as records inform us, took no further part in the politics of his country after the battle of Morgarten. He had achieved his work boldly and skilfully, if not very nobly. He merely stands in history as the representative of a free mountain peasantry, and illustrates the homely and sturdy character of his class and age. One act of private heroism is recorded of him, and worthily terminates his career. In 1354 the river Schächen overflowed its banks, and, while attempting to rescue some neighbors, he was carried away by the flood, and drowned. His name has not been forgotten by his countrymen. In the quaint market-place of Altorf, the Ducal hat of Austria has given place to the statue of the freeman who refused to bend before it. In 1388 the Canton of Uri erected a chapel on the spot where Tell landed and escaped from Gessler. Protected by overhanging rocks, and shaded by trees, "Tell's Chapel" still greets the eye of the voyager on the Lake of Lucerne.

James and Philip Van Artevelde.

THE FLEMISH GUILDS.

THE northwestern corner of the great European Continent — now divided into the kingdoms of Holland and Belgium — is commonly known in history as the Low Countries, or Netherlands, — a name strictly applicable to the flat and " spongy " soil of the district, which is, in fact, a lagune, or deposit of mud, washed down by the rivers Rhine, Meuse, and Scheldt. The hardy tribes of Batavi, Belgæ, and Frisii, which dwelt there, were conquered by the Romans, and subsequently by Charlemagne. On the partition of his empire, the Northern Netherlands fell chiefly to the share of Germany, and most of the Southern to France. The latter were generally comprised in the county of Flanders, governed by a nobleman who acknowledged the King of France as his suzerain. The Flemings, — as the people were called, — an industrious race, occupied in their woollen trade, mixed but little in European politics until the fourteenth century. The feudal system was here, as elsewhere, abused by the undue power of the nobles, to the injury of the middle classes, which had gradually acquired much wealth, and many liberties. The cities of Ghent, Bruges, Ypres, &c., like those of France and Germany, formed communes for their mutual protection, and at various times obtained charters from the Counts of Flanders. Rivalries between certain cities and trade-societies, or, as they were styled, "guilds," often proved occasions of war and serious hindrances to the common cause of liberty, and afforded frequent opportunities to the readily aggressive spirit of the feudal aristocracy.   As a rule, however, the balance of power in Flanders, during the fourteenth century, vibrated between the burghers of the communal cities on the one side, and the Counts of Flanders, with their inferior lords, supported by the Kings of France, on the other.

Louis de Nevers, Count of Flanders, who was allied, both by marriage and interest, to the reigning family of France, was justly hated by his subjects for his harsh and illegal violation of the charters given to the communes, exempting them from arbitrary taxation.   In a contest with the city of Bruges he was taken prisoner; but the jealousy of the Ghentese prevailed over their patriotism, and they forced Bruges to set Louis free.   In 1329, Philip VI. of France, being summoned by the Count to his aid, defeated the Flemings at Cassel.   Thirteen thousand of them are said to have fallen in the field.   The inhabitants of Cassel were tortured and put to death by thousands, other cities were heavily taxed, and Louis was restored to his feudal sway.   He had no firmer hold, however, on the allegiance of his subjects than military force could sustain; and this once removed, the spirit of mutiny again showed itself.   War breaking out between England and France, the power of the latter became no longer formidable; and this time it was Ghent that headed

K

the rebellion.   The leader in that city was a man of noble
descent, but by occupation a brewer, named James Artevelde.   He was one of the true demagogue stamp, endowed with much strength of will, activity, and readiness
of speech, but ambitious and plausible.   He acquired
considerable influence over the people by assiduously flattering them and disparaging the nobles.   He saw the
advantage of obtaining the assistance of England in the
struggle, and therefore urged the burghers of Ghent and
other Flemish cities to conclude a treaty with Edward
III., to which that monarch was nothing loath to assent.
Louis, who was then at Bruges, was greatly enraged at
this bold and prudent act of policy, and seizing Siger Von
Kostryk, one of the agents most diligent in promoting the
alliance, ordered his execution.   Ghent immediately rose
in arms.   The burghers marched to Bruges, where the
Count's party was most numerous, and forced the citizens
to join the rebellion.   Aided by an English army, the
insurgents gave battle to Louis, who had summoned the
nobles to his banner, defeated, and put him to flight.
He sought refuge in France for some years, during which
time Artevelde governed Flanders with a wisdom which
commanded the respect of his political opponents.   The
trade of the country was increased, and the citizens lived
peacefully and contentedly.   Philip VI. was naturally
inflamed with anger against the Flemings for their sedi-
tious support of Edward the Third's pretence to the
crown of France, and prevailed on the then Pope, Benedict XII., to issue a decree of excommunication against
them.   This produced little or no effect, for Edward, who
at once assumed the title of King of France, entered

Flanders with his army in 1338, and formally confirmed to the people their cherished privileges. In the same year Count Louis, making a bold step to recover his possessions, returned to try the effects of conciliation with his revolted subjects. He entered Ghent without opposition, but when once within the gates the burghers shut them, and took him prisoner. Artevelde even constrained him to forfeit his claim to the help of France, by signing a treaty with Edward III. in the following year. Louis, however, escaped to Paris, where he made his peace with Philip, with whom he now joined in the war against England and her Flemish allies. Two or three battles were lost and won on both sides, when Louis again attempted a peaceful compromise of the quarrel. Either from intimate knowledge of the Count's character, or for his own personal ends, Artevelde persuaded the Flemings to refuse the proposition, and Louis remained in France.

The rebellion of the Flemings was not of a republican or revolutionary character. They were not animated by any hatred to the existing form of government, or to the reigning family, but only desired to preserve their chartered rights, and be secure against the tyranny of a ruler like Count Louis. Artevelde seems to have misjudged the feeling of his countrymen, or to have over-estimated the extent of his influence over them. He made a proposition to the league of cities in 1344, that the eldest son of our Edward III. — so well known as the Black Prince — should be invited to take the office of Governor of Flanders, on condition of his making it a sovereign duchy. This scheme was very distasteful to the Flemings, and they not only rejected it, but viewed with great

suspicion all the subsequent acts of their leader. The
immediate occasion of his fall arose out of a fierce dispute
between the Fullers' Guild and Weavers' Guild of Ghent,
in 1344. It lasted during a whole day, and terminated
in the slaughter of 1500 fullers and the victory of the
weavers. Artevelde took no part on either side; but the
success of the weavers procured for Denys, their dean, or
master, such influence that he became a dangerous rival.
Artevelde, fearing probably a personal attack, introduced
into the city a band of some 500 English soldiers for his
own protection. This suspicious action was soon noised
abroad, and Denys seized the opportunity to get rid of a
troublesome antagonist. He raised the cry of "Treason!" and it was echoed on all sides by the fickle populace of Ghent. Other charges were brought against Artevelde, into the truth or falsehood of which it is difficult
and immaterial to inquire here. One of the most serious
was, that he had appropriated, without accounting for, the
government finances, and sent large sums to England.
One morning, in July 1344, he perceived from the murmurs and insults of the people that the general feeling
was strongly against him. He hastened to his house,
and barred gates, doors. and windows; but this defence
was scarcely completed, when the dwelling was assailed
on all sides by the enraged populace. He and his men
fought bravely; and during a lull in the storm he attempted to argue in his own behalf, denying the charges
brought against him, and appealing to his services and
the prosperity of the country under his rule. All was in
vain; and in the words of old Froissart, "when James
saw that he could not appease them (the Ghentese), he

drew in his head and closed his window, and so thought
to steal out by the back-door into a church that adjoined
his house; but 400 persons had entered into his house,
and finally he was there taken and slain." The fate of
this able, though probably designing man, is among the
most striking illustrations of the uncertainty of popular
impulses, and the precarious tenure of a demagogue's influence.

The fall of their insurgent leader did not affect the
position of the Flemings with respect to their exiled lord.
Louis was slain fighting on the French side at the great
battle of Cressy, in 1346. In the next year, however,
peace was made between England and France; and the
Flemish alliance was no longer of importance to the
former power. The son of the deceased Count Louis,
surnamed Male, was accordingly restored to his father's
dominions, on condition of his insuring to the Flemings
those privileges for which they had so valiantly fought.
He had not the good sense, or good fortune, nevertheless,
to remain long in the possession of the respect or allegiance of his subjects. Internal rivalries still disturbed
the country, and his imprudent connection with one of
the contending factions led to his ignominious expulsion.
In 1381 the burghers of Bruges, licensed by his authority, commenced making a channel to bring their city into
closer communication with the river Lys. This scheme
was injurious to the city of Ghent, which formerly had a
monopoly of the river traffic, and her jealousy was at
once excited. Some of the disaffected Ghentese thereupon revived a body which had fallen into disuse, —
known as the Whitehoods, from the dress of the mem-

bers, — with the view of resenting by force the wrongs
of the city. The Whitehoods stopped by threats the
progress of the channel works, but did not disband when
this end was accomplished. An arbitrary act committed
by the bailiff of the Count, in confining a burgess of
Ghent in the county prison (contrary to the city charter),
led to a remonstrance from the Whitehoods. The Count
promised to redress the injustice if this body were dis-
banded ; but the Ghentese refused to comply, and on the
Count's attempting force, they slew his bailiff and tore
his banner in pieces. This was the signal for war. Supported by Bruges, Lisle, and other cities, Count Louis II.
was for some time successful against Ghent, with which
sided Ypres, Courtray, and a few less important places.
The character of the struggle was nearly identical with
that of the late war, — the nobles, as before, ranging
themselves on the side of their feudal suzerain, and the
burghers and lower classes uniting in defence of their
rights.

Count Louis was, as we have said, for some time successful against Ghent, more especially in intercepting
the supplies of provisions which the citizens required ;
hoping by thus reducing them to want to shorten the
campaign. The result of this plan at first seemed to
answer his expectations. The Ghentese grew dissatis-
fied, and the Whitehood leaders, who had no chance of
obtaining the mercy of Louis in case of a surrender, were
in much perplexity how to act. It occurred to one of
them, named Van den Bosch, that it would create a favorable feeling in the popular mind if the influence of their
former leader could be revived. It was by a sudden

change of sentiment, and not a deeply-rooted outbreak, that James Artevelde had fallen; and now that he was dead, the fickle mob remembered his valuable services, and forgot his ambitious schemes. He had left one son, named Philip, after his godmother Philippa, Edward the Third's queen, who in the days of the English alliance had honored the Flemish leader by holding his son at the font. Philip was now in the prime of manhood, a calm and thoughtful student, mentally accomplished, and of high moral reputation. He had not mixed in politics, but lived quietly at Ghent, in the enjoyment of domestic happiness and large wealth. The Whitehood leaders, thinking him a recluse, and not penetrating into the lurking ambition of his character, considered he would be an useful tool, and accordingly applied to him. Conscious of power, really patriotic as it would seem, and at the same time not indisposed to add the glory of authority to that of wealth, Philip Van Artevelde consented to become the leader of the Ghentese. He was proposed in a great public assembly, and vociferously elected Captain of the City.

The Whitehoods soon found themselves laid aside by their supposed tool. He commenced negotiations with the Count, but, confident of eventual success, Louis would hear of no terms. Artevelde showed great firmness in this emergency. Two leading citizens of Ghent, suspected of being in league with the enemy, endeavored to persuade their fellow-citizens to surrender, but the Whitehoods put both to death; and the eloquence of Artevelde prevailed over the urgent cravings of famine. Amid the cries of fainting women, and the ill-concealed fears of the men, he thus appealed to the people: " Choose one of these three plans! Shut yourselves into the churches, commending your souls to God, and die of hunger; bind yourselves with chains, and yield to the cruel Count; or seize your arms and drive back our foes! Which will you?" The crowd seemed swayed by the will of the young Captain, and could not oppose it. " Do you choose for us!" was the answer. " To arms, then!" was his rejoinder. With a body of but 5,000 men he left Ghent on the 2d of May, 1382, and marched straight for Bruges, where the Count was stationed. The plan seemed insane, and was certainly desperate; for the assailants were few in number, and weakened by famine, while Bruges was thronged with soldiers, and abounding in provisions of every kind. Within three miles of the city Artevelde halted. In the midst of their rejoicings during a festival, the Count and his partisans in Bruges were startled by the news that the famine-stricken Ghentese had ventured to sally forth and meet death by the sword. Vainly boastful of his position, Louis issued from the city with a chosen band of knights and a motley company of Bruges citizens, all, in their own opinion, secure of victory. Artevelde had well planted his army, small as it was, by shielding it with a marsh in front, and guarding the flanks by a line of baggage-carts. He commenced the engagement by a telling fire of artillery, and then manœuvred so as to draw the Count's men into the marsh, while he charged the remaining body with such ardor that it was utterly discomfited, and the flight became general. The pursuers and pursued entered Bruges together. A panic seized the burghers, and at nightfall the city was given up to plunder, in which the rabble of Bruges itself was but too ready to join. Louis fled in disguise, and concealed himself in the loft of a house belonging to a poor woman who was in the habit of receiving alms at the palace-gate. He subsequently escaped to Lisle.

Artevelde stopped the plunder of Bruges in the morning, but signalized his victory by an act, which, unless justified by circumstances not recorded, was tyrannical and inexpedient, — the execution of the chief magistrates. His success, indeed, was fatal to his moral rectitude. He forgot his domestic duties in unlawful pleasures, assumed the airs of a monarch, and levied heavy taxes upon all the partisans of the Count. Ghent, however, benefited greatly by the alteration in the aspect of affairs; and plenty and cheapness succeeded to the miseries of famine. Most of the Flemish cities joined the revolt, and a general rising of the middle and lower classes against the oppression of the nobles was prevalent in Flanders.

The daughter of Louis had married the Duke of Burgundy, uncle of the young King of France, Charles VI.; and fearful of losing his reversionary right to the County of Flanders, the Duke persuaded his nephew's counsellors to send an army to the relief of the exiled Count, before the Flemings could, as it was probable they would, procure the support of England. Artevelde was besieging Oudenarde, one of the few cities still faithful to Louis, but advanced to meet the French army. It was victorious in an engagement at Comines, and the city of Ypres deserted the Flemish league. Both armies then marched towards the river Lys, and encountered at Rosebecque, between Courtray and Ghent. The night before the battle, it was said, was portentous of evil omen, — war-cries and the din of arms having been heard in the air, as though, says Froissart, the fiends of hell were playing " for joy of the great prey they were likely to have."

Next morning the armies met on the field. The Flemings fought like men, but were unskilfully arranged, — their lines being so close as to prevent the soldier from using his weapon with effect. The French men-at-arms pressed on them so fiercely as to increase this difficulty ; and 20,000 Flemings are said to have fallen. Philip, surrounded by his body-guard of Ghentese, was at last wounded, and beaten down, — he himself, as it is supposed, falling into a ditch, and being suffocated to death. His body was found and brought to the French camp, finally receiving honorable burial at Courtray. The war by no means ended with this battle, decisive as it seemed. The English aided the Ghentese, and carried on the campaign for some time. Louis, being assassinated in a private quarrel two years after, the crown of Flanders passed to the Duke of Burgundy, who concluded peace with the citizens in 1385, on condition of assuring their. liberties.

Both the Van Arteveldes had too short a duration of power to enable us to form a decided opinion of their characters. Able and prudent they certainly were, but tainted with the vice of ambition, and spoiled by success. They are chiefly prominent in history as the popular leaders in a contest which was in its time of great importance. Its issue, indeed, decided the line of conduct adopted by other communities similarly circumstanced.

The French cities were on the point of rising against the nobles, but cautiously waited to see the end. The rebellion of Wat Tyler, in England, was a connected movement of a like description. The sanguinary check which the Flemings met at Rosebecque probably saved the effusion of much more blood elsewhere. It certainly proved the salvation of the nobles throughout Europe, and the burghers and peasantry learned to look to patience and importunity as the surest and wisest methods of obtaining their rights secured.

Cosmo dei Medici.

THE FLORENTINE REPUBLIC.

AMONG the Italian republics, no city occupied a more distinguished position than Florence. Remarkable for the beauty of its situation, amid an amphitheatre of hills, on the banks of the Arno, and for the artistic glory of its architecture, poetry, sculpture, and painting, it was yet more conspicuous for the love of freedom, rectitude, dignity, and cultivation of its citizens. Honorable as its reputation is in these respects, its history is, notwithstanding, disfigured by the records of faction and crime, — only less common in this city than in any other during the same period. A sketch of the leading events in which Florence was concerned, from the death of Frederick II. to the commencement of the fifteenth century, may thus be given.

The Ghibelines of the city, as previously stated, united, in 1248, to expel all the Guelphs by force; but their exile did not last beyond two years. Before the death of Frederick, the leading citizens revolted against the yoke which the Imperialists sought to impose on them. At a great assembly in the Square of Santa Croce, held on the 20th October, 1250, the constitution of the republic was placed on a new footing. The *Podesta* (an officer

in imitation of the Imperial viceroys in Lombardy, instituted by Frederick Barbarossa) was no longer retained
as sole chief magistrate. With him was joined another,
named Captain of the People, and both were to act as
separate judges, without taking any active share in the
administration of affairs, which was confided to a body
of twelve, called the *Signoria*, elected by the people from
the several districts of the city, and holding office for two
months at a time. The first *Signoria*, under the new
constitution, recalled the Guelph exiles, and supported
that cause in Italy generally. Against Pisa, and other
Ghibeline cities, Florence obtained numerous successes
at this period; and the year 1254 was known as that
" of Victories."

In 1258 the Ghibelines, displaying factious symptoms,
were, in their turn, exiled. Farinata degli Uberti, their
able and eloquent leader, was well received by the rival
republic of Sienna; and having allied himself with Manfred, the King of Naples and Sicily (son of Frederick
II.), obtained a considerable force with which to recover
the defeat of his party. By intrigues and treachery in
their camp, the Guelphs of Florence were drawn into a
snare, and experienced a terrible blow at Arbia, in 1260,
where the Ghibelines attacked them by surprise, and
utterly routed them. The chiefs of the defeated faction
deserted Florence, which the Ghibelines entered, — abolishing the new government, and establishing an aristocratic magistracy, pledged to support Manfred. The
republics of Pisa and Sienna, ever jealous of Florence,
ventured to propose the destruction of the city, which
they averred to be a hotbed of Guelph democracy. Fa-

rinata, however, was a patriot still, and, with an indignant burst of eloquence, he declared that, if so monstrous a wrong were attempted, he and his party would join the Guelphs, whom they had just exiled. His arguments prevailed, and Florence was saved.

The Ghibeline rule was of short duration. In 1265, Charles of Anjou was summoned by the Pope, as already narrated, to uphold the Guelph standard. The fall of Manfred and his house soon followed. Florence rose against its Imperialist garrison, consented to receive French troops in its place, acknowledged the nominal supremacy of Charles, as they had previously done that of the German emperors, and re-established their democratic constitution. Pope Gregory X., one of the wisest and best Popes that ever reigned, used his influence to assuage the violence of faction in Italy. He endeavored to weaken the dominant authority of Charles, and balance the power of the rival parties as equally as possible. Florence, at his persuasion, restored the Ghibelines.

The concessions of Rudolph of Hapsburg to the Papal See left scarcely any room for the contention of the two factions, which now indeed quarrelled more from hereditary hatred than political opposition. Pope Nicholas III. was a Ghibeline by descent and inclination, and wholly averse to the schemes of Charles, who meditated Guelph domination in Italy. This indeed he nearly obtained, through the agency of the succeeding Pope, Martin IV., who was his creature; but in 1282 the Sicilian Vespers, and the consequent separation of the kingdoms of Naples and Sicily, distracted the attention of Charles from other than domestic politics. For several years after these events the Italian Republics were free from foreign aggression of any kind, — the power of Naples being much reduced, and the condition of Germany being such as to forbid its Emperor from attempting any designs on Italy. During this interval Florence took the lead in a peaceful rivalry of arts and literature with her fellow-states. It was at this period that her best churches and palaces, solid, simple, and beautiful structures, were chiefly built. Cimabue and Giotto, the fathers of Italian painting, and Dante, the king of Italian poets, distinguished her by their residence. Commerce, agriculture, and the graces of social refinement, were diligently and successfully cultivated, and the reputation of Florence was European. A still more democratic change was made in her constitution towards the close of the thirteenth century. The twelve magistrates who composed the *Signoria* were reduced to six, who were chosen out of the corporation of trades, and styled *Priori delle Arti*. The chief of this body was intrusted with the city standard, or gonfalon, and hence named Gonfaloner. These peaceful pursuits and constitutional changes did not, unfortunately, interfere with the progress of external or internal discords. The Guelph party maintained the upper hand, and were engaged for some years in a contest with the Pisan Ghibelines. In Florence itself, the aggressions of the nobles in 1292 led to the passing of a severe edict, excluding all nobles from the *Signoria*, and placing power in the hands of the Gonfaloner to bring to justice those who violated the laws. The curious punishment of *ennobling* unruly families, to bring them within the reach of this decree, was also devised. The strength of the aristocracy was, however, not to be easily restrained, and Florence soon found herself mixed up with a deadly quarrel, which originated in the neighboring republic of Pistoia, between two branches of the Cancellieri family, known as the *Bianchi* and *Neri*, that is, the Whites and the Blacks. The contest in Florence commenced by a division in the Guelph party, — the Neri, who belonged to the ancient nobility, adhering to the traditional principles of the party; while the Bianchi, who were chiefly nobles of recent extraction, disclaimed such illiberal ideas, and promoted a fusion of parties. The latter section, as may be supposed, subsequently sided with the Ghibelines, and the old form of dissension was revived. Pope Boniface VIII. gave his support to the Neri and Guelph cause. Inviting Charles, brother of Philip IV. of France, to wrest Sicily from the house of Aragon, he instructed him to pass through Florence. Charles announced himself as the champion of the Guelphs, and the Republic could not refuse him entrance, though it limited the extent of his power and the number of his attendants. He shamefully abused this permission by allying himself with the Neri, and sanctioning their violent assertion of authority over their opponents. The Bianchi were plundered, ill-treated, and exiled, and Charles received a large share of the spoil. He quitted Florence in 1302, after a stay of some months.

The accession of Pope Clement V.. in 1305. who was a creature of the French King. and the consequent removal of the Papal residence to Avignon, diminished for about seventy years the mischievous interference of the

Church in the political affairs of Italy. But she was
fated, almost at the same time, to enter into a struggle
for freedom with her old antagonist, the German Emperor. On the assassination of Albert I. the crown was
bestowed on the Count of Luxembourg, who ascended
the throne as Henry VII. He has already been mentioned as a just and able monarch, and his schemes in
Italy were originally prompted by no unworthy motives.
He saw that France had already succeeded in enslaving
the Papacy, and seizing the crown of Naples, and he
suspected her of designing to add to her power by further
conquests. Faction, too, was rife throughout Italy, and
a wise arbitration between the contending parties was
greatly needed. He was invited by the Ghibelines, towards whom he naturally leaned; but he at the same
time announced himself as the restorer of order, and disclaimed any political prejudices. Impartiality, however,
was not possible in such a judge between such disputants.
Entering Italy in 1310, he declared his intention of restoring the exiles, both Guelph and Ghibeline, of every
city. This was resisted in Milan, where the Guelphs
were dominant. The Ghibelines returned and drove out
their opponents, who stirred up the Guelphs of Lombardy against the Emperor. His demand of a tribute
for the support of his army — a measure which, though
perhaps legal, was certainly inexpedient — increased his
unpopularity. He reduced Brescia by force, but failed
in imposing his authority on Genoa, and his retirement
to Pisa in 1312 resembled a flight. Florence now took
part with the Guelphs, and allied itself with Robert, the
French King of Naples, to oppose Henry's claims. Un-

willingly, but almost perforce, the Emperor resorted to the aid of Pisa, which was still devoted to the Ghibeline cause, and the Bianchi of Tuscany. He was first crowned at Rome by the Pope's legate, and then set out for Florence with a large army. The Florentines prepared for war with cool determination, but bloodshed was happily spared by Henry's sudden death, in 1313.

The Guelph and Ghibeline contest was not affected by this event. Pope John XXII., elected in 1316, from his palace at Avignon, used his influence in support of the former party, of which Florence was the leading Italian representative. Pisa and Lucca, under an eminent noble named Castruccio Castracani, upheld the standard of the Empire, over which Louis, Duke of Bavaria, was elected to reign in 1322. The Florentines suffered a severe defeat in 1325, at Alto Pascio, mainly through the treachery of their Spanish commander; and hearing that Castruccio had summoned the new Emperor to his aid, they resolved to accept the protection of the King of Naples. Louis marched into Italy in 1327, but by his violent and grasping policy disgusted the Ghibelines, and increased the hatred of the Guelphs. He lavished favors on Castruccio, however, and was preparing to adopt the measures which he advised with respect to the subjugation of Florence, when the death of that skilful and ambitious general prevented the attempt. Louis returned to Germany in 1329, after a purposeless and disastrous visit. In the next year he sent John of Luxembourg, King of Bohemia, as his vicegerent. This prince was the son of Henry VII., and inherited his father's high-minded and moderate disposition. He pur-

sued the same impartial policy with more success, and,
in Lombardy especially, restored order, and obtained
oaths of obedience to the Empire. But Florence aspired
to independence and self-government. Her citizens wisely resolved to lay aside faction for the sake of insuring
liberty; and accordingly, in September, 1332, entered
into a treaty with several of the Ghibeline cities which
had already yielded to John, to reject his interference.
By the terms of this agreement, no single state was to
be allowed .to monopolize power in Italy, and the cities
which had intrusted their sovereignty to him were to be
divided among the members of the League. Florence,
it must be allowed, was not wholly free from sordid motives in making this arrangement, as by it she acquired
possession of Lucca. John, finding himself deserted by
his new subjects, gave up any attempt to recover his
influence, and departed from Italy in the next year.*
The members of the League soon quarrelled. The
powerful family of Della Scala, which had made itself
tyrant of the republic of Verona, after the death of Eccelino, was now headed by a noble named Mastino. He
succeeded in dispossessing the Florentines of Lucca in
1335, and, coveting larger possessions, formed a league
with Pisa and other Ghibeline cities. The aristocratic
republic of Venice at first united with Florence, but,
after making good terms with Mastino, deserted her.
Bologna, which had long upheld the Guelph cause, surrendered its sovereignty to the house of Pepoli in 1337,
which joined the Ghibelines. In 1341 Pisa was success-

* English readers will remember the gallant death of this prince,
when aged and blind, at the battle of Cressy.

ful in a conflict which Florence commenced to recover
Lucca; and, in short, the greatest republic of Tuscany
seemed on the brink of ruin.   In this emergency the
citizens imprudently accused their magistrates of weakness, and attributed the misfortunes which befell the state
to the want of a single leader.   They fixed upon Walter
de Brienne, a descendant of the French Crusaders who
conquered the Eastern Empire in 1204.   He still retained the title of Duke of Athens, then conferred on his
ancestors, though, since the Greek reconquest of the Empire, he no longer possessed any authority.   His abilities
were good, but he was perfidious and ambitious; and one
less fit could scarcely have been found to administer the
affairs of a free republic.   He was intrusted, in August,
1342, with the amplest powers of chief magistrate and
general; but he aspired higher still.   He intrigued
throughout Tuscany to obtain the adhesion of the lower
orders, and in Florence especially won over so many by
his bribes, that, in a month after his acceptance of office,
he was proclaimed lord of the city for life.   He soon
showed his true character, by leaguing with the Ghibeline despots abroad, and tyrannizing over his subjects at
home.   Conspiracies were organized by those who still
loved freedom in Florence.   At an assembly of the leading citizens, which he had summoned with the intention
of putting to death all whom he suspected of treason, a
concerted movement was made by the conspirators.   A
shout of "To arms!" resounded through the city.   His
cavalry were stoned and disarmed, the streets were filled
with hostile citizens, and the Duke was besieged in the
Palazzo Vecchio, to which he had retired.   Here he was

driven to yield by famine, but secretly escaped to Naples on the 6th of August, 1343.

Florence, after this happy deliverence, was forced to maintain her position against her numerous opponents without external aid. Her most dreaded foe during the next half century was Milan, now governed by the house of the tyrant Visconti. John Visconti, archbishop of Milan, was master of sixteen Lombard cities, and in 1350 obtained a surrender of Bologna from the Pepoli and Pope Clement VI. Without declaring war, in 1351 John suddenly sent an invading army into Tuscany. It was gallantly resisted and driven back; but the attempt was so unexpected that the Florentines felt their liberty constantly endangered. The great plague which ravaged Europe at about the same period, and was especially fatal in Florence, added to the disasters of the republic. The citizens were also much harassed by the aggressions of bands of soldier-adventurers, chiefly Germans, which the Viscontis and Della Scalas introduced into Italy, as mercenaries in their pay. These roving bodies, which were obedient to no laws of God or man, and acknowledged only avarice as their guiding principle, were engaged by nearly all the Italian states in turn. Repeated assaults failed to subdue the gallant spirit of the republic, and the adventurers were at last forced to withdraw.

The progress of art and literature, fostered by the study of Greek and Roman antiquities, which at this period was undertaken in Italy with the most burning ardor, amid all the interruptions of civil war, was nowhere more remarkable than in Florence. Her citizens, however, were happily proof against the weakness into which the love of the past betrayed those of Rome in 1347, where Rienzi, an imaginative enthusiast, made a vain effort to restore the ancient glory of the Eternal City. Florence cultivated learning for its own sake, and assigned it its legitimate province. Petrarch and Boccaccio are the most memorable names in her literary history at this time.

In 1354 the new Emperor of Germany, Charles IV., son of John of Bohemia, entered Italy, there to obtain recognition of his authority. His interference in politics was confined to the demand which he made for tribute from the various states, and Florence paid a heavy price for the purchase of her rights and his promise not to enter the city. He displayed an intriguing spirit, which alienated his adherents, and he was eventually forced to quit Pisa and Sienna, where he had been received with open arms. The former, however, still remained Ghibeline in feeling, and a lurking rivalry of Florence was perpetually at work in her councils. Though commercially attached to Florence by a treaty, there was an anti-commercial party in the state always ready for war. The Visconti availed themselves of this body to excite old jealousies; and after many insults, which the Florentines bore with great moderation, war was commenced in 1362, lasting two years. It weakened both cities, and strengthened the Visconti, who aspired to subdue them. In Pisa, indeed, a lieutenant of Barnabas Visconti, chief tyrant of Milan, was received as Doge. Florence saw clearly that if she would preserve freedom, she must sustain a single-handed struggle with this powerful and

anscrupulous family. The Emperor, Charles IV., and
the Pope, Urban V., indeed professed an intention to deliver Italy from the scourge of tyranny, but effected little
towards this result. Urban returned from France in
1367, and formed a league with the Emperor, the Queen
of Naples, and other Italian princes, against the Visconti;
but he was not supported by Charles, who even took
bribes from the tyrants to preserve peace, and made
himself so obnoxious to the citizens of Sienna, which he
again visited in 1368, that he was attacked and expelled
the city. Lucca, which generously received him, paid
dearly for its purchase of liberty, but was assisted by
Florence to make up the large sum which he demanded.
The Pope's excommunication of the Visconti was quite
unavailing, and his legates were actually forced to eat
the bull, of which they were the bearers, — lead, parchment, and silk together. This daring insult so terrified
Urban that he returned to Avignon. His successor,
Gregory XI., proved worse than useless to Florence by
his treacherous policy. His legate, after employing the
troops of the republic in a successful assault at Bologna,
which they wrested from the Visconti, suddenly deserted
the alliance, made a truce with the tyrants, and even
sent an English leader of mercenaries, named Sir John
Hawkwood, to attack Florence itself. This monstrous
perfidy exasperated the Florentines past bearing. They
resolved on inflicting a signal punishment on the Church
which they had so faithfully defended. Raising an army
under the standard of " Liberty," they joined, with Pisa,
Sienna, and Lucca, in a league (to which even the Visconti gave a worthless promise of adherence), the object

of which was to awaken a revolutionary spirit in the
Papal States. The hatred of French interference was
no doubt influential in promoting this unusual alliance.
The attempt was singularly successful, eighty communities freeing themselves of the Papal legates in a few
days. Bologna accomplished her independence in the
next year and allied herself with Florence. Gregory
took a frightful revenge on Faenza, one of the revolted
towns, the inhabitants of which were brutally massacred
by Hawkwood. The legate Cardinal of Geneva was a
bloodthirsty emissary of the Church, and presided at the
sack of Cesena, crying out to the soldiers to kill all the
inhabitants : " Blood ! I will have more blood ! " Gregory himself returned to Rome in 1377, in the hope of
saving his dominions, and peace was at length agreed to.
The death of this Pontiff at Rome, in 1378, led to a
great schism in the Church. The conclave of Cardinals,
in accordance with ancient usage, had to meet at the
place of the late Pope's death to choose his successor,
and thus was originated an opposition to the long-prevail-
ing influence of France over the Papacy. An Italian
was elected as Urban VI., but proved so self-sufficient
and distasteful to the Cardinals, that another Pope was
chosen, in the person of the Cardinal of Geneva, whose
cruelty has just been related. He was crowned as Clement VII. ; and, under the protection of the Queen of
Naples, first held his court there ; afterwards removing to
Avignon. The two Popes and their respective adherents
mutually excommunicated each other, and Europe was
scandalized by this exibition of disunion in the centre
of unity. The schism proved of some service to Italy,

where several cities which owed their freedom to Florence were enabled to retain it.

In the republic itself a new form of discord had broken out. The constitution was democratic, as has been shown; but the choice of magistrates was limited to the seven leading corporations of trades, out of the twenty-one that existed. This restriction was justified by the superior intelligence and wealth of the privileged bodies, which comprised the highest families of the commercial princes of Florence. A division commenced in the heart of this order, and rapidly extended. The Albizzi family was of the old Guelph party, and adhered strictly to the law which forbade any descendant of the Ghibelines from election to the magistracy. This law was strained to the exclusion of all persons of recent origin. The Ricci family headed the new party, which endeavored to abolish sect names, and aimed at the extension of municipal distinctions to a larger number of trades. Prominent in this party was the Medici family, which, though of recent extraction, was remarkable for the ability and commercial success of its members.

In 1378 Salvestro dei Medici, then Gonfaloner, proposed to suspend the anti-Ghibeline law on which the Albizzi insisted; and his proposition, though rejected by the Signoria, was approved and carried by a popular meeting. The inferior trades, thus partially benefited, increased their demands, — agitating for the extension of privileges to all classes alike. This requisition was resisted by the Signoria, who even arrested and tortured one of the lower classes on suspicion of treason. The people then rose, under the leadership of a wool-carder, named Michael Lando, who was made Gonfaloner. The palaces of the *Podesta* and *Signoria* were captured, and the whole government reorganized. Lando, considering his former position, proved a wise ruler. He preserved decorum and justice, checked the unruly spirit of his class, and passed a moderate law, by which the election of magistrates was to be made from all orders equally. The old *Signoria*, however, was not so easily displaced. Its members rejected the additions to their number, which were made by the new administration, and the Ricci party came into power. Unfortunately, some of the leaders abused it for their private ends. The Albizzi became popular; and in January, 1382, exiled their opponents, and restored the aristocratic constitution.

Florence was now called upon to resist the aggressions of Gian Galeazzo Visconti, who had dethroned his uncle Barnabas, one of the most subtle and perfidious of the Milanese tyrants. After conquering nearly all Lombardy, he turned towards Tuscany, in 1388. Bologna and Florence formed an alliance, and gave the command of their army to their former enemy, Hawkwood, whose services were open to all purchasers. The Visconti, however, were successful against the German and French armies which the Florentines summoned to their defence. Peace was made in 1392, but soon broken, through the treachery of Galeazzo, who intrigued for the purchase and enslavement of Genoa, Pisa, Sienna, Bologna, Lucca, and Perugia, which he eventually obtained.

Happily for Florence and Italy generally, he died of the plague in 1402, at the height of his power. In the confusion which followed this event, many of the con-

quered cities changed their sovereigns, or recovered their
freedom. Pisa, however, was still governed by Gabriel,
a natural son of Galeazzo. The possession of this city
was of great importance to Florence, as its hostile attitude prevented her needful communication with the sea.
Having vainly attempted to purchase Pisa, the Florentines resorted to war. After a year's gallant resistance,
the Pisans, through the treachery of Gambacorta, their
Captain of the People, yielded in 1406; but Florence
tried in vain, by a just and generous policy, to appease
the ancient hatred which existed between the two cities.
The leading families removed elsewhere; and Pisa, so
long a free and flourishing commercial republic, became
politically dead.

A new antagonist now presented himself in Ladislaus,
King of Naples, the son of Charles III., of the house of
Anjou, who, after defeating his rival, Louis II., Duke of
Anjou, in 1399, commenced a succession of aggressive
acts on the States of the Church and Tuscany. Finding
herself wantonly assaulted, Florence set up Louis II. as
opponent to Ladislaus, and chose as their general an able
Perugian noble, named Braccio da Montone. He reconquered Rome from Ladislaus in 1410, but failed in
preventing his success in Tuscany. The death of that
monarch, in 1414, terminated the struggle.

This was no sooner over than another commenced with
the new Duke of Milan, Filippo Maria Visconti, who
revived his father's schemes against Florence. He had
a skilful general in a Piedmontese, named Carmagnola;
whereas Florence was deprived of the services of Braccio by his death, in 1424. Six defeats did not weary the

patience or exhaust the courage of the brave Florentines,
who, as a last resort, sent to request the aid of Venice.
The ambassadors had not much influence, until seconded
by the unexpected appearance of Carmagnola, who had
been suddenly dismissed by the cruel and capricious
Duke of Milan. The arguments of the fugitive prevailed, and war was commenced in 1426. It lasted for
several years, the Venetians taking the most prominent
part in checking the power of Filippo. Carmagnola, as
their general, obtained several successes, but suffered a
defeat in 1431, which subjected him to the punishment
of death by the disappointed and stern Venetians. Florence also was worsted in an attempt on Lucca in 1430,
but managed to hold her own in Tuscany. Still, her
situation was disturbed with both external and internal
discords, and a genius of wisdom and peace was greatly
needed to put an end, if possible, to the existing causes
of strife.

We have dwelt at such length on the history of Florence prior to the political appearance of Cosmo dei Medici, because the spectacle of turbulence which it discloses
cannot fail to heighten our estimate of that man who was
able to reduce the chaos to order and beauty. The liberal sentiments of his relative, Salvestro, have already
been referred to. Cosmo's father, Giovanni, was as eminent for wisdom and moderation as for wealth, which he
derived from his extensive commercial relations throughout Europe. Without seeking any political distinctions,
all that the republic could afford were conferred upon
him in the course of his life. On his death-bed, in the
year 1428, he thus addressed his sons : " I die content,

after living the prescribed time, and leaving you, my
sons, in affluence and health, — placed in such a station
as, if you follow my example, will enable you to live
here honored and respected. I reflect upon nothing in
life with so much pleasure as on having given offence to
no one, and having endeavored to serve all men as far as
possible. I advise you to act thus, if you would live
securely, accepting only such honors as are conferred on
you by the laws and favor of the state; for it is the exercise of power which has been violently, not voluntarily,
obtained, that occasions hatred and strife." These words,
which breathe the maturity of good sense and political
experience, seem to have been accepted by Cosmo, the
elder of the two young men to whom they were addressed,
as the talisman of his career. He was born in 1389, and
spent his youth and early manhood in the mingled occu-
pations of commercial and public life; acquiring by the
former immense wealth, which he distributed with as
large a generosity, — and in the latter, filling the honorable place of leader of the opposition to the Government.
This was, and had been for half a century past, vested in
the aristocratic faction headed by the Albizzi. By means
of a *balia*, or select commission of the Parliament, the
magistracy was confined to this party. The administration had been on the whole just, and decidedly successful,
yet partook of the abuses consequent on exclusiveness.
The Parliament was a tool in the hands of the Council
of Dictators, and did not represent the people. Party
spirit was preferred to patriotism; ambitious wars were
rashly undertaken; and the finances squandered by irre-
sponsible officers. Against these abuses Cosmo declared

a steady, though constitutional opposition. The head of
the state since the year 1427 had been Rinaldo degli
Albizzi, whose pride and jealousy proved fatal to his
house. He determined to check the growing influence
of Cosmo, whose acuteness, firmness, and kindliness won
him the admiration and affection of all classes. Secretly
intriguing with his partisans, Rinaldo, in 1433, procured
the election of none but his own friends to the new *Signoria*. Their first act was to summon Cosmo as an of-
fender against the state, and commit him to prison. The
Parliament acted obediently to its instructions, and Cosmo
and his friends were sentenced to exile. He retired to
Venice, where that republic received him with much
respect ; but his absence from Florence was but brief.
The *Signoria* of 1434 was less partial than its predecessor. Donati, the president, was attached to Cosmo,
and revenged his expulsion by attacking the acts of
Rinaldo ; who, however, refused to obey his summons,
and held out by force. The docile Parliament, nevertheless, obeyed Donati's voice, — the Medici were recalled and the Albizzi banished.

While Rinaldo meanly employed his exile in exciting
the Duke of Milan to make war against Florence, Cosmo,
now at the head of the republic, availed himself of the
opportunity to tranquillize and strengthen the Government. The process was too gradual to present any features of striking interest. He has been censured for selfish
and ambitious views in the means which he employed;
but his conduct is open to another construction. His
boundless wealth, and the vast circle of influence which
he acquired by his munificence and patronage, might

have procured him sovereign power. To this he never attempted to rise, and avoided all appearance of wishing to obtain it, by keeping his personal expenditure within the limits of a citizen's pretensions. He was no doubt animated by the desire of authority, and spared nothing to insure it; but as compared with his contemporary, Francesco Sforza (of whom more anon), and others similarly placed, Cosmo's moderation was conspicuous and admirable. Though he supported tyrants, he did not imitate them; and both his foreign and domestic policy may have been guided by the love of order rather than power. The constitution of Florence remained as he found it, — still aristocratic, but no longer, like that of the Albizzi, unpopular. By measures sometimes rigorous and even unjust, but generally quiet and firm, the spirit of faction was repressed. The duties of peace were steadily performed. Commerce was sustained; art and literature were cultivated; and all that patronage could accomplish was lavished on their professors. The revival of Plato's philosophy in Europe, and the foundation of the great Laurentian library at Florence, are due to Cosmo's wisdom and liberality. Abroad the republic was respected, without making itself detested by conquests. It must, indeed, be admitted that Cosmo did not carry out in office the principles which he avowed in opposition. The corrupt system, which the Albizzi had introduced, of silencing the popular voice in the national Parliament was not abandoned; and an attempt made in 1455 to establish a legitimate representation of the people was, after a trial of three years, forcibly put down. It would, however, be unjust to charge upon him the result

of a long series of despotic acts, for which the whole
body of the aristocracy was really responsible. If a
tyrant, Cosmo dei Medici was among the wisest and least
arbitrary that ever obtained the name. Florence, in accepting his rule, did not surrender her freedom ; for during at least half a century previous the government which
she acknowledged was an oligarchy. This form Cosmo
attempted not to change, but to improve, by securing its
basis in the affection of the citizens. In this he certainly
succeeded ; and on his death, in 1464, the *Signoria* expressed the general sentiment by inscribing on his tomb,
" The Father of his Country."

Francesco Sforza.

THE history of Milan during the period at which we have been considering that of Florence, has far less interest, — less in proportion to the difference, in an Englishman's eyes, between a lapse into slavery and a struggle for freedom. As typical, however, of the Lombard cities generally, Milan has an historical importance which demands our attention.

During the two great wars between those republics and the Empire, and the Empire and the Church, it will be remembered that Milan stood at the head of the Guelph faction. The shameful ingratitude of Innocent IV., however, in 1251, after the death of Frederick II., sufficed to turn the scale, which had already at times vibrated between the Guelphs and Ghibelines, considerably to the latter side. Unmindful of the faithful support and generous sacrifices constantly afforded by the Milanese in his behalf, he treated them as his slaves, and for some offence against ecclesiastical privileges threatened them with excommunication. The Ghibelines, profiting by the resentment occasioned by this dastardly conduct, strengthened their position in the city. The nobles here, as elsewhere, were prominent in the ranks of this party. A

9   M

temporary union took place between the rival sections in 1259, against the tyranny of Eccelino, who, after Frederick's death, aspired to the sovereignty of Lombardy. A crusade was declared against him, in 1256, by Pope Alexander IV.; but the tyrant, with the aid of Milan and Brescia, which did not then suspect his views, was for some time victorious over the Papal armies. His crimes, however, made him distrusted, and in September, 1259, his allies deserted him. He was wounded and captured, dying a few days after, from an obstinate resolve neither to have his wounds healed or take any food.

The influence of the aristocracy in Lombardy made itself felt sooner, and to a more dangerous extent, than elsewhere in Italy. Admitted as citizens, yet proud of their lineage, and secure in the possession of armed horsemen and strong castles, the nobles could afford to despise and plunder the burghers. In opposition to this power, the citizens often had recourse to the expedient of making one of the more popular nobles head of the state, both in a military and civil capacity. Professing popular sentiments, but at heart true to his order, he frequently abused his authority by despotic acts, and prepared the way for a perpetual tyranny. The family of Della Torre was thus raised into importance. It sprang from Valassina, of which it possessed the feudal lordship. The principles of the house were Guelph; and after the defeat of the Milanese by Frederick II. at Cortenuova, in 1237, Pagano della Torre had sheltered the fugitives in his territory, and protected their return to Milan. This service was acknowledged by the grateful city to five generations of the family, each lord holding the office of Captain of

the People, and ranking superior to the Podesta and the
judges. Other Lombard cities followed this example,
and Philip della Torre, in 1264, was Governor of Como,
Vercelli, and Bergamo also. As a counterpoise to the
growing strength of this house, the Popes commenced to
favor the Visconti, — a Ghibeline family in the neighborhood of Milan; and thenceforth private rivalry often obscured the interest of political faction. Both, however,
united in 1277 to substitute the tyranny of the Visconti
for that of the Della Torre family, and to secure the
Ghibeline power in Milan. Otho Visconti, Archbishop of
Milan, who was exiled by Napoleone della Torre, Captain of the People, suddenly raised an army of his political friends, attacked, and captured his rival at Desio.
Otho was received with joy by the Milanese, whom Napoleone had irritated by his injustice and pride; and was
admitted to the same posts and influence. The chiefs of
the Della Torre languished in the confinement of an iron
cage, and a new dynasty ruled over Milan. An attempt
to restore the exiled family was successful in 1302, but
for a brief period. The impartial endeavor of the Emperor Henry VII., in 1310, to restore alike Guelph and
Ghibeline exiles to their cities, has already been mentioned. Guido della Torre, who was then Captain of the
People in Milan, opposed this policy, which was fatal to
his despotic schemes. It was, however, carried into effect, and Matteo Visconti, who had been driven out by a
Guelph league in 1302, returned with his Ghibeline
friends. The demand of Henry for a tribute to his army
led to a commotion in Milan, which ended by the expulsion of Guido della Torre and the Guelphs, and Matteo

recovered his former seat. He governed Milan with considerable vigor and popularity, and acquired the title of *Great* in his time. His chief exploits were performed in a war which he carried on for some years against the Lombard Guelphs, supported by the French, the King of Naples, and Pope John XXII. Visconti succeeded in taking Pavia and other cities; besieged the King of Naples in Genoa, where he had fled; and drove Philip de Valois (afterwards Philip VI.) back into France. But while successful against the Church in temporal things, he was spiritually its slave. A weak fear of losing his soul, in consequence of Papal excommunication, seized upon him in 1322. He abdicated in favor of his son, and died shortly afterwards. Galeazzo, his successor, was not at first acknowledged by the Milanese, who expelled him, and proclaimed the republic. But tyranny and intrigue had taken too firm a hold of Milan to be shaken off. The exile was summoned back, and resumed his father's rule.

The imprudent and mischievous interference of the Emperor Louis in Italian affairs, in 1327, lost him the attachment of Milan, among other Ghibeline cities. He was well received by Galeazzo Visconti, who surrendered into his hands the iron crown of Lombardy, and supplied him with a body of cavalry. Jealous either of Visconti's independent power, or of his treasures, Louis suddenly arrested his host and the leading members of the family, confined them in a dungeon, and threatened torture, unless their wealth was yielded up.

Azzo Visconti, son of Galeazzo, contrived to purchase the sovereignty of Milan from the Emperor in the next

year; and on his father's death, in 1329, succeeded to
his rank. The power of this family greatly increased
during the fourteenth century. Genoa, after invoking
its aid in a disastrous naval war with Venice, in 1353,
gave up the *Signoria* of the city into its hands. Pavia
fell before its victorious arms, in 1359, after a gallant
attempt to achieve her freedom made by Jacopo de Bus-
solari, who, though a monk, was an earnest patriot and
a man of cultivated intellect. By means of their " com-
panies of adventure," the Visconti kept their rivals in
awe, and endeavored to weaken the stability of all free
governments. Florence, as already related, was greatly
in danger from the attacks of John Visconti, who was
both Archbishop and Lord of Milan.

On his death, in 1354, two of his three nephews, Barnabas and Galeazzo, after poisoning their brother, divided
their uncle's territories. A successful attempt was made
by Genoa to recover its freedom in 1356; but a league
of the Della Scala, tyrants of Verona, Este of Ferrara,
Gonzaga of Mantua, and Carrara of Padua, with the Marquis of Montferrat against the Visconti, failed, through
the treachery of the mercenaries employed by the league.

The intrigues of Barnabas Visconti in Pisa, against
Florence, and his defiance of the Pope and the Emperor,
have been sufficiently dwelt on in the last biography.
His nephew, Gian Galeazzo, after succeeding to the share
of his father, in 1378, formed the design of dispossessing
his uncle and cousins of the rest. Assuming habits of
retirement and devotion, he impressed Barnabas with
the idea of weakness, and disarmed suspicion. In May,
1385, Gian sent to his uncle, stating that on his way to

a shrine near Milan, he should be glad to meet him. Barnabas and his two sons accordingly went to meet Gian. On his uncle's approach the young man leaped from his horse to embrace him; but at the moment of greeting called in German to his soldiers, "Strike!" The attendants of Barnabas and his sons were overpowered, and they themselves captured and imprisoned. The old tyrant died a captive in December, 1385, and Gian Galeazzo obtained the throne. He carried to its height the aggressive policy of his family, and seemed to aim at the conquest of all Italy. Personally suspicious and fearful, his public acts were conducted on a principle of intrigue, which served to cover the boldness of his ambition. Nearly all his allies found out, too late, the error of forming alliance with one so untrustworthy and covetous. The best mercenaries, domestic and foreign, were in his pay, and he spared no pains to strengthen his position by matrimonial and other relations abroad. His daughter Valentina was married, in 1389, to the Duke of Orleans, brother of Charles VI. of France, — a marriage which subsequently gave a color to the designs of the French on Italy.

In 1395, for the sum of 100,000 florins, Gian purchased the fief and nominal dukedom of Milan, which he had so long virtually held, from the weak Emperor Wenceslaus. By this title Visconti secured his possession of Pavia and twenty-five other cities in Lombardy. This sale was repudiated by the next Emperor, Robert; but, on his attempting to enforce his Imperial authority, Gian defeated him and his Florentine allies, near Brescia, in 1401, and drove him back to Germany.

Among the first of the Duke's conquests were those of his fellow-tyrants, the Della Scala family of Verona and the Carrara of Padua. The revenge of Venice on the latter for having assisted her rival, Genoa, gave him the opportunity he needed. Attacked by Antonio della Scala, at the instigation of Venice, Francesco da Carrara accepted the aid of Gian. Verona was taken by his arms ; but he had the treachery soon afterwards to league with Venice for the conquest of Padua. It, too, fell in 1388. Francesco was secretly got rid of. His son fled to Florence, while Gian turned to threaten his imprudent ally, Venice. By the aid of Florence, the young Carrara recovered Padua, in 1390. In Ferrara Gian incited the Marquis d'Este to commit acts of violence towards certain members of that family, and thus schemed to bind him firmly in allegiance to Milan. Pursuing the same policy in Mantua, by a horrible intrigue in the palace of Francesco da Gonzaga, who had married the daughter of the late Barnabas Visconti, Gian persuaded her husband of her unfaithfulness, and procured her unjust death. But for the brave opposition of Florence to the designs of Visconti in Tuscany, they must have prevailed. No other city of importance held out. By a series of assassinations, plots, and open attacks, Pisa, Genoa, Perugia, Sienna, Bologna, and Lucca, fell into his hands one after another. The plague, as before stated, proved the best friend to Italian freedom, by carrying off the despot, in September, 1402.

His two sons, Gian Maria and Filippo Maria, were declared heirs to his dominions ; but as both were too young to rule, their mother, Catherine, and the leading generals of the deceased Duke, were constituted guardians. The profligate and cruel acts of Catherine incited her subjects to rise, and in 1404 she was imprisoned and put to death by poison. The generals, who were only *condottieri*, or hired captains, and felt no attachment to the Visconti family, took advantage of the youth of their wards to obtain power for themselves. The Duchy was split up into independent states, which quarrelled one with another; and acts of violence filled every city in Lombardy with blood. The elder of the two boys, Gian Maria, became a puppet in the hands of Facino Cane, one of his guardians, but was allowed sufficient liberty to exhibit his character, and give cause for gratitude that he was not allowed more. A nature so wantonly cruel and grossly passionate has seldom disgraced humanity. His chief pleasure seemed to consist in giving pain, and when tired of the chase, he would hunt human prey with his hounds in the streets of Milan by night. Criminals were surrendered to him by the judges for this brutal sport. After ten years of mock sovereignty, thus abused, he was assassinated by his nobles in May, 1412. Facino Cane died on the same day, and left the road to power open to the strongest aspirant. This was Filippo Maria, the second son of Gian Galeazzo. He arrived in Milan within a few days, and at once married the widow of the deceased general, thus securing his army and influence. By a series of victories during a period of ten years, Filippo's armies, under the leadership of Francesco Carmagnola (who has been already named), won back to the Duchy nearly all of which it had been deprived at the death of Gian Galeazzo. Filippo himself, however, rarely was present in the field. His character was a curious compound of boldness and fearfulness, and though eminently subtle in intrigue, his fickleness and jealousy of others lost him the advantage of his most ingenious schemes. He carried out his father's policy in Tuscany and other parts of Italy, but met with the same opposition from Florence. In these wars he was wise enough to secure able generals for his armies, and at various times the best *condottieri* in Italy were engaged in his service. But his capricious temper soon disgusted his servants, and his perpetual jealousy of their power, and distrust of their designs, led him to act unjustly and suspiciously. Among the most eminent of those who were once his commanders, and subsequently his opponents, was Francesco Sforza, whose history now claims our attention.

His father, Jacopo Attenduolo (who acquired the surname Sforza at a later period), was born of peasant parentage at Cotignola, near Faenza in Romagna. Of great personal strength and courage, the laborer soon spurned his simple vocation, and one day determined to decide by lot what life he should follow. Tossing his pickaxe into a tree, he vowed, that, if it remained among the branches, it should be an omen of a stationary life, but if it fell, of an adventurous career. It fell, — and Jacopo took an early opportunity of joining a band of adventurers, then famous as the company of St. George, commanded by Alberico, Count of Barbiano, — a man of more respectable character than most of the *condottieri*, and whose soldiers, all Italians, were trained with the utmost military science and discipline. Under this leader, Jacopo

distinguished himself in the wars of 1375 – 8; the company being first engaged by Barnabas Visconti and
Florence, against the Papal legates; and afterwards by
Pope Urban VI. against his rival, Clement VII. In a
battle at Ponte Molle in 1378, the Breton mercenaries
of the latter — the most dreaded of their class — were
defeated by Alberico's band, which thenceforth ranked
first. At the beginning of the next century we find Jacopo an independent *condottiere*, and with but one rival
in eminence, — Braccio da Montone, previously named.
These captains were identified with two distinct systems
of warfare, the latter having adopted an alteration of the
old routine, by placing his troops in small bodies, each
with an officer, and trusting for success to rapid and
dashing charges; while Jacopo improved the older system of moving men in vast sections, and maintaining a
steady front. After a term of service with Gian Galeazzo, Sforza was hired by Florence to lead her expedition
against Pisa in 1405. He conducted the siege skilfully,
and with final success, Pisa yielding up her liberty in
November, 1406. In the war that soon after broke out
between Florence and Naples, the former intrusted her
armies to the command of Braccio da Montone, while
Sforza transferred his services to the adventurous and
unprincipled Ladislaus, then King of Naples. The
States of the Church, and the Eternal City itself, were
the objects of his avarice, and Sforza was his unscrupulous tool. The only bar to his progress in Tuscany also
was Florence, and Braccio gained two or three victories
over Sforza in 1410 – 11, but was worsted in the next
campaign, which terminated by the death of the King in

1414. His sister, Joan **II.**, reigned in his room, but soon had a contest to wage with Alfonso, King of Aragon, whom, having no children, she at first adopted, but afterwards displaced in favor of Louis III., of the house of Anjou. Sforza was now in great honor. In addition to large territories in Naples, he held the office of Great Constable, as well as that of General. It was by his influence that Louis of Anjou was brought forward, — his motive being jealousy and fear of Caraccioli, the queen's favorite, who was an adherent of Alfonso. As the commander of Louis's army, Sforza won several battles in the kingdom of Naples; but in 1424, while attempting to ford the swollen river Pescara, in the Abruzzi, was drowned.

His son, Francesco, was born in 1401, and at an early age was ennobled by the Queen of Naples. He stepped into his father's place as general of the queen's army, and succeeded to his possessions.

The Neapolitan war was not long confined to a quarrel between two dynasties. Filippo Maria Visconti supported Louis, and Florence allied herself with Alfonso. This resulted in the former's successful campaign of 1423 – 5, which has already been noticed. Florence, after long resisting the Duke single-handed, obtained the aid of Venice, and both united with Alfonso against Milan. Carmagnola, who had been dismissed by the Duke, commanded the allied armies; but Filippo engaged in his service three or four generals of equal eminence. A pupil of Braccio da Montone (now deceased), named Nicolo Piccinino, brought with him the best of the Bracceschi, as Braccio's soldiers were called, while

Francesco Sforza headed his father's band, the Sforzeschi.

The great campaign of 1426 – 31 was, as we have seen, for some time unfavorable to the Duke, in spite of his distinguished commanders. Francesco was taken prisoner at the battle of Macalo, in 1427, where the Milanese were utterly defeated, but was released by the courtesy of Carmagnola. After several defeats fortune turned, and Francesco was the hero of the battle of Soncino, in 1431, which retrieved the Duke's cause, and proved fatal to the generous Carmagnola.

Peace was now made, but lasted only a short time. On the expulsion of Rinaldo degli Albizzi from Florence, in 1434, he repaired to Milan, and excited Filippo against the republic. War was recommenced in that year, but Sforza no longer led the Milanese armies. Ill-rewarded by the Duke, he left his service, and now appeared at the head of the Florentines. He defeated Piccinino, the Milanese general, in several engagements during this campaign, which lasted, with occasional breaks, till 1447. Sforza meantime developed talents far above those of a mere general. He cultivated an intimacy with Cosmo dei Medici, who often assisted him with money, and doubtless imparted to him much of that political wisdom which distinguished his own rule. After severe losses, Filippo showed an apparent desire for peace, and with this view made overtures to Sforza in 1441; promising to give him his natural daughter, Bianca, to wife, with the dower of Cremona and Pontremoli. Francesco, seeing in this match a stepping-stone to the Dukedom, — for Filippo had no son, — consented, and the marriage was celebrated

in the same year. The Duke's jealousy of his son-in-law
led to a rupture of peace. Sforza had obtained from
Pope Eugenius IV. a grant of the March of Ancona as a
fief. Into this territory Filippo treacherously sent his
general Piccinino, with an invading army, and at the
same time incited the Pope and Alfonso, now King of
Naples, against Francesco. The latter, with his duties
as general of Florence, had, by this additional task of
repelling invasion, work enough on his hands for two
men; but he bravely sustained his burden, — carried on
the war against Filippo in Lombardy, and against Piccinino in Romagna. The Duke was at last so hardly
pressed by the Venetians, that he proposed terms of reconciliation with Francesco, who, no doubt from politic
motives, and not from faith in one so traitorous, agreed
to desert his post and join the Milanese. His treachery
was not carried into execution, as, on his way to Milan,
he received news of Filippo's death, in August, 1447.

Milan, so long crushed beneath a despotic yoke, was
not yet utterly degraded. The fertile soil of Lombardy,
the garden of Italy, favored the toil of the husbandman
and the skill of the manufacturer. In spite of tyranny
and civil war, the commerce of Milan and other Lombard
cities was extensive, — while the citizens, saved by despotism at least from the oppression of an oligarchy, were
not overburdened by taxation. Thus circumstances were
not so wholly unfavorable as they seemed to the growth
of liberal ideas, and in the heart of Milan there yet beat
a pulse of freedom. On the death of Filippo Visconti
without lawful heirs, or any male issue, the title of Duke
was extinct. An opportunity thus being afforded them,

four of the leading citizens, Trivulzio, Cotta, Bossi, and Lampugnani, ventured to proclaim the republic. The mass of the citizens joined them, and engaged the best *condottieri* of the late Duke in the service. This seemed a death-blow to the schemes of Francesco Sforza; but he was not easily discouraged, and bided his time. He volunteered to join the republic with his army, — conditionally on the confirmation to him of Cremona, which he had received in dower with his wife.

Filippo Visconti had, some years previously, been compelled to yield Brescia, Bergamo, and other places, to the Venetians; and one of the objects of his late war was to recover these possessions. On the proclamation of the republic of Milan, peace would have been made had Venice agreed. But the Doge, Foscari, aimed not only at retaining the ceded territory, but acquiring more, and refused terms of peace. Meantime the Duke of Orleans (cousin of Charles VII., then King of France) claimed the Duchy of Milan in right of his mother, Valentina, daughter of Gian Galeazzo Visconti, and sent an army to invade it. Sforza was on terms of intimacy with the Dauphin of France, afterwards the perfidious Louis XI., and therefore would not himself command the Milanese against the French. He first put down a rising in Piacenza, which aspired to independence, and cruelly plundered it. Siding with the Ghibelines, — a party which still existed in Milan, — he incited them to reject a proposition made by the Guelphs of the city for peace with Venice. Then advancing against the Venetian army, he gained three or four decisive victories, and in October, 1448, made a treaty with that republic, by which he yielded up Brescia and Bergamo, on condition of obtaining its assistance in conquering Milan for himself. This shameful treachery was first made known to the Milanese by his refusing to obey the instructions of their Commissioners; and the news of the treaty excited the utmost surprise and anger. Sforza was, however, supported by several of the Lombard cities, which were jealous of Milan. Its brave citizens procured some troops from the Duke of Savoy, and prepared for resistance. Venice, now fearful of Sforza's power, played false to him, by making a treaty with Milan, in 1449, to acknowledge the republic, but at the same time agreed to secure the General's claims on the cities which had declared for him. He meantime craftily concealed his disappointment, consented to the treaty, and withdrew his invading army from Milan. Waiting until the citizens were short of supplies, he suddenly reappeared, and besieged the city. The succor of Venice was in vain. He defeated its troops, and continued the siege. Famine at last reduced the citizens, in February, 1450, and Francesco Sforza entered as Duke of Milan.

He signalized his success by a moderation scarcely to be expected of him. By a mild and yet firm policy he reconciled the people, in great measure, to their slavery. Justice was secured to all; taxation was kept upon its former footing; and the crown officers were chosen from natives instead of foreigners. These wise measures, which were probably owing in some degree to the sound advice of his friend Cosmo, were followed up by a liberal expenditure on the improvement and adornment of the city, which served to employ the poorer classes and gratify

the higher.   The Ducal Palace, a large hospital, and the
canal which unites the city with the river Adda, are due
to Sforza's hand.

He was for many years opposed by Venice, but held
his own in Lombardy.   Cosmo dei Medici, influenced
alike by personal friendship and political interest, secured
him the support of Florence, and a reconciliation was
effected with the Pope and Alfonso of Naples.   Louis
XI. of France still remained his ally; and the refusal
of the irresolute Frederick III., Emperor of Austria, to
acknowledge the new Duke of Milan, gave him no con-
cern.   Finally, after a desultory war with Venice on the
one hand, and the Duke of Savoy on the other, Sforza
made peace with both, ceding Brescia, Bergamo, and
Crema, to the former, and fixing the river Sesia as the
boundary between the latter and his own territory.   In
1455 a general league was happily accomplished between
the four leading Italian powers, — Florence, Venice, Naples, and Milan.   One of the objects of this alliance was
to secure Italy against the probable assault of the Turks,
who had recently captured the city of Constantinople,
and conquered the Eastern Empire from the Greeks;
thus finally extinguishing the ancient dominion of Rome.

One of Sforza's last acts was the acquisition of Genoa.
He achieved this by throwing his power in the scale in
favor of Ferdinand (son of Alfonso, King of Naples,
recently deceased), who, on his father's death, had to contend for the throne with the descendants of the house of
Anjou.   Joan II., and Louis III. of Anjou, her adopted
son, died in 1435, and René, the brother of the latter,
was named by the Queen's will as her heir.   Alfonso of

Aragon, however, by the assistance of Filippo Visconti, overcame his rival, and reigned in peace from 1442 till his death. Genoa, which had accepted the sovereignty of Visconti, was attached to the Anjou dynasty, and, on his favoring the Aragonese, revolted. Sforza always bore in mind this loss, and aspired to retrieve it. On the death of Alfonso, in 1458, his son Ferdinand, though illegitimate, was acknowledged his successor; but having offended the Neapolitans by his tyrannical conduct, they set up John, son of Réné of Anjou, as a competitor. This prince looked for Sforza's assistance, which had been given to the Anjou dynasty hitherto; but at this moment Genoa, torn by internal factions, placed itself under the protection of the French King, Charles VII. Sforza coveted Genoa, and feared the power of France. He therefore refused to help John of Anjou, and prevented his obtaining aid from Florence, where Cosmo dei Medici was still dominant. This policy was wisely conceived, and proved fortunate. John, who governed Genoa as a viceroy of Charles VII., disgusted the citizens by heavily taxing them to support his ambitious views. Ferdinand succeeded in Naples; Genoa expelled its French garrison, and after a brief period of anarchy gave up its sovereignty to Sforza in 1464.

His rule extended over the cities of Milan, Pavia, Piacenza, Cremona, and Como, together with Lodi, Novara, Alessandria, and other cities which form part of the present kingdom of Sardinia. To these he added Parma, in Central Italy, and now Genoa. After a reign of sixteen years he died of the dropsy, in 1466, at the age of sixty-five. Though unscrupulous in obtaining power,

N

Francesco Sforza was a favorable specimen of the Italian tyrants, as whose representative we have taken him. His private life was dishonored by no excesses; and, though ruthless as a conqueror, he was humane as a sovereign. His masterly political genius entitles him to the first intellectual rank in that school of diplomacy and intrigue which, about this period taking root in Italy, has spread so extensively throughout Europe down to the present time.

Christopher Columbus.

THE DISCOVERY OF AMERICA.

It is a relief to turn from the feverish excitement of selfish ambition, and the clamorous ferocity of the battle-field, to the calm enthusiasm of selfless science, and the noiseless daring of the field of maritime discovery. There the destroyer, — here the creator rules ; there the turbulent passions of man overpower and obscure his higher attributes, — here the goodness of God and the wealth of nature supply fresh food for mental culture, and open new channels for the spread of religion and civilization.

During the period which we have been considering, the Italian cities of Genoa, Pisa, and Venice took the lead in commerce with the East. The fifteenth century brought Portugal as a new competitor into the field, but its distance from the great seats of traffic led to enterprises being undertaken in other directions. The South and the West were yet unexplored. Some Spanish adventurers, however, having lighted on the Canary Islands in 1393, Don Henry, the accomplished Infante of Portugal, sent a vessel in 1412 to explore the African coast. Madeira was discovered in 1418 by another Portuguese expedition, or at least rediscovered, for a legend exists

of an Englishman named Macham, who was accidentally
wrecked there in the previous century.   Later expeditions resulted in the exploration of the whole coast of
Western Africa and the Cape of Good Hope in 1486.
Vasco de Gama, a Portuguese nobleman, subsequently
crowned this discovery by pursuing the route to India,
and thus applying science to the enlargement of commerce.   The invention of the astrolabe, for ascertaining
the altitude of the heavenly bodies and determining lati-
tudes at sea, and the application of the magnet as the
mariner's compass, greatly contributed to these results.

Spain in the fifteenth century began to occupy a prominent position in Europe.   The Moorish power had, by
a series of encroachments on the part of the Christian
states, gradually dwindled down to the possession of the
single province of Granada.   These states were now
resolved into three, of which Navarre was comparatively
isolated from the other two, which were of great size and
importance, Castile and Aragon.   The marriage, in 1469,
of Isabella, the high-minded and beautiful heiress of Castile, with the able though crafty Ferdinand, heir to the
crown of Aragon, reduced under a solid government the
hitherto divided races of Spain, and resulted in the final
fall of the Moorish dominion.   The attention of the sovereigns was soon directed to the condition of their commerce.   Jealousy of the Portuguese trade inbittered the
political "War of the Succession" between Spain and
Portugal, which occupied nearly five years at the outset
of the new reign.   The war, which arose out of a dispute
as to the crown of Castile, terminated in 1479 by the
defeat of Portugal; but a clause was fortunately intro-

duced into the treaty of peace, reserving to the latter the sole right of traffic on the African coast. But for this, Spain might not for centuries have been led to undertake expeditions in the West, and Christopher Columbus might not have been the hero of the adventurous enterprise with which his name will be eternally connected.

Cristofero Colombo (as his name is in Italian) was born in the state of Genoa, about the year 1441, or perhaps somewhat later. His parents were of humble origin, and poor, but contrived to send him to the famous school of Pavia, where he devoted his time to his favorite studies of geometry and astronomy. An enthusiasm for the sea induced him to leave school at the age of fourteen. He made repeated voyages to various parts of Europe, and engaged himself as captain in the service of Naples and Genoa. The dissensions of his native state drove him to Lisbon, where he married. Thence he took a voyage to the North, and seems to have reached Iceland, and even Greenland. He visited also the Guinea coast, and resided some time at the newly discovered island of Porto Santo, of which the father of his wife was governor. Here he heard rumors of a vast continent far out to the west, the outline of which the islanders to this day believe they occasionally see. Driftwood curiously carved, and the bodies of strange men thrown upon the western shores of the island, indicated the existence of unknown races. These rumors were confirmed to the mind of Columbus by his devout belief in the Scriptural predictions of the universal sway of Christianity; and he burned to be the harbinger of truth and civilization to the new world. This continent he identified with the Cathay (Northern China) and Zipangu (Japan), of which the Venetian, Marco Polo, had been the first European explorer in the thirteenth century; and which were placed by geographers so far to the east, that Columbus, adopting the conjecture of the earth's spherical shape, considered they would be reached soonest by voyaging west.

Full of these hopes, he applied first to his native country for assistance in his schemes, but without success. He fared no better at the court of Portugal, where he obtained indeed a hearing, but was rejected. He soon after had the mortification of learning that his project was secretly carried out by the Portuguese, who sent a vessel in the direction indicated on his charts. The pilots, lacking his courage and spirit, put back after a short trial, and ridiculed the scheme as visionary. Angry at such unworthy treatment, he repaired in 1484 to the port of Palos, in Andalusia, and thence set out for the Spanish Court. Stopping at the convent of La Rabida, near Palos, to beg some refreshment for his son Diego, — for Columbus was much reduced in funds at this period, — the Superior, an intelligent ecclesiastic, named Marchena, engaged him in conversation. A discussion of the project ensued, which so delighted Marchena that he gave Columbus a letter of introduction to the Queen's confessor, and, meantime, undertook the care of young Diego. The confessor, Talavera, a narrow-minded scholar, gave the adventurer no encouragement; but by this acquaintanceship Columbus made hmself known at Court, and gradually interested some of the leading courtiers in his views. A council was at last

appointed by Ferdinand to discuss them, but after a delay
of five years it came to an adverse decision. Columbus
had actually quitted the Court in disgust, and determined
to apply to the Court of France, when, in repassing La
Rabida, the friendly Marchena pressed him to await the
result of another application. The friar himself took a
journey to Granada, and had an interview with the
enlightened Isabella. This led to an invitation being
given to Columbus, who again repaired to the Court.
Here, at an interview with Ferdinand and Isabella, he
stimulated the interest of the former, by representing the
wealth of the countries which Marco Polo had described,
and the zeal of the latter, by picturing the extension of
Christianity to the heathen. He demanded only the
reasonable reward of a tenth of the profits of whatever
lands he might discover, and the title of Admiral and
Viceroy for himself and his heirs. This was refused ;
and he once more turned his face towards France : but
his numerous friends at court convinced the Queen how
fair were the conditions proposed. She immediately entered into the scheme with the utmost enthusiasm, —
volunteering to pawn her jewels if needed, and undertaking to charge the expenses on her own Castilian revenue. Columbus was recalled, received a courteous
greeting from the Queen, and finally, in 1492, after a
delay of eight years, the agreement between the Court
of Spain and himself was signed. Three vessels were
fixed on as suitable, though of small size : the Santa
Maria, which was commanded by Columbus ; the Pinta,
by an eminent navigator, Alonzo Pinzon ; and the Nina,
by his brother Ganez. The expedition was so unpopular

with the Spanish, that criminals who volunteered as
sailors were promised exemption from punishment.   The
crew at last amounted to about one hundred and twenty ;
and on the 3d August, 1492, the fleet set sail.

After a brief stay at the Canary Islands it put out to
sea.   When beyond sight of land, many of the crew lost
courage, — shedding tears, as though persuaded of the impossibility of returning home.   Columbus restored their
hopes by his eloquent promises, and had recourse to an
expedient for keeping them in ignorance of the distance
they were voyaging, by having two reckonings, — one
accurate for his own use, and the other inaccurate for the
crew.   Flights of birds seemed to suggest the vicinity of
land in various directions, but steadily bearing in mind
the cherished vision of a continent, Columbus refused to
go aside in search of small islands.   The wind, which
had blown from the east till the 20th of September, then
changed to southwest, and the crew clamored to take
advantage of it, and return home.   With admirable wisdom and patience Columbus combated this movement, —
threatening some and assuring others.   But the continu-
ance of the unfavorable wind, and the frequent disappointments which were experienced by appearances of
land, that vanished on closer inspection, drove the crew
into actual mutiny, and Columbus was called upon to exercise his utmost vigor and presence of mind.   His life
was in danger, but he never yielded his claims upon their
obedience, and had succeeded in partially appeasing the
revolt, when at midnight, on the 11th of October, there
was a cry of " Land! "   For several days the indications
of its being near had been increasingly numerous, but

had so often proved untrue, that they failed to insure belief. Now there could be no doubt, and the manifesta-
tions of joy and hope among the crew exceeded the recent
outburst of discontent and despair. All watched sleep-
lessly during the night, — anxious for the dawn. It broke
upon a coast of verdant hills and valleys, and by sunrise
the vessels reached the shore. Columbus, bearing the
royal standard, landed with his crew, and at once planted
a crucifix, before which they knelt with tears of gratitude.
He then took possession of the island, as it proved to be,
in the name of the King of Spain, and entitled it San
Salvador. It is now identified as one of the Bahama
group. The crew then assembled round their admiral,
and swore fealty to him as Viceroy, asking forgiveness
for the trouble they had occasioned him by their attempted
mutiny.

The shore was peopled with naked and painted savages
of both sexes, who seemed timid rather than fierce, and
had to be coaxed into familiarity. When their wonder
at the complexion and habits of the Spaniards was sa-
tiated, they readily exchanged their golden earrings for
beads and other trifles. Seven natives were retained on
board as interpreters, and after a short stay the fleet
sailed southwards, and discovered the islands to which
were given the names of Conception, &c.. Having ascertained from the gestures of the natives that their gold
came from a southern country which was called Cuba,
Columbus steered in that direction, and on the 27th of
October came in sight of the island. From its name, as
pronounced by the people, he at first deemed it must be
the Zipangu of his search, but was soon compelled to re-

ject the supposition. The Cubans proved to be savages, possessing similar characteristics to those of the other islanders, — wholly unlike the civilized inhabitants of Japan, as described by Marco Polo. For years, however, the new world was held to be part of India, and hence the people were known as *Indians*. At Cuba, Alonzo Pinzon deserted with his vessel, — animated by an avaricious desire of first reaching the island of Hayti, which the Cuban islanders reported as the chief gold country. Columbus reached it in December, and anchored near the spot where the town of Cape François was afterwards peopled. The natives were so timid as to preclude intercourse, until one of them, who was accidentally upset in his canoe, was rescued by the Spaniards, and treated so kindly that the others flocked to the vessels. Their chief, or cacique, came to meet Columbus, who received him with great respect. Gold was readily bartered by the islanders for trifling articles; but the mines whence it was derived were said to be in a country further east. The fleet sailed in that direction, but the Santa Maria struck on a reef, and Columbus and his crew were forced to escape in the Nina. The cacique of Hayti gave every assistance to the Spaniards, and nothing was stolen from the wreck by the natives. Columbus, at the request of the chief, erected a fort on the bay of Caracole, and manned it with thirty-eight Spaniards, to aid the Haytians against the attacks of the Caribs, — a fierce tribe, which invaded the island in ships. Thus was established the first European colony. In January, 1493, Columbus met Alonzo Pinzon on the northern coast of the island, and generously forgave his desertion. Both vessels set out on the homeward voyage in the same month. A heavy gale separated them near the Azores, and proved almost fatal to the Nina, in which the Admiral was. He even despaired of life, but, anxious to save his discovery, wrote two accounts of it on parchment; threw one, fixed in a sealed cask, into the sea, and left the other on board. Happily the storm ceased, and the Nina anchored at the Azores in safety. It reached the port of Palos in March, at about the same time that the Pinta arrived at a northern port. Columbus was greeted with transports of joy at Palos, and entered Barcelona, where the Court was stationed, amidst a public procession. Some of the natives from the islands followed in his train, and the gold and other curiosities which he had brought were duly displayed. Ferdinand and Isabella received him at a full court, — raising him from his knees as he bent before them, and ordering him to be seated. He then recounted his adventurous voyage, and exhibited his treasures. A confirmation was accorded to him of his privileges, and other honors were conferred on him.

A second expedition was immediately set on foot, with greater preparations than previously. Materials for stocking and cultivating the new territory were amply supplied by the Treasury, — seventeen vessels chosen, and a colony of artisans, miners, and others speedily collected. Twelve missionaries accompanied the fleet, and Columbus received full instructions to treat the islanders with kindness, and extend by every fair means the spread of Christianity. A bull of Pope Alexander VI. was then obtained, confirming to the Spanish Crown the possession of all the lands recently or thereafter to be discovered by its enterprise. The fleet set sail from Cadiz, in September, 1493. Upwards of 1,500 persons of all ranks embarked on board, and the government of this motley assemblage soon occasioned serious anxiety to Columbus. As a foreigner, and a successful discoverer, he was exposed to the jealousy of the Spanish adventurers, who accompanied the expedition in great numbers; and as an earnest, high-minded enthusiast, he had nothing in common with their avarice and selfishness. Constant mutinies disturbed the voyage, and were only quelled by his manly and dignified firmness. The discovery of Jamaica and the Caribbee Islands was the result of this expedition, and the colonization of Hayti (which was also known as St. Domingo, or Hispaniola) was extensively carried out. But the licentious and unruly conduct of many of the Spaniards exasperated the simple natives into revolt, while the neglect of agriculture in the search for gold, detracted from the success of the colony, and brought odium on the name of Columbus. The rebellion of the islanders led to their severe punishment, — an act of authority which the Admiral was unwillingly compelled to discharge, and for the cruelties attending the execution of which he must not be held responsible. He was assailed with unjust calumnies by the colonists, but on his return to Spain, in 1496, had the gratification of being received cordially by the sovereigns, before whom he cleared his character. The Queen, especially, favored him with her warm and sincere patronage. He made his famous third expedition in May, 1498, with but six vessels, — the scanty exchequer of Spain, drained by a war in Italy, not allowing a more liberal supply. This voyage resulted in the discovery of the Parian coast of South America, and the mouths of the river Orinoco. In Hayti, whither he next repaired, he found the utmost confusion prevalent, and it occupied him upwards of a year to reduce the colony to order. His exertions in this work, which obliged him to punish severely many of the leading colonists, brought upon his head a discharge of rage and slander, which lost him the favor of Ferdinand, and even weakened the confidence of the Queen. Several of the colonists returned to Spain, and represented the Admiral as aspiring to sovereign power in Hayti, and misappropriating its revenues. His adoption of the common Catholic doctrine that heathen nations had no civil rights, as being out of the pale of the Church, and his zeal for the conversion of the islanders, led him to sanction their enslavement as the shortest road to that end. This well-meant imprudence — which she disavowed by cancelling the decree of slavery — was the chief cause of Isabella's consenting to the proposition of her council, that a special commissioner should be sent to supersede Columbus. A knight named Bobadilla, who, though chosen with some care, proved a most unfit person, was accordingly despatched, in July, 1500. His instructions were very large, but he exceeded them in his treatment of Columbus, whom he loaded with fetters, and sent home as a criminal. The Admiral, deeply wounded, but firm of heart and conscience, made no resistance, and the vessel reached Cadiz, bearing the discoverer of the New World as a prisoner to the Old World, which his discovery had enriched. Both the sovereigns, and all who were honorable and generous in Spain, felt indignant at this shameful sight. Isabella was especially concerned at learning the indignity put on so illustrious a man. He was at once released, and furnished with a retinue and money for his expenses. He had an interview with the sovereigns at Granada, where the kindness of the Queen so touched his wounded spirit, that his firmness gave way and he burst into tears. He was promised redress of his injuries; but it was considered prudent to send out another governor to the colony, where his name was in such ill-favor. Nicholas de Ovando was sent out in 1502, and Bobadilla was ordered home for trial; but perished on the route, with all his fleet, save that vessel only which contained the private property of Columbus. This remarkable retribution seemed to many a special interference of Providence on behalf of this deeply injured man.

Though now of advanced age, the enthusiastic pioneer of science would not relinquish his long-cherished scheme of finding a passage to the Indian Ocean between Cuba and South America, which, from the character of the coast, he rightly inferred must exist, though ignorant that it would prove to be an isthmus. He was supplied with a small fleet for this expedition, and set sail in March, 1502.

At Hayti he was actually denied shelter by the governor, Ovando, and was driven by storms to the Gulf of Honduras, whence he vainly essayed to find the southern passage. He attempted to colonize the coast, but was prevented by the attacks of the savages, and thence returned to Hayti, where he was at length allowed to enter, though treated with discourtesy and ingratitude. His crew, which had been mutinous throughout the voyage, was nevertheless generously treated by him, and a vessel for the homeward passage was fitted out at his own cost.

After a perilous voyage he arrived at the port of St. Lucar, near Seville, in 1504. The news of the Queen's death speedily reached him, and the cold nature of Ferdinand gave him little reason to expect an extension of that patronage which Isabella had afforded him. He was unprepared, however, for the treatment he actually received. Though met with outward marks of respect, the share of revenue to which he was entitled, by the agreement made with the Crown before his first voyage, was withheld; and now in his old age, and suffering from disease, he was reduced to poverty. After vainly applying for redress, he lingered another year in neglect, only sustained by conscious rectitude and faith in God, and died at Valladolid in May, 1506, at the age of nearly seventy years.

Such was the fate of one of the noblest martyrs of science. Animated with a lofty and devout aim for the extension of religion and civilization, and the increase of knowledge, he stands foremost in the rank of discoverers. No lust of gain or power led him to cross the seas, and imperil life, fame, and fortune, in the service of ungrateful foreigners. Deliberately just and generous in his treatment of his fellow-laborers, and the tribes with which he came in contact, he may be pardoned for ever having injured either by indulging too freely his imaginative dreams, or carrying out too zealously his religious convic-

tions.   His is one of the few names which can be recorded with satisfaction as that of a colonizer, who exercised the privilege of Man to subdue the earth, without
abusing it for the sake of national glory or private interest.

Niccolo Machiabelli.

THE life of a statesman, though not exciting in itself,
is the cause of excitement in others. Kings, armies —
even nations — are often but the puppets of a single
man, who is seldom seen out of the council-room. A
decree of his framing, an intrigue of his devising, may
open or close a civil war, put thousands to death, or develop new materials for the support of the human race.
This vast authority was more especially capable of being
exerted at a period when, in the absence of an open parliament and a free press, popular influence was weaker
than is happily the case in our own day. The life of
Machiavelli, who was the moving spring of Italian politics during his time, may be taken as a fair illustration of
this historical condition.

The history of Florence, since the death of Cosmo dei
Medici in 1464, must first be briefly sketched. His son,
Pietro, succeeded to his father's position of chief of the
republic, but governed with far less popularity, and a severity which evidenced conscious weakness. Many distinguished citizens emigrated, and the people were only
kept quiet by being amused with splendid festivals and

spectacles. Pietro's infirm health obliged him to surrender the administration into the hands of his officers, who abused their trust to his prejudice.

He died in 1469, leaving two young sons, Lorenzo and Giuliano, who, on reaching manhood, gave signs of a tyrannical disposition. A feeling of discontent meantime agitated the breasts of many, both in and out of Florence, who loved their country. A slight attempt was made, in 1470, at the town of Prato, to shake off the yoke which the Medici were now manifestly seeking to impose; but it failed for want of prudent management.

In 1478 an organized conspiracy was set on foot by the Pazzi family, one of high rank and position in Florence. The conduct of the Medici which gave offence in this case was their refusing to allow any of the Pazzi to be called to the *Signoria*. The leading members of the house secretly formed a scheme, to which a large number of persons was made privy, for assassinating the tyrants and restoring liberty to Florence. Pope Sixtus IV. gave the conspiracy his sanction, and promised aid; being prompted by his hatred of the Medici, who opposed his selfish plans for endowing his nephews with the richest benefices in the Church. Salviati, Archbishop of Pisa, whom the brothers had refused to acknowledge, was also one of the conspirators. The murder of Lorenzo and Giuliano was fixed for the 26th April, 1478, at the time of a religious ceremony at which they were to be present in the cathedral. All were in readiness on the day appointed. At the elevation of the host, the two conspirators who had undertaken to stab Giuliano effected their purpose; but the attempt on Lorenzo failed. He escaped, and the conspirators were taken or killed. The plot miscarried in other places through a series of blunders. The populace supported the cause of the rich despots, and revenged the death of Giuliano, instead of rising at the cry of " Liberty." The result was the confirmation of tyranny on an increased scale. Lorenzo was addressed as a prince, and lived in a manner becoming that rank. His title of *Magnificent* has been handed down to modern times. It was better deserved for the splendid patronage which he gave to literature and art,* than for any political glory that he obtained. His rule was neither prosperous at home nor successful abroad. Sixtus IV. united with the King of Naples and the republic of Sienna against him in 1479, and signally defeated his army. His only ally was Milan, which was now under the government of the widow of Galeazzo (son of Francesco) Sforza, a profligate and ferocious tyrant, who had been assassinated in 1476 by three young noblemen of Milan. The Swiss of Uri, hired by the Pope, defeated the Milanese troops which the Duchess had raised to support Lorenzo; and shortly afterwards she was deprived of the throne in favor of her son, Gian Galeazzo, a youth, who nominally ruled under his uncle, Ludovico Sforza, the real sovereign. Lorenzo, in this perilous position, threw himself on the consideration of Ferdinand of Naples. By threatening that he must have recourse to France (the Anjou dynasty of which still asserted a right to Naples) if not supported by Ferdinand, and promising

* The illustrious scholar, Politiano, and Michelangelo Buonarotti, equally celebrated as architect, sculptor, and painter, glorified Florence in this reign.

to render assistance in obtaining the government of Sienna for the King's son, Lorenzo prevailed. A treaty
was signed on these terms in 1480, which would have
been carried out to the ruin of Tuscany, had not an unexpected landing of a Turkish force on the southern coast
of Calabria recalled the Neapolitan army, and put an end
to Lorenzo's alarm. He made use of this freedom from
external aggression to enslave Florence more effectually.
The Parliament, and the *balia*, or committee which it created, were superseded by a council of seventy, which was
to be perpetual, and to exercise an arbitrary power in
selecting the magistrates of the republic. The finances
of the state were then fraudulently employed in disburs-
ing the debts acquired by the extravagance of the Medici
family. Lorenzo was reconciled to Sixtus IV. in 1480;
but the avarice of that pontiff, who leagued with Venice,
in 1482, to part between them the possessions of the Duke
of Ferrara, occasioned another dispute, in which Florence
sided with Naples and Milan against the League. The
war terminated by the death of Sixtus, in 1484. Lorenzo
was engaged in wars or plots throughout his reign, — aspiring to put down the last spark of liberty which occasionally gleamed in the republics of Genoa, Sienna, and
Lucca, and allying himself with the tyrants of Milan and
Naples. He died in 1492, in the prime of life.

His eldest son, Pietro, succeeded to his rule, but
proved without strength to support it. A revolutionary
spirit was at work in Florence, mainly through the
influence of Savonarola, an earnest, though fanatical
reformer both in politics and religion. The timid policy
of Pietro with respect to the invasion of Charles VIII.

of France, in 1494, whose attempt on the kingdom of
Naples will be hereafter noticed, led to the restoration
of the republic. In fear of being attacked by Charles,
Pietro sought an interview with him, and weakly surrendered several important fortresses into his hand. The
enraged Florentines drove out the Medici, and, by adopting a firm tone in treating with Charles, obtained his
promise to restore the fortresses at the close of the war.
By the advice of Savonarola, the Council instituted by
Lorenzo dei Medici was enlarged, so as to assume the
character of a Parliament. The career of this zealot terminated by his martyrdom in 1498, through the instru-
mentality of the depraved Pope Alexander VI. (Borgia);
but the republic still maintained its self-government.
Pisa made herself independent at the moment of the
Medici's expulsion, after a slavery of eighty-seven years,
and obtained the assistance of Venice and Milan in resisting Florence. The claims of Louis XII. of France
on the duchy of Milan, in right of his grandmother,
Valentina Visconti, gave the Florentines an opportunity
of allying themselves with him, and procuring his aid to
reduce Pisa. The intrigues of Pope Alexander VI. to
procure the elevation of his natural son, Cæsar Borgia,
as Duke of Romagna, led him to seek the alliance of
France on the one hand, and to threaten Florence on the
other, — the restoration of the Medici to which would
have favored his schemes. Venice, meantime, steered
between the conflicting parties, allying itself now with
Milan to support Pisa, then attacking Florence with the
view of restoring the Medici, and afterwards making a
treaty with Louis XII. against Milan. Lastly, the Em-

peror Maximilian of Germany began to reassert the rights of the Empire in Italy, and to interfere in the Pisan war by sending troops to the besieged. Amid this web of politics the form of Machiavelli first appeared in 1498.

He was born at Florence in 1469, of a good family, and at an early age became secretary to the Ten, or Board of Foreign Affairs. He was soon noted for his singular discretion and penetration, and was employed by the republic on its most dangerous and delicate missions. After two or three minor engagements, he was despatched, in the year 1500, as a commissioner to the Florentine army, which was besieging Pisa. Louis XII. had just succeeded in deposing Ludovico Sforza, the Duke of Milan, and effecting the conquest of Lombardy. He then allied himself with Florence, whose assault on Pisa he assisted with a body of French and Swiss troops. But these auxiliaries proved mutinous, and insulted the republican officers; finally throwing up the siege, and even possessing themselves of portions of the Florentine territory. Cæsar Borgia, meantime, was pursuing his course of perfidy, selfishness, and cruelty in Romagna; menacing Florence, and intriguing for the help of Louis XII. Machiavelli was accordingly sent, in July, 1500, to France. Here he skilfully performed his difficult task of reconciling the republic and its offended ally. In spite of Borgia's machinations through his partisans at the French Court, Machiavelli succeeded in awakening against him the fears and jealousy of Louis. The result of this mission was shown soon after, when Borgia suddenly attacked Florence, but was ordered to desist by the French King. A treaty between Borgia and the republic was then agreed to.

In 1502 the two ablest politicians in Italy set themselves against each other in a match of diplomacy. Borgia had reconciled himself with Louis XII., and obtained promise of aid in conquering Romagna, of which he was nominally Duke, though resisted by the Bentivogli, lords of Bologna, and a few petty princes. He had endeavored also to excite an insurrection against the Florentines in Arezzo and other of their dependencies. Meantime, some of his captains, angry at his perpetual bad faith, and suspicious of his intentions against themselves, revolted, and invited the assistance of Florence. This was not given, for fear of France, with which the republic desired to be on good terms, but Machiavelli was sent to Imola, where Borgia was stationed, to profess friendship, yet at the same time watch his movements. It must have been deeply interesting to witness the remarkable display of intellectual acuteness which this mission called forth. To those who have seen the portraits of the two combatants, and remember the dark and cruel beauty of the lithe and diminutive Borgia, and the cold, subtle wisdom of the tall and attenuated Machiavelli. the scene will suggest an encounter between a tiger and a serpent. Each hated and feared the other, yet both were anxious to secure the alliance of France, and accordingly made the most cordial advances. The reports of his proceedings which the Florentine sent home to the republic are still extant, and are held to be models of political writing. He was a spectator of the savage and treacherous revenge which Borgia took at Sinigaglia, on several of the revolted captains whom he invited to a conference. Another, named Petrucci, who occupied Sienna, would have fallen by the same hand, but for the timely intimation of Machiavelli to his own government. Borgia, under professions of close alliance with Florence, endeavored to persuade Machiavelli that it would be politic to obtain for him the command of the republican army; but this, too, was thwarted by the ambassador's craft. He procured from Borgia a safeguard for Florentine merchants through Romagna, and returned home in January, 1503. Soon after he was sent to Rome, to be present at the election of Pope Julius II., who had succeeded Alexander VI., on the death of that pontiff by the poison — as it is thought — which he had prepared for another. Julius signalized his accession by attacking and overcoming Cæsar Borgia, of whose fall in 1504 Machiavelli was a spectator. By his advice the tyrant's troops were disarmed by the Florentines, and Italy was freed from its most fearful scourge.

The country, however, was still an arena of unceasing wars and intrigues, ravaged on all sides by foreign aggressions and worn by internal dissensions. The Spanish monarch, Ferdinand, after promising help to the Aragonese house of Naples, treacherously agreed with Louis XII. of France to divide the kingdom of the two Sicilies, and then possessed himself of the whole, by driving out the French. Louis XII. was master of Lombardy, and Genoa, with its surrounding dependencies; and to strengthen his position still further, leagued with the Emperor Maximilian of Germany and Pope Julius II. to conquer and divide the republic of Venice. This league.

was known as that of Cambrai, where it was signed in 1508. Florence, meantime, was employed in guarding itself against the plots of the Medici, now represented by the two brothers of Pietro, who had died in 1503. It retained its free government under the wise guidance of Pietro Soderini, who was chosen perpetual gonfaloner, or chief magistrate, in 1502, and worthily fulfilled his trust. He accomplished, in 1509, the task of reducing Pisa, which had long held out against the republican forces. Machiavelli, as foreign secretary, was engaged in various capacities during these years; and especially directed his attention to the subject of standing armies, which he urged the republic to employ instead of mercenary soldiers, whom he justly considered dangerous tools.

The League of Cambrai was carried into execution in 1509. Venice had excited the anger of the Pope by the aggressions which, on the fall of Cæsar Borgia, it deemed itself strong enough to make with impunity on the States of the Church. France and Germany were merely actuated by love of conquest and hatred of a republican form of government. The war was carried on with varying fortune by the allies, when Pope Julius II., who, though passionate and revengeful, was not tyrannical or unpatriotic, became convinced that it was the intention of his allies to enslave all Italy. He commenced his plans for preventing this result by levying mercenary troops in Switzerland, a country which was nationally opposed to Germany, and ill-disposed towards the haughty and insolent French. Florence, though taking no part in the war, was in alliance with France, and looked with fear on the success of the Pope's designs, lest it should lead to the restoration of the two Medici, — the elder of whom, Giovanni, was a Cardinal and Papal Legate. In July, 1510, Machiavelli, who had deeply studied the political condition of Italy at this time, was despatched to France. His object was to strengthen the alliance of the republic with that country, to urge Louis to prevent the Swiss from enlisting in the Pope's service, and with this view to maintain the League of Cambrai. In numerous interviews with the French King and his ministers, Machiavelli developed his ideas on the subject of Italian politics. Their soundness was fully borne out by the events. During his absence from Italy, a concerted movement had been set on foot by the Papal emissaries in Switzerland, and the French were attacked in several places at once. Julius deserted the League of Cambrai, and formed a new league (called the Holy) with Spain, England, Switzerland, and Venice, against France and Germany. Machiavelli succeeded in confirming the alliance of Florence with France, and returned home in September, 1510.

The young French general, Gaston de Foix, Duc de Nemours, a youth of twenty-two, by a series of rapid movements took Bologna, which the Pope's general, Raymond de Cardona, had besieged, — retook Brescia, which, after its conquest from the Venetians, had revolted against France, — and at the great battle of Ravenna, fought with the Papal army on the 11th of April, 1512, died in the arms of victory. The Emperor Maximilian, however, suddenly and treacherously deserted his ally, and recalled his German troops. Attacked at the same time by the armies of Spain and England, the French lost the advantages recently obtained. Lombardy was regained by Maximilian, son of Ludovico Sforza, and Genoa proclaimed a republic. The Holy League then turned on Florence. The citizens had offended the Pope by their French alliance, and as a punishment were sacrificed to the Medici. The latter readily gratified by ample promises the avarice of the Spanish and Swiss mercenaries, who undertook the task of enslavement. The cruel massacre of the citizens of Prato by the Spanish, who assaulted it in August, 1512, terrified some of the leading Florentines, who, after obtaining from Giuliano, the younger of the two Medici, a pledge that many of the republican privileges should be maintained, admitted him in the following September. Cardinal dei Medici, who entered soon after, violated this pledge in spirit, by restoring the parliamentary *balia*, and insuring the sovereignty of the state in the hands of his family. Among the members of the old government and popular party, who were in consequence banished, was Machiavelli.

He was considered to be implicated in a conspiracy against the Medici in the following year, and was put to the torture; but, confessing nothing, was soon after released by order of the Cardinal, now Pope Leo X., so famous for his patronage of art and letters.* Machiavelli then retired into private life for some years, and employed his leisure in writing, among other works, his treatise

---

* It must suffice to name only as their chief representatives the immortal Raffaelo Sanzio, the prince of painters, and the fascinating poet, Ariosto.

called *The* **Prince,** in which he expounded the lessons which his long political experience had taught him. There is more worldly wisdom than morality in the principles which he here lays down ; but great allowance must be made, in our judgment of his moral character, for the time in which he lived, and the education which he had received. Only the highest and noblest natures are able to uphold their standard of right in days when perfidy and injustice are the ruling laws of society. Machiavelli can neither be ranked in this exceptional class nor in its opposite. Though led astray by an admiration for genius which blinds his eyes, he is not insensible to the beauty of virtue. He seems to possess an inherent regard for truth, — disappointed by repeated failures to find it. Living among men whom he suspects, and who suspect him, he points out the most expedient methods of managing them ; among which he includes the employment of their own weapons against them. This is not a defensible system, but at the same time should not be branded as that of an unscrupulous and unprincipled teacher, — epithets too often applied to the great Florentine.

He wrote this work for the perusal of one of the Medici family, with which he became reconciled, and whose power he desired to see established in preference to that of a foreign ruler, with which Lombardy and Naples were cursed. Machiavelli's historical works and comedies evince original thought and extensive observation. He again mixed in political affairs after 1521, but not prominently, and died in 1527.

The Chevalier Bayard.

THE FRENCH INVASION OF ITALY.

In the mountainous province of Dauphiné, on the southeastern frontier of France, there stood, in the fifteenth century, the fine old Gothic Château de Bayard, — a fortress and a residence in one, as was usual at that period. Here, for many generations, the Seigneurs de Bayard had fixed the seat of their feudal lordship, — gallant warriors all of them, living and dying for country and king. In a chamber of this mansion, one day in the year 1488, its lord, the Seigneur de Bayard, lay dying. It was rarely that a chief of this family died on any bed save the battle-field; and one may fancy that the old soldier, who had received many a wound, and often met Death face to face in the recent wars, lamented as he lay that his fate had not been ordered like that of his ancestors who fell at Cressy and Poictiers. His mind was no doubt engaged in these reflections when, shortly before his death, he sent for his four sons, and asked them what kind of life they wished to follow. The eldest answered that he would remain at home, and fulfil his duty to his parents; the two youngest said they desired to rise to honors in the Church; the second son, Pierre, a boy of thirteen, alone replied, with the spirit of his ancestors,

" My choice is a soldier's life ! " Cheered by these words, the old warrior died in peace, and was gathered to his fathers. His son Pierre prepared to fill his place. To support the ancient reputation of the family for gallantry and martial skill, it was needful that the boy should be regularly educated in the profession of arms. Accordingly, his mother obtained him a position as page in the household of the Duke of Savoy, where he would be certain to mix in the society of valiant and experienced soldiers, and might chance to see actual service in the field. The boy's head was filled with romantic ideas of his future career, and when the day of his departure from home arrived, he was eager to go. One of his biographers thus describes the way in which his mother bid him adieu : " The poor lady was in a tower of the castle, bitterly weeping ; but when she knew that her young son was on his horse, impatient to be gone, she went down to take leave of him, and, as earnestly as a mother could advise a son, gave him three commands. The first was to love God above all, recommending himself to God night and morning, and serving him in every way, as far as possible without offence. The second was to be courteous to all men, casting away pride ; not slandering, lying, or talebearing, but being temperate and loyal. The third was to be charitable, and to share whatever gifts God should bestow upon him with the poor." A simple, yet a wise sermon this, which Pierre never forgot, but set himself to follow throughout his life, — a life exalted by the highest principles of honor and purity, unstained by a trace of meanness or selfishness. At the court of the Duke of Savoy, Bayard remained five years, which were steadily devoted to the practice of knightly duties and accomplishments. He displayed the greatest fitness for the profession he had chosen, and attained extraordinary skill at tilting especially. At the age of eighteen he carried off the prize in a tournament, at which some of the most famous French knights were his rivals. At the same age he entered the service of Charles VIII., King of France.

This monarch was one after Bayard's heart, — daring, generous, and gentle. Rashly ardent and impulsive, he was guilty of a thousand follies, but few crimes. He had fed his mind from childhood with chivalric romances, to the exclusion of solid reading, and burned to equal the exploits of Charlemagne. Persuading himself that he was destined to be the conqueror of Italy, which France had long lusted to possess, and founding his pretensions upon a worthless will of the King of Provence, who, as representative of the Anjou dynasty, had bequeathed the crown of Naples and Sicily to Louis XI., Charles asserted a claim to the former kingdom, then held by Ferdinand, son of Alfonso of Aragon. A general attempt on Italy was, at the same time, invited by Ludovico Sforza, Duke of Milan, whose plans to enslave it required assistance. Against the advice of his most experienced counsellors Charles assembled an army, scantily provided with money or provisions, but animated with a fiery enthusiasm. In addition to his troops, a band of young noblemen volunteered to accompany him, and Bayard was foremost in the ranks. There seemed but little probability of the attempt succeeding, but the heroic spirit of such men as Bayard prevailed over every obstacle. Charles crossed the Alps in August, 1494, marched through Italy, not only without opposition, but in triumph; and in January, 1495, advanced towards Naples. Its king, Ferdinand, had recently died, and Alfonso, his successor, was unequal to the occasion. He fled to Sicily, leaving his son Ferdinand to lead the army. At the approach of the French, however, the Neapolitans fled, and Charles subdued the kingdom with ease. After wasting much time in diversions at Naples, he retraced his steps to attack the armies of the Pope, Spain, Germany, Venice, and Milan also, which in the interval had been leagued against him. The opposition so suddenly exhibited by the last-named state, at whose invitation Charles had entered Italy, was occasioned by Ludovico's suspicions of the ultimate designs of France on his dukedom; to which, indeed, it had already asserted a right, in virtue of the marriage of Valentina Visconti with the Duc d'Orléans.

Charles left a considerable body of troops in Naples; and on reaching Fornuovo, a town at the foot of the Apennines, near Parma, where the allied army, amounting to 40,000 men, was stationed, found that his own did not exceed 9,000. The materials of which it was composed, however, now became apparent. In spite of these fearful odds Charles determined to attack the enemy. The battle-field was a narrow valley at the passage of the river Taro. On the 6th of July, 1495, the two armies encountered. Settling themselves in a body, the French rushed forward and charged the dense mass of the allied Italian army. Bayard was in the thickest of the fight, — a boy of twenty only, but an arch-hero among heroes,

— performing feats of prodigious valor. Two horses were killed under him; but he fought on still. The result of this and similar acts of courage was, that the French, outnumbered as they were, utterly routed the Italian forces, broke through the ranks, and pursued their march, losing only eighty men, but leaving 3,000 of the enemy slain on the field. This success, however, did not suffice to establish the French in their conquest of Naples, from which they were soon after driven out by the Spanish troops which King Ferdinand called to his assistance.

However groundless may have been the claim of France to the throne of Naples, in support of which this foolhardy expedition was undertaken, the title was no doubt considered valid by the French nation. If we duly reflect on the character of the feudal system, which, by enforcing the rigid obedience of every tenant to his superior lord, rendered loyalty a sacred duty, and private conscience less important than military discipline, we shall judge leniently of such good and true men as Bayard, when we find them engaged in unrighteous wars. He seems to have felt no scruples in joining the army which, on the death of Charles VIII., was raised by his successor, Louis XII., to renew the attempt on Naples. Louis made a secret treaty with Ferdinand of Spain, whereby the two monarchs agreed to assist each other in first conquering, and then dividing, that kingdom. The armies of France and Spain united to carry out the former part of this treaty, and succeeded in expelling the weak prince who filled the Neapolitan throne; but the latter part of the treaty was not so easily fulfilled, and the conquerors soon quarrelled among themselves.

11   P

In 1502 Louis declared war against Spain, and commenced the task of expelling his late allies. The French army was commanded by the Duc de Nemours; and that of Spain by "the Great Captain," Gonsalvo de Cordova. Bayard distinguished himself at the siege of Canosa, a fortified town in Apulia, garrisoned by the Spaniards, against which he headed two desperate assaults. The siege was finally successful, and the garrison capitulated.

Trani, on the Adriatic, was the next scene of his exploits; and here he was the hero of a personal adventure. The knights on both sides were in the habit of showing their prowess, by engaging in tournaments and single combats during the intervals of regular fighting. A Spanish knight, Alonso de Sotomayor, on one of these occasions, charged Bayard with discourtesy to him when a prisoner, — an accusation which Bayard denied, and defied the Spaniard to prove in duel. Sotomayor, knowing his antagonist's fame as a horseman, chose to fight on foot.

On the appointed day, February 2, 1503, the lists were prepared, and the two knights entered, clothed in mail, but having the visors of their helmets up, and armed with swords and daggers. Each knelt to pray, and rose up to fight; "the Good Knight, Bayard," says one of his biographers, "moving as light of step as if he were going to lead a fair lady in the dance." He was not powerfully made, and was at the time weakened by a recent fever; but possessed great bodily agility and masterly skill. Sotomayor was a man of unusual size and strength, upon which he relied for success. And now the eyes of the two armies are upon them, as they advance to the struggle. The Spaniard strikes heavily and fiercely, as if to crush his foe to the earth. The Frenchman parries the blows, and darts rapidly from side to side, striking seldom, but surely. At last, Sotomayor overbalances himself by a false thrust, and Bayard dashes in, — his sword cleaving the gorget, and entering the throat of his foe. With one fierce and agonized effort Sotomayor seizes Bayard in his arms, and the combatants fall together. With a sudden motion of his left hand, Bayard thrusts his poniard through the open visor of the Spaniard, and pierces the brain. The day is won, but at a heavy cost; and when the songs of the minstrels are heard proclaiming the conqueror's glory, Bayard sternly silences the unseemly joy, kneels to give thanks to Heaven, and then sadly leaves the lists, uttering a heart-felt lament that, in order to vindicate his personal honor, it had been necessary to sacrifice a brave man's life.

In the latter part of this year (1503) Bayard performed achievements, as far more arduous as they were nobler than any of his previous acts. After the loss of two battles, and the death of their commander, the French found themselves opposed to the Spaniards on the banks of the river Garigliano, on the northern frontier of the Neapolitan dominions. A bridge over this stream was the great centre of action, and scenes of fearful carnage occurred in the repeated attempts of each side to seize this strong position. On one occasion the French succeeded in crossing the river, but were driven back by the Spaniards. Bayard was in the vanguard when the repulse commenced; and while retreating, still kept his face to the foe. The Spaniards pressed on ardently, but did not reach the bridge soon enough to cut off the retreat. The main body of the French recrossed the river; but Bayard, like another Horatius Cocles, remained upon the bridge alone. Two hundred Spaniards attacked him; but, single-handed, he kept his ground for upwards of an hour, and drove back each assailant, until he had allowed time for all his countrymen to make good their passage, and form on the opposite bank. Then he, too, slowly retired to join them.

Another desperate act of valor is recorded of Bayard in the same campaign. The final and disastrous defeat of the French on the Garigliano was temporarily retrieved by a gallant charge of their knights at Mola di Gaeta. The Spaniards were in full pursuit; but at the bridge before this place the French turned, and stood at bay. After a fierce conflict, in which Bayard had three horses killed under him, accompanied by a few daring comrades he made a bold dash into the enemy's ranks, and was carried so far by his impulsive charge that, but for the succor of his friend, Sandricourt, he would have fallen or been captured. No efforts of personal courage, however, could suffice to restore the broken fortunes of the French army. Gonsalvo and the Spaniards obtained complete victory, and Naples was lost to France.

The life of Bayard is almost an epitome of the history of the wars in which France was engaged during his time. Wherever the oriflamme waved, he and his men-at-arms might be seen fighting beneath it. In 1507 Genoa revolted, and Bayard conducted a daring assault

on an outpost at the siege of that city. His next remarkable appearance was at the memorable defeat of the
French by our Henry VIII., which took place at Guin-
gette, near Terouenne, in Picardy, on the 16th August,
1513, and was known as "the Battle of the Spurs."
Here the good Knight and a few kindred spirits alone
preserved their honor amid the disgrace which fell upon
the whole army of France. Owing to some panic, or
mistake of orders, the French cavalry fled before the
English; and the battle — as its popular name imports
— was decided rather by swiftness of horse's foot than
strength of man's arm. Had it not been for Bayard, the
whole army would have shared in this shameful flight.
But he. true to his practice of facing his enemy, slowly
retired, sword in hand, fighting as he went. At length
he halted with but fourteen men-at-arms at a small
bridge, where only two could pass abreast: "We will
halt here," he cried; "the enemy will be an hour in
gaining this post. Hie to the camp, and tell them to
reassemble during the interval." Here stood Bayard,
firm as a rock, hewing down all who ventured to assail
him, until the retreating French had time to reassemble;
and then, as his work had been accomplished, he yielded
to the pressure of numbers, and voluntarily surrendered
himself prisoner to a knight, whom he had himself for
that purpose first captured. Led into the presence of
Henry VIII., that monarch, then young and chivalrous,
received his gallant opponent with respect. When Henry's ally, the Emperor Maximilian of Germany, gave
utterance to a taunt that he thought Bayard never fled;
"Sire," was the manly answer, "if I had fled, I should
not have been here."

Owing to the peculiar circumstances of his capture, Bayard was set free without ransom, and soon rejoined his comrades in arms. The treaty of Orleans, however, between Louis XII. and his enemies, and the speedy death of that King, for a brief period silenced the sounds of war. His successor, Francis I., was a prince whose education, like that of Charles VIII., had been based upon the reading of the romances of chivalry; and he, too, soon aspired to carry out fiction into fact. With greater prudence, nevertheless, than Charles had shown in undertaking his Italian expedition, Francis raised a brilliant and powerful army, and set out for Milan. Bayard, who had been recently raised to the post of Lieutenant-General of his native province of Dauphiné, hastened to join in the campaign, and occupied a distinguished place near the person of the King. Crossing the Alps by a new and difficult road, so as to avoid attack from the Swiss troops of the young Duke of Milan, — Maximilian, son of Ludovico Sforza, — the French descended into the Stura valley on the Italian side. Prospero Colonna, the Milanese general, was then quartered at the fortress of Carmagnola, and showed his contempt of the French by neglecting to defend his residence. Bayard and some other captains, hearing of this imprudence, proposed the audacious plan of capturing the general in person. After careful preparations they stealthily reached Carmagnola, but not finding Colonna there, tracked him to Villafranca. The town was taken after a short struggle, and the General's house at once surrounded. Colonna was sitting at dinner when, to his surprise and bitter mortification, Bayard entered with a summons to surrender. There was no help for it, and Colonna gave up his sword to his courteous captor, only exclaiming in a natural emotion of self-reproach : " Would God I had met you in a fair field, albeit I had perished there !" Milan, however, was not to be captured so easily as its general, and an immense army of Swiss disputed the passage of the French at Marignano, in the neighborhood of the city. On the 13th September, 1515, the armies met, and the encounter lasted for two days. It was a fearful contest. The Swiss were animated alike with personal hatred of a body of German troops, which were conspicuous in the French army, and with a greedy desire for the spoil which had been promised by the Italian leaders. The French were elated by recent success, inflamed with hope of conquest, and enraged at the failure of an attempt to buy over their mercenary opponents. The mountaineers advanced in a close band, armed with enormous pikes and two-handed swords. The French cavalry for a long time failed in making any impression on this dense mass, until, after repeated charges, an onset of the young King and his men-at-arms at last destroyed its compactness. Bayard was again the hero of the day.· His horse was killed under him, and he mounted another. In the charge he let his bridle drop, and the animal thus unrestrained, borne away by its own excitement, carried him into the Swiss ranks, where it stumbled and fell. Bayard leaped from the saddle, threw away his helmet, and crept back by a ditch into the French lines. He was at once known by his friends, obtained a third horse and armor, and was again in his place. On the second day the Swiss gradually gave way, and, though at tremendous sacrifice, the French were victorious. "A war of giants," was the characteristic expression which one of the French generals, who had witnessed a score of battles, applied to this terrific conflict. Bayard, satisfied with having done his duty, thought nothing of personal reward, and it was to his extreme surprise that, after the battle was over, he received an honor from Francis I., the most ennobling to both giver and taker that could have been possibly devised. This was no less than an entreaty that Bayard would dub him a knight. After a slight remonstrance the good Knight yielded, and the King knelt to his subject, Bayard praying, as he struck his shoulder with the sword, that the new knight might never turn his back upon an enemy. Then, with the generous courtesy of his nature, the warrior dispossessed himself of all appearance of vainglory by turning to his sword, and saying: "Thou art fortunate, my trusty sword, to-day, in being chosen to confer knighthood on so great a king; thou shalt henceforth be kept as a sacred treasure, and never be unsheathed save against the infidels!"

Milan was taken, and the dukedom of Maximilian Sforza compensated for by money; but possession was not long kept. A quarrel broke out in 1522 with Charles V., the young Emperor of Germany, who had been elected to that dignity in spite of the intrigues of Francis, who coveted it for himself. This young monarch, who was likewise King of Spain, Naples, and Sicily, resumed that authority over Italy which had been exercised by the earlier German Emperors. He agreed with Pope Leo X. to set up one of the Sforza family as Duke of Milan, and drive out the French.

War was declared between France and Germany; and
Bayard was intrusted with the defence of Mezières, a
frontier fortress on the Meuse, where an invading force
had made its appearance. "No place is weak which is
defended by brave men," said the good Knight, when
told that the place was too weak to resist. He summoned his tried friends, and at the sound of his name a
legion flocked to his side. Ordering all the inhabitants
who could not work to withdraw into the town, Bayard
bound the authorities by an oath not to surrender. "We
will eat our horses and boots, if provisions fail," was his
calm assurance to his garrison. The place was invested
on two sides by the Emperor's army, amounting to 35,000
men; while Bayard's band numbered but 1,000. Relying
on the constancy of his men for success, he not only suffered but assisted the escape of deserters. "We shall be
stronger without them," was all he cared to say. To the
summons of the enemy to surrender he returned a defiant
retort, and steadily gave back fire for fire. At last, however, finding his position precarious, he resorted to a
stratagem for getting rid of the blockade; and accordingly, by means of a letter passed into the Imperial camp,
put one of the generals on a false scent, and stimulated
the jealousy of a rival commander. Confusion so much
prevailed in the besieging army, that the siege was raised,
and Bayard received as a reward from the delighted
Francis the badge of the Order of Philip Augustus, and
the princely privilege of commanding a hundred men-at-
arms.

But the good Knight was not destined to win many
more such trophies. He had yet to earn one, — the best

11 *

of all, in his own idea, — a glorious death. The scene of warfare was transferred to Italy, where the Constable Duc de Bourbon, once the most illustrious noble of France, but expelled for alleged treason from his country, was traitorously commanding the Imperial army. The French were led by the Admiral Bonnivet, an unskilful general, and a personal enemy of Bayard, who also held a high post. The Emperor's attempt on Milan had been successful, and the French were now seeking to recover their loss. After failing in an attack on the city, Bonnivet withdrew towards the Alps, in the neighborhood of the river Ticino. During the retreat he endeavored to cut off the supplies which were being continually sent in from the provinces to Milan, and accordingly despatched Bayard to the village of Rebec, to intercept any food or money which might be sent from thence. Rebec was wholly unprovided with shelter, and close to the camp of the enemy; nevertheless Bayard would not refuse the enterprise. He asked for a large body of troops, but this Bonnivet denied him, and with but 200 horse and 2,000 foot Bayard set out. Arrived at Rebec, and seeing his danger, he sent for reinforcements, which never arrived. For several days he kept to his post, never doffing his heavy armor, and scarcely sleeping, until at last reduced from illness. During one of his intervals of rest the enemy came upon him, — hundreds of soldiers crying out eagerly for the chance of capturing such a noble prize. Springing from his bed of sickness, Bayard seized a weapon, and followed by a few men, repulsed the attack for a time; but at last, finding defence useless, ordered a retreat. It was successfully accomplished, and he reached the French head-quarters, where he reproached Bonnivet for his neglect in sending reinforcements, a neglect which is considered to have been designed treachery. A series of mistakes on the part of Bonnivet obliged him to withdraw from Biagrasso, his last fortress, and move homewards. Leaving Novara, the French reached Romagnano, a hamlet on the river Sesia. The enemy pursued, and met them there. The good Knight and his men-at-arms performed a subordinate part in the battle which ensued, until Bonnivet's arm was broken, when the command devolved upon Bayard. He had just assumed it, and made his first charge, when a stone shot from a hacquebouse struck upon his spine, and broke it. He fell from his saddle, with the words, "Jesus! my God! I am killed!" Then raising his cross-shaped sword-hilt, he kissed it reverently and prayed. As he was borne off by his soldiers, he begged them to stop, and place him against a tree, that he might face the foe in death. The battle ceased, for the French were powerless from grief, and the enemy was too generous to follow up the success. All men knew and honored the good Knight. The Marquis of Pescara, one of the Imperialist commanders, came up to Bayard, whose hand he kissed, and uttered with earnestness his deep sorrow at the sight. "May God be my help!" he cried: "I would rather have given half of what I am worth than that this should have been." And after Pescara came up Bourbon, the traitor, to express his pity also; but the loyal Knight would not accept it. "I thank you," said he; "but I need it not. I die a true man to my king and country. Keep your pity for yourself, who are armed against your

fealty, your king, and your nation." Though tended with
the kindest courtesy by Pescara, who had a tent pitched
on the field for him, Bayard sank rapidly, and, after a
space of agony, once more uttered his old battle-shout,
" God and my country !" and then closed his lips forever.
The body was embalmed, and carried back to Dauphiné
with the most solemn rites, — the Duke of Savoy ordering royal honors to be paid to it as the procession passed
through his territories, and peers and peasants coming
out to meet it. The warrior's remains were buried at
Grenoble, where a tomb has since been erected over
them.

Bayard may stand as the last great example of a
mediæval hero, — the best representative of the feudal
chivalry, which died out with him. The next age witnessed the growth of popular constitutions, and a reformed Church, which the increasing intelligence of the
world demanded. He exemplifies, however, the value
and beauty which the older forms of government and
religion possessed, during periods when obedience to a
wise and able king, and a holy and well-ordered Church,
was the only safeguard against anarchy, barbarism, and
licentiousness. Such is his interest for us moderns, when
we view him as the type of an epoch. Regarded as a
man simply, what need is there to praise him ? In the
virtues of true manliness — sincerity, courage, firmness —
can we find his equal ? As, to those who lived in his
own day, the star of his glory was thrown out into
brighter lustre by the dark clouds of disaster amid
which it always shone ; so to us who read of him, his
golden fame gleams clearer amidst the gloomy records of

perfidy and cruelty with which the history of his age is overshadowed. Centuries have crumbled into dust his body of clay, and will crumble his marble tomb; but while the world lasts, the name of Bayard, embalmed with the rich perfume of his brave deeds, and enshrined in the reverent love of his countrymen, will immortalize him as " *The good knight without fear and without reproach.*"

Martin Luther.

THE REFORMATION.

THE spiritual power of the Church of Rome waned when its moral corruption reached its height. A succession of profligate, faithless, and cruel Popes during the fifteenth century, destroyed popular belief in their infallibility ; and the prevalence of vice among the priesthood and monastic orders rendered their teachings practically worthless. The name of a monk or a nun was a byword, and of the former it was said, that he " did what the Devil was ashamed to think." Christianity was no longer a system of faith or a check on the passions, but an engine of spiritual tyranny, supporting a large ecclesiastical government at the expense of the laity, which was cheated with hollow services, performed by ignorant clerks, with tawdry ceremonies and sham miracles. The sale of indulgences for crime, instituted by the later Popes, crowned the list of abominations. These documents actually encouraged immorality, by fixing its price at so much a sin, and granting absolution on payment of the sum. These manifold and overwhelming abuses did not, as we have seen, pass without remonstrance at various periods. Abelard, and Arnold of Brescia, had eloquently declaimed against them in universities and popular assemblies. The peasants of Provence and the Pays du Vaud had attempted a practical reform. Huss and Jerome of Prague, in Bohemia, and Wicliffe in England, had manfully protested with the same object. But all these symptoms of a revolutionary spirit had been ruthlessly crushed. The Inquisition, established by Pope Innocent III. to chastise heresy, fulfilled its design by means of the rack, the gibbet, and the stake. Thousands of earnest and devout men and women, who dared to worship God according to the dictates of their reason and conscience, and to rebel against the yoke of his assumed vicegerent, paid the price of liberty with life. But this violent oppression proved fatal to itself. A secret abhorrence of the system which upheld its power by such practices, doubts of its claim to divine authority, and contempt of its professors, spread gradually but surely in the mind of Germany, and other parts of Europe. The circulation of ancient literature, and the intellectual enlightenment to which it gave rise, had its due effect on the higher classes; and the invention of printing in the early part of the fifteenth century contributed to diffuse liberal ideas amongst all grades of society. The translation of the Bible, moreover, enabled the laity to see how vast was the difference between the teachings of Christ and those of the Church. In short, a reaction against the dominant form of religion had commenced throughout Europe before the opening of the sixteenth century. There was yet needed a man of clear head, true heart, and active sympathies, to unite the scattered elements of doubt and indignation into a settled form of protest; one eloquent breath to kindle the sparks

of truth into a flame, that should refine the golden faith
of Christ from the impure alloy of tyranny, falsehood,
and superstition. Such a man was Martin Luther.

He was born in 1483, at Eisleben, in Saxony, his
father being a miner in humble circumstances, but sufficiently prosperous to allow of Martin's entering the
University of Erfurt, where he studied law and theology.
In 1505, when walking with a friend, a flash of lightning
struck the latter dead. A hasty impulse of thankfulness
for his escape induced Luther to take monastic vows, and
he accordingly assumed the habit of the Augustines, a
branch of the Franciscans, and of good repute for virtue
and learning, as compared with other orders. He visited
Rome in 1509 on a mission from this body, and there
imbibed his first disgust at the stagnant corruption which
rotted away the very life of the Church at that period.
Julius II. was then Pope, — a conqueror who governed
by fear, not love. The priests were infidels and repro-
bates, rather than ministers of religion and morality; and
there, at the fountain-head of faith, could be tasted nothing but polluted waters. The shrewd and simple-hearted
monk observed, lamented, and pondered. He returned
to Germany, and was soon after appointed Doctor and
Theological Professor of the new University of Wittenberg, founded by the Elector of Saxony, Frederick "the
Wise," an able, just, and powerful prince. This University was known as the seat of the Humanists, or professors
of liberal learning, as opposed to the dry and lifeless
teaching of the Schoolmen, who had for centuries absorbed the work of education. Luther, without actively
joining the new party, was influenced by its views, and

his work on *German Theology*, published in 1516, was directed against the Scholastic tenets. His practical bent was called into play in 1517. Leo X., now Pope, resorted, as a means of filling his treasury, to an increased sale of indulgences, which he intrusted to the Dominicans, who traversed Europe for this purpose. One of their leading monks, named Tetzel, carried this detestable traffic to an unwonted pitch, inventing horrible and unheard-of crimes, and publicly declaring in the churches and assemblies to which he came, that all these monstrosities would be at once expiated on payment of a due sum to the Pope. Luther was filled with indignation at this degrading exhibition, and endeavored, though in vain, to stop it by appealing to the bishop of the diocese, and then to the Archbishop of Mentz. Failing to obtain a reply, he, on the 31st of October, 1517, boldly posted up on the church at Wittenberg Castle ninety-five *theses*, or propositions, against the indulgences, and which he offered to defend. In these articles he denied the right of the Pope to deal with God's decrees, and asserted that sins could be remitted by repentance only, not for money. He was applauded by the wisest and best scholars of his day, but vehemently attacked by Tetzel, and Eck, a famous controversialist. Happily, the state of the political world favored his daring. The Emperor Maximilian was not on good terms with the Pope, and refused to surrender Luther when called upon. On the Emperor's death in 1519, the Elector of Saxony, Luther's stanch patron, was made regent of the Empire, and during his term of office faithfully supported the new views. Luther was burned in effigy at Rome, and every en-

deavor was made to procure his execution; but, cheered
by the voice of Germany, he held on his way to a yet
higher point of boldness. He published a work on the
Babylonian Captivity of the Church, which denounced in
the clearest terms the idolatry of the mass and Papal supremacy; and busied himself in the practical reformation
of the German Church, wherever his influence extended.
The Latin service was given up, and prayers and psalm-
ody conducted in the native language of the people. The
Pope was now roused by the terrified doctors of Rome to
publish a formal condemnation of Luther's teachings.
The bull was brought to Germany by Cardinal Alcan-
der; but his life was in danger from the anger of the
people, who vehemently supported the Reformation. The
students of Erfurt tore the copies of the bull from the
booksellers' shops, and threw them into the river.
Luther himself at once published a pamphlet against
"the execrable bull of Antichrist," and finally crowned
his resistance by a signal act of defiance.

On the 10th of December, 1520, a vast concourse met
at the eastern gate of the city of Wittenberg. Grave
Professors of the University in their robes of office;
young students, sober, enthusiastic, and careless; burghers of the city, and a motley crowd of both sexes, and
all ranks and ages, flocked to a cross which was erected
just without the walls, and beside which a huge pile of
wood had been laid and lighted. The homely, burly
figure of a man habited in the plain garb of an Augustine
monk, stood alone by the pyre. His features were somewhat coarse, but worn by care and study; and an expression of intense earnestness gave them a beauty not their

own. In a clear and penetrating voice he addressed the crowd, stating the occasion of the meeting to be the necessity of declaring in the name of God the freedom of religious conviction which the Papacy had endeavored to inthrall. He then took from the hands of an attendant a parchment document. The speaker held it up, and announced it as the last bull of Pope Leo X. against himself, Martin Luther. Amid the shouts of the multitude he threw it into the burning pile, where it was consumed to ashes. He then produced a massive volume, which he announced as the Decretals, or collection of Papal decrees, embodying the principles of the canon law of the Church of Rome. " Thou hast tormented the Lord's holy one," cried Luther, as he cast the book into the flames ; " may the everlasting fire torment and consume thee ! " Other volumes of theology and law shared the same fate. When the great assembly dispersed, all felt that the rupture between the Church and the Reformers was decisive. In this daring conduct Luther was countenanced by the Elector of Saxony, who blamed the Pope and Cardinal Aleander for their presumption in interfering with the progress of reforms in the German Church.

In 1521 Charles, grandson of the late Emperor Maximilian, heir to the possessions of the Hapsburgs, and, on the death of Ferdinand of Spain, the acknowledged king of that country and the Two Sicilies, was elected Emperor of Germany. As a devout Catholic, he was opposed to the Reformation ; but desiring to keep on good terms with the powerful Elector, moved cautiously in attempting to suppress it. Luther, however, was cited to appear at a great Diet held at Worms, in April, 1521.

The monk did not hesitate to comply with the demand, though urged by his friends to refuse. "I will go," said he, "though there should be as many devils as tiles on the house-roofs." He was triumphantly greeted by the people as he passed from Wittenberg to Worms, and on his arrival was accompanied to his lodgings by 2,000 persons. At the council he maintained a calm and majestic bearing. Summoned to retract his opinions, and the charges he had brought against the Church, he steadily refused, to the irritation of the Emperor, and the great joy of many of the leading princes and nobles. Four hundred of the latter, it was said, were pledged to defend him. The safe-conduct which he had received from the Emperor before starting on the journey was respected; and though Luther was put under the ban of the Empire, he was not touched, and departed on his way home. On the road a body of horse seized him, and conveyed him in secret to the Castle of the Wartburg. This was a stratagem of the Elector of Saxony to shield him from any possible violence of his enemies; and Luther, who believed himself a prisoner, found to his delight that he was under the protection of his patron. From this re-treat the Reformer, and his friend Melancthon and others, conducted the progress of the Reformation. Its principles were explained to the people in simple language, and the Bible was translated into German. The imprudence of a party of Reformers, who, by their rejection of infant baptism, acquired the name of Anabaptists, called Luther to Wittenberg. Under their leaders, Thomas Munzer and Carlstadt, they had destroyed various images and orna-ments in the churches, — an act wholly opposed to the

BOLTON. Sc.

views of Luther, who loved and respected art. He ventured forth from the castle, and preached for eight days in the city, finally succeeding in quelling the tumult. Meantime the Reformation was extensively spreading in Switzerland, under Zwingli and other teachers. In various parts of Germany, especially in the cities of Nuremberg, Breslau, and Dantzic, the priests were expelled, and Lutheran teachers — who were married men — substituted.

A dangerous reaction arose, in 1522, against the new theology, in consequence of the support which it seemed to give to political disturbance. The peasantry of Suabia and Thuringia, oppressed by the nobles, and hearing the welcome sounds of religious liberty on all sides, applied the same principles to politics, and rose in revolt. The acts of violence committed in this rebellion were laid at the door of Luther, and he felt called upon to disavow the whole movement. He endeavored to act as peacemaker between the conflicting parties; but Munzer and Carlstadt, who led the peasants, would hear of no terms, abused him as a traitor to the cause, and roused their followers to the most atrocious deeds of cruelty. Seventy nobles who were taken prisoners were compelled to run between two ranks of spears, which pierced them as they passed. Luther no longer hesitated to throw all his influence in the opposite scale, and aided the nobles by writing and preaching. After a terrible war, in which thousands perished, the insurrection was put down in 1525.

Luther was now involved in a controversial strife with some of the leading Swiss and Rhenish reformers; and, still more seriously, with the eminent Erasmus of Rotterdam, the king of literature in his time, who, though adopting the principles of the Reformation in part, lacked the earnestness of the great German, and exhausted his fine genius in subtle discussions on doctrine. The controversy was conducted with heat and bitterness, and much injured the general cause of truth, by dividing the Protestant army into sects and parties.

In 1525 Luther completed his defiance of ecclesiastical rules, by cancelling his monastic vows, and marrying a fugitive nun, named Catherine von Bora, a woman of great beauty, who bore him several children. He was extremely poor, in spite of his fame as a writer; and though willing to earn his bread, even by handicraft, was fain to accept the bounty of his friend, the Elector John, who had succeeded his father, Frederick, in the government of Saxony. The Lutheran Church was now firmly established in Saxony, Prussia, and other parts of Germany; and the new King of Sweden, Gustavus Vasa, adopted it as that of the State. In England, Henry VIII., after acquiring the name of Defender of the Faith, by attacking Luther, was now a zealous Reformer. George, Duke of Saxon Thuringia, and the Elector of Brandenburg, were the chief opponents of the cause in Germany.

With the doctrines of the Reformation, as opposed to those of the Catholic Church, we are not here concerned, further than to state that they professed to be based exclusively upon the Scriptures, — the right to interpret which was declared to be vested in *private judgment*, and not the voice of the Church, as uttered by the Fathers, or in General Councils. Many of the corruptions which had gathered over the simple teaching of Christ and His Apostles — such as the doctrines of transubstantiation, meritorious righteousness, the worship of the Virgin and Saints, the infallibility of the Pope, the obligation of confessing sins to a priest, the exclusion of the laity from the cup at the communion, praying for the dead, purgatory and indulgences, the celibacy of the clergy, and the inviolable character of monastic vows — were more or less repudiated and condemned by Luther and the leading Reformers. Differences of opinion between them, touching one or more of these subjects, led to the formation of the various parties into which Protestants are now divided.

In Saxony, where Luther himself was authorized to settle the constitution of the Church, he fully developed his own views. Monasteries were abolished, and their wealth was applied by the State to education and other purposes. The monks and nuns were enjoined to marry, and adopt a profession. The election of bishops was placed in the hands of the State, and pastors were appointed over each commune. The churches were cleared of superstitious ornaments, the service performed in the native tongue, and the schools enlarged.

It was not long before Protestantism became an important political engine. Germany was threatened by a terrible invasion of the Turks, under their Sultan, Suleiman II., who, after capturing Rhodes, and disposing of the Hungarian throne, marched into Austria in 1529, and besieged Vienna. After vainly attempting to carry it by storm, the Turks were repulsed, but ravaged the country, and carried off thousands into captivity.

Charles V., who saw the necessity of combining all Germany against the foe, was compelled to be moderate in dealing with the Reformation. A Diet, however, was held at Augsburg, in June, 1530, at which the progress of Protestantism was a principal subject of consideration. Luther, being under the ban of the Empire, could not attend ; but Melancthon was present, and drew up a confession of faith, which, under the name of the Augsburg Confession, has ever since been taken as the Protestant charter. The Diet closed by an edict of the Emperor, calling on the Reformers to retract; but no attempt was made to enforce it, as the Protestants threatened to withhold their assistance in repelling the Turkish invasion. An alliance of the leading German princes who supported the Reformation was made, in 1531, against the Emperor, but in the next year he yielded. Suleiman II. was on his way to Vienna with a large army, raised, as he avowed, to subdue the Empire. Charles, in alarm, signed a treaty at Nuremberg with the Protestants, whereby he agreed to acknowledge the Reformation for the present as an accomplished fact, subject to a future settlement of the question. On this concession, the princes gave him their support ; and Suleiman, who had counted on their withholding it, on hearing the news, suddenly retreated.

Luther, in his desire of reforming the Church, had no original intention of separating himself from the Catholic body. This act, which cost him many a hard struggle and anxious doubt, was forced upon him by the obstinacy of the Pope and Cardinals in refusing reform. He gladly joined, however, in the attempt made by Melancthon, soon after the Diet of Augsburg, to make use of the Pope as an agent of general reformation; but it failed, as might have been expected. Both Catholics and Protestants united in repudiating the monstrous excesses, which, under the sanction of Protestantism, the Anabaptists of Munster committed in 1534. A fanatical enthusiast named John of Leyden, a tailor by trade, excited his party by his assertions that revelations had been communicated to him from Heaven. He drove out the town council and leading citizens, proclaimed himself king, and declared a community of wives and goods. His follies and crimes were terminated by the success of the Bishop of Munster in his assault on the city, who put John and other chiefs of the Anabaptists to a cruel death in 1536.

The latter years of Luther's life were saddened by the conviction, which was forced on him, that the great work of spiritual reformation which he had set in motion was rapidly becoming a political tool in the hands of the warlike and intriguing princes who had adopted its principles. He had, however, the gratification of seeing the spread of Protestantism in parts of Germany where it had previously been rejected. The Emperor, Charles V., was still its strenuous opponent; and the efforts of the Papacy were unceasing to revile its doctrines and assail its professors. In 1545, the Council of Trent (the decrees of which are to the Catholic what the Confession of Augsburg is to the Protestant) was opened by the Pope; and the Emperor summoned a Diet at Ratisbon for the next year, with the view of enforcing by temporal power what the spiritual could not effect alone. Luther looked to the event of these proceedings with much interest, but did not live to behold it. Having journeyed from Wittenberg to Eisleben, on a mission of reconciliation between two Protestant princes and brothers, the Counts von Mansfeld, he was seized with a return of a long-existing malady, and died after a few weeks' illness, in February, 1546, at the age of sixty-three. He was buried at Wittenberg with the greatest honor.

No representative man was ever more suited to his age than Martin Luther. With a spirit devout, pure, and ardent; a mind clear, acute, and practical, yet not wanting in imaginative power; with generous emotions, and a vigorous, active frame of body, he was qualified to attract the sympathies of the really earnest members of the old faith, to wrestle successfully with its subtle theologians, please the taste of the higher and more refined classes, and win the hearts of the middle and lower classes of Germany. Whatever errors in judgment may be attributed to him at certain periods of his life, — and although he may have occasionally overstepped the bounds of charity, good-temper, and courtesy in his discussions, — alike for wisdom and true-hearted zeal he occupies a rank among religious reformers, to which we think no other can presume to attain. To him we owe the boldest expression of that conviction, without which all progress in religious or political freedom is impossible, — the right of private judgment. To him we owe the best employment and widest diffusion of those intellectual weapons which the Church of Rome had so long retained in her own custody, and by the exclusive use of which she alone upheld her despotic power.

Hernando Cortes.

THE CONQUEST OF MEXICO.

WE have seen Spain at the close of the fifteenth century, entering, through the ability of Columbus, upon a course of scientific and commercial enterprise. It remains to see how the spirit which he evoked was turned aside, by the love of conquest and of gain, into a path, which, if it led to the wealth and fame of one country, was productive of death and misery to myriads of the human race.

Following in the direction which Columbus had endeavored to penetrate, the Spaniards, before the year 1518, had surveyed the eastern shores of both North and South America, coasting from the Bay of Honduras, by the Isthmus of Darien, down to the Rio de la Plata. But as yet the lands lying round and beyond the Mexican Gulf were unexplored. Here lay the vast Mexican Empire, which had existed for nearly two centuries, unknown to Europe, in a flourishing state of comparative civilization. It extended from the Atlantic to the Pacific, over a large and varied territory, rich in natural beauty, vegetation, and minerals. The government was an absolute but elective monarchy; the administration of justice was strict and equal. The military discipline of the Aztecs, or Mexicans, was excellent, though their tactics were rude. In science and art they had made great advances, possessing an astronomical scheme superior in some respects to that of the Egyptians, and a system of picture-writing only inferior to theirs. In social refinement the Aztecs had likewise attained remarkable progress, and their manners and customs evinced a careful regard to moral restraints. Notwithstanding all this civilization, the national creed was a degrading superstition, which, if capable of explanation by the more enlightened priests, was to the people only a yoke of cruel slavery. Blinded by fanaticism, they became callous to the horrors of human sacrifice, and even cannibalism, which formed part of their devotional rites. Such was the country and such the people of Mexico at the commencement of the sixteenth century. The condition of the State, however, was not then so prosperous as previously; the reigning monarch, Montezuma, though eminent for political wisdom and warlike prowess, having alienated the affection of his subjects by his profuse expenditure, which demanded heavy taxation to support it.

The coast of Yucatan was first discovered in 1517, by a Spanish colonist from Cuba, named Cordova, who was driven from his course to the Bahamas by strong winds. He was astonished at the civilized character of the natives, but was unable to make any exploration of the country on account of their hostile disposition. On returning to Cuba, he represented the discovery to the Governor, Velasquez, who sent out an expedition under his nephew, Grijalva, in May, 1518. He succeeded in establishing a friendly intercourse with the natives, and obtaining from them, in exchange for his trinkets, some superb jewels and golden ornaments. These, which he sent back to Cuba in a vessel which preceded his arrival, excited the avarice of Velasquez, who, without waiting for his nephew's return, despatched an expedition to conquer so valuable a country. Ho chose for its leader a man named Hernando Cortes.

The future conqueror of Mexico was born in 1485, of good family, resident in the province of Estremadura. Relinquishing the law, to which he was designed, for an adventurous life, he quitted Spain in 1504, and settled in Hayti, where he displayed much military skill in suppressing the revolts which broke out at times among the injured islanders. He acquired at the same time a disreputable character for profligacy. In 1511 he joined the expedition with which Velasquez undertook to conquer Cuba; and after the subjection of that island, settled there,—marrying happily, and realizing by his agricultural industry a moderate fortune. Velasquez, perceiving his ability, determined to intrust him with the command of the new expedition to Mexico, under the title of Captain-general. The responsibility of the post effected a great change in the character of Cortes, who from gay became grave, and from thoughtless, reflective. He eagerly procured a troop of 300 men and six vessels. His instructions from Velasquez were to aim at the conversion of the natives, and induce them to enter into commercial relations with the Spaniards,—carefully to survey the coast, and ascertain the nature of the country and the government. Cortes, in spite of his early excesses, was a sincere bigot, and aspired to show his zeal for

the Catholic faith by the utmost efforts for its extension.
He may be reasonably credited, moreover, with an ambition not less ardent, but more selfish. Suspicions of
his character were excited in the Governor's mind before
the fleet sailed, and he determined to revoke his trust.
But being apprised of the intention, Cortes on the same
day made ready to start, and at midnight set sail. Though
pursued by messengers of Velasquez, he managed to
evade them. He obtained ample stores of ammunition
and food at various ports, and increased his force to the
number of eleven vessels and 500 soldiers, with a crew
of 100 mariners, and a body of Indians amounting to
200. Small as this force was for the conquest of so vast
a country as Mexico, its members were prevented from
feeling alarm by their ignorance of the difficulty, and
animated by an enthusiasm able to surmount it when
known. On the 18th of February, 1519, the fleet set
sail for Yucatan.

A storm drove Cortes to take shelter in the island of
Cozumel, where he treated the natives kindly, and, as
usual, bartered his trifles for their gold. He fulfilled his
aim of extending Christianity by means of the teachings
of two missionaries, who accompanied the expedition, and
by his own plan of destroying the idols, and thus demon-
strating their powerlessness. He here obtained a valuable assistant in the person of a Spanish captive, who
knew the Yucatan language, and joined him as interpreter. After a brief voyage, the squadron anchored off
the Rio de Tabasco, where Cortes attempted to land, but
was received with hostile gestures on the part of the
natives. Through his interpreter he proclaimed his pa-

cific intentions, but a shower of arrows was the reply; and the river banks were thronged with armed warriors, prepared to dispute the passage. Dividing his troops into two detachments, he ordered an officer, named Avila, who commanded one, to land at a point whence a road led to the town of Tabasco; while the other detachment, under his own command, advanced in the same direction from the opposite point. The landing was effected with great difficulty, owing to the determined resistance of the natives. But once on shore, the fire-arms of the Spaniards terrified and bewildered their opponents, who fled to shelter. Avila had meantime disembarked, and came upon the town by surprise. It was soon taken, and Cortes fixed his quarters in the chief temple. An immense force of natives threatening his position, he sent forward his infantry and artillery to attack it in the plain where it was encamped. He himself skirted the camp with his cavalry, so as to assail the rear. When the plain was reached, the natives, who were infinitely superior in numbers, pressed hard upon the invaders; but were met by a deadly fire, which thinned their dense ranks. The fight had lasted an hour, and they were still courageously sustaining their ground, when Cortes and his cavalry suddenly attacked their rear. Unaccustomed to the sight of horse-soldiers, the natives fled in terror, and the battle was won after a fearful carnage, — in which the defeated might be counted by thousands to the conquerors' units.

Cortes, instead of pursuing his conquest further, declared, through the interpreter, that all who yielded to his arms should be freed from molestation, but that resistance would be punished by death. The chieftains, or caciques, in the vicinity, at once made their submission, presenting the conqueror with gifts of slaves, &c. Among the female slaves was a girl whom Cortes named Marina, and soon adopted as his mistress. She proved of great assistance to the Spaniards from her knowledge of the language of Mexico, of which country she was a native.

After establishing Christianity in Yucatan, Cortes returned to his vessels, and setting sail, reached the Mexican coast in April. After holding intercourse with the natives on the coast, who were amicably disposed, he landed on the spot where Vera Cruz is now built, and encamped on the plain. In fortifying his situation he was assisted by the natives, by the order of the Emperor's viceroy, Teuhtile. This officer visited the camp next day, and was courteously received; Cortes stating that he was sent as an ambassador from the mighty King of Spain to the great Emperor of Mexico, with gifts which must be delivered to him in person.

Montezuma had from his viceroy a faithful account, by means of picture-writing, of the wonderful advent of the fair-skinned strangers, with their cavalry and artillery, the latter especially having astonished and terrified the Mexicans as much as it had done the natives of Yucatan. He was considerably alarmed at the news, in consequence of a floating prophecy that a banished deity, named Quetzacoatl, represented as fair-skinned and bearded, was destined to return, and rule over Mexico. Splendid presents were sent to Cortes, including vessels and ornaments of gold and silver, rolls of cotton cloth, and richly embroidered articles of feather-work. The

ambassadors who carried these at the same time expressed
their regret that, owing to the difficulties of the journey
to his capital, and the state of the country, the Emperor
could not receive the messengers of the King of Spain,
to whom he, nevertheless, desired them to convey his
profound respects. Cortes was not dejected at this refusal, and sent back a courteous reply, that he could not
return after so long a voyage without having fulfilled his
mission. He forwarded by the ambassadors a few presents, including some Holland shirts and a gilt Florentine
goblet. In ten days the Mexican ambassadors returned
with another present of great value, but a decided refusal
to admit the Spaniards. Cortes on this occasion treated
the envoys coolly; and one of the Spanish missionaries informed them that it was their intention to establish Christianity in Mexico. The ambassadors at once dropped
their friendly bearing, and retired during the night.

Having no intention of complying with Montezuma's
orders, Cortes looked about for a more favorable situation
than that in which the army was stationed. He met,
however, with opposition from some of his soldiers, who
were anxious to return to Cuba. While he was trying
to allay the mutiny, a turn was given to the dispute by
the arrival of some Indians from Totonac, a recently conquered dependency of Mexico, and greatly disaffected.
The envoys, who desired a visit from the Spaniards, were
received by Cortes with much honor, and a promise to
comply with the invitation. The wily Spaniard saw in
this visit an easy opening to the conquest, which he had
always kept in view. A spirit of disunion was clearly at
work in the Empire, and his policy was to increase it.

12 *   R

He first directed his energies to soothing the discontent
of his followers. By readily consenting to return to
Cuba, since it was the wish of the army, he excited a
strenuous opposition to that course in the well-affected
party; and on the day after the order to set sail was
given, he was entreated by a majority to withdraw it.
Yielding, as he made it appear, to the prevalent feeling,
he then with a show of humility offered to resign his
office of Captain-general; but the resignation was refused with acclamations. A colony was then projected,
of which he was to be Chief-justice, with the share of
one fifth of all the produce of conquest or trade. Good
feeling being thus restored, the fleet coasted down to
Chiahuitzlan, where was the intended site of the new
city; while Cortes marched to Cempoalla, the capital of
the Totonacs, to pay his promised visit. The Spaniards
were well received by the cacique; and after obtaining
information as to the nature of the Mexican government
and territory, Cortes promised the Totonacs his aid in
breaking off the yoke of Montezuma. During the interview, five Aztec nobles, sent by that monarch to receive
the tax laid upon the Totonacs, entered the town, and
blaming the cacique for receiving the Spanish strangers,
demanded as a punishment the surrender of twenty
youths, of both sexes, for sacrifice. Cortes, accounting
this an insult, directed the Totonacs to imprison the envoys; but at night he secretly enabled two of them to
make their escape, apologizing for the dishonor done
them by the imprisonment, and promising to release their
comrades. This promise he fulfilled next day, by removing the captives from the custody of the Totonacs

to his own vessels. He then stirred up disaffection to the Mexican rule in the neighboring towns, whose citizens eagerly embraced his cause against Montezuma, and took oaths of fealty to the Spanish king. By native aid he next carried into execution his design for the new city, which rapidly grew in size.

The conduct of Cortes towards the envoys had its due effect on Montezuma, who sent his acknowledgments, together with costly presents. Cortes treated the envoys hospitably, and returned a message to the Emperor that the Spaniards would soon visit him in his capital. At the port of his new city, which received the name of Villa Rica, Cortes was one day surprised to find a vessel with a Spanish cavalier on board, in command of a small troop, who told him that Velasquez had obtained authority from Spain to found a colony in the new country. Cortes at once decided on securing for himself the result of his own labors. He sent off a vessel to Spain with an account of the discovery, and a petition from the citizens of Villa Rica that the proceedings of Cortes, and his appointment as their general, might be confirmed. With the despatches were sent the treasures which he had acquired from the Mexicans, and the army was prevailed upon to surrender its own share also. The vessel was pursued by two ships of Velasquez, who received news of its departure; but succeeded in safely reaching the port of San Lucar, in Spain.

A conspiracy of those who wished to return to Cuba broke out in the camp, but Cortes quelled it with much firmness, and determined to prevent its recurrence by taking the bold step of destroying his fleet, and thus rendering return impracticable. The pilots were induced to declare the vessels unfit for service, and all but one were sunk. Loud clamors arose against this act, but Cortes was master of the occasion. Calling the army together, he reminded them of his own labors in their behalf, and how thoroughly he was identified with their own success or failure. For himself, he said, he would stay — let all beside depart. The remaining ship was at the service of all who wished to go. The appeal was decisive. None accepted the proposal, but a general enthusiasm for their General and their cause pervaded the camp, which resounded with cries of "To Mexico!" Cortes then prepared his forces for the march to the capital of Montezuma. His own men did not exceed 400 foot and 15 horse, but he was accompanied by upwards of 1,000 Indian soldiers, and porters to carry his artillery and baggage. Forty hostages from Cempoalla acted as guides and interpreters to the expedition. After crossing the great Mexican table-land, with its varied scenery of rich vegetation and barren plains, the Spaniards reached the territory of the Tlascalan Republic. Here they were attacked by the natives, a warlike race, constantly engaged in contests with the Mexicans, with whom they concluded the Spaniards to be at peace. After one decisive engagement, in which the Tlascalans were signally defeated, they yielded, and formed an alliance with their conquerors. On the march from Tlascala, the Spaniards had to pass through the Mexican dependency of Cholula. A large force of Tlascalan volunteers accompanied the Spaniards, but was not allowed to enter the city. The reception was at first hospitable, but on the arrival of some messengers from Montezuma, symptoms of hostility appeared. Cortes suspecting a plot, set Marina at work to discover it. She ascertained, from the wife of one of the caciques, that a massacre of the Spaniards, as they quitted the city, was to be effected by the Cholulans, with the aid of a Mexican force. Cortes lost no time in charging the Aztec ambassadors with the plot, who denied any knowledge of it. He professed to believe them, but kept them in guard, and prevented their corresponding with the Cholulans. Towards the latter he assumed a friendly tone, and informed them that he intended leaving the city next day, requesting the assistance of a large reinforcement for the carriage of his guns. On the next morning he had prepared his army for the struggle, — guarding the gates, and arranging with his Tlascalan allies to join him at a signal. When the Cholulans made their appearance with the reinforcements demanded, Cortes charged them with their treachery. In their terror they confessed it, but laid the blame on the Mexicans. He replied by a declaration that their punishment should be in proportion to their crime. At his signal, the Tlascalans outside the city joined his troops, and a fearful massacre of all the Cholulans ensued. Some fled to the chief temple ; but, failing to obtain help from their gods, threw themselves from its pyramidal summit. As many as 6,000 are said to have perished in one day.

Montezuma, in alarm at this terrible vengeance, sent at once his ambassadors, laden with presents, to deny any share in the plot. Cortes concealed his disbelief and anger, and received the embassage with respect. He continued his march to the capital, observing on his way various evidences of an existing disaffection to the reigning monarch. The spectacle of the great valley of Mexico, studded with cities amid its woods and lakes, excited the desire of the Spaniards to possess so goodly a land; but such were the signs of civilization, that all save Cortes were fearful of the result of their hostile attempt. He cheered his troops with his wonted eloquence, and succeeded in impressing them with his own persuasion of an eventual conquest. He was the more confirmed in this belief from the tone adopted by the ambassadors of Montezuma at each successive interview. The Emperor's fears at last prevailed so far as to induce him to offer an immense bribe to Cortes, with the promise of an annual tribute to the Court of Spain, if he would but return home. Cortes declined the offer, which disclosed its proposer's weakness; and Montezuma, concealing his terror, sent his nephew with a superb present and courteous greetings to welcome the strangers to the capital. They entered on the 8th of November, 1519, in number about 7,000 men, of whom only 400 were Spaniards. The Emperor, a tall, slender man, of dignified presence, and splendidly attired, was borne in a palanquin to the city walls to meet Cortes. The interview was brief, but amicable, and the Spaniards were then conducted to their appointed quarters.

The magnificence of the city astonished them. It was built at the edge of a vast lake, with which it had numerous causeways of connection. The buildings were of stone, and included some lofty and spacious temples and palaces. The chief street extended in a straight line for several miles through the centre of the city. Canals intersected the streets at intervals, and were crossed by bridges. The Imperial palace was on the grandest scale, — the immense rooms being ceiled with perfumed woods, and draped with rich hangings.

At his first interview with Montezuma, Cortes touched but slightly on the professed object of his mission ; but at the next, warmly advocated the cause of Christianity against heathenism, though without producing much effect. Montezuma's tone, however, was suppliant ; he admitted the superiority of the Spanish monarch, and promised to accede to all the wishes of his ambassadors. Cortes, nevertheless, as though in danger of attack, took the precaution of fortifying his quarters by a strong wall, which bristled with his guns, and before which walked his sentinels. Among the buildings of the city the great central market, with its crowds of busy traders, and surrounded by a court of justice for the punishment of fraud, first attracted the notice of the Spaniards. Thence they proceeded to the chief temple, having five stories, in height about a hundred feet, and resting on a base of three hundred feet square. In the interior was an altar, by which stood a huge image of the god of war, with three human hearts as a sacrifice before it. Cortes and his companions could not conceal their horror and disgust at the scene, and the former represented to Montezuma his surprise that so wise a king could worship an idol manifestly an image of the Devil. The devout Emperor seemed much shocked at this slander on the gods. He, however, permitted the Spaniards to convert part of their own residence into a Christian chapel. In the process of alteration a hall was discovered in the ancient palace which Cortes occupied, full of treasure, but carefully sealed up. The sight of this wealth did not diminish the desire of the Spaniards to dispossess the Emperor of his dominion.

After a week's sojourn, Cortes became uneasy at his position in the capital. He resolved, by one daring measure, to put an end to his difficulties. This was nothing less than the seizure of the Emperor as a hostage. The pretext for this act was an insidious attack made upon the Spanish garrison at Vera Cruz, two soldiers of which had been invited to visit a neighboring cacique, who murdered them. In revenging this crime, the garrison had been defeated and its commander killed. Some of the Indians were taken prisoners, and accused Montezuma of having instigated the murder. Cortes accordingly requested an interview with the Emperor, whom, after a cordial greeting, he informed of the news just received. Montezuma averred his innocence, and promised redress; but Cortes, though professing to believe him, declared that he should not feel secure without a hostage for the good faith of the Mexicans at large, and therefore begged the Emperor to remove his residence to the Spanish quarters. In vain did the unfortunate monarch protest against this outrageous demand. Violence was at last threatened, and he was fain to give way. He was carefully watched, but allowed apparent liberty for some time. All endeavors, however, to convert him to Christianity proved ineffectual. His dependent condition aroused the anger of his nephew, Cacama, who ruled over the neighboring state of Texcuco, and a league of tributary chiefs against the Spaniards was formed by his influence. The plot was discovered and defeated by Cortes, who caused Cacama and the other members of the league to be seized, and brought to Mexico in chains. This success completed the fall of Montezuma, who now acknowledged his inferiority to the King of Spain, and put the revenues of the kingdom, and all his private treasures, at the command of Cortes. A booty of nearly £1,500,000 was thus secured; a fifth of which was reserved for the Spanish Crown, and another fifth for Cortes, the remainder being divided in certain proportions among the army, to the dissatisfaction of the common soldiers, who received a very small share. Cortes, however, again soothed their murmurs by the eloquence of which he appears to have been such a consummate master.

The Mexicans were not so complaisant as their sovereign to the despotic acts of the Spaniards. Cortes, in his zeal for the faith of Christ, violated the sanctity of the great heathen temple, by clearing one of its altars for the use of his followers. A violent sentiment of indignation possessed the people, and Montezuma warned Cortes that it might become uncontrollable, unless he withdrew from the city. While in this state of threatening danger, the Spanish general received news of yet more alarming import. Velasquez, enraged at the success of Cortes, had fitted out an expedition, under the command of a cavalier named Narvaez, to supersede him in Mexico.

Narvaez reached Villa Rica with a fleet of eighteen vessels, 900 Spaniards, and 2,000 Indians, in April, 1520. The governor of the garrison seized a few soldiers sent

on shore, and forwarded them as prisoners to Cortes;
who, however, treated them kindly, and returned a pacific
message to Narvaez, asking for his co-operation in the
work of subduing Mexico. That leader treated the message with contempt; but the priests who brought it
greatly impressed the soldiers with the advantages to be
derived from uniting with their comrades. Cortes, accordingly, left two thirds of his men as a garrison in
Mexico, under an officer named Alvarado, obtained a
thousand Cholulans as a reinforcement, and marched
against Narvaez with the remainder of his force, amounting to only 266 Spaniards.

Relying on his greater numbers, Narvaez was careless and imprudent; stationing his troops beside a river,
which he relied on the inability of Cortes to cross. The
General, however, effected the passage by night, and
came suddenly on the slumbering army. The surprise
was complete, the artillery was silenced, Narvaez
wounded and made prisoner, and his followers induced
or compelled to surrender. By a division of the spoil
found in the camp among the conquered Spaniards,
Cortes secured their adherence to his own army. He
had scarcely concluded this arrangement, when news
came of an insurrection in Mexico. He obtained an
additional force of Tlascalans, and with an army of Spaniards, now 2,000 in number, hastened back to the capital,
perceiving on his way symptoms of hostility among the
natives. Entering the city, he found from Alvarado that,
owing to information received by that officer of a contem-
plated rising among the citizens, he had violently assaulted and massacred a large number of the nobility,

assembled at a religious festival. The citizens rose in
arms, and would have retaliated on the Spaniards but
for the intercession of Montezuma. They had, however,
withheld provisions ever since, and starvation was threatening the garrison when Cortes returned.

The insurgents were soon seen in full force; the Emperor's brother, Cuitlahua, who had been sent by Cortes
with the hope of calming their anger, heading their
ranks, and besieging the Spanish quarters. A terrible
conflict ensued, in which the artillery of the Spaniards,
and the bravery of their Tlascalan allies, scarcely succeeded in overcoming the obstinate fury of the immense
host which stormed round the palace. On the third day,
Cortez determined to make use of his Imperial captive
as an intercessor. He consented to address the people;
but immediately he declared himself well disposed to the
Spaniards, a shower of stones was thrown at him, one of
which struck him to the ground. He was borne away
senseless; but on recovering, refused to have the wound
dressed. Weary of his dishonored life, he expired a
few days after, commending his family to the mercy of
Cortes.

Meantime the siege of the Spaniards, and their counter
attacks, proceeded. In one of the latter, made upon the
great temple, where a body of Mexican nobles was stationed, Cortes was nearly killed by two warriors, who
endeavored to hurl him from one of its terraces. By a
vigorous effort he released himself, and threw over one
of his opponents from the same height. The temple and
many adjoining buildings were then fired, and hundreds
miserably perished in the flames. Still the Mexicans

showed no signs of yielding, and the retreat of the Spaniards was hindered by the destruction of the chief canal bridges. Cortes made a final effort to secure the possession of the few yet remaining. This was successful, and he then resolved to quit the capital. Cacama, the nephew of Montezuma, and some of the family of the deceased Emperor, were carried away as prisoners.

On the 1st July, 1520, the Spaniards commenced their retreat. On reaching a canal, for the purpose of crossing which they had brought a portable bridge, it failed to act, and at this moment a vast body of the enemy fell upon them. Hundreds were pushed into the water, and choked the passage. The slaughter was immense, the Spaniards being taken at disadvantage, and overpowered by numbers. The loss of their baggage and treasure proved the safety of the small band that escaped the furious attack of the enemy, who stayed pursuit to seize the spoil. 450 Spaniards and 2,000 of their allies are said to have fallen, and the remainder were deprived of those weapons on which they mainly depended for future success against a barbarian foe, — every musket being lost. The Mexicans put to death Cacama and all the other prisoners, several Christians being sacrificed to the gods.

The broken line of Spaniards continued its retreat, — Cortes being deeply affected at his misfortune, but not yet wholly disheartened. The army underwent the greatest privations from want and fatigue in its march across the plains, and, on reaching the valley of Otumba, found a large army of the enemy there encamped. Cuitlahua, the successor of Montezuma, had levied troops

from all the dependencies of Mexico to oppose the Spaniards, and all the great caciques of the empire were
present. Notwithstanding the number of his assailants,
Cortes determined to give battle. He inspirited his
troops with his own ardor, advising them to thrust their
lances and swords in the faces of the foe, which were
unprotected; and especially to aim at the chieftains,
whose fall would be sufficient to insure the flight of their
followers. The result proved the wisdom of his tactics.
The swords of the Spaniards cleared a road for them
through the dense ranks of the enemy. After a fight of
several hours, however, the Indians were gaining on their
opponents, when Cortes, who saw at a distance the Mexican commander, made a bold dash in that direction, with
a few cavaliers. The little knot of officers round the
chief was reached, and Cortes plunged into its midst,
hurling his lance at his antagonist, and bringing him to
the ground, where he was slain. The attendants fled,
and the death of their chieftain was communicated to the
whole army. The flight became general, and the day
was won by the Spaniards. As many as 20,000 Indians
are said to have fallen. After a prayer of gratitude, the
Spaniards loaded themselves with the treasure left by the
fugitives, and resumed their march. On reaching the
capital of Tlascala, they were kindly received by the
caciques of the republic, who renewed their alliance.

Cortes, after refreshing his troops for some time,
strengthened his position in the empire, by punishing
several tribes which had acted treacherously towards his
soldiers at Vera Cruz and elsewhere. He received an
addition to his force by the desertion of the crews of

two ships, which had been sent by Velasquez to Vera
Cruz, and of three other vessels, sent by the Governor
of Jamaica to found a new colony. Now, therefore,
feeling himself strong enough to retake the capital of
Mexico, he set out in the middle of December, 1520.
His Spanish troops amounted to about 600 men, —
some of whom were armed with muskets. His allies
were very numerous, probably several thousands in number, armed with bows and pikes. Crossing the snowy
mountain-chain which obstructed its progress, the army
entered the Texcucan territory, and reached its capital
on the last day of the year 1520. Thence, by several
successful expeditions, Cortes induced many of the tribu-
taries of Mexico to desert their allegiance, and unite with
him in breaking off their bondage. He next sent a message to the new Emperor of Mexico, Guatemozin, who
had recently succeeded Montezuma's brother on the
throne, offering to secure his power, on condition of his
acknowledging the supremacy of Spain. Guatemozin, a
youthful and valorous prince, who bore a mortal hatred
to the invaders, returned no reply, but busied himself in
strengthening the city and animating his people.

In the spring of 1521, Cortes, having procured thirteen
vessels for the use of his army on the great Mexican
lake. left a garrison at Texcuco, and advanced towards
the Imperial capital. He was, however, called aside to
subdue several cities in the valley, where Aztec garrisons
had been placed, which continually harassed his soldiers ;
and, though meeting everywhere with determined resistance, he inflicted, in return, the most severe penalties.
A new canal for his vessels was dug by his Indian allies,

and joined to the lake. The besieging army was then
formed into three divisions, each of which had a separate
camp stationed at the head of the causeways over the
lake which communicated with the capital. An attack
on the Spanish vessels, made by Guatemozin with a fleet
of canoes, was successfully resisted, the whole Mexican
flotilla being shattered to pieces by the artillery, which
was brought to bear upon it. Thus, being masters of the
lake, the Spaniards proceeded to block up all other channels of communication between the besieged and the
neighboring district. This being accomplished, the besiegers advanced down the main causeway which led
into the city. They met with opposition at every point.
Behind every breach was a band of spearmen ; on every
flat house-roof a crowd of slingers. Ramparts of stone
protected the sides of the canals, and wide ditches without bridges intersected the roads. By means, however,
of his artillery, Cortes destroyed the strongest defences.
and drove the defenders for shelter to the temples. His
inroads were made day by day, the troops retreating at
night to their quarters. Guatemozin, meantime, actively
exerted himself to repair the devastation thus caused,
and, by means of sorties, to harass the foe. Famine,
however, began to commit its ravages in the city.
Though the ruin of the empire was at hand, nothing that
courage could perform was spared to avert it. A bold
assault which Cortes made upon the central market-place
was unsuccessful, many of his soldiers being slaughtered
or drowned, sixty-two taken prisoners, and he himself
scarcely escaping. The unfortunate captives were all
sacrificed, and their heads sent by the Emperor to the

allies of the Spaniards. This for a time availed to thin
the ranks of the besiegers; but, on the failure of a rash
prophecy uttered by the Aztec priests, that eight days
would witness the ruin of the Spaniards, most of their
allies returned. Having obtained an increase of military
stores, Cortes determined to pursue no longer his generous policy of sparing the buildings of the capital, but to
end the siege at once. The palaces and temples were
accordingly thrown down, and the canals blocked up.
The Imperial palace was next fired, and finally the great
temple destroyed. The market-place was soon afterwards captured, and the Spaniards were masters of the
city. They found famine and pestilence holding a revel
in its interior; hundreds dying in the streets, and resting
there unburied; the survivors gliding about like their
ghosts. Yet Guatemozin held out still, with a large and
desperate band, among which women and children fought
like men. The Spaniards swept down thousands with
their artillery, and the streets were soaked in blood like
water. The final act of carnage was committed on the
15th of August, 1521, when the Mexicans resisted for
the last time, and were butchered in such masses that the
streets were piled with dead bodies. The Emperor, in
an attempt to escape, was captured, and led into the presence of Cortes, who received him with respect, and
promised him protection. Between one and two hundred
thousand Mexicans are said to have perished in this fearful siege. But little booty was found in the city, most of
it having been destroyed. The clamors of the soldiers
induced Cortes to put Guatemozin to the torture, in
hopes of forcing him to discover if any treasure had been

hidden; but no confession was extracted, and Cortes ashamed of his cruelty, released his courageous prisoner in time to save his life.

Mexico having fallen, the empire was practically subdued, and the caciques sent in their submission. The capital was rebuilt, the conquered people being pressed into the service of reconstruction, and performing the work with great rapidity. Cortes forwarded home a full account of the conquest; and, though at first his services were overlooked through the malignant influence of Velasquez, the interest of powerful friends prevailed, and the conqueror was appointed by Charles V., in .1522, Governor and Chief-justice of New Spain. He remained in Mexico some years, during which time he zealously carried on the rebuilding of the capital. A Christian cathedral was erected on the site of the heathen temple, the Governor's palace and a Franciscan convent also occupying prominent positions. Christianity was diligently preached; and, if we may believe the statements of the missionaries, no less than nine millions of the native population embraced the faith within twenty years from the conquest. Spaniards were invited to settle in the country, and brought with them European grain and plants, which, in a short period, effected nearly as striking a change in the natural aspect of Mexico as its national character exhibited by the alteration of government.

In 1524 Cortes was called into Honduras, where he had established a colony, by the tidings of an insurrection. The journey was tedious and dangerous, and many of his soldiers perished from want and fatigue. On the route, a conspiracy broke out against him, in which the

13   s

deposed Emperor, Guatemozin, and some Aztec nobles were concerned. It was discovered, and the rebels punished with instant death, — an act of severity for which Cortes has been much blamed by those who consider that the alleged conspiracy was not sufficiently proved against Guatemozin. From his influence over the natives, it was doubtless convenient to get rid of him on the slightest pretext. After quelling the rising in Honduras, Cortes returned to Mexico, where an insurrection had arisen on the false report of his death. His presence sufficed to restore order, but he was permitted only a brief repose.

In July, 1526, he was astonished by the intelligence that, owing to the malicious slanders of some of his personal enemies, who charged him with misappropriating the Mexican revenues, and aspiring to the throne, he had been superseded in the government until a commission had reported on the truth of the accusation. Estrada, the Royal Commissioner, exceeded his duty, and treated Cortes with indignity. The conqueror, therefore, determined to return home, and seek from the King in person a redress of his injuries.

He reached Spain in May, 1528; and, in spite of the charges brought against him, was received by Charles V. with the utmost honor. He was ennobled as Marquis of the Oaxacan Valley in Mexico, where he obtained the grant of a large territory. His military command was restored to him, but he was not reinstated in his civil appointment. After marrying a second time, on the death of his first wife, he returned to Mexico in 1530. The slanderous imputations were not withdrawn by the commissioners, one of whom was his personal foe; but no further proceedings took place. Finding that the authorities who exercised the civil government of Mexico interfered with his military duties, he resigned his office and retired to his estates.

In 1532–3 he fitted out two squadrons on voyages of discovery, which were unsuccessful. Another expedition was more prosperous,—the squadron sailing round the coast of California for many miles. Being aggrieved by the opposition of the Mexican government to his schemes, Cortes returned home, in 1540, to seek redress. Charles V. had lost his interest in the progress of science, or the merit of Cortes, and paid no attention to his petitions. After a final and dignified appeal to his ungrateful sovereign, which obtained no answer, Cortes determined to return to Mexico. He died at Seville, on his road to the coast, in December, 1547, at the age of sixty-two. His services were recognized immediately after his death, and his burial was performed with the most solemn rites.

The genius, the virtues, and the vices of a conqueror, are all to be remarked in the character of Cortes. His firmness, patience, observation of human nature, and ingenuity, are beyond praise. Unscrupulous in effecting his purpose, he was not wholly without a conscientious motive for his most selfish designs. His bigotry is his most laudable characteristic, violent and fierce as it was. In his lust of power and gain, and the stern cruelty by which he achieved the satisfaction of both, he typified the spirit which, under the cover of Christianizing zeal, animated the leading enterprises of Spanish adventurers during the sixteenth century. A mongrel Christianity was, indeed, propagated by the conquerors in the heathen lands

which they subdued.   But, sown by those who exhibited
as results of their faith deeds of murder, fraud, and licentiousness, the seeds of the religion of love, justice, and
purity, could scarcely be expected to bring forth good
fruit.   If, in the final issue of events, the conquests thus
cruelly won proved to be instruments of Christianity, civilization, and science, the beneficial result must be ascribed to the overruling wisdom and goodness of Him
who decrees that even "the wrath of man shall praise
Him."

Gustavus Vasa.

THE inhabitants of the ancient Scandinavia were only known throughout the middle ages as bold pirates by land and sea. As Danes and Norwegians, they ravaged the coasts of England, and for a space even usurped the throne. As Northmen, or Normans, they invaded France, and obtained a grant of the large and valuable duchy, called after them, Normandy. Some roamed further south, and founded kingdoms in Sicily and the coasts of Italy; while others first invaded the territory, and then entered the service, of the Eastern Emperors, where, under the name of Varangians, they were long the most trustworthy guards of the Byzantine throne. This Northern race was essentially Gothic in constitution, and strikingly displayed its characteristic·features, — a love of orderly freedom, strong religious and poetic feeling, coupled with violent passions and a lax conscience. Of the three countries into which, owing to natural boundaries, or separation of races, Scandinavia was divided at an early period, Denmark and Norway speedily adopted a monarchical form of government, but Sweden remained for a longer time severed into small independent states. At last the race of Odin, the reputed leader of the Goths who subdued the original Finnish tribes, established its sway over both the conquerors and the conquered in Sweden. Constant wars, arising out of the absence of national affinity, disturbed the country till the eleventh century, when the Odinic dynasty terminated. A temporary union took place under the rule of Stenkill and his successors, but did not long continue. In the twelfth century a compromise was effected between the two races, according to which a Gothic and a Finnish king were alternately elected. This system, though giving rise to endless disputes, was not changed until 1389, when Albert, a German prince of the house of Mecklenburgh, who succeeded his cousin Eric XII., was overthrown by Margaret, Queen of Norway and Denmark. The chief event in the history of the three nations, prior to their occupying a prominent position in European history, was their union into a triple kingdom by this princess. She was the widow of Hakan, King of Norway, the daughter and heiress of Waldemar, King of Denmark, and the conqueror of Albert of Mecklenburgh, King of Sweden. Both inheritance and conquest were by her added to the possessions of her late husband, by the Treaty of Calmar in 1398. The junction was not happy; for, though it served to terminate the old quarrels, which had so long agitated the three nations, it gave rise to new jealousies, owing to the impossibility of securing an equal distribution of honors and advantages between three admittedly equal states. Denmark, as the native country of Margaret, was naturally favored by her and her successor, Eric XIII.; and Sweden, as the only conquered country, was naturally slighted. The oppression of the

Danish officers in Sweden at last drove the people of Dalecarlia to revolt, and Eric was forced to resign the crown. Carl Cnutson, a powerful Swedish noble, who headed the revolt, was finally elected King of Sweden in 1448, and maintained its freedom against Christian I. of Oldenburg, who wore the united crowns of Norway and Denmark. After the death of Carl, his nephew, Steno Sturé, was elected King, and defeated the Danes in an important battle in 1471, which prevented any attempts on the freedom of Sweden for some years. In 1483, however, the Treaty of Calmar was renewed, and the three crowns were united under John, the son of Christian I. Dissatisfaction with his government soon produced a revolution in Sweden, and Steno Sturé was chosen independent Regent in 1501. The title was continued to his relatives, Swanté and Steno, successively, who courageously sustained the conflict with Denmark. On the death of King John in 1513, his son, Christian II. succeeded; and it was in the early part of his reign, and the antagonistic regency of Steno Sturé the younger in Sweden, that the hero of our present sketch, Gustavus Vasa, made his first historical appearance.

His surname was Ericson, that is, the son of Eric, Vasa being the name of his family, which was of ancient, if not royal descent, and had produced several members of the State Council. He was born about the year 1496, near Stockholm; his father, Eric Johanson, being a State Councillor, and his mother sister-in-law of Steno Sturé the younger. He was educated at Upsala, where he was known while a boy for a frank, daring disposition, combined with shrewdness and patience.

At the age of eighteen he was received at the Swedish Court, and there imbibed a zealous sentiment of hatred against the Danish invaders of his country. The leading politician of Denmark at this period was Trollé, Archbishop of Upsala, a haughty, unprincipled man. Gustavus first drew his sword in an engagement which took place in 1517, between the Swedes and a Danish army sent to relieve Trollé, who was besieged in his castle of Stekeborg by Steno Sturé. The castle was taken, and the Archbishop compelled to renounce his see, and retire to a monastery. In the following year, Gustavus bore the great banner of Sweden at the battle of Brankyrka, fought between the Regent and King Christian II. The King was defeated, but after the engagement opened negotiations for peace; Sturé, meantime, supplying the Royal troops with provisions. Christian, taking advantage of this generosity, proposed a conference on board his vessel, but Sturé was not permitted by his councillors to comply. Six nobles were therefore sent as hostages for the safety of the King, who came on shore, and among them was Gustavus. No sooner had they entered a boat to convey them on board, than the treacherous Danes seized it, and bore the hostages as prisoners to Denmark. Gustavus was committed to the custody of a relative, at a castle in North Jutland. Here he suffered little bodily restraint, but the acutest mental disquietude at the tidings which ever and anon reached him from Sweden, against which Christian was preparing a vast army of invasion. Gustavus at last could bear his confinement no longer, and availing himself of a favorable opportunity, in the autumn of 1519, escaped from the castle in the disguise of a drover. He fled to Lubeck, where the burgomaster and council of this flourishing commercial city, influenced partly by compassion and partly by suspicion of the designs of Denmark upon the Hanse towns, refused to give him up, but permitted his returning to Sweden. He reached Calmar, and thence traversed the country in disguise, sounding the popular feeling, and stirring up disaffection to the Danish yoke. During his wanderings, he learnt tidings of the tragedies which had been and were being enacted.

In January, 1520, the Danes had signally defeated the Swedes under Sturé, who died of the wounds received in the battle. None was found brave enough to fill his post, and many of the nobles submitted to Christian, upon an amnesty for past offences being accorded them. The peasants still held out in certain districts; but Stockholm and the leading towns yielded, and the conquest of Sweden was held to be achieved. The King resolved to secure it by an act of diabolical perfidy. He summoned the highest nobles of Sweden to attend his coronation, on the 1st of November, 1520. Trollé, the Archbishop of Upsala, performed the ceremony. Amid the festivities attendant on this event, and the apparent cordiality of the King and Archbishop towards their recent enemies, ninety-four of the latter, including two bishops, twelve nobles, among whom were the father and brother-in-law of Gustavus, and several burgesses of Stockholm, were suddenly arrested for the crime of having deposed Trollé and destroyed his castle of Stekeborg, — an act just pardoned, among other political offences, by the King's solemn oath and treaty. Condemned by a packed tribunal,

13 *

after a brief trial, the victims of this monstrous treachery were publicly beheaded or hanged in the market-place of Stockholm, on the 8th of November, — even the last rites of religion being refused them. Many of the friends and retainers of the sufferers were then pitilessly massacred. This event is known in Swedish history as the Bloodbath.

Roused to a burning anger at the murder of his kinsmen, and a patriotism scarcely less ardent at the fall of his country, Gustavus devoted his life to the work of vengeance. He passed into Dalecarlia at the close of the year 1520, where he relied on the sturdy character of the Dalesmen for support in his enterprise. Here he took service with the miners and farmers, — running the most hairbreadth escapes of detection on several occasions. He was once or twice discovered by his dress and manner, and soldiers were sent in search of him. At a barn in Isalaby he was one day concealed among the straw of a wagon of his protector, a forester named Elfson. Some troopers searched the place, and in thrusting their spears through the straw, wounded the leg of the fugitive. The blood flowed down on to the snow, but Elfson concealed its real cause by secretly gashing his horse in the leg at that moment, and thus deceived the soldiers, who went off in another direction. At another time Gustavus was hidden for three days in a fir-tree, and fed by the peasantry. This class he roused to insurrection by his glowing eloquence in describing the story of the Bloodbath. Success attended his exertions. At Mora, the chief village of the Dales, he was elected Captain-general of the kingdom.

In February, 1521, he took possession of the great

copper mine, and seized the royal revenues. Thence he traversed Gestrickland, and obtained promises of support from Gefle and other towns. Meantime, Trollé and the authorities, who, on Christian's departure for Denmark administered rule in Stockholm, sent an army of 6,000 men to put down this peasant insurrection, as it was deemed. Swenson, an able Dalesman, whom Gustavus appointed General during his absence in Gestrickland, completely routed the Danes on the banks of the Dalelfven. Gustavus now issued a proclamation of war against Christian, whom he denounced as a perjured and blood-stained usurper, from allegiance to whom all good Swedes were absolved. He followed up this declaration by an attack on the important town of Vesteras, where Slaghec, one of Christian's chief favorites, commanded the Danes. They were defeated mainly through the vigor of Gustavus. After a partial victory, his first detachment had commenced pillaging the town, and thus given time to the Danes to form anew, when he sent in a fresh reserve, and decided the struggle. His next step was to attack the Archbishop of Upsala in his palace. Owing to the careless contempt of Trollé, the assault was successful, and the palace was burnt; but he himself escaped. As a result of this achievement, the Assembly or Council of the States, which met at Vadstena in August, 1521, feeling confident of the final triumph of Gustavus, offered him the crown of Sweden. He was too wise and too patriotic, however, to accept this dignity at the hands of a section of the people, and therefore assumed only the title of Regent, which gave him full power to command the military forces, and direct the policy of the State.

His career from this date is not marked by the records of any memorable battles, but was a gradual progress towards final success. Stockholm was besieged by his forces, which were reinforced by a fleet from his former friends at Lubeck, and it finally yielded in June, 1523. The treachery of Christian so disgusted his Danish subjects that they deposed him, and elected Frederick, Duke of Holstein, as their king. This change of government determined the Swedish nobles to press upon Gustavus the offer of that crown; and as their voice was echoed by that of the nation, he consented to be elected in June, 1523.

As a king, Gustavus fully justified the choice of the Swedes. He soon made peace with Frederick, who but feebly supported the claim of Denmark to the possession of Sweden. Adopting the Lutheran tenets from principle, Gustavus favored their propagation in the country, but checked the excesses to which they had given rise in Germany, and tempered the zeal of the new converts with his own moderation.

In 1527 he proposed a measure, which was adopted at the same time in England; viz. the appropriation by the Crown of the Church revenues. Finding the Council indisposed to grant him an uncontrolled authority over such large wealth, he announced his abdication as the only alternative, — an act evincing the highest integrity, or the firmest assurance in the affection of his people. The storm of enthusiasm with which he was greeted by the burghers and peasants, during the deliberation of the colder nobles on the alternatives he had submitted, convinced the latter that his confidence had not been misplaced. He, meantime, showed no anxiety as to the result, but passed his time in diversions of various kinds. The effect of this policy was soon manifest. The Council, warned by the exhibition of popular feeling, and roused to a sense of the value of Gustavus, yielded his demands. The measure was passed unanimously, and his power secured amid the joyful acclamations of the whole nation.

The remainder of his reign was not free from internal dissensions, or foreign wars, but none were of importance sufficient to demand a detailed narration. He sedulously promoted commerce and the general improvement of the country, — evincing, in his correspondence with his officers, an intimate acquaintance with the practical machinery of the reforms which he suggested. Under his rule Sweden enjoyed the greatest prosperity, and took a high rank among European states. His latter years were somewhat imbittered by domestic anxieties, arising out of the jealousies of his sons by different mothers. He was himself the unintentional cause of these disputes, by having imprudently anticipated in his lifetime the future distribution of his possessions by will. He was thrice married, and left several children. After a gradual decay of strength for some time, he expired, amid the consolations of his faith and the affectionate tears of his people, on the 29th September, 1560. It would be possible to point out certain failings in the character of Gustavus, but the task would be alike ungracious and unprofitable. Considered in his public or private capacities, as patriot, judge, and statesman, — as husband, father, and friend, there are few kingly names which can be pronounced with such satisfaction as that of Gustavus Vasa.

Ignatius Loyola.

THE JESUITS.

The corruptions of the Church of Rome, which gave
rise to the Protestant Reformation in the North of Europe, produced a Catholic Reformation in the South.
With men of thoughtful and inquiring minds, doctrine is
more important than practice. The reverse is true of
passionate and impulsive temperaments. Thus in Germany, England, and Sweden, the flagrant violation of
the doctrine of God's free grace, exhibited in the sale of
Papal indulgences, gave far greater offence, and originated a much deeper sentiment of resistance, than the
flagrant violation of virtue and decorum exhibited in the
condition of the monastic houses. In Spain and Italy,
on the other hand, it was the perfidy, profligacy, and
worldliness of the highest dignitaries of the Church, and
the powerlessness of its agencies for good thence resulting, that produced a strong reaction of practical improvement, at the very same period when the doctrinal reforms
of Protestantism were being effected. The majestic
beauty of the Romish theory and ritual, to which the
colder Northerns were but slightly sensitive, fascinated
the ardent Southerns far too strongly to be obscured by
any blemishes in practice. To remove these by zealous

measures of reform, was the ambition of earnest believers. The hero of the movement, and type of Catholic reformers, was Ignatius Loyola.

He was born in 1491, of a noble Biscayan family in Spain. Trained to the military profession in the service of Charles V., he embraced its romantic side with a chivalric ardor, rare even in a Spaniard, and fitter for the times of Charlemagne or the Cid than his own. He entertained an imaginative passion for a princess of exalted station, in whose name and for whose sake he aspired to the loftiest achievements of prowess in the field, and enterprise throughout the world. His dreams were soon ended, or rather, altered. At the assault of Pamplona, which was besieged by the French and Navarrese, he received a wound that confined him to his bed for many months, and crippled him for the remainder of his life. Solitude and sickness changed his thoughts and prospects. His career had been that of a reckless and frivolous soldier. Influenced by the convictions of conscience and the study of religious works, he rose from his bed of sickness, resolved that his future should be the very opposite of his past. The Church, the Virgin Queen of the world, was to be the object of his idolatrous devotion. To cleanse her garments from the stains of sin, and render her a pure spouse, meet for the heavenly bridegroom, was now the ambition of his life. Full of this hope, and buoyed up by a restless and diseased imagination, yet with a fervent piety and charity, Loyola entered upon his mission of reform. He practised ceaseless penances and watchings, undertook a journey to the arid sands of Syria, and worshipped at the Holy Sepulchre.

He returned to Europe in 1526, and commenced his career as preacher in the University of Alcala, where he succeeded in impressing some of the students with his own views. A tinge of wildness in his tone, and the novelty of his high moral standard in that corrupt age, attracted the attention of the Inquisition to him, and by the authority of that deadly foe to reforms he was silenced by imprisonment for two years. Not discouraged, on his release he repaired to Paris, and gave up some time to study. Here he made the acquaintance of several enthusiasts of his own character. After numerous discussions, the conclave met in the underground chapel of Montmartre Abbey. Here they finally concocted a scheme for the radical improvement of the Church, — a scheme afterwards developed into the foundation of a new order. From Paris Loyola went to Venice, and enrolled himself as a member of a monastic body called " The Theatines," whose object was to convert and minister to the poorest classes, which the regular clergy neglected. At the convent of this order Loyola remained some time, and employed himself in the zealous discharge of his office. He seemed to live almost without food and clothing, so scanty were his meals, so ragged his dress. After assiduously waiting upon the poor and sick at the hospitals, he would wander about the squares and streets of the city, and, by his strange gestures, and stranger words, attract round him knots of listeners, to whom he preached of the glory of the Church and the blessedness of her faithful children. Other cities in Spain and France were the witnesses of his self-denying labors and street preachings.

In 1534 he repaired to Rome, and sought an audience of the Pope. Being destitute of position or patronage, it was long ere Loyola obtained an opportunity of announcing to the successor of St. Peter a scheme for the confirmation and extension of his authority. The time, however, arrived; and after many rebuffs and disappointments, the Spaniard's ardent plan for instituting a new mechanism of reform was sanctioned by Pope Paul III., in 1536. The foundation of the Society of Jesus was thus established. Its aims were to purify the Church and to propagate the faith, both by attacking heretics and converting the heathen. Little did the pious and misguided Spaniard foresee how gigantic the engine which he had constructed would eventually become, — gigantic for evil not less than good! He did not live long enough to have his eyes fully opened to the result of his exertions. He laid the constitution of the Order on a military basis, arranging its government in grades, until the post of Superior was reached, over whom none had any control save the Pope. This form accounts for the favor with which the Popes regarded the new Order. The monastic bodies generally were self-governed and democratic in character; whereas this served to exalt the absolute despotism of the Papacy. In 1541 Loyola was made Superior of the Order. After a rigorous life of self-mortification, he died in 1556.

A few words must suffice to describe the workings of the spirit evoked by Loyola's influence. On one side, no doubt, there was, and has been, a change for the better. In place of worldly and dissolute Popes, the See was generally filled by men of earnest souls and saintly lives.

T

The character of the clergy and monastic orders was improved, and placed under due inspection. Christianity, unaccompanied by the fatally persuasive eloquence of the sword and the musket, was preached in heathen lands, and heretics were combated with a bigotry, in which the element of sincerity must justly be severed from that of ferocity. The cause of education also has been a gainer by the writings of learned Jesuits. On the other hand, the principles of that diabolical policy, which men have learned to execrate under the name of Jesuitry, were given forth to the world, in the name of the true and holy Jesus. Founded originally with the aim of purifying the Church, as a means of glorifying God and benefiting man, the Society of Jesus was speedily perverted, by the craft of designing prelates and politicians, into a tool for glorifying the Church, at the expense of God and man. "The end sanctifies the means," is its motto, — *obedience* its guiding principle. Devoting themselves to an idea, — the supreme dignity of the Order, which represents the Church, — the members of the Society are only men in so far as they are Jesuits. Every feeling of right or wrong, pleasure or pain, is deliberately sacrificed to the higher consideration of the benefits accruing to the Order. Mixing either openly or in secret with the world, as priests, monks, statesmen, professors, students, soldiers, or merchants, — prominent in the conclave, the court, the council, the university, the battle-field, or the exchange, — employed in the heart of a great city or the solitude of an Indian prairie, — the Jesuit remains the same, bound by indissoluble ties to his profession, in constant communication with the governing body of his Order. Into any intrigue, from the most subtly political to the most grossly passionate, he may not scruple to enter, if any advantage to the Society can be derived thereby. Repeatedly put down, or weakened even by Papal authority, and expelled from every European state in turn, the Order yet flourishes. The annals of this formidable and pernicious system — could they be written — would unfold the blackest pages in the chronicle of human nature.

William the First of Orange.

By the marriage of Margaret, daughter of Louis II., Count of Flanders, with Philip, Duke of Burgundy, the county became annexed to the duchy in 1385. The most eminent of the dukes of Burgundy, after the annexation, was the turbulent and tyrannical Charles, surnamed "The Bold," whose reign was a perpetual scene of crime and bloodshed. He misruled his country, and was in a state of constant war with his suzerains, Louis XI. of France and Frederick III. of Germany. He met a sudden death by drowning in 1477, and was succeeded by his daughter Mary, known in history as the lovely and sweet-hearted Mary of Burgundy. Her marriage with Maximilian, son of the Emperor Frederick, and afterwards Maximilian I., secured peace to the troubled land for a few years, but on her lamented death, in 1482, the Flemings revolted against Maximilian, who, with all his good qualities, was, from his ignorance of the duties of a king and the rights of a free people, unfit to govern. The revolt was put down after a great effusion of blood, but the Flemings obtained favorable terms. The seventeen provinces of which the Northern and Southern Netherlands were then composed became part of the German

Empire on the accession of Maximilian to the throne. His grandson, Charles V., who united Spain to his other vast possessions, abdicated in 1555, and ended his days in a Spanish monastery. His brother Ferdinand succeeded as Emperor, but the Burgundian territories descended to Charles's son, Philip II. of Spain, with which country they were formerly united by a Pragmatic Sanction in 1548.

The principles of the Reformation had taken deep root in the hearts of the free Netherlanders. Charles V., though respecting their civil liberties, attempted to repress by force what he deemed their religious heresy. But his persecutions were as nothing in comparison with his son's. Philip, who was naturally cold, suspicious, and cruel, superadded a bigotry of the narrowest and gloomiest cast. In a storm at sea he took a vow of exterminating the heretics, and kept it to the best of his ability. His violence was not openly resisted until he attempted to introduce the Inquisition, which had recently acquired general execration, in consequence of the martyrdoms which had been perpetrated by its authority in Spanish America. A petition for its suppression having produced no effect, a revolt broke out, in which both the nobility and people were implicated. It was put down by Count Egmont, the royal general, who, though attached to the popular cause, loyally supported his master. Philip restrained his anger, and proclaimed an amnesty ; but sent a large army into the Netherlands, under his universally detested general, the Duke of Alba, — a man whose personal character was as repulsive as his aspect.

On his approach, Count Egmont and Count Horn, the

most eminent of the loyally disposed nobles, persuaded
their fellows to act with moderation and respect. Many,
however, viewed the designs of Philip with the utmost
apprehension. William of Orange, Count of Nassau,
the wealthiest and ablest nobleman of his time in the
Netherlands, was foremost in this body.

He was the head of the Nassau family — which was
prominent among the Rhenish nobility — and Prince of
Orange in Provence. He likewise held the important
post of Governor or Stadtholder of the provinces of
Holland, Zealand, and Utrecht. He was born in 1533,
and bred up by his father as a Protestant ; but having
obtained favorable notice from Charles V., was by him
removed to the Court, and instructed in the Catholic
faith. William's calm and reserved temperament, with
which were united an unselfish ambition and dauntless
courage, procured him the esteem and confidence of
Charles, who took counsel of him in difficult cases when
he was but twenty years of age. The favor of Charles
was the reverse of a guarantee for that of his son, and
Philip soon had as much reason to fear as to hate
William. Among other nobles, the Count was sent to
France in 1559, as a hostage for the peace of Château
Cambresis, which terminated a war between Spain and
France. Here the French King, Henry II., who had
recently joined in a secret treaty with Spain to suppress
Protestantism, communicated the information to William,
who had obtained, for his discretion, the name of "The
Silent," and was naturally supposed to be as much a
confidant of Philip as he had been of Charles.

On his return to the Netherlands, William soon threw

off the profession of Catholicism for that of the Reformed Calvinistic system, and revealed to his religious brethren the news which he had heard. Philip soon discovered the detection of the treaty, but could not openly display his anger. During the government of the Duchess of Parma, who ruled in the name of her brother Philip, before the Duke of Alba's arrival, William exerted all his influence to frustrate the Spanish policy. He well knew what fate to expect when the approach of this monster of cruelty was announced; and having failed to persuade Egmont and Horn of their imprudence in remaining, he sought safety in retirement to his Rhenish provinces of Nassau. "I fear you will be the first over whose corpse the Spaniards will march," was William's farewell warning to Egmont. The event fulfilled the prophecy.

Alba entered Brussels in the summer of 1567, with a Spanish and German army. He began by showing much mildness to all the late rebels, and the utmost cordiality to Egmont and other nobles. This treachery was only enacted for a few weeks. Having invited Egmont and Horn to an interview, he placed them under arrest; and fearing that, in spite of their loyalty, they would offer a formidable resistance to the crimes which he had in contemplation, he ordered their execution in the following year. A court, composed of Spaniards and a few Dutch traitors, was then established to pass sentence on all who confessed heresy, or who were concerned in the late revolt. Several were condemned without any crime whatever being proved against them, and a wholesale system of persecution was ruthlessly put into operation. Rob-

bery was added to murder. The victims were first tortured to confess where their treasures were hidden, and
then given over to be executed.

William, whose flight had arisen from his apprehension of danger to himself personally, rather than to the
country at large, received tidings of this tragedy with
feelings of the bitterest indignation. Rousing to arms
the Princes of Nassau, his brothers, he headed an army
which, though raw and undisciplined, gallantly maintained for years a desultory warfare with the Spaniards,
but without much success. Alba, meantime, continued
his barbarous system in the Netherlands, out of which
he vaunted that he could extract more gold than Peru.
His victims amounted to upwards of 18,000, and the
country roads were poisoned with the effluvia of the car-
casses which rotted on the gallows. After a short pause,
the war was renewed with vigor in 1572, when Egmont's
friend, the Count von Lumay, who had vowed not to
comb or cut his hair till he had avenged the murder,
captured a Spanish fleet, and the town of Briel. This
success encouraged the citizens of the chief towns of
Holland to throw off the Spanish yoke. The Southern
Netherlands also revolted, and Louis of Nassau, by a
sudden surprise, captured and garrisoned the town of
Mons. It having been besieged by the Spaniards, William, who had raised a German army, marched to its
defence. He failed, however, in relieving it, and a noc-
turnal attack of the enemy on his camp was nearly fatal
to him.

A band of 600 arquebusiers, led by a knight named
Romero, entered the Dutch camp by stealth, cut down

the sentinels, and made for William's tent. His guards were all asleep, save one, and that a little spaniel, which lay upon his bed. At the sound of intruding steps it barked angrily, and woke its master by scratching his face with its paws. He leaped up just in time to mount his horse, which was kept saddled, and escape into the night. His secretaries, steward, and servants, were all too late, and fell by the weapons of their assailants. The camp was burnt, and soon afterwards William was forced to retreat. To the day of its death he kept the spaniel in his bedroom. The figure of this faithful creature is sculptured on his tomb.

Alba marched against Mechlin, captured, and plundered it, — massacring the citizens. His son Frederick, after outrivalling his father in barbarity at Zutphen, advanced on Naarden, where he persuaded the inhabitants to capitulate under promise of safety, and then murdered them. Haarlem held out for a whole winter, — a troop of 300 women being foremost in the ranks of the garrison. William marched to its relief, but in vain; and it capitulated by stress of famine in 1578. Frederick's revenge for the loss of his men in the siege was among the most horrible events of this war. After beheading so many that his executioners could not work from fatigue, hundreds of victims were tied back to back, and cast into the sea. At Altmaar, however, he was worsted through the brave defence of its men and women. At the same time the Netherlanders were victorious at sea, and captured the Spanish fleet.

Alba's tyranny having failed to secure success to Philip's designs, a more merciful governor, named Requesens, was substituted in 1574, but without effect. The Dutch no longer believed in Philip, and maintained hostilities. Two of William's brothers fell in an engagement near Nimuegen, in the same year; but the Spaniards met with a signal disaster at the siege of Leyden, in 1575. The city was blockaded on all sides, and a fleet which was sent to its assistance was unable to land its troops. 6,000 citizens are said to have died of famine. In this emergency, William suggested the desperate expedient of cutting the dykes — which here, as elsewhere throughout Holland, communicated from the city to the sea — and letting in the water upon the land. The people assented with the cry, " Better to spoil than to lose ! " The dykes were cut through, and the tide flowed in under the favoring influence of a northwest wind, — filling the Spanish trenches, and bearing upon its surface the Dutch vessels. The Spaniards fled, and 1,500 were drowned or slain in the pursuit. The starving citizens were relieved with provisions, and Leyden was saved. Its University was erected in memory of this great deliverance.

Spain was now severely punished for her tyranny, and the finances of the country were at the lowest ebb. The soldiers were unpaid and mutinous, but revenged themselves by pillaging the Flemish cities. At Ghent, which they had previously treated less severely on account of its taking little part in the revolt, an attempted assault in 1576 led to a revolution, and the admission of a garrison sent by William's orders. The sack of Antwerp, in the same year, where 5,000 citizens were massacred, completed the catalogue of Spanish crimes. William took advantage of the hatred excited by these events to promote a spirit of union among the Netherlanders. This aim was crowned with success at Ghent, in November, 1576. A new commander, sent out at this time by Philip,— his natural brother, Don Juan, — was forced to acknowledge the union, but consented only in appearance. He stirred up jealousies among the other nobles against William ; but that wise and unselfish leader defeated the scheme by voluntarily surrendering the prominent position which the course of events had given him. Don Juan's treacherous dealings were discovered, and the Flemings, by William's advice, invited the Archduke Matthias, son of the Emperor Maximilian II., to take command of their army. The object that William had in view, in taking this step, was to unite the country with Germany against Spain. Ghent was recaptured by the people from the hands of a partisan of Don Juan, who had seized it ; but the Protestants sullied their success, and lost favor by their cruel persecution of their Catholic opponents. In 1578, the young Duke of Parma (Philip's nephew) headed the Spanish forces, and defeated the Dutch at Gemblours. This loss excited fresh disunion in the Protestant party ; and the interference of the Duc d'Anjou, brother of Henry III. of France, with a hope of obtaining the government, added to the confusion. William appeared once more as the genius of harmony, calming the turbulence of the Ghentese bigots and demagogues, and restoring order, in December, 1578. The Duke of Parma, however, and the Catholics, still retained a hold on the Southern provinces, and prevented their alliance with the Northern Netherlands. The union, so long advocated by William, was finally adopted by the seven provinces composing the latter, which, in January, 1579, by the League of Utrecht, renounced their allegiance to Spain, and formed a republic, over which William was placed as Stadtholder-General.

In Flanders the Spaniards carried on the war successfully, capturing Dunkirk, Maestricht, and Mechlin, among other places. Enraged at the revolt of the Northern Netherlands, Philip issued a manifesto, ascribing the cause to William's intrigues, setting a price of 25,000 ducats on his head, and promising to ennoble his assassin. William, nevertheless, held on his course, appeasing the disturbances at Ghent in 1580, and procuring its adhesion, with that of Bruges, to the League of Utrecht. The Archduke Matthias had already withdrawn, and the Duc d'Anjou been expelled from the government of the Flemish councils. An attempt was made on William's life, in 1581, by a French assassin, anxious to win the reward promised by Philip; but the wound inflicted by the shot was, happily, not mortal. The intrigues of the Duke of Parma to dissever the alliance of Ghent and Bruges with the new republic were carried on with great ability, and, unfortunately, with success; both admitting a Spanish garrison in 1584. This event defeated the wise policy which William had so steadily pursued, and originated that separation which, after many attempts at union, still exists between the Northern and the Southern Netherlands, now known as Holland and Belgium.

On the 10th of July, 1584, another assassin, named Gerard, stimulated by the bribe of Philip II., accomplished the murder of the good Stadtholder. William was at Delft, whither Gerard proceeded with despatches, and representing himself as in want of money, was generously relieved. With the money was bought the pistol with which his benefactor was shot. The Prince had just left the dinner-table, and was passing through a vestibule which opened on the street, when the murderer, who had concealed himself in a sunken arch by the door, suddenly stepped forward, and pulled the trigger. The Prince fell back, with three poisoned balls in his breast. " God have mercy upon me and upon this poor nation!" was his last prayer. His death followed in a few minutes. The murderer was seized and put to death ; Philip fulfilling his vile promise, by ennobling the Gerard family with the title, " Destroyer of Tyrants ! "— a name which the juster Muse of history will rather bestow upon the victim. Thus, in the vigor of his days, perished this wise and manly prince. As the Liberator of Holland, William deserves the affection with which his name is still regarded. Though not free from faults, for which his bad political education must be mainly held responsible, his career is yet eminently remarkable as an example of high-minded and unselfish policy. To the subsequent exertions of his son, Maurice, must be ascribed the military success of the Republic ; but to William it owed its firm foundation of political and religious freedom.

Henry the Fourth of France.

THE WARS OF THE LEAGUE AND THE HUGUENOTS.

THE most important events in the history of France, during the fourteenth and fifteenth centuries, were the English wars, and the triumph of the kingly over the aristocratic power. With the particulars of the former, from the defeat of Philip VI. to the success of Charles VII., every English reader may be supposed to be familiar. The conquest of feudalism is due to the ability of Louis XI., who, by his minute but perpetual encroachments on the rights of the nobles, his subtle and perfidious intrigues in their councils, and his ferocious punishment of their rebellions, achieved their fall; and, though by the worst means, and with the most selfish intention, attained the desirable result of strengthening the popular power, as well as his own. The Italian invasions of Charles VIII., Louis XII., and Francis I., which have already been noticed, ushered in the sixteenth century, the leading event of which in France was the religious war between the Catholic Church and the Protestant Reformers.

The origin of hostilities was the cruel persecutions of the Protestants of Provence by Francis I., in 1535 and 1546. He at the same time threw doubt upon the sin-

cerity of his zeal, by supporting the Lutheran princes
of Germany, who were leagued against the Emperor
Charles V. Henry II., who succeeded Francis in 1547,
was equally inconsistent, — publishing barbarous edicts
against his own subjects, and yet aiding their religious
brethren in Germany. His wife, Catherine dei Medici
(a member of the great Florentine family), who, after his
death in 1559, ruled over France, in the names of her
sons, Francis II. and Charles IX., is the Catholic heroine
of these religious wars. Henry IV. is the Protestant
hero.

He was the son of Antoine de Bourbon, Duc de Vendôme, a prince of the blood royal (through his ancestor,
Robert, son of Louis IX.), who married Jeanne d'Albret,
heiress of the King of Navarre, and in 1535 became
king in her right. Henry was born in 1553, at the
beautiful town of Pau, in the Béarn. In the seclusion
of his native province, trained to natural and simple
enjoyments, and unspoilt by the flatteries and vices of a
court life, Henry was brought up under the care of his
mother, a sensible and devout adherent of the system of
the Reformer, Calvin. His father, Antoine, in virtue
rather of his rank than of his talents, was regarded as one
of the leaders of a political party which opposed that of
the Queen-mother, Catherine dei Medici, and her sharers
in the government, Francis Duc de Guise, and his brother,
the Cardinal de Lorraine. The perfidy of Catherine and
the ambition of the Guises created a strong hatred against
them amongst the French nobles, and the barbarity of
the persecutions, which were sanctioned by the government, incited the Protestants to ally themselves with the
opposition.

In 1560 was formed the famous Conspiracy of Amboise, in which the King of Navarre, his brother, the Prince de Condé, and the Admiral de Coligny, were said to be implicated, among other Protestant leaders. Its object was to crush the Guises, from whose custody the King (Francis II.) was to be forcibly removed. The plot was betrayed, and failed of success, — the result being a cruel slaughter of the Protestants. The King of Navarre was threatened with death, and his brother was even condemned, though subsequently released. The death of Francis II. in the same year, and the accession of his brother, Charles IX., a child of ten years old, somewhat altered the aspect of affairs. Catherine became Regent of the kingdom, and henceforth the influence of the Guises, and that of the Crown, no longer weighted the same scale. The Queen, from political, not religious motives, began to lean to the side of the Protestants, — liberating Condé, and making the King of Navarre Lieutenant-general of France. The Guises, on the other hand, allied themselves with Phillip II. of Spain, the most bigoted champion of Catholicism in Europe.

After an ineffectual edict, in 1561, which served to exasperate, while professing to benefit, the Protestant party, and a theological congress, which also came to no result, the wise Chancellor of the kingdom, Michel de l'Hôpital, mediated between the factions, by obtaining a new edict in 1562. Toleration was thereby accorded to the Reformed congregations, the members of which may henceforth be spoken of under their common (though unexplained) name of Huguenots. The peace was short, owing to the fickleness of the King of Navarre, who was won over to the Guise side by the promise of Sardinia, as a gift from Philip II. The unprovoked attack of the Duc de Guise on a small Protestant congregation in Champagne, opened the war. The Queen in vain attempted to join Condé, who now headed the Reformers. The young King was seized by the Guises, and she followed him to Paris. The Catholics, under the fanatical Constable de Montmorency, carried fire and sword into the Protestant provinces and towns; while Condé and Coligny, who headed the Huguenots, carried on the work of attack and devastation in an opposing direction. Antoine of Navarre, who besieged Rouen in the Catholic interest, in 1562, was slain in the assault; leaving Henry, still a child, to succeed him on the throne.

The battle of Dreux, in Normandy, was fought in the same year. The issue to both sides was singularly equal: the Catholics, under the Constable de Montmorency, and the Marshal de Saint André, being defeated, — the former general being taken prisoner, and the latter killed, — while the Huguenots, under Condé, were routed by a vigorous charge of the Duc de Guise, their leader falling into the hands of the victors. The Guises seemed triumphant; but their success was suddenly terminated in the following year, at the siege of Orleans, where the Duke, who commanded the besiegers, was assassinated by a Huguenot named Poltrot. The assassin, when put to the torture, accused Coligny of having instigated the crime, — a charge which, however unfounded, was believed by the son of the murdered man, Henry, now Duc de Guise, who headed the Catholic party. A treaty of peace and toleration was made in the same year between Catherine, as Catholic Regent of the kingdom, and the Huguenots; but there was no sufficient guarantee for its observance.

The Queen allied herself with Philip II., and took counsel with his minister, the Duke of Alba, whom we have seen an unrelenting persecutor of the Reformed party. She also took a tour throughout France, accompanied by the young King, with the object of ascertaining the condition of the Huguenot interest. The real character of this crafty woman was soon exhibited, and Condé summoned the Huguenots to arms in 1567. An attempt to seize the person of the King was unsuccessful; and at the battle of St. Denis the Catholics obtained a partial advantage, though losing their general, the stalwart old warrior, Montmorency, who fell, at the age of seventy-four, covered with wounds. A truce was patched up, but was soon broken, and Catherine lent herself to the perpetration of the most horrible barbarities upon the Huguenots, who retaliated, and the land was deluged in blood.

Henry, now King of Navarre, after having spent his early youth in Béarn, was sent to the French Court for a few years, but was recalled by his mother in 1566, soon after she had been proclaimed a heretic, and declared to be deposed, by a Papal bull fulminated against her. Though quite young, he showed such ability and courage that he was permitted to join the Huguenot army, of which his uncle, the gallant Condé, was now chief. Henry was first engaged at the battle of Jarnac, in 1569. Here the Huguenots were taken at a fearful disadvantage by the Catholics, under the nominal leadership of the Duc d'Anjou, brother of Charles IX. Condé's arm was in a sling, and his leg was broken by a kick from his horse ; but he mounted afresh, harangued his troops, and maintained a desperate fight for some hours. At last he was forced to surrender, but made a promise of his life the condition. He was carried from his horse, and placed on the ground, when a captain of the Royal Guard suddenly came behind him, and shot him through the head. This loss was a terrible blow to the Huguenot party, which now turned to Henry of Navarre as the hope of its cause. The good Jeanne stimulated its activity by her courageous conduct. At Cognac, in Anjoumois, she joined the defeated army, accompanied by Henry and her nephew, the son of the lamented Condé. Before a large assembly, she stepped forth, holding a hand of each prince. " I offer you," she said to the soldiers, " my son, and confide to you the son of the prince for whom we grieve." Henry then addressed them with the words : " I swear to defend our common religion, and maintain our common cause, till death or victory shall secure to us all the freedom for which we fight." The enthusiastic shouts of the army were a fitting acceptance of the Queen's offer, and he was at once proclaimed General-in-command. Owing to his youth, however, Coligny exercised the duties of that post. The battle of Roche-Abeille soon followed, in which the Huguenots were victorious, and the young King greatly distinguished himself. But at the battle of Moncontour the Catholics gained sufficient advantage to induce Coligny to desire peace. A treaty was thereupon signed at St. Germain in 1570.

As a pledge of peace and order, Catherine and her son, Charles IX., now of age to rule by himself, invited the leading Huguenots to court. The Queen of Navarre, Henry, and his cousin, accordingly accompanied Coligny to Paris. They were received with apparent cordiality by Charles and his mother; and a marriage was soon proposed between Henry and the King's sister, Margaret of Valois. The Pope at first opposed the match; but after an interview with Charles, the legate forbore further remonstrance. He was secretly assured that the union of a Catholic princess to a heretic would never have been proposed but as a cloak of treachery. The princess herself was averse to the marriage, having, it was said, bestowed her affection on the Duc de Guise, but was forced to yield by her imperious mother. During the preparations, Jeanne of Navarre died, as some thought, by poison, but probably from natural causes only. The marriage was celebrated on the 18th of August, 1572, and the court was a scene of festivities of every description. But under the mask of gayety was concealed the most atrocious perfidy. The Huguenots were invited to Paris in great numbers, while, at the same time, the Catholics were armed and prepared. On the 22d of August, an attempt was made upon the life of the old Admiral Coligny, by the instigation of Catherine; but the assassin only wounded him. Charles at once hastened with his mother to the house of their victim, with the loudest expressions of condolence and indignation. A guard was sent for his protection; and, under pretence of preventing the escape of the assassin, the city gates were shut, so that no Huguenots might be spared. On the

23d of August a great consultation was held at the Tuileries Palace, between Catherine, her son Henry (Duc d'Anjou), and the leading Catholic chiefs. The final arrangements were then made for the intended tragedy of the following day, which was nothing less than the massacre of all the Huguenots in Paris and other cities. The sound of the tocsin, or great bell of the palace, was to be the signal for the Swiss Guards of the King, and the militia of the city, to set upon their victims. A white cross in the hat, and a scarf on the left arm, were to be the tokens of recognition among the Catholics. As the appointed hour approached on St. Bartholomew's day, Charles, who was not wholly hardened in crime, displayed striking evidences of agitation, — trembling in every limb, and perspiring at every pore. Catherine, an adept in villany, and her worthy accomplice and son, the young Duc d'Anjou, had great difficulty in extracting a command for the massacre to begin; but, on obtaining it, anticipated the signal by ordering the bell of St. Germain l'Auxerrois to be rung at daybreak. The death-note sounded, and the city was filled with armed soldiers. The Duc de Guise, whose adhesion to the plot arose mainly out of hatred to Coligny, the supposed murderer of his father, headed a troop, and marched to the Admiral's house. The old man was in his bedchamber at prayer, and lay disabled by his recent wounds. The leader of the band, a German named Besme, ascended the stairs, and entered the room. "Art thou Coligny?" he demanded of the Admiral. "I am he," was the answer. "Respect my gray hairs, young man!" A mortal wound was the reply, and the muti-

lated body was thrown into the street, where the Duke
awaited it.   The head was cut off and sent to the Queen,
while the body was first gibbeted, and then burnt.   During the enactment of this scene, the miserable Huguenots
throughout Paris had been aroused from slumber, and
driven half-naked into the streets to be murdered by the
soldiery.   The leaders of the Catholic party presided
over the butchery, — Charles, who soon recovered from
his fit of remorse, actually firing from his palace window
upon the flying Huguenots, and Catherine with her ladies
looking down upon the bodies which were piled up in the
court.   The massacre was continued for three days in
Paris, where 5,000 persons of all ranks are said to have
perished.   In Orleans, Lyons, Rouen, and other cities,
the same scenes were transacted, — the governors of a
few towns only refusing to stain their consciences with
such a crime.   Some Catholics also in Paris hazarded
their lives to save those of their Huguenot friends, and
from motives of policy a few of the heretical party were
omitted from the massacre.   Amongst the latter were
Henry of Navarre, and his cousin, the Prince de Condé.
During the three days, they were shut up in the Louvre,
and were adjured, both by promises and threats, to change
their creed.   " Death or the mass " were the alternatives
at last presented to them by Charles.   With a weakness
that would have been less culpable, had it been an exceptional instance, Henry yielded, and his cousin followed
the example.   They were, nevertheless, watched closely,
lest they should escape from Paris.

The tragedy of St. Bartholomew, applauded at Rome
by Pope Gregory XIII. as an act of Divine vengeance,

and regarded by Catherine and her son as the security of their rule, was execrated by the Protestant powers abroad, and in France had the effect of **exasperating** the Huguenots to a more determined resistance. The civil war recommenced; Rochelle, where the Protestants predominated, holding out successfully for six months against the assaults of the **Duc d'Anjou, who enforced** Henry and Condé to accompany the army. Nismes and other places were still held by the **Huguenots, and they at length agreed to a treaty of peace, on** favorable **terms to themselves. A plot to deliver the** Navarrese **princes, who managed to make** known their forced abjuration of Protestantism, was **soon after set on foot.** It was carried into execution during the Carnival, and the Prince de Condé succeeded in making his escape; but Henry was less fortunate, and was closely guarded till the death of Charles IX. This event, which was hastened by the pangs of remorse for his share in the massacre, **took place in May, 1574, when he was at the age of twenty-four.** His brother, the **Duc d'Anjou, who had recently accepted the kingdom of Poland, hastened to return, and** succeeded **him, by** the title **of Henry III.**

One of the first events of his reign was the outbreak of a new religious war; commenced by the Huguenots, in their natural mistrust **of a king who** had been a chief actor in the tragedy of St. Bartholomew. Condé headed the army, and won over several nobles to his side. The cause soon **received a distinguished, but** worthless **adherent, in the** person of the King's brother, the Duc d'Alençon, who was jealous of his mother's partiality for Henry III. And in February, 1576, the young hero of the Huguenots himself escaped from his splendid captivity, and the vicious influences with which Catherine had surrounded him. At the Protestant camp, he formally abjured the faith which a fear of death had alone led him to adopt. His wife remained at the French Court, where her dissolute life dishonored the reputation of his house, and worthily fulfilled that of her own. Fortified by the assistance of the Elector-Palatine with a strong force, the Huguenots compelled Henry III. to deliver up to them six towns, and agree to a truce. By this weakness he lost the regard of the Catholic party, and obliterated the memory of the pious vengeance which he had helped to wreak on the heretics. His scandalous and frivolous mode of spending his time at Paris, moreover, proved him unfit for the throne which he had just been called upon to fill. Catherine, by her able policy, endeavored to supply the deficiencies of his government, and, by means of her ladies, intrigued to create a division in the Huguenot camp. She succeeded in winning back the Duc d'Alençon, her son, (who took the title of Duc d'Anjou,) and procured the cessation of active hostilities on the part of the other leaders. Meantime a new and formidable party had arisen in the Catholic ranks. A union of the sternest bigots was formed in defence of the faith, under the title of "the League of the Holy Trinity." Its avowed objects were the protection of the Church and the Crown, and the annihilation of the Protestants; but the chief Leaguers also secretly purposed to punish the Duc d'Anjou for his late perversion, and to depose Henry III. in favor of the Duc de Guise, whose asserted descent from Charlemagne was considered superior to the pretensions of the house of Capet. The Duc himself was General of the League, which obtained the support of Pope Gregory XIII. and Philip II. of Spain. In 1576 Henry III., having become aware of the nature of this plot, awoke to some sense of his dangerous position. He frustrated the ambition of the Duc by himself assuming the generalship of the League. Guise so far yielded, for the sake of their common cause, as to lead an army against the Huguenots. The fortune of the campaign leaned to the side of the Catholics, but peace was made in 1577, whereby full toleration was accorded to their opponents.

War broke out again in 1580, owing to the intrigues of the despicable King, who endeavored to separate Henry of Navarre from his wife. The attempt failed, and Navarre, by a rapid and gallant attack on the town of Cahors, possessed himself of it as a guarantee for the King's good faith. The Duc d'Anjou, who had designs on the county of Flanders, which was offered him by the Flemings, now in revolt against Philip II. of Spain, interfered to make peace between his brother and the Huguenots, of whose troops he was in need. After a partial success, his tyranny incited the Flemings to banish him, and he died of shame and rage in 1584. By his death Henry of Navarre became heir to the throne. The fear of a Huguenot's shortly succeeding the childless Henry III. renewed the activity of the League. Under the cloak of supporting the claims of the Cardinal de Bourbon, uncle of Henry of Navarre, as heir to the throne, the Duc de Guise, instigated by Philip II., with whom he made a treaty of alliance, aroused the partisans of the League throughout France. Henry III., forced by the menaces of the people, who clamored for war, became reconciled to Guise, and violated his pledge of toleration to the Huguenots. The eighth war accordingly broke out in 1584, and was known from the Christian names of the King, Navarre, and Guise, as "the War of the three Henries."

The ability of our hero now showed itself. Aided by Condé, Rosni, and other valiant leaders, he raised a powerful army; and, thus fortified, endeavored to avoid bloodshed, by first proposing an assembly of the States, and then a single combat between himself and a Catholic champion, as modes of deciding the dispute. His efforts failing, he carried on the war with amazing vigor and speed. Languedoc and Guienne were rapidly subdued, and he then gave battle to the royal army under the Duc de Joyeuse, in October, 1587. The combatants met at Coutras, in Périgord. When his troops were drawn up in order of battle, Henry advanced in the centre, and ordering them to kneel with him, prayed for the help of God. After a spirited address to his men he turned to Condé and his other cousins, reminding them of their Bourbon blood, and promising to prove himself a worthy chief of the family. The signal for battle was then given, and by their resistless charges the Huguenots completely destroyed the Catholic army, — Joyeuse falling in the engagement. Henry's conduct after the victory was eminently humane. This success was considerably damaged by the subsequent loss of a large German force, which, in marching to join the Huguenots, was cut up by Guise. In the next year, the death of the pious and manly Condé, by poison, was another serious blow to the Protestant cause.

The Leaguers soon made themselves so obnoxious to Henry III., who only desired means of indulging his paltry and licentious tastes, and took little heed to the government, that he determined to ally himself with Henry of Navarre, and break with Guise. This powerful noble was, meantime, securing a vantage-ground in the affection of the people. The "Sixteen," or Municipal Council of Paris, were also in his interest. Plots were formed with the view of deposing the King, who, however, obtained an insight into their design through his spies. He at last, in the spring of 1588, sent an order to Guise not to enter Paris. This was sufficient to determine the popular favorite on defying his sovereign. He entered the city in May, amidst the enthusiastic shouts of an immense crowd. The King was obliged to yield, when urged to promise that he would declare war against the Huguenots, and reform his Court. He endeavored to support his authority by means of a body of Swiss; but Guise summoned the citizens to his aid, and the Swiss were suddenly surrounded by enemies, and their retreat blocked up by barricades. When the King had been sufficiently humbled, Guise quieted his allies, and saved the Swiss; but Henry, fearful of further violence, fled from the city. Guise, whom Catherine apparently supported, now dictated his own terms to Henry, with whom he consented to be reconciled. An edict was obtained against the Huguenots, — Henry of Navarre was disinherited, and Guise was named General-in-chief. The King concealed his rage, and planned revenge. At a meeting of the States-General in December, 1588, Guise was present, and was treated by the councillors as the true

King of France. Henry professed the most cordial friendship for him, and they received the sacrament together as a pledge of good faith. At that very time the plot of assassination had been arranged. A guardsman named Lognac, with nine others, had been instructed to set upon Guise with their poniards, at the moment of his attending the King on a false summons. In spite of repeated warnings, the victim remained at court. On the 23d of December, he was summoned to the Council, and obeyed; but was refused entrance, and told that the King wanted to see him. He turned to enter the royal closet, when the assassins fell upon him. He gallantly resisted, but was stabbed to death with repeated strokes, — the King, who immediately came in, trampling his enemy's body under foot. The Cardinal de Lorraine, the Duke's next brother, was then murdered in prison; but the Ducs de Mayenne and d'Aumale, two other brothers, were suffered to escape. They soon stirred up the people to revenge; and Henry's neglect in securing Paris proved his ruin. Catherine dei Medici died at this juncture, — anxiety at the aspect of affairs having inflamed her illness. The new Pope, Sixtus V., united with the Guises, by refusing to absolve Henry from the murder. Mayenne was declared Lieutenant-general of the kingdom, and proceeded to invest Tours, where Henry had retired. The King turned, in his despair, to Navarre, whom he had just disinherited, and met with a generous reception. The monarchs met in April, 1589, and agreed to reconciliation and alliance. Their united armies of 38,000 men advanced to besiege Paris, which Mayenne was only able to defend with a small force.

An unlooked-for event changed the position of affairs. A fanatical monk named Jacques Clément, instigated by the Duchesse de Montpensier, sister of the murdered Duc, obtained admission into the King's room, under the pretext of presenting a petition. Clément delivered the paper with one hand, and stabbed the King with the other. Henry pulled out the knife, and struck at his assailant, who was soon slain by the guards; but his own wound was mortal : and after sending for the King of Navarre, whom he named as his successor, and urging him to abjure the Huguenot tenets, he expired in his arms.

Henry of Navarre, now Henry IV. of France, by right of descent, and the choice of his predecessor, had yet to win the confirming votes of the nobles and the people. The task was scarcely feasible, to all appearance. As a Huguenot, he had to contend against the Pope, the League, and the influence of Philip II.; and as a member of the house of Capet, against the pretensions of the Guises. His army was greatly reduced on the late King's death, by the withdrawal of nine regiments and a large body of knights; and finding it inadequate to sustain the siege of Paris, he retired to Normandy. Thither Mayenne, the eldest surviving member of the Guise family, who declared himself the general of the Cardinal de Bourbon, prepared to follow. The Cardinal was, in reality, Henry's prisoner at Tours; but it was convenient for the Guises to make him a tool, and they accordingly proclaimed him King, as Charles X. The enthusiasm of the people at the murder of Henry III. was immense. Jacques Clément was declared a martyr, and almost can-

onized; while the utmost abuse was showered upon
Henry IV., both as a heretic, and an ally of the late king.
Strong in the number of his army, which now amounted
to 25,000 men, and in the support of the Catholic party,
Mayenne gave out that he was going to capture "the
Béarnese," as he contemptuously styled his opponent.

Leaving Paris at the head of his army, the Duc
attacked Henry in his camp at Dieppe. The Huguenots
mustered only 7,000 men, but gallantly sustained the
assault; and at last gave battle in the open field, near
Argues, where they gained the day. Some flags having
fallen into the hands of Mayenne, he sent them as tokens
of victory to Paris, where the people celebrated a triumph. They were in the midst of the rejoicings when,
by a sudden movement, Henry, who had been joined by
a body of nobles, and an English force, marched to the
capital, and seized upon the faubourgs, driving the citizens into the interior of the city. The faubourgs were
pillaged for the use of the troops; but the churches and
monasteries were spared, and acts of violence kept in
check.

In Paris he found the Sixteen his most formidable
opponents, having been bribed by Phillip II., with the
hope of placing on the throne his daughter, Isabella, niece
of the late king. Henry, perceiving that he could not
retain Paris, left it for Normandy, part of which he subdued. Mayenne marched to meet him, and the two
armies met in the plain of Ivry. Mayenne's troops were
greatly superior in numbers; but Henry did not hesitate
to give battle, and would make no preparations for retreating. "Let there be none but the battle-field," was

his reply, when these were suggested. At daybreak, the
two armies were seen in order, on opposite sides; — the
white jackets and scarves of the Huguenots forming a
striking contrast to the crimson badges of the Catholics.
Advancing on horseback in complete armor, Henry bared
his head, and prayed aloud in the presence of all: "O
Lord, thou knowest my secret thoughts: if it be good for
my people that I should reign, defend thou my cause, and
prosper my arms!" Then putting on his helmet, above
which a large feather nodded in the breeze, he cried to
his men: "My children! should you lose sight of our
standards, follow my white plume; it will be found
always on the road to honor!" Then, at his signal, the
Huguenots shouted "Henry of Navarre!" and charged.
The Catholics gave way before the desperate onset, and
were slaughtered by thousands, — the whole army being
broken up. Henry at once marched on the capital, which
he blockaded. Famine and pestilence committed terrible
ravages among the citizens, and his generous heart was
deeply moved at the spectacle. He refused to take the
city by assault, — spared the lives of all who threw
themselves on his mercy, and even allowed provisions to
be secretly introduced. Meantime, Mayenne had obtained the assistance of Alexander Farnese, Duke of
Parma, one of the most eminent generals of Phillip II.,
and forced Henry to raise the siege in August, 1590.
Discussions among the Leaguers divided their interests,
but Henry's cause was still unpopular. The war was
carried on with vigor. Rouen was besieged by the
Huguenots in 1591, but relieved by the Duke of Parma.
At the battle of Aumale, Henry was defeated and

wounded; but, by a series of daring stratagems, he recovered his loss, and hemmed in the army of the League between his own, the sea, and the river Seine. The Duke of Parma, in this dilemma, performed the brilliant exploit of building a bridge over the Seine in a single night, — May 22, 1592, — crossed with his army, and escaped. He died of fever in the winter of the same year.

In 1593 the States-General met at Paris to elect a king. Harassed by the difficulties of his position, of which the principal arose from his profession of the Reformed faith, Henry, whose attachment to it had always been lukewarm, began to think seriously of renouncing it. What decided him on taking this step was the proposal made by Philip II. of Spain to ally his daughter to a French noble, if she were elected Queen. This election, however, as contrary to the Salic law, had its Catholic opponents, especially in the Parliament; and when Henry offered to abjure his faith, a strong party was formed in his favor. Mayenne withstood him but feebly, and the people refused to obey an order which was issued to forbid their witnessing the ceremony of Henry's abjuration, which took place at St. Denis, on the 25th July, 1593.

This act can only be palliated by the consideration that, to a man of Henry's practical bent and liberal sentiments, a change of faith was much less a matter of conscience than of expediency. There can be no doubt that he was actuated in a great measure by private ambition, but he may also be fairly credited with the desire of avoiding further bloodshed. It is a striking proof of his personal popularity, that his adherents were so little offended at what in another would have been considered an act of shameful treachery. The Pope still refused him absolution ; and Mayenne took occasion to announce this as a fatal barrier to Henry's election. The Parliament, and many of the people, thought otherwise, and Mayenne quitted Paris in the following year. Henry opened negotiations with the Comte de Brissac, governor of Paris, who deceived the League by his professions of zeal, and secretly arranged with the Mayor to deliver up the city. Henry entered it on the night of March 22, 1594. A small body of Spanish troops only were put to the sword, the remainder yielding, and being dismissed next day. The King was received by his children, as he called the Parisians, with enthusiasm, and extended his generous forgiveness to all his enemies. War, however, still continued in other parts of France, the advantage steadily increasing on the Royal side.

Mayenne, now relinquishing his claims as a Guise, took up the quarrel of the Infanta of Spain against Henry, but was defeated in a brilliant engagement at Fontaine-Française. The Pope's absolution being obtained in 1595, all grounds for Mayenne's opposition were removed, and he acknowledged the new king as his master.

The remainder of Henry's reign must be disposed of in a few lines. The war with Spain terminated by the peace of Vervins, in 1598, whereby all the fortresses which Philip II. had occupied were surrendered. In the same year Henry issued the famous Edict of Nantes, which secured the rights of Protestants in France, permitting them the exercise of their religion, the ministers of which were endowed by the State ; admitting them to all offices, and ordaining a chamber in each Parliament, composed of magistrates of both persuasions. Henry's course as a sovereign was not clear from serious difficulties, which he increased by his own errors. The unruly character of the nobility, which the late wars had encouraged, gave him much trouble. A pretext for revolt was afforded them by a rash promise of marriage which he made to his mistress, Henriette d'Entragne, the daughter of one of their number. The conspiracy of the Marshal de Biron arose out of this affair. He was one of Henry's ablest generals, and a man of great ambition. Bribed by the Duke of Savoy, he consented to command the army of that prince, and arouse France in favor of Henriette's son, against the pretensions of the Dauphin, son of Henry by his second wife, Maria dei Medici. The plot was betrayed to the King, who would have pardoned his rebel subject, had he consented to confess. Persisting in a denial, Biron was justly executed, in 1602. Under his just and wise minister, Rosni (Duc de Sully), Henry thoroughly reformed the whole system of French commerce, agriculture, military discipline, and finance. Roads, bridges, and public buildings benefited and beautified the country and chief cities. France was never so prosperous as under his rule.

One fatal blot on Henry's scutcheon dishonored the close of his reign. Becoming enamored of the bride of the young Prince de Condé, his intemperate passion drove her and her husband to quit France, and seek protection from Spain and Austria. Blind to the injustice of the act, Henry declared war against both powers. Preparations were made for the campaign; and the coronation of the Queen was performed, in order to secure her authority as Regent during his absence. On the 14th May, 1610, the day after this ceremony, the King went to visit Sully, who was indisposed. The royal carriage was stopped in a narrow street by two other vehicles, when a man named Ravaillac leapt upon the wheel, and plunged a knife twice into the King's breast, who died instantly. The assassin was a fanatical Catholic, who declared that his belief in the insincerity of Henry's abjuration of Protestantism was the motive for the crime. He was put to death with great cruelty; but no torture seemed to the French nation sufficiently keen to expiate the crime of murdering such a king. The land was one great house of mourning. "We have lost our father!" was the general lamentation. The verdict of posterity has confirmed the justice of that epithet. In painting the picture of this great man's life, the historic artist should never fail to make it evident how much the black shadows of tarnished honor and turbid passions are relieved by the brilliant light and warm coloring of justice, freedom, and humanity.

Wallenstein.

THE conviction of the great founder of Christianity that he "came not to bring peace, but a sword," receives its completest justification in the history of Europe during the sixteenth and seventeenth centuries. Ignorant of the constitution of the human mind, and blind to the absurdity of attempting to enforce opinion, the adherents of the old and the reformed faith, during these two hundred years, scarcely sheathed their swords. The offenders, it is just to say, were generally, but by no means invariably, the Catholics; and the retaliation of the Protestants was seldom inferior in ferocity to the offence received. The "Thirty Years' War" was the bloodiest, as happily it was the last, scene in this great religious tragedy. The Catholic hero of this period was Wallenstein.

After a term of peace, consequent on the Diet of Augsburg in 1555, which secured toleration to Protestantism in Germany, persecution recommenced in 1578, under the weak Emperor, Rudolph II. His cousin Ferdinand, Duke of Styria, a pupil of the Jesuits, was the most deadly foe of Protestantism, which had taken deepest root in Bohemia and Transylvania. The incapacity and bigotry of the Emperor at last provoked his subjects to bring about his deposition, and, in 1610, he was forced to abdicate in favor of his brother Matthias. He, though himself tolerant, unwisely committed the government to Ferdinand, whose tyranny in ordering the destruction of the Protestant churches in Bohemia led to the expulsion of his officers, and the Jesuits, in May, 1618, and the commencement of the Thirty Years' War. Matthias died in the following year, and Ferdinand was elected Emperor.

In 1619 the name of Wallenstein first became prominent. Albrecht von Waldstein, as he was properly called, was the third son of a Bohemian baron, of old family, and was born in September, 1583. As a boy, he displayed signs of a singularly proud and independent temper, and foreshowed his bent by the delight which he took in the society of military men. His family was Protestant; but, having lost his parents when quite young, he was educated, by the wish of his guardians, at the Jesuit college of Olmutz, and soon changed his faith. In Italy, where he next studied, he made great advances in mathematics, law, languages, and the delusive science of astrology, in which he was a firm believer ever afterwards. On his return to Germany, he fought in the Imperial army against the Turks, who invaded Hungary. He had considerable estates in Bohemia, which were increased by his marriage, in 1606, with a rich Moravian widow, who died in 1614, and left him her property. In the peaceful occupation of farming he spent several years, and acquired great wealth by his skill and economy. In 1617, he took part in a campaign against the Republic of Venice, with which Ferdinand had quarrelled, and, on the termination of the war in the same year, was ennobled as Count. The lavish generosity of Wallenstein during this war greatly endeared him to the army.

Such was his popularity, that in 1619, on the Bohemian revolution breaking out, he was offered by the insurgents the command of their army, although a Catholic. But he steadily refused the offer, and warmly espoused the Imperial cause, upon which the Bohemians confiscated his estates. He, however, soon retrieved his fortunes by a second rich marriage, and the favor of the Emperor. The Bohemians, under their heroic leaders the Counts von Mansfeldt and Thurn, ventured to march upon Vienna, and threaten Ferdinand in his capital; but Wallenstein, on the 10th of June, 1619, gained a signal victory over their army, and saved his master's throne. In the following year the Bohemians and Hungarians formally renounced their allegiance; the former setting up Frederick, Elector-Count Palatine of the Rhine, as their king; and the latter, Bethlem Gabor, Prince of Transylvania. Frederick, who was the son-in-law of our James I., was as unfit to govern as his father-in-law, and spent his time in a frivolous parade of his rank. He obtained but a doubtful support from the Protestant princes in Germany, who were jealous of his popularity. Ferdinand, assisted by Spain and other Catholic powers, sent a large force into Bohemia, under the command of Maximilian, Duke of Bavaria, and totally routed Frederick's army at Prague, — the King fleeing to Breslau, and thence to Holland. The Palatinate was then declared forfeited to the Empire, and was devastated by the Spanish commander, Spinola. Wallenstein, during this

campaign, spent his treasures in the Imperial cause with
the utmost readiness and liberality, and obtained as a
reward the lordship of Friedland, which brought him a
large revenue. To this he added by the purchase of
several forfeited estates in Bohemia, and thus became
possessed of immense wealth. In 1621 – 3 he distinguished himself by defeating Bethlem Gabor, the new
King of Hungary, and forcing him to surrender his
claim to the crown. For this service Wallenstein was
created Duke of Friedland.

A cruel persecution of the Protestants in Bohemia and
Silesia dishonored the Emperor's success; and the attempt of his officers in Austria to suppress Lutheranism
by force, produced a revolution in 1625. It was put
down by the energy of Tilly and Pappenheim, two of the
greatest generals of their day. The Count von Mansfeldt gallantly upheld the Protestant cause in Westphalia,
and other parts of Germany, but was defeated by Tilly,
who imposed Catholicism upon all the revolted provinces.
In their despair the German Protestants applied for aid
to their northern brethren. Gustavus Adolphus, the
young and brave King of Sweden, an ardent champion
of the Reformed faith, and Christian, King of Denmark,
responded to the appeal, — the latter immediately invading the Empire. The Imperial finances being considerably reduced by the war, Ferdinand was glad to avail himself of an offer made at this crisis by Wallenstein, to levy
an army at his own cost. This offer was abundantly fulfilled. In a few months an army of 30,000 men was collected, as if by magic. Wallenstein was enviously suspected of being in league with the Devil; but the secret

of his sway was the fascination of his bold and generous
nature.   He maintained at once thorough toleration, and
strict discipline in his ranks.   These results, however,
were not attained without injustice.   Contributions were
levied on the most fertile districts, as yet undesolated by
war, to the extent, as it is said, of 60,000,000 dollars in
seven years.   His popularity with the army procured him
the jealousy of Tilly, who, in the campaign of 1625 – 6,
outrivalled him, by successfully combating the invasion
of Christian and his Danish forces, and driving them beyond the Elbe.   Wallenstein, nevertheless, in the following campaign, won his laurels, both as a statesman and a
general, by his intrigues and conquests.   Displaying the
greatest ardor in the cause of the Empire, he attempted
to render it an absolute despotism.   After routing Count
Mansfeldt on the Elbe, he marched into Hungary, and
defeated the united armies of the Count and Bethlem
Gabor.   Christian of Denmark having assembled a new
army in 1628, Wallenstein marched to meet it; and, by
a series of brilliant successes, recaptured all the towns
garrisoned by the Danes, and forced the King to sue for
peace.   At the Congress of Lubeck, in May 1629, this
was accorded on favorable terms to Denmark.   Wallenstein during these campaigns astonished his compeers,
and excited their envy, by the wondrous rapidity of his
movements, and the skill with which he surmounted difficulties that seemed insuperable.   He was rewarded with
the duchy of Mecklenburg, which was forfeited to the
Empire by the treason of its former owner.

The envious schemes of Tilly, and Maximilian, Duke
of Bavaria, induced Ferdinand to remove Wallenstein

from his rank of commander in 1630. He had hardly withdrawn to his Bohemian estates, when Gustavus Adolphus, who had been hitherto prevented from affording active assistance to the Protestant party, landed in Pomerania with a small but highly disciplined army. This illustrious monarch, eminent for virtue and piety, no less than for political wisdom and military skill, was now the sole hope of the Reformation in Germany. The princes who professed its tenets were lukewarm and unready, — divided by jealousies among themselves, and careless of all but their own worldly interests. He, on the contrary, was devoted to the cause of his faith, and his solemn disavowal of personal ambition in undertaking its championship is stamped with sincerity.

He soon commenced a career of conquest. New Brandenburg and other districts yielded to his arms, and he formed an alliance with France, now under the sway of Cardinal Richelieu, which the Emperor had vainly negotiated to prevent. The rich city of Magdeburg declared for him, and was accordingly besieged by Tilly. The selfishness of the Lutheran leaders, the Electors of Brandenburg and Saxony, in not responding to the appeal of the Protestants in the city, led to its fall in 1631, before Gustavus could reach it. The most atrocious cruelties were perpetrated by the Catholics at the sack; no consideration of age or sex availing to prevent the massacre, which lasted for two days, and extended to 30,000 of the inhabitants. This monstrous crime was severely avenged by the indignant Gustavus. He forced the Electors of Brandenburg and Saxony to render him assistance, and, with an augmented army, hesitated not to give battle to

15 *

Tilly at Leipzic. The Swedes, though inferior in discipline, were far superior in spirit and enthusiasm to the Imperialists, and, by a judicious distribution of his forces, Gustavus outgeneralled the stratagems of Tilly. The Saxons were repulsed on one side, but, by a bold movement on the flank of their opponents, the Swedes captured their artillery, and routed them with their own weapons. The disordered Imperialists were put to flight on the 7th of September, 1631. The Protestants took courage and joined Gustavus in great numbers. He continued his victorious march, defeating the enemy at Merseberg, capturing Wurzburg, then advancing on the Rhine, and reducing on the way Frankfort-on-the-Maine, Mentz, Spires, Mannheim, and other cities. He next turned to Bavaria, where Tilly and Maximilian entrenched themselves at Rain-on-the-Lech. The former was killed by a cannon-ball during the siege, in 1632. Gustavus marched through Augsburg, where the citizens did him homage, and besieged Munich, which speedily surrendered. He now threatened to subdue Bavaria and Austria, when his progress was stopped from an unexpected quarter.

The Emperor, justly mistrusting the loyalty of Maximilian, who was in league with France, now saw himself deprived of his ablest generals, and felt his power failing. He turned to Wallenstein, as the only man who could save the Empire. That leader was meantime living in retirement, and secretly glad at the success of Gustavus. He refused at first to take the command of the Imperial army, and only consented at last on condition of having sole and absolute authority, with the right of disposing as

he pleased of his conquests. These humiliating terms were accepted by Ferdinand, and in a few months after the death of Tilly, Wallenstein was in the field with a large and powerful army, raised, as before, by his own exertions. He drove the Saxons from Bohemia, and thence marched to Leipzic, which capitulated. At Nuremberg, where Gustavus offered him battle, he wisely refused, and for three months the two camps remained close to each other, each general trying to exhaust the patience of his adversary, and relying on the destructive effects of famine and pestilence. Gustavus was forced to withdraw, after losing 20,000 men; a yet heavier loss, nevertheless, having befallen Wallenstein, whose numbers were better able to bear it.

Gustavus marched southwards, but soon turned to attack Wallenstein, who had moved northwards, and was pillaging the neighborhood of Leipzic. The two armies met at Lutzen on the 6th of November, 1632. A dense fog shrouded the movements of each side from the other, and created a fearful confusion. Wallenstein ranged his infantry in squares, having a ditch in front, and flanked by his cavalry. Gustavus headed his men, and charged the enemy across the ditch. But his own infantry was borne down by the black cuirassiers of Wallenstein, and, as he turned to attack them, the thick fog concealed their approach. His horse was wounded, and he himself had his arm broken. In moving off the field he was shot in the back, and falling from the saddle was dragged in the stirrup. He fell into the hands of the cuirassiers, — one of whom, as the Swedes came up to the succor of their King, shot him through the head. His corpse was discovered after the battle, and honorably buried. The death of their king caused the deepest affliction to the Swedes, but aroused instead of enfeebling their courage. A charge of the Duke of Weimar, one of the Protestant leaders, threw Wallenstein's infantry and cavalry into disorder. An attempt of the Imperialist General Pappenheim, who now came up with a reserve to retrieve the battle, was for a time successful. But as the tide of fortune seemed turning against the Swedes, a reserve of their own army made a last desperate charge, carried the ditch which protected Wallenstein's infantry, and won the day; the Imperialists fleeing in all directions, and their great leader escaping into Bohemia.

This defeat was the death-blow to Wallenstein's fortunate career. The Swedes continued to carry on the war successfully under the able minister of Gustavus, Oxenstiern, and the valiant Duke of Weimar. Meantime Wallenstein, after some slight victories in Saxony and Silesia, remained inactive. He at the same time assumed an air of extreme pride and self-sufficiency, which exasperated his enemies, and gave occasion for their slanders. He was accused to Ferdinand of designing to seize the Empire, — a charge which seemed the more credible, on account of an offer having been made by France to assist him in obtaining the Bohemian crown. This proposition, however, he had firmly refused. The Emperor's intention of removing him from the command of the army having reached his ears, he declared he would resign, but was persuaded to remain by his officers, who signed a promise of inviolable attachment to his person. This, too, was interpreted by his enemies as a conspiracy against the Emperor. His destruction was resolved on by the Duke of Bavaria, and others; among whom an Italian mercenary general, named Piccolomini, was the most perfidious and savage. A plot was formed against him by certain traitors among his own officers, — the names of Devereux, Butler, Gordon, and Leslie, to the shame of their nations, appearing in the list.

On the 25th of February, 1634, an entertainment was given to the whole body of officers by Gordon, who commanded the castle of Eger. where Wallenstein was residing. He himself being indisposed, had retired from the table to his chamber. He was roused by loud cries proceeding from the mess-room, where his faithful officers were being murdered by the traitors. He opened the window to inquire the cause of the disturbance, when Devereux entered, with thirty Irishmen at his back. The cowards shrank at the sight of their great general, standing calm and stern, unarmed, and at their mercy. But Devereux, a callous and brutal soldier, in a moment stepped forward, and cried: "Art thou the traitor who wilt ruin the Empire?" Wallenstein did not speak, but opened his arms, as if to accept the blow which was aimed at his heart. He was slain at the age of fifty-one. His wealth was chiefly shared among his enemies.

Though undoubtedly ambitious and intriguing, Wallenstein's alleged treachery to the Emperor, whom he kept informed of all his schemes. has never been proved, and by many recent historians is disbelieved. He fell a victim to the jealousy of his rivals, which he augmented by his own pride. His fall, however, reflects lasting disgrace on the character of the Emperor Ferdinand. and was justly avenged by the subsequent humiliation of the German Empire. The succeeding narrative of the Thirty Years' War belongs to the history of France.

Cardinal Richelieu.

THE REIGN OF LOUIS XIII. OF FRANCE.

ON the death of Henry IV. of France, in 1610, his widow, Maria dei Medici, was appointed Regent, during the minority of her son, Louis XIII. She was the daughter of the Duke of Tuscany, to which rank the Medici had now raised themselves. Her character was imperious and selfish, and she neglected the country to enrich the Court. Her chief favorite was an Italian, named Concini, who rose from the ranks to the highest dignities. His upstart arrogance and mistaken policy so disgusted the old nobility that the Prince de Condé, who was at their head, retired from his courtly attendance, and soon appeared as chief of a league against the government. By timely concessions, the Queen-mother prevented an outbreak, and convoked the States-General — the greatest assembly of the nation — in 1614. The policy which she adopted to shield herself and her favorite from enforced reforms was to set one estate of the realm against another, and thus divide their councils. This plan succeeded, and no decision was arrived at by the Assembly.

Among the representatives of the clergy on this occasion, was the tall and strikingly handsome Armand John du Plessis Richelieu, Bishop of Luçon. He was born of noble ancestry at Paris, in 1583, and destined for the army; but an opening to Church preferment occurring, by his brother's resignation of the bishopric of Luçon, Richelieu studied theology, became a Doctor of the Sorbonne at the age of twenty-two, and soon after Bishop. He attracted the notice of the Queen-mother at the Assembly just mentioned, who made him her Almoner, from which post he soon worked his way to yet higher distinction. Her disputes with the nobles still continued, and a new cause of dissatisfaction was afforded in 1615, by the zeal with which she promoted the young King's marriage with Anne of Austria, the Infanta of Spain, daughter of Philip III., — an alliance opposed to the political views of the Condé party. After the marriage, however, Maria became reconciled with her enemies by the treaty of Loudun, in 1616. Condé came into power, but the Queen-mother procured the appointment of Richelieu as Secretary of State. The new arrangement did not work well. Condé and Concini (whom Maria had created Maréchal d'Ancre) soon quarrelled, and the young King, who now aspired to reign alone, disliked both. By his orders, Condé was suddenly arrested on a charge of treason, and committed to the Bastile. A worse fate was reserved for the now triumphant Maréchal. In April, 1617, as he was on his way to attend the Council, he was stopped by Vitry, Captain of the Royal Guards, who demanded his sword, and at the same moment signalled to his men to fire. Concini fell instantaneously. Louis XIII. openly avowed his sanction of this murder, and took the opportunity of declaring himself king. Under the influence of his favorite, the **Duc de Luynes**, he banished his mother to Blois, and appeased the discontents which her government had excited. Richelieu obtained permission to attend Maria to her retirement, but is supposed to have been secretly commissioned by the Crown to act as a spy upon her movements. He soon distinguished himself by his skilful management of an intrigue which was set on foot to deliver the Queenmother. She effected her escape by the agency of the Duc d'Epernon and an Italian named Rucelai, who placed a ladder of ropes at the window of her château. The King demanded that d'Epernon should be surrendered to him, as the price of his mother's freedom from molestation at Angoulême, whither she had fled; but Richelieu, by his wise counsels, made peace without this condition being enforced. Louis, however, released Condé, and restored him to power, as a check on Maria's influence. Her partisans, feeling aggrieved, left the Court, and threatened hostilities, — d'Epernon and other leaders advising her to fortify herself in Guienne. This step, however, Richelieu, who was in communication with the King, prevailed upon her to reject as imprudent. War actually commenced, and Condé defeated the troops of the Queen-mother at Cé. Richelieu again interfered, and made peace. Maria returned to Paris, and the rebellion was put down. As a reward for his treacherous dealings, Richelieu was promised a cardinal's hat.

He seems to have set before him three main objects in his political career, in all of which he succeeded, — the humiliation of the Huguenot party, of the nobility, and of the Empire of Germany. To attain these results he

spared no time or pains. Having, it is to be feared, really
in view only the extension of his own power as a minister, he contrived to make it appear that he aimed only
at the extension of his master's power as king. Louis
never loved him, but found him so necessary that,
throughout a long political life, Richelieu was scarcely
once in serious disfavor. The accomplishment of his
first object was a work of years; and some progress had
been made towards it by others. Béarn, where the Huguenots were in the majority, was restored, in 1620, to
the Catholic faith, which Jeanne d'Albret had abolished.
A general league of the party in 1621, for the purpose
of organizing an armed force, led to the Catholic invest-
ment of Rochelle and the siege of Montauban. The
failure of the latter was imputed to De Luynes, the
King's favorite. He died in the same year, and peace
was then made, the Edict of Nantes being confirmed.
Richelieu now obtained the cardinal's hat, which had
been promised him, and was soon after admitted, by the
Prime Minister La Vieuville, to the Council. Here he
acquired a vast influence over the King's mind, and soon
stepped into the position of La Vieuville, who was disgraced.

Now minister, Richelieu governed with a high hand.
Passing over events which bear upon the success of his
second great object, we proceed to notice the accomplishment of the first. After seeming to befriend the Reformed party, by supporting the Protestants of the Swiss
Grisons against the Catholics of the Valtelline, with
whom they were at war, — advocating the marriage of
the King's sister, Henrietta Maria, with our Charles I.,

and treating with moderation a revolt of the Huguenots in 1625, he took vigorous measures, on the occasion of the next outbreak, to crush the whole party. Rochelle, the Huguenot stronghold, was fortified by the family of Rohan, the most illustrious Protestant leader in France; and the English sent a fleet under Buckingham to its relief. Richelieu himself commanded the attack, and displayed as great military as political skill. He cut off the besieged from communication with the sea, whence they expected supplies of food and ammunition, by the construction of a vast mole, half a mile in length and sixty feet in breadth. The sea twice carried away the works, but he persevered, and completed them. The English fleet could not force the passage, and at last sailed away, the besieged being reduced to the miseries of famine. Their mayor, Guiton, evinced the most heroic courage, declaring that, if but one man remained in the city, he should still shut the gates against the foe. But when all hope of assistance was gone, the Rochellois were constrained to surrender, after a year's resistance. Richelieu gave them favorable terms, allowing them the exercise of their religious rights, and securing toleration by an Edict, in 1629. As a political party, however, the Huguenots were henceforth crushed.

In the prosecution of his second aim, the humiliation of the nobles, the Cardinal had to contend with great difficulties. Gaston, Duc d'Orléans, the King's brother, was his chief rival, and had many partisans. Ornano, one of these, had been favored by Richelieu, but turned against him, advising the Duc to marry against the Cardinal's wish. The penalty paid for this advice was Ornano's perpetual imprisonment. Chalais, another friend of Gaston, formed a plot, in which the Queen Anne of Austria and the Duke of Buckingham were implicated, to overthrow the great Cardinal. Among other objects of this plot was, it is said, the deposition of Louis, and the marriage of Gaston to the Queen. Richelieu soon discovered and revealed it to Louis; but, with a show of humility, offered to resign his post. Unable to govern without him, the King gave him the fullest powers to act as he thought best. Gaston, accordingly, was forced to marry Mademoiselle de Montpensier; Chalais was tried and executed for treason; his mistress, the Duchess de Chevreuse, banished; and the Queen herself strictly confined to her own apartments.

In 1629 – 30, a war broke out between France and the duchy of Savoy, in which Victor Amadeus, then duke, and brother-in-law of Louis, was worsted. The Queen-mother, who favored her son-in-law, reproached Richelieu with this result, and endeavored to procure his dismissal; but he triumphed over her intrigues, — obtaining her banishment from Court in 1631. She retired to Flanders, while Gaston, who espoused her cause, excited a rebellion in Lorraine, where — his wife being dead — he made a second marriage with the sister of its duke. Richelieu arrested the chief partisans of the rebels in France, two of whom, the Maréchal de Marillac and the Duc de Montmorency, with some subordinates, were executed. The Duke of Lorraine lost his possessions; but Gaston, whose character was cowardly and selfish, deserted his mother and his party, made peace with Louis, and returned to France. He attempted, at a later period, to have the Cardinal assassinated, but the scheme miscarried through his own hesitation. Other nobles of less importance ventured their strength against Richelieu's, and equally failed. The Duc de Vendôme, the King's natural brother, was banished, and D'Epernon, the Queen-mother's partisan, imprisoned. One last attempt to overthrow the powerful Minister may here be mentioned, though it occurred at the close of his career. He had placed near the King a young nobleman named Cinq-Mars, who, perceiving that the tie between the King and the Cardinal was one of fear rather than love, schemed to betray his patron. He accordingly leagued with the Queen, the Duc d'Orleans, and a rival minister, the Duc de Bouillon. By his spies, Richelieu obtained information of the plot, and revealed it to the King, from whom he obtained permission to crush it. Cinq-Mars, and his friend De Thou, were arrested; and, on the evidence of the dastardly Gaston, were condemned and executed. He himself escaped and retired into privacy; while the Duc de Bouillon lost his possessions as a condition of pardon. Richelieu remained triumphant. On the occasion of one of Gaston's conspiracies, the Parliament ventured to oppose the royal ordinance, declaring his partisans guilty of treason before bringing them to trial. Richelieu resolved to humble it also. The judges who composed the Parliamentary Court were summoned to attend the King, with the record of their refusal to sanction the Edict. On their entrance into the council room, the record was taken from them, and burnt in their presence. The chief members of the court were then either banished or removed from office.

The humiliation of the Court of Aids, where the decrees for the state expenditure were recorded, soon followed a similar act of resistance; and the foundation of a new tribunal for trying political criminals — the members of which were appointed by Richelieu — placed in his hands almost absolute power.

His third aim was to depress the power of Germany, the most formidable continental rival of France. To achieve this result, he did not scruple to ally himself with the Protestants. Gustavus Adolphus, as we have seen, was in treaty with him, and received a subsidy to prosecute the war. After the death of the Swedish king, and his great opponent, Wallenstein, the Thirty Years' War was carried on under the leadership of the Archduke Ferdinand as the Catholic, and the Duke of Weimar as the Protestant champions. In 1634, the victory of Nordlingen over the Swedes, and the peace of Prague, by which the Elector of Saxony deserted his party, seemed fatal to the Protestant cause. But Richelieu gave it his support, — allying himself with the Dutch republic, and with the Duke of Weimar in 1635, and thus defying both Spain and Austria. In the next campaign, of 1636, France was invaded by the armies of both these powers, and Paris was even threatened; but Richelieu's courage and firmness sustained the nation. He aroused the popular enthusiasm, and procured by his exertions a powerful army, which forced back the tide of invasion. The war was prosecuted with varying success in particular engagements, but with progressive advantage to France and Sweden, which, with rival aims, formed a close alliance. The gallant Duke of Weimar died in 1639, but his troops were generalled by French officers, and led to conquest. The Cardinal did not live to see the successful result of the war, which was terminated in 1648 by the peace of Westphalia. By this important treaty, the religious liberty of Germany was secured in the toleration of Lutheranism and Calvanism, and the admission of Protestants to the Imperial Chamber and Aulic Council, — the highest political and judicial courts of the Empire. To this great result the policy of Richelieu, though pursued with a very different object, must be held to have mainly contributed. His own object was at the same time attained by the humiliation of the Empire, and the cession of Alsace and other important provinces to France, which gave her a foothold that she did not fail to employ to her future advantage.

At the height of his success and fame, just after the failure of the conspiracy of Cinq-Mars had crowned the fall of his enemies, Richelieu was taken ill, and died on the 4th December, 1642, at the age of fifty-eight. On his death-bed he sent for the King, whom he assured of his constant fidelity, — declaring that all his political schemes had for their aim the glory of France. Louis felt relieved at his death, but pronounced his eulogium in terms as just as they are brief: — "There is a great politician dead!"

Richelieu was probably sincere in his assertion that he had aimed at the glory of France, but deserves no credit for patriotism on that account, since her glory was identified with his own. He was virtually king under the name of minister, and no government was ever more despotic than his. His grasp of mind was immense, and whatever he undertook he seemed able to achieve. Under his guidance, France attained an influence in Europe superior to that of any other power; and a social stability, as potent as any which is attainable by a despotic government. Her rivals were permanently humbled, and her territories enlarged. The nobles and the Parliament were subdued to the will of the Crown; and the political importance of the Reformed faith destroyed, without the dangers of intolerance being incurred. The national army and navy were placed on an increased footing of strength; literature and the arts were encouraged; and commerce extended. The foundation of the French Academy in 1635, and the formation of the French East India Company in 1642, are among the country's debts to his wisdom.

It is scarcely needful to observe on the utter unscrupulousness of the great Cardinal, since his whole life is an example of it. He did not hesitate to avow the fact, in the famous words, — "I dare undertake nothing, without having well reflected on it; but once having taken my resolution, I advance straightforward, — throwing or cutting down everything in my way, and then covering all with my red robe." No portrait could be more faithful. Under the red robe — the symbol of his sacred office — he cloaked the most unholy ambitions and practices. Proud, treacherous, revengeful, and vain, he governed men by the weapon of fear only, and probably never obtained the love of any human being. It is, perhaps, a redeeming feature in his character, that he was not insensible to the fascination of beauty. He was even suspected of a secret passion for the Queen; and a story is told of her having endeavored to cure him of it, by persuading him to dance before her in a fancy dress, and exposing him to her courtiers while in this ludicrous position. His weakness on this score at least links him with his fellow-men; from whom his towering intellectual stature, and lack of moral principle, seem utterly to divide him.

Condé the Great.

LOUIS XIII. survived his minister only six months; and his widow, Anne of Austria, was appointed Regent of the kingdom during the minority of her son, Louis XIV. On his death-bed, Richelieu had named Cardinal Mazarin as his successor; and his wish was confirmed by the choice of the Regent. This eminent statesman, an Italian by birth, was originally sent to France as Ambassador from the Pope; but having attracted the attention of Richelieu by his talent for diplomacy, was retained in his service. The new minister carried out to the full the policy of his predecessor. The Thirty Years' War was drawing to a close; but the later campaigns were marked by battles scarcely inferior in importance to any that went before them.

Among the first events of the reign of Louis XIV. was the victory of Rocroy over the Spaniards. The hero of the day was Louis, Duc d'Enghien, son of the Prince de Condé, and a youth of twenty-two. He was born at Paris in 1621, and as a boy was noticed by Richelieu, who predicted his future success. At an early age he evinced such military knowledge and ability, that he was intrusted with the command of the royal army in

16

Flanders. It amounted to 23,000 men; and though the Spaniards had a larger force, he determined to march to the relief of Rocroy, which they were besieging. The battle which ensued is one of the most sanguinary on record. By three bold charges of his cavalry, D'Enghien broke the renowned Spanish infantry, and won the day, leaving 8,000 of the enemy dead on the field, — the Comte de Fuentés, their leader, among them, — and taking 6,000 prisoners. He followed up this success by capturing the important town of Thionville. In 1643 the French sustained a serious defeat at Dutlingen, by the Imperial forces under Mercy and other officers. D'Enghien, and the Maréchal Turenne, son of Richelieu's rival, the Duc de Bouillon, and an illustrious general, were sent, in 1644, to retrieve the failing fortunes of the Protestant cause. Friburg was besieged by Mercy, and thither the French hastened; but arrived too late to prevent its capture. The armies, however, met in the vicinity, and a fearful contest ensued. D'Enghien evinced on this occasion the daring which was the leading feature of his character, and the chief element of his glory as a general. To animate his men, he threw his commander's bâton (or staff) into the trenches of the Imperial camp, and vowed that, sword in hand, he would recover it. He kept his word, after a desperate struggle with the foe. Both sides claimed the victory; but Mercy testified to his defeat by evacuating his position. In the following year Turenne was defeated at Mariendahl; but D'Enghien gained another victory at Nordlingen, where Mercy was killed. It was on the tomb of the latter that was engraved the famous inscription, — "*Sta, viator ; heroem calcas.*" (Traveller, stop; you tread upon a hero.)

In 1646 D'Enghien was at Dunkirk, which he reduced in sight of the Spanish army that was sent to its relief. His father dying in this year, he became Prince de Condé, by which name he is always known in history. His last great successes in the Thirty Years' War were the capture of Ypres, and the subsequent battle of Lens, in 1648. The Archduke Leopold, brother of the Emperor, commanded the united German and Spanish armies. Condé's address to his men was brief, but inspiriting: "Soldiers, remember Rocroy, Friburg, and Nordlingen!" Its effect was shown in the total rout of the enemy, with the capture of thirty-eight guns and a hundred standards. The peace of Westphalia soon followed this memorable victory.

Thus far Richelieu's policy was ably carried out by his successor, but Mazarin drew upon himself deserved odium by his unjust methods of recruiting the State exchequer, especially the sale of offices, and the prohibition of building beyond certain limits. The Parliament at last refused to sanction these monstrous edicts, and, on the arrest of two of its most factious members, the people of Paris rose in revolt. The party opposed to the Government was known as the *Fronde* (from *fronder*, to censure), and its head was the turbulent De Retz, afterwards Cardinal. The Regent, at the tidings of outbreak, fled to St. Germain, where she was reduced to considerable privations by the withholding of her revenues. Condé, on his return after the peace, at once took up her cause, but Turenne allied himself to the Fronde. Paris was besieged by the former, and soon gave way; peace being made in 1649, and the old order of affairs restored.

Condé and Mazarin, however, who both aspired to independence, soon quarrelled. The former veered between the Government and the Fronde, but made himself unpopular to both parties by his haughty temper; the latter determined to avail himself of this fact, and silence all opposition. Condé, and two of his relatives, were seized and imprisoned, in January, 1650. This bold step failed to secure the minister's safety. The discontent of the nobility and people at last became so great that the Regent was forced to release Condé and his relatives, and dismiss Mazarin, who retired to Cologne in disgrace. Condé was now in power, but misused it. His contemptuous treatment of the Queen induced her to apply to De Retz, who was ready for any scheme that promised to advance himself. He readily intrigued to procure Condé's downfall, and succeeded in leaguing the Fronde and the Parliament against him. The Prince left Paris, and retired to Guienne, where he negotiated with Spain (which still remained hostile to France) for assistance. The Regent made peace with Turenne, whose. services she needed, and recalled Mazarin, who became as powerful as before.

Civil war now commenced in earnest. Condé was joined by the ever-intriguing Duc d'Orléans, who emerged from his obscurity, sent him a body of troops under the Duc de Nemours, and despatched Mademoiselle de Montpensier, his own daughter, to secure Orleans. Turenne was defeated at Blenau in 1652, but pursued Condé in his march to Paris, and contested its possession with him. The adroitness of Gaston's daughter, who made her way to Paris, and won over the city author-

ities to Condé's side, secured his success. After a variety
of minor events, the war terminated by the Regent's consenting to banish Mazarin. The fickle Parisians now
deserted Condé also, and forced him to quit the city,
whence he departed to Flanders. The wily De Retz
was for a time in power, but, being discovered to be
implicated in a conspiracy, was soon afterwards imprisoned. Louis XIV., now of age to govern, was received with joy by the nation. He soon signalized his
possession of power by recalling Mazarin, whom, with
their usual instability of sentiment, the Parisians were
delighted to welcome. The Cardinal speedily procured
the condemnation of Condé as a traitor. In the war
which ensued, the latter appeared as the Spanish leader.
Turenne commanded the royal army, and the campaign
of 1654 was favorable to the French. Condé, however,
displayed masterly skill, even under disadvantageous circumstances, and his retreat from Arras, the siege of
which Turenne obliged him to raise, was as brilliant as
many a victory. In the next campaign, of 1656 – 7,
which was also fought in Flanders, Turenne quitted the
defensive position which he had hitherto held, but was
defeated by Condé, who rewon his laurels by forcing the
French to raise the siege of Valenciennes. England
now made her influence felt in this continental war. The
illustrious Cromwell was at the head of her councils, and
found it necessary to combat the exertions which the two
sons of Charles I. were making to procure aid from
France. His alliance was sought by Spain also, but he
gave it to Mazarin, on the conditions, that the Stuart cause
should be abandoned, and, that if Dunkirk were taken by

the French it should be ceded to England. These terms being agreed on, Cromwell sent a fleet and 6,000 soldiers. Charles and James then left the camp of Turenne for that of Condé. The Prince was defeated near Dunkirk in 1658, and the city was surrendered to England.

Philip IV. of Spain was now weary of the war, and opened negotiations for peace. Mazarin, on this occasion, displayed remarkable acuteness, and the Peace of the Pyrenees (or Bidasoa), signed in November 1659, is one of his most memorable achievements. By it, Roussillon, Pignerol, and Alsace, were yielded to France, together with many towns in Flanders. The submission of Condé was one of the conditions of peace, and Louis, who recognized his value, restored him to his full honors. The marriage of the King with Maria Theresa of Austria, daughter of the King of Spain, happily concluded this war.

The death of the astute and unprincipled Mazarin, in 1661, relieved Condé of a dangerous antagonist, and Louis of a nominal servant, but a real master. The young King henceforth governed alone, making choice of able men, such as Colbert and Louvois, but using them as instruments of his own will. There is a considerable fascination about the character and career of Louis XIV.; but the splendid bubble breaks when handled. He was dignified, affable, and generous, and possessed great firmness and political sagacity; but an overriding selfishness perverted his qualities of heart and mind to the most immoral ends. " *L'etat c'est moi* " was his motto, and his whole reign was its illustration. To exalt his own glory as " le Grand Monarque," he degraded the independent spirit of his nobles by lavishing honors upon them; flattered the people by his superb state, but yet despised and oppressed them; subdued the Parliament into a mere echo of his will; persecuted the Protestants, but at the same time opposed the exacting spirit of the Papacy; and abroad, rendered himself formidable by unjust aggressions upon all States, both free and despotic, which presumed to compete with or resist him. His extension of commerce, and patronage of literature and art, were means to the same end, rather than patriotic labors; and he must be regarded only as the creator of a magnificent despotism, which culminated long before his death, and of which the next century attested the insecurity. While it lasted, however, the illusion was gorgeous. Condé, from his restoration to power to the close of his life, was a main instrument of his master's glory abroad. The humiliation of Spain was his first achievement. On the death of Philip IV., in 1665, leaving a son, Charles II., under age, Louis laid claim to the territory of Flanders in right of his wife, the elder child of the late king. The claim was unfounded, as the law of Brabant, giving daughters the preference to younger sons, in ordinary cases of descent, — upon which he professed to rely, — had no bearing upon the succession to the crown. The Emperor Leopold of Germany, however, supported France. Flanders was partially conquered by Turenne, but Brussels and Antwerp resisted him successfully. The brilliant feature of the war was due to Condé, who, in the space of a fortnight, invaded and made himself master of the province of Franche-Comté.

Alarmed, however, at these successes, England, Hol-

land, and Sweden, formed a league against France in
1688, the originator of which was William of Orange,
afterwards so memorable as our greatest English King.
Louis concluded peace at Aix-la-Chapelle in the same
year, — retaining Flanders, but surrendering Franche-
Comté. He was much incensed against Holland for its
interference, and resolved on vengeance. He found a
frivolous pretext for war in 1672; and Condé and Turenne led his armies. The capture of Wesel was the
former's first success, only outshone by his famous passage of the Rhine in sight of the enemy. Here he was
wounded, and obliged to surrender the chief command to
Turenne. The Dutch, under William of Orange, made
the most heroic resistance to the demands of Louis, who
aimed at the annihilation of their republican form of government and Protestant faith. The two De Witts, who,
as Grand Pensionary and Admiral, had served Holland
faithfully, were torn to pieces by the people, on suspicion
of being in communication with France. The dykes
were cut through, and the country was flooded, with the
hope of expelling the invaders. This gallant opposition
at last moved Europe to decide against Louis, — Germany, Spain, and the Elector of Brandenburg leaguing
against him. England, which had given him naval assistance, withdrew it also. The King, however, was not
discouraged. Franche-Comté was again invaded, and
overcome in six weeks. At Senef, in Flanders, in 1674,
Condé gave battle to William of Orange. For fourteen
hours the two armies contested the field, — Condé having
three horses killed under him. The enormous number
of 27,000 men is said to have been the united loss on this

occasion. The great French commander met with his match in the youthful Prince of Orange, whose courage in rallying his men, after the day seemed lost, prevented the French from obtaining more than a doubtful victory. Condé then relieved Oudenarde; but in the following year (1675) was called into Alsace, to take the head of Turenne's army,—that great general, after a victorious campaign against the German forces, having been killed by a stray cannon-ball near Saltzbach, in Baden. Condé finally compelled Montecuculli, the German commander, to evacuate Alsace. This was the Prince's last campaign; ill-health compelling him to retire from military command. He lived to see the successful close of the war, which terminated in 1678, by the peace of Nimeguen. Holland was weakened, and Spain lost Franche-Comté and several towns in the Netherlands, of which, together with Alsace, France obtained possession.

Condé retired to his princely estate of Chantilly, where he lived in much splendor, surrounded by men of letters, — among whom Racine and Boileau were prominent, — until his death, in 1686. He obtained the name of "*the Great*" for his military prowess, and deservedly, but cannot be praised for any other greatness. Like his master, he seems to have been governed throughout his career by selfish motives only, joining the Government or the Fronde, France or Spain, as it best suited his own ambition and pride. We have selected him as the hero of his age, because of his prominence both as a general and politician. His campaigns especially illustrate the nature of the means by which Louis XIV. made himself formidable.

Condé is the last hero whose name belongs to the seventeenth century. With the foregoing sketch of his career terminates this biographical outline of the history of Europe, during the millennium that elapsed between the eighth and eighteenth centuries. A new period of history then opens. France falls from the pinnacle of her power; and England, which for centuries had scarcely interfered in foreign politics, — having recently achieved domestic freedom, — is the agent of her rival's downfall, and the architect of her own continental reputation. Spain, though strengthening her position in Italy, gradually sinks into the national insignificance in which she at present appears; while the sudden rise of three new States into importance weakens and represses the power of Germany. Russia, till then scarcely known beyond the limits of its own territories, becomes, under the policy of Peter the Great, an organized and aggressive despotism; while Prussia and Savoy, elevated into kingdoms, oppose an armed barrier north and south. Italy — a helpless prey to her invaders — scarcely evinces, save in the direction last named, a trace of life. Thus is established that "balance of power" in Europe, which all the storms of the succeeding century and a half have not materially or permanently disturbed.

THE END.

Cambridge : Stereotyped and Printed by Welch, Bigelow, & Co.

www.ingramcontent.com/pod-product-compliance
Lightning Source LLC
Chambersburg PA
CBHW030825110726
47900CB00006B/1746